PRAISE FOR THE VAMPIRE SLAYERS' FIELD GUIDE TO THE UNDEAD

This is just about the best factual book about vampires that I've ever read. I had no idea that there were so many vampire stories the world over, and I've been a student of the subject for thirty years. The Hopping Vampires of Hong Kong alone are worth the price, but then so are the Asasabonsam, not to mention the ghastly Impundulu. Plus, the illustrations are fabulous and loads of fun. This is a superb effort, deserving of attention, awards and a long, long, LONG life!

> - Whitley Strieber, author of *The Hunger*, *The Last Vampire*, and *The Wolfen*

From hopping vampires to white ladies to redcaps, this vibrantly illustrated reference guide to the world's essence-sucking predators is a must-have for fans of the macabre, scholars of the undead, and even the uninitiated. It leaves nothing out, joining the contemporary realm of fiction, film, and vampire role-playing with ancient legends and a history of crime for an enlightening read that's also engaging and provocative.

> - Katherine Ramsland, author of *Piercing the Darkness* and *The Science of Vampires*

The Vampire Slayers' Field Guide To The Undead is the best resource I've read about vampires in myth and legend from around the world. Packed with information, beautifully illustrated, this is a keeper for the shelf.

> - Douglas Clegg, author of *The Priest of Blood*

The Vampire Slayers' Field Guide To The Undead is a literary and visual masterpiece, and could well be the finest book ever written on vampire folklore. Kudos to Shane MacDougall for giving us this wonderful collection.

> - Owl Goingback, author of *Breed*, *Shaman Moon* and *Crota*

Shane MacDougall's *The Vampire Slayers' Field Guide To The Undead* is an impressive compilation of fact and fiction (and everything in between) concerning vampires and the undead. Beautifully produced, with some amazing artwork, it's a heady mixture of legend and folk beliefs that will prove to be a wonderful resource for the researcher or the casual traveler

> - Rick Hautala, author of *Bedbugs* and *The Mountain King*

Gloriously illustrated and thoroughly researched, *The Vampire Slayers' Field Guide To The Undead* is an essential and endlessly fascinating resource no globe-trotting vampire slayer should be without. Shane MacDougall has unearthed a frightening array of all things vampiric by delving into the world's vast store of myth, folklore, and legend and by examining today's pop culture representations of the undead in literature and film. An A to Z crash course in recognizing, surviving, and slaying the vampires who walk among us!

> - John Passarella, Bram Stoker Award-Winning author of *Wither's Rain*

The Vampire Slayers' Field Guide To The Undead is an astonishing piece of research and should be on the bookshelf of every writer, educator, and fearless vampire hunter.

> – P.D. Cacek, author of *Night Prayers* and *Night Players*

Hold the garlic! MacDougall's international compendium of folklore, superstition, and fantasies adds up to more than the sum of our fears about immortality's dark side. In documenting the astonishing prevalence of vampire legends in so many civilizations, MacDougall shows how myth, legend, and the occasional cheesy horror flick illuminate eternally human concerns about grief, decay, contagion, violation and sexual frenzy. *The Vampire Slayers' Field Guide To The Undead* is recommended for appetites natural and supernatural.

> - Bill Kent, author of *Street Hungry*

The Vampire Slayers' Field Guide To The Undead is probably the most comprehensive and "all-inclusive" study of the undead throughout history to be published. This book effectively mixes a plethora of information about actual and mythical predatory monsters (including werewolves, ghosts, zombies, witches, and more)—throughout history and from every corner of the world—with current pop culture icons and entertainment stereotypes, such as Dracula and Buffy. The tome studies ties to Christianity, SIDS, blood fetishes, superstitions, burial methods, traditional weapons, medicines, and more in a manner that remains interesting and engaging. I thought I knew a lot about vampires until I read *The Vampire Slayers' Field Guide To The Undead*! The vampire dictionary, timeline, bibliography, websites, and newsgroups are priceless. A lot of time, effort, and love obviously went into this highly informative book. The facts are here and you will believe that vampires really exist! *The Vampire Slayers' Field Guide To The Undead* will WOW you!

> - Jim O'Rear, star of *Vampire Wars*

Shane MacDougall's *The Vampire Slayers' Field Guide To The Undead* is a tremendous resource for anyone who wants to write fiction about vampires, revenants, and the nosferatu (you'll even learn what that word actually means, which is more than Bram Stoker knew). More than that, it's informative and entertaining reading in its own right. Turn anywhere in the book and I guarantee you, no matter what you think you know about vampires, MacDougall's book will show you more. Most highly recommended.

- Gregory Frost, author of *Fitcher's Brides*

From the strigoi to the vrykolaka and all the nightcomers beyond—*The Vampire Slayers' Field Guide To The Undead* is a wonderfully entertaining and informative tour de force through Vampirology 101 with a man who knows his territory!

- Karen Koehler, author of the *Slayer* series: *Slayer* and *Slayer: Black Miracles*

Shane MacDougall's book, *The Vampire Slayers' Field Guide To The Undead*, is both meticulously researched and energetically written. Simply put, it's a gold mine of ideas for writers of supernatural fiction. I suspect it will become an essential tool for every working horror/fantasy author. It's also an entertaining tour of how other cultures view the undead, and probably belongs on the shelf with your Joseph Campbell books and your copy of the *Larousse Encyclopedia of Mythology*.

- A.L. Sirois, Editor of FarSector SFFH (www.farsector.com)

The Vampire Slayers' Field Guide To The Undead is the most detailed reference on vampires currently available. It's an excellent resource. You'd be dead without it!

- Steve Gerlach, author of *The Nocturne*, *Love Lies Dying*, *Rage* and *Hunting Zoe*

How sharp do wooden stakes need to be? And does holy water really work? The night is full of questions; this book is full of answers. Chronicling the worldwide activities of things that go flap in the night, *The Vampire Slayers' Field Guide To The Undead* is an encyclopedia of survival skills for the Van Helsing in everyone. (Nor are the wampyr's various kith and kin neglected, from the loup-garou to—my favorite—the Jersey Devil.) How many other reference works provide so many hours of chilling entertainment? This collection of lore and literature is exhaustively researched, lavishly illustrated and delightfully clever. Don't leave home without it, especially not after sunset.

- Robert Dunbar, author of *The Pines* and *BATS!*

Several of us had the chance to review Shane MacDougall's *The Vampire Slayers' Field Guide To The Undead*, and we found it to be a true gem. It is a treasure trove of information and ideas that horror writers can use to breathe life into their gruesome tales of the living dead and their grizzly world. What a treat to read and page through! It sucks you in like the welcoming embrace of a voluptuous succubus and holds your interest with its overpowering allure to define the gruesome. Horror writers, novice and pro, will welcome such an addition to their shelves of reference books; such knowledge at one's fingertips makes it a true find. Kudos!

- K. A. Patterson, Senior Editor of *AlienSkin* Magazine

Shane MacDougall has set a standard I challenge anyone to meet. *The Vampire Slayers' Field Guide To The Undead* is an amazingly interesting work aimed toward those desiring the true meat. MacDougall has provided us with a reference that goes beyond any other and it is worthy of our attention.

- John Paul Allen, author of *The Gifted Trust*

Comprehensive and definitive, *The Vampire Slayer's Field Guide to the Undead* surpasses other reference sources and deserves a place next to such works as *The Golden Bough*. Shane MacDougall's new book combines an easy-to-read style with scholarly research and obvious affection for the topic. He has created a masterful tour-de-force that, to steal a line from the intro to an old TV sports show, "Spans the globe to bring you the constant variety of vampires ...."

And span the globe the book does, citing vampire legends in just about every culture. Packed with obscure and interesting information, this book tells you everything you need to know to go out and slay some vampires. Or you could just curl up with it and enjoy its lively style and occasionally puckish humor. Either way, the reader is in for a treat.

My one regret is that this book has not been available until now. Its vast scope of information—ranging from the well known to the unknown—would have been invaluable to writers, movie makers, and those just interested in vampires. I recommend it, and I plan to add it to my library of reference sources.

- Gary A. Markette, Senior Editor of Anotherealm

The Vampire Slayer's Field Guide To The Undead is a great book on vampire lore and other things that go bump in the night. I especially liked the section on the Jersey Devil. This is a must-read for horror fans.

- Art Bourgeau, author of *Wolfman*

THE VAMPIRE SLAYERS' FIELD GUIDE TO THE UNDEAD

By
Shane MacDougall

Strider Nolan
PUBLISHING

Library of Congress Catalog Card Number: 2003108127.
ISBN: 1-932045-13-9

First Edition Paperback 2003
Printed in Canada.

Strider Nolan Publishing, Inc.
68 South Main Street, Doylestown, PA 18901
www.stridernolan.com

·DEDICATION·

This book is dedicated to two extraordinary women ....

Maude Blanche Flavell, my grandmother. Born on Halloween, psychic and strange and thoroughly wonderful, she taught me to read tarot cards when I was eight and told me tales of vampires and werewolves on dark and stormy nights.

And to my loving wife, Sara Jo, who proves to me every single day that real magic exists.

·ACKNOWLEDGEMENTS·

A lot of wonderful people have helped in various ways with the creation and development of this book.

- Sara Jo West for just about everything.
- My publisher, Michael S. Katz, for believing in the project and bringing it to life.
- Mary Wilsbach-Katz, for such clear artistic vision and the cover painting.
- To Glo and Bill Delamar for guidance and friendship.
- My wonderful artists: Robert Patrick O'Brien, Marie Elena O'Brien, Jason Lukridge, Breanne Levy, Matej Jan, Bill Chancellor, Sarah Kirk, Stefani Rennee de Oliveira Silva, Krista McLean, Kevin Converse, Alberto Moreno, Philip Straub, Eldred Tjie, Pedro Lara, Adam Garland, Anton Kvasovarov, Vinesh George, Jack Schrader, and Denise Lawrence.
- Lilian Broca, for generously allowing us to reprint some of her wonderful Lilith paintings.
- Steve Belden, Andy Burnham, and Alan Wilson for allowing me to use their magnificent art.
- Jill Katz, for doing a thousand things all at once, and getting them all right.
- My new friends in the Horror Business: Douglas Clegg, Jim O'Rear, John Passarella, John Paul Allen, Karen Koehler, Katherine Ramsland, Owl Goingback, Rick Hautala, Rob Dunbar, Steve Gerlach, P.D. Cacek, Gregory Frost, and Whitley Strieber.

- Rachel Altomare for the first edit.
- Carolyn Lynn for those long chats about Horror and Science Fiction way back in 1974.
- The Horror Writers Association
- The Authors Guild.
- The National Writers Union.
- Mary SanGiovanni and the Garden State Horror Writers Group.
- Kelli Dunlap of Horror Web (www.horrorweb.com)
- Cathy Buburuz of Champagne Shivers (http://www.samsdotpublishing.com/expressions.htm)
- HorrorFind.com
- PSFS: Philadelphia Science Fiction Society.
- The Philadelphia Writers Conference.
- Al and Paula Sirois for sharing a moment of cosmic harmony.
- Dave Juliano for his excellent research on the legends of the Jersey Devil.
- Bill Kent for moral support and a truly weird sense of humor.
- Art Bourgeau for running the best bookstore in the country (Whodunit? Books in Philly)
- The Elkins Park Crew–Fran & Randy Kirsch, Charlie & Gina Miller, Rit & Cindy Rubino, and Alan & Merle Hockstein. It was over dinner at (appropriately enough) The Raven in New Hope, chatting with them about vampires, that I came up with the idea for this book.
- John West, thanks for everything you do.
- Rex Gilroy author of <u>Giant from the Dreamtime-the Yowie in Myth and Reality</u> and director of the Yowie Research Institute in Australia; and Greg Foster, also of the Yowie Institute.
- Our models: Tovah Cornman the Slayer, Sid the Slayer, victim Paul Scott, and vampires Marie O'Brien, Jill Katz, Mike Mazzoni, Wendy Goldberg, Jodi Holman, Joanna Vulakh, and Joshua McGann.

·CONTENTS·

·ABOUT THE AUTHOR·

Shane MacDougall is the pen name for award-winning writer and lecturer Jonathan Maberry, author of more than 500 articles and several books. MacDougall is an 8th degree black belt in jujutsu, an artist, and a devoted folklorist. He lives in Elkins Park, Pennsylvania with his wife and stepson.

Shane MacDougall may be reached at stridernolan@yahoo.com, or by mail at P.O. Box 286, Jenkintown, PA 19046.

·AUTHOR'S NOTE·

The Vampire Slayers' Field Guide To The Undead is not just a book about vampires. It is about all kinds of supernatural predatory monsters that have plagued the nights and the lives of people around the world since the dawn of recorded history. Besides, the standard concept of a vampire with cape and fangs is an image that was created for books and movies and bears no resemblance to the monsters people have believed in for thousands of years.

The vampires of folklore and myth come in many bizarre shapes, sizes, and species. Each one is strange and deadly in its own way, and often the line between what is a vampire and what is, say, a werewolf or zombie, is considerably blurred. Some vampires are even half witch or part ghost. In fact, few vampires are *only* vampires; most of them possess other unholy qualities, which makes identifying and destroying them very, very difficult. For the purposes of this book, the word "vampire" is used for a large and varied group of creatures that take some vital essence from their victims, be it blood, sexual energy, breath, or the essence of life itself.

VAMPIRE CATEGORIES

Astral Vampire: A term coined by Theosophist Franz Hartmann to explain the type of vampirism that involves the astrally projected spirits of living people who prey on other humans, often draining them of life force or spiritual energy. This differs from most kinds of Psychic

Vampire in that Astral Vampirism is a deliberate method of attack, whereas many humans who use Psychic Vampirism do so without conscious knowledge.

Essential Vampire: This type of vampire, sometimes called a Pranic Vampire, consumes life energy or sexual essence from its victims. Many Sexual Vampires are also Essential Vampires.

Human Vampire: These are living people who are not supernatural but choose to live as vampires. In rare instances, the term is used to describe human serial killers who practice cannibalism.

Living Vampire: These are supernatural creatures that prey on humans in a vampiric manner but are not undead creatures or ghosts.

Psychic Vampire: Humans who use charisma, passive aggression, or co-dependency to drain others of emotional, mental, and psychological energy. This is often a side-effect of mental or emotional illness and is seldom deliberate.

Revenant: A corpse that has been reanimated and has risen as a vampire, ghost, zombie, or angel. For the purposes of this book, Revenant will be used as a term to describe those vampires that are human corpses that have returned from the dead. These vampires are often pale and shambling, their bodies showing signs of decay.

Sexual Vampire: A form of vampirism that primarily feeds on sexual energy. In the case of females sexual vampires (by far the most common) they are frequently called Seductress Vampires.

Vampire: A general term referring to any creature–natural or supernatural--which feeds on the blood, psychic energy, emotion or life essence on others.

VAMPIRE SUB-GROUPS

Blood Drinker: Any person or creature that consumes blood. This ranges from human Blood Fetishists to parasites like mosquitoes, to vampires and werewolves.

Nightcomer: A vampire who travels only by night and generally cannot abide the light of day.

Shapeshifter: A creature capable of changing its physical form, usually into other animal shapes.

·PART ONE·
EVERYTHING I KNOW ABOUT VAMPIRES I LEARNED FROM MOVIES
(... AND IT GOT ME KILLED!)

"Red is the Color of Blood"

"For I think of you, flung down brutal darkness;
Crushed and red, with pale face.
I think of you, with your hair disordered and dripping.
And myself, rising red from that embrace."

Conrad Aiken
From <u>The Charnel Rose</u>
1918

If the only information about vampires available was that which can be found in novels, poetry, movies, and TV, how well would a modern vampire slayer be protected against an attack by one of the undead?

Not very well, actually.

First, would he know how to identify a vampire? According to popular culture all of the following would be tip-offs:

- Vampires are pale, gaunt creatures with dark eyes and exaggerated canines.

- They don't cast shadows, won't have a reflection in a mirror, and won't appear on film.

- They can't cross running water.

- They can't abide any holy items such as the crucifix (or, more popularly lately, the cross), the Host, or Holy Water.

- They can't enter a church or sacred ground.

- They may not enter any house where they have not been invited.

- Their hearts don't beat, nor do they breathe.

All of which should make them easy to identify, right? Sure, but only if the books and movies have the information correct.

Next, having identified one of the undead, how would a modern vampire slayer dispose of it?

- Do silver bullets work on vampires, or are they just for werewolves?

- What about a stake through the heart? That's supposed to be the ace-in-the-hole for any slayer.

- Could a slayer just tear down the curtains and give the vampire a fatal dose of UV?

- Will running water kill it?

- How about using a cross? Would that do the trick?

The ugly truth is, *no*.

If these were the methods a vampire slayer would pick to destroy one of the undead, then the slayer himself would most likely be the main course at a bloody banquet.

The problem is that the qualities which identify a creature as a vampire according to folklore, religion, and mythology do not match very well against those found in fiction. The same goes with the methods of disposal for these undying monsters.

Bram Stoker. Archival photo.

Novelists, poets, and screenwriters have taken a lot of liberties with the vampire over the years by changing this, modifying that, completely fabricating the other—all in an attempt to create a new slant or a novel twist. From an entertainment standpoint this is great because it keeps the genre from getting stale; but for a vampire slayer researching ways of destroying the undead this is misinformation that will get him (or her) killed.

For example, in his classic novel *Dracula*, Bram Stoker suggested that vampires do not cast reflections in mirrors, that they shun sunlight, can shapeshift into wolves and bats, and cannot cross running water. Armed with this information, Van Helsing and company were able to track Dracula to his lair and destroy him. Yet Van Helsing's team would have been in real trouble if they'd come up against the monsters that actually haunt the cold Romanian forests, such as the Pryccolitch (a vampire-werewolf hybrid that fears no cross and is extremely difficult to kill), or the Strigoi (a pernicious ghostlike predator who not only gets stronger as it feeds but can eventually rejoin humanity, raise a family, hold a job, and has no fear at all of religious icons or sunlight).

London At Midnight. **Original artwork by Robert Patrick O'Brien.**

Oddly, the Chiang-Shih of China does possess the qualities ascribed to the vampires in *Dracula*. Running water, garlic, mirrors, shapeshifting; all of it affects them. But this vampire is an anomaly and by no means the standard.

Prior to the misinformation found in popular fiction, the rise of Christianity—and the emphasis on the Christian rituals and practices in fiction—had a powerful impact on the way the old tales of vampires were handed down. The desire by early Christians to consider everything in relation to church doctrine caused many legends to be rewritten, often resulting in existing legends being replaced with new official versions of each folktale. From the medieval Christian perspective, all of the practices of supernatural beings were viewed as direct affronts to God. Even creatures who used their supernatural powers in defense of humanity, such as the Stregoni Benefici and the Benandanti, were denounced by the Inquisition as unholy.

When fiction writers began telling tales of vampirism, they took the position that supernatural beings were in direct opposition to the church and established new "traditions" to retell the stories of vampires in relation to purely Catholic concepts. For example, the idea of a vampire trading blood with its victim to create a new vampire was a twisted variation on the ritual of communion, where Christians drink wine that symbolizes the blood of Christ and as a result are "reborn." The transformation from human victim to newborn vampire taking three days is clearly modeled after the three days it took Jesus to rise from the dead after his crucifixion.

Such concepts began to be taken as established legend. For example, the inability to face a crucifix was invented by fiction writers, but presented with such deftness that it appeared as if the fiction writers were using established folklore practices as back-story in much the same way that Michael Crichton uses established genetic science as back-story for his fictional dinosaur novels. The proliferation of similar vampire novels made it clear that the general populace was accepting the newly-created methods, powers, and limitations of the vampire as a new kind of gospel.

On the other hand, there were some ties to Christianity that could be found in the established folklore, such as rituals of exorcism used to destroy vampires. As late as the seventeenth century, vampire slayers were using bullets blessed by priests to shoot corpses suspected of being vampires. Stoker cited this in *Dracula*, though no folktales really tell whether these "sacred bullets" actually worked or not. As a practice it did not spread very far and eventually died out.

Using religion as a weapon against evil is not confined to Christian countries or even to the Christian era. Vampires are tied to various religions around the world, from widespread religions like Hinduism, Buddhism, Judaism, and Islam to the less common religions of the druids and Native Americans. In every country, vampire stories have been influenced by religious beliefs and popular fiction so that the original folkloric beliefs are often muddied, and in some cases, entirely lost. This makes it very difficult for the vampire slayer to know the nature and specifics of his unnatural enemy because he cannot trust most of what is "popularly" believed.

Count Orlock killed by sunlight. Archival photo.

By way of example, nearly all vampire movies and books use a vampire's inability to cast a reflection as a nice trick for establishing that a person is actually a vampire. But this bit of information cannot be found in *any* vampire folktales, except in China. As far as crossing running water, few vampires have that restriction, and there are several vampires who actually live in water. The Kappa of Japan and the Animalitos of Spain are water-dwelling demon-vampires, as are the Green Ogresses of France. In the movie *Dracula Prince of Darkness*, the titular count falls through a break in a patch of ice and the rushing water beneath kills him. However, that would not have worked against any of the true Romanian vampires who could easily cross bodies of water.

Photo by Robert Patrick O'Brien.

There are no records of a cross, the Eucharist, or Holy Water being a proof against any of the world's many species of vampires. Again, this belief is mostly the work of Bram Stoker and his literary followers, and the movies have taken the thematic baton and really run with it. In some movies the cross itself is not just a protection but also an actual method of destruction, as shown in the Hammer Films classic, *The Brides of Dracula*. And in that film, a real holy cross isn't even used— Van Helsing turns the vanes of a windmill so that their shadow falls across a fleeing vampire and that alone destroys him. In *Horror of*

Dracula, candlesticks are used to form a cross and, combined with the rays of the sun, turn the Count to dust.

Sunlight has little actual power against true vampires (again with the exception of the Chiang-Shih). Even in the novel *Dracula* the count was able to move around in sunlight, though his powers were diminished. The idea that sunlight is fatal to vampires was concocted by film director Friedrich Wilhelm Murnau as a way of disposing of his Dracula-pastiche vampire, Count Orlock, in the silent classic *Nosferatu*. Since then it has been accepted as gospel in vampire stories, but in folklore most vampires can exist during daylight hours. The Upierczi of Poland, for example, rises at noon and hunts until midnight. The Bruja of Spain lives a normal life by day and only becomes a vampire at night, as do the Soucouyan of Dominica and the Loogaroo of Haiti, along with many others.

The stake through the heart business is a tricky one because it does appear in folk tales of vampires from all over the world, but it is not used to *kill* the undead. Despite the quick, clean "dustings" shown on *Buffy The Vampire Slayer*, or the bloody stakings in so many vampire films, the stake was not a weapon used to actually destroy a vampire but a tool in a more elaborate exorcism. In cases of ritual destruction of a vampire, a stake (of wood or metal) was driven through the body (chest, stomach, wherever) of a resting vampire. This did not end the vampire's life (or un-life) but rather pinned the vampire either to its coffin or to the ground, preventing it from rising. Once restrained in this fashion, the vampire slayers would decapitate the creature, often filling the mouth with garlic. The corpse was then either re-interred or burned. It is the decapitation and burning, not the staking, that does the job. The Kozlak of Dalmatia is the only vampire that will perish from a staking.

Fictional accounts of vampires shapeshifting into animals are a bit closer to the mark than most information found in books and movies, though there are very few legends that say anything about bats. Only about a third of the world's vampires possess shapeshifting powers at all, and out of the hundreds of vampire species around the world, only a handful (the South African Azeman, the Jaracacas of Brazil, the Croatian Kudlak, the Dalmatian Kozlak and the Bhuta of India) can transform into bats. The most common creature for a vampire to morph into is a bird. Owls, crows, ravens, hens, and turkeys are far more common shapes. Cats are another popular beast-shape for vampires, as recounted in the Japanese legend of O Toyo and Prince Hizen, the Chordewa of Bengal, and the Jaracacas of Brazil. Other shapes seen in vampire folklore include such diverse creatures as the moth, snake, wolf (again, not as common as the movies suggest), fly, dog, tick, flea, mouse, rat, or bee.

Artwork by Denise Lawrence.

Several vampires also take the form of fireballs or something resembling a will-o'-the-wisp. These include the Soucouyan of Dominica, the Hungarian Lidérc Nadaly, the Zmeu of Moldavia, the Obayifo of Africa's Gold Coast, the Loogaroo of Haiti, the Asema of Surinam, and the Vjestitiza of Montenegro.

Vampire fiction also insists that no vampire can enter a house uninvited, a theme used heavily in everything from *Dracula* to *Fright Night* to *Buffy* and *Angel*. However, this is not something found in legend; just the opposite, in fact. Special precautions usually have to be taken to keep a vampire out. Various rites, spells, or herbs are employed by different cultures to bar a vampire from entering. In the absence of those protections, the vampire can enter freely and of his own will.

On the subject of vampire strength, all of the sources—from folklore to the most current direct-to-video fang flick—seem to agree: they are very, very strong. Nearly all of them are at least twice as strong as a human, and some are a great deal stronger. The Draugr of Scandinavia, for example, is a vampiric ghost that inhabits and reanimates the bodies of dead Viking warriors, creating a monster so strong that no weapon can harm it. The Chiang-Shih of China actually entertain themselves by ripping their victims limb from limb with their bare hands, as do the Callicantzaros of Greece and the Czechoslovakian Nelapsi. Since the vampire is so powerful, getting close enough to one to fight it is generally a fatal gambit.

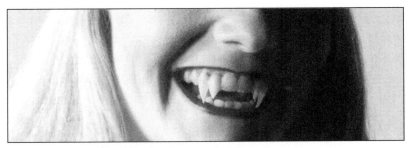

Photo by Robert Patrick O'Brien.

Some vampires do not need physical strength to kill their victims; some can do it merely by the intensity of their gaze. The Jigarkhwar of India and the Russian Eretica both possess lethal stares. Strangely, the Aswang vampire of the Philippines is best defeated by engaging it in a staring contest and waiting until it backs down and slinks away.

Another point on which many legends do jibe with fiction is that vampires hate garlic. Nearly all of them do, and the only reason there are exceptions is because there is no mention of it in their lore, not because these vampires actually demonstrated any resistance to it). Still, there are differences. In the movies, garlic wards vampires off but otherwise does little harm. In the film *The Lost Boys* it does no good at all. But for a vampire slayer, garlic is like arsenic to the undead.

In countries and cultures all over the world, garlic is used to fend off vampires as well as to insure that they are truly dead. In Bavaria, for example, the Blautsauger is kept from entering a house by smearing the windows and doors with mashed garlic. In some countries, including Bavaria, garlic paste is lathered onto livestock to keep them safe from vampiric attack.

The most common use for the plant is to stuff a decapitated vampire's mouth with fresh cloves. This somehow breaks the bond between reanimated flesh and demonic spirit and prevents the vampire from making the mutilated corpse rise again. There are tales aplenty of vampires who, having merely been staked, rise again to trouble the living, but when garlic is placed in the mouths of the dead, they simply do not rise again.

Decapitation is also a handy tool against vampires, whether in the movies or in real life. Sadly, popular fiction doesn't use this method enough, perhaps because it is too quick and simple a solution. A skilled swordsman, a woodsman with an axe, or a reaper with a scythe would each be ideal as a vampire slayer or slayer's assistant. The downside of this method of disposal is that one has to identify and locate the vampire, then get close enough to swing the weapon. Vampires are secretive by nature, and being unnaturally fast and powerful, they generally offer a strong resistance.

The movies and television have one other thing right, and that is the fact that fire destroys vampires, just as it destroys everything else. It is often called "the great purifier," and in the battle against undead evil it certainly lives up to that claim. When a slayer is unsure if a ritual has been properly performed, or when confronted by a species of vampire whose complete nature is unknown, the best fallback is a nice bonfire. In many countries cremation of a suspected vampire is done regardless of any other rituals or rites. There are no known cases of a vampire returning from the ashes.

In Czechoslovakia, when the vampiric Nelapsi is burned, the ashes are spread over fields and along roads as a final charm against evil. In Romania, the ashes of a destroyed Strigoi are mixed with water and fed to the members of the Strigoi's surviving human family to cure them of any sickness or evil taint. In many world cultures a "need fire" (also called a "living fire") is made of the vampire's pyre, a kind of purifying bonfire used to cleanse the evil taint from anyone who passes through its smoke.

One last—and very significant—point that is often presented entirely wrong in books and movies is the method by which a person becomes a vampire. The idea of trading blood—a vampire must bite its victim and then offer its own blood—was started in *Dracula* and is now popularly believed to be the case. Not so, however. For the most part, all that is required for a person to become one of the undead is to die in a horrible fashion—violent deaths, suicides, hangings, battlefield deaths, murders, stillbirths, death during delivery, death by plague, and so on. Being born under a curse can also lead to a vampiric life, including being born with teeth, born with a caul (an amniotic membrane covering the face), born between Christmas and the New Year, being born out of wedlock, being a seventh son or daughter, or even being born on Christmas day. In some rare cases a person returns from the dead if they were bitten by a vampire, without having had to drink the vampire's blood. In more than a few cases, if a werewolf dies it comes back as a vampire. That's not something seen in movies, which is a shame because it makes for a nice and very frightening twist.

Another power that vampires possess that is never addressed in movies or books, but is extremely common to vampires around the world, is the spread of disease. Vampires are frequently plague carriers, and either infect with their bite, or carry with them a pervasive air of pestilence that can wither humans, livestock, and crops. Even the word "Nosferatu," mistakenly defined as "undead" by Bram Stoker, actually means "plague carrier."

The most important thing for a vampire slayer to do when facing one of the undead is to first define which kind of monster it is, then do some homework; not cribbing information from books, TV, or movies, but reading folktales and listening to the wisdom of village elders who know what will, and will not, destroy a vampire.

The Vampire Slayers' Field Guide To The Undead is a directory of vampires and similar creatures from around the world and throughout history. The book is intended to provide useful information on how to identify these monsters, how they are created, what their powers are, how they hunt, and how they can be fought. These vampires and their kin are organized by country.

So gather your garlic, sharpen your stake, fetch your gravedigger's shovel, and prepare to face the world of the undead.

Photo by Robert Patrick O'Brien.

·PART TWO·

VAMPIRES AROUND THE WORLD

A–F

"Vampyre"

The choir then burst the fun'ral dome
Where Sigismund was lately laid,
And found him, tho' within the tomb,
Still warm as life, and undecay'd.

With blood his visage was distain'd,
Ensanguin'd were his frightful eyes,
Each sign of former life remain'd,
Save that all motionless he lies.

The corpse of Herman they contrive
To the same sepulchre to take,
And thro' both carcases they drive,
Deep in the earth, a sharpen'd stake!

John Stagg
The Minstrel of the North
1810

VAMPIRES OF ALBANIA

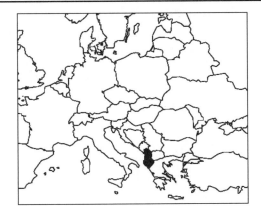

GJAKPIRË

The Gjakpirë is an Albanian vampire about which little is known today. It is generally considered to be a Revenant and a blood drinker, much like the Lugat, though it is not as difficult to kill.

Folk tales suggest that the Gjakpirës were cowardly vampires because they could easily be killed. Therefore, they used deception and trickery to gain access to a sleeping person, then would take just a little blood but not enough to cause alarm.

The Gjakpirës traveled by night, often in the form of dark night birds, and would change back into their natural shapes (that of reanimated corpses) prior to attacking their victims.

Often a Gjakpirë would lay by the side of a road, appearing to be simply an injured traveler, and wait for a good samaritan to come along and offer aid. Once the well-intentioned person was within reach the Gjakpirë would stab him in the groin or throat with a sharpened stick, then wait for the victim to become weak with blood loss before attacking and lapping up the blood.

DARK NIGHT BIRDS

The Gjakpirë is one of many supernatural creatures who adopt the form of a dark night bird. Crows, ravens, and magpies are tied into the darker legends of nearly every culture around the world. Sometimes they are seen as beings of evil, sometimes as forces for good, and sometimes merely as omens of impending events. Here are some of the more common supernatural beliefs regarding crows, ravens and magpies:

- Roadkill as good luck? Apparently, finding a dead crow on the road is considered so.

- Church yards aren't considered safe havens for those who find a raven there. It's considered bad luck.

- One crow flying over a house is considered a bad omen, perhaps intimating a death to come. "A crow on the thatch, soon death lifts the latch."

- In Wales, the black cat superstition is replaced by a single crow crossing your path leading to bad luck. However, if a second crow joins his pal, it becomes good luck. "Two crows I see, good luck to me."

- In New England, however, two crows flying from left to right across your path are considered bad luck.

- In the darker ages, European peasants believed a quiet molting season meant that crows were gearing up to pay tribute to the devil with their discarded feathers.

- Although pairs of doves are often released at weddings, pairs of crows have also been released at weddings in order to foresee the outcome of the marriage. If the pair fly off as a duo, it is expected that the couple will have a long happy marriage. If the two birds fly away from each other, the newlyweds may soon also part.

- In Chinese mythology, the number three is the number of goodness and light. A three-legged crow is therefore used to represent the Sun, the ultimate embodiment of these characteristics.

- The size of a group of crows or magpies is a harbinger of what is to come, as suggested in the following rhyme:

    > *One for sorrow, two for mirth,*
    > *Three for a wedding, four for a birth,*
    > *Five for silver, six for gold,*
    > *Seven for a secret not to be told.*
    > *Eight for heaven, nine for hell,*
    > *And ten for the devil's own sel'.*

Artwork by Robert Patrick O'Brien.

- If you aren't fond of the magpie counting fortunes, you can cast a spell of protection by making the sign of the cross, raising your hat to the bird, or spitting three times over your right shoulder and saying, "Devil, devil, I defy thee."

- Because magpies didn't wear all black to Jesus' crucifixion, it is assumed that God has since cursed them.

- In Scotland, it was thought that Magpies were so evil, they must have a drop of the Devil's blood under their tongues.

Artwork by Shane MacDougall.

- In Somerset, England, people would carry an onion with them for protection against magpies and crows.

- Also in Somerset, they took tipping their hats to ravens quite seriously so as to appease the birds.

- Instead of the Bogeyman, Yorkshire children were scared with threats of the Great Black Bird coming to take them away if they were bad.

- Never steal a raven's eggs. It is thought to cause the death of a baby.

- King Arthur was supposed to have turned into a raven, clearing the birds of some bad press and giving them a royal air.

- Alexander the Great had two ravens sent from heaven to guide him out of the desert.

- "A House Divided Shall Not Stand." Not in England anyway. The Tower of London, home to ravens for a millennium, represents the crown of England. It is assumed that if the ravens ever leave the Tower, then the Tower will fall. In turn, so goes the crown and country.

- In Wales, a raven perched on your house means there is some prosperity to come.

- In Scotland, if a raven circles above a house, someone in the house will die.

- Rain can be predicted by rooks feeding close to their nests or on the streets in the morning. If they feed far from their nest, it should be a nice day.

- When a landowner would die, the new landowner was to stand beneath the rookery and announce the news to the birds. The new landowner would usually add the promise that only he or his friends would be allowed to shoot the birds. However, if the new landowner did not perform this ceremony, the rooks would leave their home. This was considered a bad omen of financial downfall to come.

- In France, a priest gone bad is thought to become a crow, while an evil nun is thought to become a magpie.

- The Greeks say "Go to the crows" the same way Americans say "Go to Hell."

- For something thought impossible to do, the Romans say "To pierce a crow's eye".

- An Irish expression, "You'll follow the crows for it" means a person will miss something once it's gone.

- "I have a bone to pick with you" used to actually be " I have a crow to pick with you".

- Shooting crows seems to be a popular protection racket:

  To protect seed, one should shoot rooks and carrion crows.

  To protect baby birds, shoot crows and magpies.

  And for protection for young lambs, ravens should be shot.

Archival artwork.

SAMPIRO

Legend has it that any Albanian who is of Turkish ancestry will, upon his death, rise again as a vampire called a Sampiro. At this point, the creature will construct steel shoes and, still wrapped in its burial shroud, haunt the countryside, spreading death and disease.

Vampire slayers look for a will-o'-the-wisp and follow it back to the Sampiro's grave. If the disinterred corpse looks like someone who has just died—or worse, like someone who is still alive—then it is proof that they have found the resting place of the evil Sampiro.

Once the corpse is exposed, the vampire slayer will drive a long ashwood stake through the creature's chest. This does not kill the vampire, but it does irrevocably pin the vampire into its coffin, making it unable to rise and feed. Devoid of nourishment, the vampire's body, will eventually wither and decay into dust over the coming years.

In cases where this preventative measure has not proved sure enough, or when a slayer wants to play it safe, the staked vampire is decapitated, the mouth filled with garlic, and the head turned backward in the coffin so that it will constantly look downward to Hell. The body is re-buried, and chopped garlic is mixed into the grave dirt as an added protection.

SHTRIGA

The Shtriga is a vicious female witch-vampire whose special prey are infants. Many legends suggest that the Shtriga is a woman who was barren or whose child died young, and now seeks revenge on the world for the injustices of Fate. Other tales cast her as a spinster who has never known love and has therefore grown bitter and old. She has turned to black magic to strike back at the people who shunned her and—by her perceptions—denied her the grace of love and family.

The Shtriga is a shapeshifter that transforms into a moth, bee, or other flying insect. It will steal in through an open window, settle on a sleeping child, and drain away its life essence.

The Shtriga has been the hated villain in the bad dreams of many a parent, and has been blamed for many Sudden Infant Death Syndrome

(SIDS) losses as late as the twentieth century. These crib deaths, inexplicable even now, could have no other explanation to simple villagers, who felt there had to be some dark supernatural agent at work.

Children are not the Shtriga's only victims. These evil creatures also prey on adults by spreading diseases and bringing discord to the community.

By day the Shtriga is able to live undiscovered among ordinary people, passing herself off as a member of the community and even attending church. But once a person had been suspected of being a Shtriga there are two potential methods of detection. During a church service the suspect would be handed a piece of the Host (in this case it would be a piece of bread rather than a wafer) spiced with garlic. Like most vampires, the Shtriga cannot eat garlic and will be visibly repelled by it—alerting the rest of parishioners to the demon in their midst.

The Shtriga. Artwork by Robert Patrick O'Brien.

The second way of detecting the presence of a Shtriga is to place a small cross made from the bones of a pig on the doors of the church after the service has begun and everyone is inside. When the service is concluded, the Shtriga will not be able to cross the threshold to exit the church.

Another charm works quite well against the Shtriga but is very dangerous to obtain. A person has to follow a Shtriga that has assumed mortal form back to its home. Legend has it that the Shtriga will vomit up some of the blood she's consumed. Once she leaves or goes to sleep, the intrepid vampire slayer has to scrape some of the blood onto a silver coin, wrap the coin in cloth, and wear it constantly. The Shtriga is unable to inflict harm on the wearer of a charm such as this.

VAMPIRES OF AMERICA

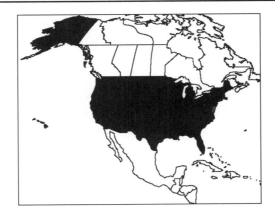

America has two kinds of vampires–domestic and imported.

The domestic vampires are creatures from the various Native American cultures (*see* Vampires Of Native American Cultures), but European settlers and African slaves brought their own species of vampires with them. Since America is the "melting pot" it's not surprising that many vampire legends from others cultures have blended together and overlapped to create new versions of old horror tales.

In American monster folklore there are plenty of tales of shapeshifting monsters such as werewolves and cat people, life-draining sorcerers, reanimated corpses, and more. Some of these legends are tied into the African-based religions of Voodoo and Santeria, and others are based on influences from Native American beliefs from the United States and, more often, Mexico.

The many Native American nations have their own legends of monsters, some of whom drink blood although they are not considered "vampires" as the rest of the world might define them. Most of the Native American monsters are flesh-eaters and shapeshifters, which makes them cousins to the werewolf. But as the werewolf is inextricably linked to vampirism, that makes them targets for the vampire slayer.

The culture and fascination with vampires is arguably stronger in America than anywhere else on earth. The whole movie industry has one foot in the grave, so to speak. Dracula is one of the most frequently featured characters in movies, as are all of the Dracula clones (Count Yorga, etc.), the romanticized vampires of Anne Rice's books and movies, and the post-modern vampires of films ranging from the nihilistic *Near Dark* to the allegorical *The Addiction*.

Many forms of American vampire fiction, especially films, utilize vampires as symbols of various forms of social dysfunction such as drug abuse, gang mentality, teenage rebellion, xenophobia, and so on. Nineteenth century European writers like Bram Stoker, Lord Byron, and Sheridan LeFanu have handed the baton to American film makers, who have run with it all through the twentieth century and into the twenty-first. It is has become Hollywood that decides what a vampire is, what it looks like, how it can be created, how it can be killed. American films now modify vampire mythology, constantly changing the specifics of the nature of vampirism to further their plots. These movies, as wonderfully entertaining as they are, are full of misinformation and disinformation.

Even so, are there undead monsters haunting America? Are there creatures who came over in the settlers' ships? It is difficult to say with any certainty, but in the nineteenth century, during an outbreak of tuberculosis, there were quite a few suspected cases of vampirism that resulted in a large number of corpses being disinterred. This occurred mostly in the New England states of Connecticut, Vermont and Rhode Island. In 1896, the *New York World* even published an account of disinterment in Rhode Island. A clipping of this article found its way across the Atlantic and into the hands of Bram Stoker. *Dracula* scholars have often postulated that this news story may have been a contributing factor to Stoker writing that novel.

BIGFOOT

See Sasquatch in Vampires Of Canada, p. 142.

THE JERSEY DEVIL

Though not a vampire *per se*, the Jersey Devil has been associated with the mass slaughter of animals and stealing of children, ostensibly to feast upon both.

The Jersey Devil has haunted the New Jersey Pinelands for well over 250 years, making it the oldest folk legend among the non-Native Americans. There have been several thousand sightings of the creature, many by what are believed to be unimpeachable sources.

The original stories of the creature vary, often wildly. One of the most common tales has it that a Mrs. Shrouds (sometimes called Mother Leeds or Abigail Leeds) of Leeds Point, NJ, burdened with twelve children, made a vow that if she ever had another child she would want it to be a devil (or, in some histories, the child of the Devil). When she bore her inevitable thirteenth child it was misshapen and horribly deformed, with goat-like legs, a human torso, bat wings, and an elongated snout variously described as similar to that of a wolf, horse, fox, or crocodile. When Mrs. Shrouds tried to suckle the infant, it spread its wings and escaped up the chimney.

The second most common story tells of a young girl from Leeds Point who fell in love with a British soldier during the Revolutionary War. The townspeople felt that she betrayed her country, so they cursed her. When she delivered the love child, it was a devil.

Dozens of other histories abound, sometimes placing the site of birth as Burlington, Hammonton, Green Bank, or elsewhere. Whichever is closest to the truth, the creature apparently came into being in Leeds Point in Atlantic County, New Jersey. It has never left, although it may have strayed occasionally (there have been sightings in Maryland and Pennsylvania). The year of birth is most often agreed upon as 1735.

Different stories tell that the child was the 6th, 8th, 10th, 12th, or 13th child of the misfortunate woman. Some stories state the child was born human but soon transformed into a monster. Theories on what the creature might be range from some species of vampire, to an immortal though deformed child, to a new kind of predator bird. Theories that it might be a surviving dinosaur or pterodactyl have been forwarded (in one case by a scientist at the Smithsonian Institution). Whatever it is, it appears to be immortal and has a definite thirst for blood and destruction.

The Jersey Devil. Artwork by Robert Patrick O'Brien.

NOTABLE SIGHTINGS OF THE JERSEY DEVIL

Much of the information in this section generously provided by Dave Juliano.

- In the 19th Century, Commodore Stephen Decatur of the U.S. Navy was engaged in artillery testing at the Hanover Iron Works in Hanover, NJ. A strange creature flew across the test range. He fired at it and hit it, but the creature flew away, apparently uninjured. Decatur claimed that the creature was easily nine feet long from head to tail.

- Joseph Bonaparte, former king of Spain and brother of Napoleon, encountered the creature while living in exile in the United States under the name Count de Survilliers. He had come to the U.S. in 1815 following his brother's defeat and purchased 1,800 acres in Bordentown. While hunting in 1841 he spotted the Jersey Devil and recorded it in his diary. He claimed that he released his hunting dogs but the hounds would not pursue the creature.

- In 1840-41 there was a massive slaughter of chickens and sheep, reportedly by a creature that uttered a piercing scream and left strange hooflike tracks in the muddy soil.

- In the years between 1859 and 1894, the Jersey Devil was very active. It was blamed for attacking animals and children, and carrying them off into the woods in and around Haddonfield, Bridgeton, Smithville, Long Branch, Brigantine, and Leeds Point.

- In 1899 there was another massive slaughter of livestock, this time around Vincentown and Burrsville. The ground was marked once more by huge hoof prints. Hunting hounds brought in to track the creature would not go near the woods.

- 1909 saw the greatest spate of Jersey Devil sightings, with more than one thousand sightings across thirty towns all over the Delaware River line. Again the creature was described as being nine feet tall and horrifying to behold.

- In 1927, a cab driver stopped to fix a flat tire and while he was working the Jersey Devil landed on the roof of his car. Though it shook the car back and forth with great violence, it did not attack him and flapped off into the nearby woods.

• On the night before Pearl Harbor was attacked in 1941, the Devil was spotted by several people. These sightings led to the belief that the creature is a harbinger of evil. There were similar sightings prior to the Vietnam War and the World Trade Center disaster.

• In 1953 the creature was even spotted in the town of Salem, New Jersey, crouching in the street.

• On a starlit evening in 1961, four young folks were "parking" in a secluded spot in the Pine Barrens. They heard a loud scream from outside, then the roof of their car was smashed in by something immensely strong. They fled with-out injury, but their car was destroyed.

• In 1966, a farm was attacked and ducks, geese, cats, even two guard dogs--one of which was a fierce German Shepherd--were slaughtered.

• In 1987, another German shepherd was found torn apart, the body gnawed upon. The corpse was surrounded by strange hoof prints.

Photo by Jason Lukridge.

LOUP-GAROU

The French word for "werewolf" is *Loup-Garou*. These creatures seem to have invaded the United States along with early French settlers.

The werewolf and the vampire are closely linked in many cultures. In Byelorus, when a werewolf is killed it comes back as a species of vampire called a Mjertovjec. The Loogaroo of Haiti are witches who shed their skins at night to become vampire/werewolf hybrids. The Romanian Pryccolitch is a vampire/werewolf hybrid. The Portuguese Lobishomen is regarded by many scholars to be as similar to a true werewolf as it is to a vampire. In Greece, when a wronged person is killed (a common source for vampire legends) it is reborn not as a vampire but as a werewolf called a Farkaskoldus.

A werewolf is any person who changes into a wolf or wolflike creature. In folklore this was something that happened by force of will, but in more recent fictional accounts (books and movies) it is related to a curse and only happens during the three days of the full moon.

The name is probably derived from *vargulf*, a Norse expression meaning murderer or predator. In fact, many the accounts of early "werewolf" attacks were closer to the murderous methods used by human serial killers. The Greek term *lycanthrope* (wolf-man) is also commonly used. More general terms for the metamorphosis of people into animals include shapeshifter, turnskin, or turncoat.

Most European cultures have stories of werewolves, including Greece (Lycanthropos), Russia (Volkodlak), England (Werewolf), Germany (Werwolf), and France (Loup-garou). In northern Europe, there are also tales about people changing into bears. In European mythology, the legends of berserkers may be a source of the werewolf myths. Berserkers were vicious fighters dressed in wolf or bear hides. They were apparently immune to pain and in battle were vicious killers, slaughtering their opponents with the single-mindedness of wild animals. In Latvian mythology, the Vilkacis was a person who had been changed into a wolf-like monster, though the Vilkacis was occasionally benevolent.

Many of these legends came to American shores with visitors as early as the Vikings, and more steadily with the colonists. Of the European werewolf legends, the Loup-garou, or d'Loup-garou (pronounced loo-guROO) is by far the most common, especially among the Cajuns of Louisiana.

One common Cajun legend is used to frighten children into good behavior. A Loup-garou lives deep in the swamps of Louisiana and comes out when the moon is full. According to local stories, this creature is "the meanest, smelliest, ugliest monster." It can smell when a child has been mean, comes to their house, and "eats bad lil' girls an' boys—from d'tip o' dey hair to dey baby toenails."

The Loup-garou can be killed in any number of ways, from firearms to burning, but it can be warded off by a charm called a *gris-gris* (*see* Vampires Of Ghana (p. 215) and "The Religion Of Vodoun" (p. 221) for further details).

The Loup-garou is not confined to the bayous and swamps of Louisiana. In Vincennes, Indiana, legends of the Loup-garou suggest that a person can be cursed to transform into a wolf, cow, horse, or some other animal. Once under the spell of this demonic spirit, the unfortunate victim becomes an enraged animal that roams through the fields and forests at night. The curse only lasts for a specific span of time, usually 101 days. During the day, the Loup-garou returns to his human form, but will afterward be plagued with poor health and depression.

The only way for the Loup-garou to be released from the curse is for someone to recognize him as a human that has transformed to an animal, then somehow draw blood from him while in his transformed state. This is difficult and dangerous and is usually only possible while the creature sleeps. However, the curse states that even if the spell is broken neither the victim nor his rescuer can mention the incident, even to each other, until the original 101 days were over. Otherwise they would both suffer even worse enchantment.

Vincennes, Indiana has been the center of more than a century of werewolf legends. Even today there are plenty of people who look closely at any animal acting strangely, and make the sign of the cross to ward off the possible Loup-garou lurking within.

Photo by Jason Lukridge.

HUMAN VAMPIRES

In America (and to a lesser degree around the world) there is a culture of non-supernatural vampirism that has grown up over the last few decades. These are living people who are not supernatural but choose to live as vampires. Human Vampires range from devotees of the massively popular *Vampire: The Masquerade* role-playing game, to members of the Goth culture, to other groups whose dress, names, and manners reflect some aspect of vampire culture, largely based on the more romantic presentation of vampires from fiction. The works of Anne Rice, whose vampires are cultured, intellectual, and beautiful, are major influences on the lifestyles of many Human Vampires.

Within the Human Vampire community there are major distinct sub-groups. Rarely do the groups overlap:

- *Lifestylers* live the vampire life constantly and identify with vampires as kindred spirits.

- *Role Players* adopt vampire clothing, personalities, manners and speech patterns as part of their participation in games such as *Vampire: The Masquerade*.

- *Real Vampires* are self-named for their addiction to activities involving real blood, often involving sado-masochistic cutting (of themselves and their willing partners) and sometimes the ingestion of blood.

- *Mundanes* are anyone who is not part of the vampire culture, especially those who are oblivious to its existence. Mundanes are often jokingly referred to as "mortals."

These Human Vampires often dress in stylized Gothic clothing, sometimes dye their hair jet black, bleach their skin to a milky white, and have custom fangs made for themselves. A much smaller sub-group, called Blood Fetishists, even drink human or animal blood. This is a dangerous lifestyle choice in this day of AIDS, but on the other hand, drinking blood is not really that far away from eating sushi or steak tartare, which is, after all, raw flesh (albeit animal).

Human Vampires have their own forms of music and their own clubs. One very famous club, the Long Black Veil in Manhattan, has established a code of conduct for proper vampiric behavior on the premises, known as the Black Veil or the "13 Rules of the Community." The Black Veil is the foundation of the Sanguinarium community, as it sets a standard for common sense etiquette. The original Black Veil was composed in 1997 by Father Sebastian of House Sahjaza, and revised by Michelle Belanger of House Kheperu in the spring of 2000.

The Sanguinarium community has its own sub-groupings:

- *Born Vampires* are those persons who have always believed that they were vampires, and that they did not adopt vampirism as a lifestyle choice.

- *Fashion Vampires* dress and act as vampires but do so as a fashion statement rather than a lifestyle choice.

- *Latent Vampires* are persons whose vampirism has not yet blossomed, so they need to be drawn out by others who are already empowered as vampires.

- *Made Vampires* are those persons who have been inducted into the vampire community through ritual "transformations."

- *Pranic Vampires* are persons who feed off vital energy, also called Essential Vampires. "Prana" is an Indian concept of a life force that courses through the body along spiritual path-ways called meridians. It is equivalent to Chi (Chinese) or Ki (Japanese), and forms the basis for acupressure and acupuncture.

- *Sanguinarians* are Real Vampires who drink blood and engage in Blood Sports.

- *Sexual Vampires* feed off of sexual energy or are empowered during sexual encounters.

> **SANGUINARIAN:** Derived from the Latin word *sanguineus*, which means bloodthirsty. Sanguinarians are people who have a physical craving for blood. People acting out because of this disorder may be one of the many non-supernatural causes of vampire folktales.

There has frequently been some confusion caused by some Human Vampires referring to themselves as Living Vampires. For the purposes of this book Human Vampires and Living Vampires are treated as two different groups, as in the definitions given in this section and in the Vampire Dictionary in Appendix I.

The term Human Vampire has also frequently been given to a radically different and much smaller sub-group of humanity: serial killers who sometimes demonstrate cannibalistic behavior. But the true Human Vampire community has rarely been associated with any kind of violence. It is actually a quite nonviolent, mutually supportive culture.

The degree of involvement in the Human Vampire culture ranges from a peripheral involvement for those who just like to attend vampire

Photo by Robert Patrick O'Brien.

parties to those for whom it has become a true lifestyle. This is not something taken as a lighthearted joke by these "true" vampires; it is their life choice and their practices and interactions with others of their kind are taken very seriously.

Within the culture of Human Vampires, there are some who believe that vampires exist or used to exist. These people generally regard vampires as tragically misunderstood figures rather than predatory monsters, and refer to them variously as the Old Ones, the Lonely Ones, the Wise Ones, the First, and so on.

Another small sub-culture embraces the darker species of vampires and models itself after them regardless of what the non-vampire society might think of them. They do not consider this to be antisocial behavior, but rather behavior appropriate to the complex societies they have developed.

Vampires symbolize power and freedom from social and cultural restraints, a liberation from the extremes and complexities of human emotions. Vampirism is therefore very appealing to those who feel that "normal" society is too inhibiting and prohibitive of truly open expression.

Most people seem to regard vampire societies as merely extreme off-shoots of the Goth subculture, but that is neither entirely accurate nor entirely fair. It is easy for outsiders to mock the Human Vampire lifestyle, but people frequently tend to mock what they don't under-stand, don't belong to, or fear. Any culture that is honest about what it wants, what it believes, and how it chooses to live is as correct as any other and should not be mocked for its differences.

There is one disturbing thought, though: if true vampires do exist, then it would be very easy for them to find sanctuary among these vampire societies. This concept has been presented in various works of fiction, from movies like *The Hunger* and *Blade* to the novels of Anne Rice. The possibilities send a shiver down the spine.

BLOOD FETISHISM

Fetishism is a state of mind in which an individual's sexual impulses become fixated on a symbol that acts as a substitute for a real, love-based objective. In the case of the Blood Fetishist, the fixation is on blood. It is the blood--not sex, or sex alone--that is the driving need and substitutes for more conventional forms of intimacy.

Blood Fetishism is blood drinking and/or bloodletting, done either for erotic gratification or as a method of intimacy or bonding. This blood consumption ranges from taking small amounts of blood to drinking much larger quantities. In many cases this practice is tied into the sexual practices of Bondage and Discipline, and Sadism and Masochism.

A Blood Fetishist is different from other kinds of human blood drinkers such as Sanguinarians, who suffer from a psychological compulsion to drink blood. The difference is one of choice: the Sanguinarians must drink blood, whereas the Fetishist craves it for erotic gratification. The presence of violence also separates Blood Fetishists from Sanguinarians: blood arousal and violence are linked in many (though certainly not all) cases. Certainly this degree of fetishism has far outpaced the less destructive forms of blood drinking shared by those who enjoy S&M and B&D.

Blood Fetishism has been documented for well over a century. One early and very important book on sexual deviation is Richard von Krafft-Ebbing's *Psychopathia Sexuali*, a pioneering collection of case studies that catalogs and defines various forms of perversion, including fetishism, incest, and others. The book is considered one of the most important documents in modern humanity's efforts to understand and define itself.

Another aspect of blood fetishism is Blood Play (sometimes called Blood Sports) which involves willing participants cutting themselves or each other for ritualistic or, more commonly, sado-masochistic thrills.

Blood drinking has also been discovered as a practice of quite a number of serial killers.

PSYCHIC VAMPIRES

In modern America, psychologists and holistic healers have coined a term for people who prey on others and, essentially, "drain them" of emotional energy: Psychic Vampires. These vampires are clearly human (no fangs, no rising from the grave), but they nevertheless possess a tremendous power over others. Psychic Vampires use a variety of tools, from passive aggression to co-dependency, to sap the psychic, emotional, and even physical energy out of their victims.

These Psychic Vampires are generally not evil or even mean. They are normal and unaware of the damage they inflict. Much of their power comes from a kind of charisma, and they intentionally or unintentionally exploit other people for their own benefit.

Psychic Vampires generally don't look too closely at themselves or their motives and practices, much in the way that fictional vampires avoid mirrors. Self-examination is anathema to them and they avoid it the way a folkloric vampire avoids garlic. Having avoided this introspection, they can easily deny responsibility for any damage they do.

The attacks of Psychic Vampires may seem of little consequence on the surface, but like folkloric vampires who only take small amounts of blood at a time, it is the cumulative effect that matters. After repeated attacks by a Psychic Vampire, a person feels totally drained, even to the point of physical, emotional, or mental exhaustion, and that is certainly dangerous.

The methods of "attack" used by Psychic Vampires can take many forms:

- Taking responsibility for another's achievements in work, among family, etc. leads to frustration and stress levels that can adversely affect one's health.

- Stealing the limelight in almost any circumstance by turning any situation around to be "about them." For example, if a relative dies, no matter how distant, the Psychic Vampire will become dramatically and tragically distraught, forcing others in the family away from their grief in order to succor him or her. This feeds the Psychic Vampire and drains energy from the rest of the family.

- They can be a smothering or cloying parent who cannot yield control of a growing child's life to the child, thereby socially or emotionally crippling that person.

- Some are religious extremists who pollute the minds and hearts of their children with bigotry toward anyone who doesn't believe in the same rigid and exclusive practices that they do.

- Sexual predators are often Psychic Vampires. Their methods of attack can range from seduction that appears to be romantic but is actually self-gratifying exploitation of another, to far more insidious seductions of the innocent (of any age).

And so on, with great variety.

In folklore, the line between human Psychic Vampires and supernatural vampires who prey on humans in order to feed on emotions and life essences is often indistinct. Many of the supernatural Psychic Vampires are of the subspecies called Essential Vampires, named so because they feed on sexual or vital energy rather than blood.

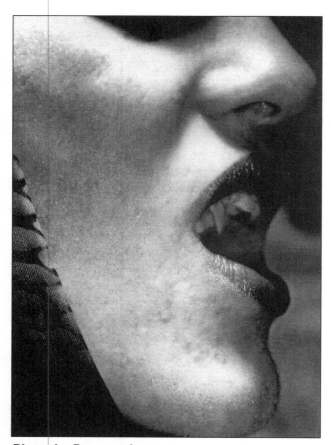

Photo by Breanne Levy.

THE VAMPIRES OF EDGAR ALLEN POE

The great American poet and writer, Edgar Allen Poe, used vampirism in one form or another in several of his classic works. In his 1838 short story, "Ligeia," the narrator longs for a long-dead love who then returns in the undead flesh, in what promises to be something less than a happy and romantic reunion. In the novel, _The Fall Of The House of Usher_, Roderick and Madeline Usher each display several of the classic traits of vampires. Roderick, for example, has a "cadaverousness of complexion," "ghastly pallor of the skin," and eyes that possess a "miraculous lustre." He also shuns lights. Madeline mirrors may of these same qualities.

Poe's vampires tended to be more ghostly than substantial, haunting the minds and hearts of his characters much in the same way that a Psychic Vampire preys on the living in order to feed on emotions and psychic energy.

Edgar Allen Poe. Archival photo.

Many of Poe's characters are obsessed with the dead, often willing the dead to rise from the grave to return to them in any form, no matter how unnatural. Vampirism, with its terrible energy exchanges and lesions, is ultimately Poe's analogy for a love that persists beyond the grave--an all-consuming passion that knows no peace until undead reconciliation is effected.

VAMPIRE: THE MASQUERADE

In 1991, a card and dice role-playing game was introduced called *Vampire: The Eternal Struggle*. Invented for White Wolf games by Mark Rein-Hagen, the game established a vampire-themed story-line. The story's directions were based on rolls of the dice. During the game, the players use various strategies to acquire blood; failure to accomplish this ends in death (that is, losing the game.)

Two years later the game evolved into *Vampire: The Masquerade* (VtM), which replaced the dice with coded hand signals. Shortly after, the game moved to the Internet. Once there it spread like wildfire and is now immensely popular all over the world.

The story lines have evolved, establishing rich histories and creating detailed vampire clans that war with one another in the "reality" called the World of Darkness (WoD). Each game is overseen by a Storyteller who sets the scene and controls the action. Players often develop very ornate and complex histories for their characters and assume the personalities of their characters while they are playing. Their adherence to the WoD is very strong and they consider is very bad form to break character during a game.

White Wolf has released a whole library of books to provide Storytellers and players alike with game rules, plots, histories, alternative actions, and more. Spin-off books number in the tens of thousands, and players may be in the millions.

In the VtM world, vampires are called the Kindred, all of whom are descended from Caine (same as the Cain who slew Abel). Cursed by God, Caine became the first vampire and later created others, many of whom formed their own bloodlines, or clans. Each clan has its own history and attributes that set it apart from the others. The clans are like extended families and serve to provide strong archetypes for character development. Players choose the clan with which they most identify, or may also choose to play one of the Caitiff, the Clanless, if they feel that their character vision does not fit any of the given clans or if they would simply like to play an outcast.

The clans of VtM are:

THE CAMARILLA

- *Brujah*: These are the renegades and street thugs. A smaller faction of this group tends to be intellectuals who shun society and its ways.

- *Malkavian*: All Malkavians are thought to be insane, but each Malkavian is more likely crazy like a fox.

- *Nosferatu*: A group of extremely ugly vampires (think the Master from *Buffy*) that keeps to itself and yet knows many secrets of the other creatures in their city.

- *Toreador*: The Toreadors are the high-fashion upper-crust type. They favor the fine arts and tend to be quite high-strung.

- *Tremere*: This is an exclusive group of warlocks that developed through ancient magic. They tend to keep to themselves and guard their magics closely.

- *Ventrue*: The nobility of the Camarilla, this group is considered by many to be leaders of the clan. They respect the old ways and traditions.

SOLITARY CLANS

- *Assamites*: This clan is comprised of assassins.

- *Cappadocians*: This clan has not existed since the Middle Ages, but was greatly feared and respected. Known as "the Clan of Death," this group and their leader, Cappadocius, strove to extract every bit of knowledge about vampires, including death and what came after.

- *Daughters of Cacophony*: This group consists of beautiful musicians. It developed sometime around the eighteenth century. It is possible they were an offshoot of the Toreador or the Malkavians.

- *Followers of Set*: Set is the god of evil and darkness. This clan is not favored by any of the other clans. The Settites intend to create a race of slaves for themselves and their evil master.

- *Gangrel*: Gangrel are shapechangers who can turn into wolves, bats, or other animals. Until recently, they were a part of Clan Camarilla. They tend to be isolationists and keep to themselves.

- *Giovanni*: This clan is most like the Italian mafia. They maintain a respectable, affluent business façade on the outside while performing dirty deeds behind closed doors.

- *Ravnos*: Ravnos are most like gypsies and hoboes, wandering throughout Europe. Very strangely, all Ravnos will attempt to kill each other if they see another of their kind.

- *Salubri*: Only seven in number at any given time, this clan hates their vampire lives. They can pass as humans, although they have a hidden third eye. Other clans dislike them.

- *Samedi*: A relatively new bloodline, the Samedi are thought to have developed out of the Nosferatu or Giovanni clans.

THE SABBAT

- *Lasombra*: This alluring group of Cainites is comprised of superior predators who consider themselves to be the height of Vampiric existence. They believe that theirs is the Divine Right.

- *The Antitribu*: This group is formed by clan members of the Camarilla and some independents. Subgroups of the Antitribu include the Tremere Antitribu, the Salubri Antitribu, and the Settite Antitribu. The Tremere Antitribu no longer exists, as they were all vanquished by the Salubri Antitribu. The Settite Antitribu are considered the Serpents of the Light.

- *Tzimisce*: An especially cruel group, the Tzimisce have plagued Europe from the beginning of time. Their dwellings are found in the Carpathian mountain range.

VAMPIRES OF ARABIA

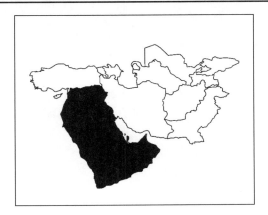

ALGUL

An Arabic vampire, whose name translates as "horse leech," the Algul is most often a female blood drinker who preys on children. Like the vampires of Europe, the Algul lives in or around cemeteries and comes into houses at night to attack children, or lures them into dark places with promises of treats and then pounces.

Also known as a bloodsucking Jinn, the Algul is reputed in some places to feast only on the newly buried corpses of dead children. In these stories the Algul shares more of the characteristics of a ghoul than those of the vampire. But either ghoul or blood drinker, the Algul is a vicious and heartless monster.

Often at night the Algul can be heard howling in the darkness, often mimicking the calls of night birds and desert scavengers such as the jackal. The Algul most often appears as a sickly, wasted human being,

and in this form deceives travelers and good hearted people who think they are encountering some unfortunate who has just wandered in from the desert. Using this ploy the Algul tricks people into deserted spots and then attacks them, using stones, knives, staves, or its own unnatural strength to slaughter and feast.

The Algul was mentioned in <u>*The Thousand And One Nights*</u>, as well as in hundreds of folktales and countless nightmares.

Algul. Artwork by Robert Patrick O'Brien.

THE THOUSAND AND ONE NIGHTS

One of the greatest storybooks ever written, *The Thousand And One Nights* was introduced to European readers by the French scholar Galland. Galland discovered the Arabic original and translated it into French in the early eighteenth century. No one knows for sure when the original stories were written, but copies have been dated to as early as the tenth century.

The framework of the book tells of a King who maintained the rather gruesome habit of killing his wives after the first night of marriage. He was led to abandon this practice by the cleverness of the Vizier's daughter. After marrying the King she would nightly tell him a tale which she left unfinished at dawn. His curiosity would lead him to spare her so the tale would be completed the following night.

There are scores of versions of the *Thousand And One Nights*, many radically different from the others. For example, Oriental editions do not include the famous story of "Ali Baba and the Forty Thieves." It was probably drawn from another source and added by Galland.

Stories mentioning the Algul, however, are found in even the oldest Persian copies of the manuscript.

Medard Tytgat's rendering of Scheherazade entrancing the Sultan with her tales of the 1001 Arabian Nights, which included several references to the cannibalistic vampires, the Ghul and Algul. Archival artwork.

GHUL

The Ghul (known in other parts of the world as "ghoul"), is spoken of all throughout Muslim folklore. The Ghul is most often a female demon that haunts the desert, often near the sites of old battles, in deserted oases, graveyards, and other remote places where the unwary can easily be attacked. The Ghuls of the deep desert are able to assume the shapes of various animals and birds.

An evil spirit, the Ghul mostly satisfies its hunger by robbing graves and feeding on the fetid flesh of the dead. In other cases Ghuls lure travelers into the desert, often enticing them by posing as prostitutes or "willing" women. Once they have their victims in some secluded spot they attack and devour them.

Unlike the Algul, the Ghul does not use brute force to overcome its victims. Rather it lulls them to sleep and then either slits their throats or smashes their heads in with sharp stones. The Ghul is also known to haunt the fringes of a battlefield, looking for wounded soldiers to attack, often assuming the guise of a nurse or water-bearer.

In some cases the Ghul is a person who was cursed while living and, after death, has risen as a flesh-eating ghoul. In such cases it can haunt an area for generations until a holy man has exorcised the area with seven days of prayers to Allah.

The Ghul. Artwork by Robert Patrick O'Brien.

GHULS AND OTHER ZOMBIES

Ghuls are mentioned several times in *The Thousand And One Nights*, including this reference in the story called "The Seventh Voyage Of Sinbad":

> "It was not long before I discovered them to be a tribe of Magian cannibals whose King was a Ghul. All who came to their country or whoso they caught in their valleys or on their roads they brought to this King and fed them upon that food and anointed them with that oil, whereupon their stomachs dilated that they might eat largely, whilst their reason fled and they lost the power of thought and became idiots. Then they stuffed them with coconut oil and the aforesaid food till they became fat and gross, when they slaughtered them by cutting their throats and roasted them for the King's eating, but as for the savages themselves, they ate human flesh raw."

They are also mentioned in the story "Abu Kir The Dyer And Abu Sir The Barber":

> "Allah ease thee, O King of the Age, even as thou hast eased me of these Ghuls, whose bellies none may fill save Allah!"

In modern fiction the Ghul has been transformed into a new cinematic creature: the Zombie, also known as the living dead. In most Zombie films these creatures are mindless cannibals who attack both the living and the dead to eat their flesh and drink their blood. Like the Ghuls of folklore, cinematic zombies are Revenants who prey on the living and require specific methods of destruction in order to be stopped.

The term "Zombie" is used quite inaccurately in these films, because the creatures therein are actually closer to the Craqueuhhe of France, Germany's Brukulaco, Neuntoter, Nachzehrer, and Blautsauger, and the Pontianak of Java. All of these creatures are reanimated corpses who feast on flesh as well as blood. Therefore, the Zombie attack in the classic horror film *Night of the Living Dead* could easily be a tale of any of these vampire species.

Some of the better zombie/living dead films include:

• *Night of the Living Dead* (1968). The film that really started the genre, this black and white classic was produced in 1968 for $114,000. Filmed on location in Beaver County, Pennsylvania, the film still has considerable power to shock over 32 years later.

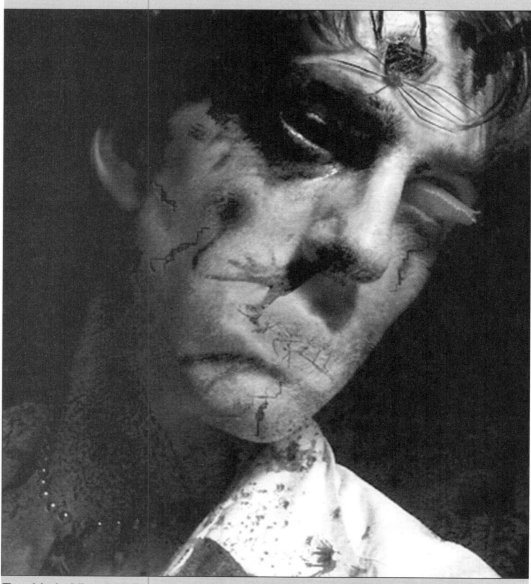

Zombie by Vinesh V. George. Used with permission, (c) 2003.

- *Children Shouldn't Play With Dead Things* (1972). An above average film about a group of hippies who experiment with witchcraft and accidentally make the dead rise as flesh-eating Revenants. The acting is terrible and the special effects are obvious and cheap, but the film somehow manages to overcome all of this and be quite entertaining. But only for those with strong stomachs.

- *Dawn of the Dead* (1978). Director George A. Romero's epic sequel to his legendary *Night of the Living Dead* is actually better than the original. It blends a siege story with inventive and intelligent heroes, some truly black humor, and a biting social satire.

- *Day of the Dead* (1985). The last of the Romero trilogy and also the least. The gore is over the top, but the story is dead on its feet, with too much talk and not enough of a logical story.

- *Return of the Living Dead* (1985). A horror comedy by Dan O'Bannon, with real chills and real humor. It was panned by critics but is a cult favorite among Zombie film lovers. It was followed by two sequels that were not nearly as good, though still interesting.

- *Re-Animator* (1985). Technically a science fiction film loosely based on the writings of H. P. Lovecraft, this movie manages to reanimate a number of corpses who savagely attack humans, biting them and tearing them apart. The film was followed by two excellent sequels.

- *Dead Alive* (1992). This film deals with a housewife who gets bitten by a Sumatran Rat Monkey, dies, and is reanimated as a flesh-eating zombie. Over-the-top gore and hilarious comedy, including a kickboxing priest. It was directed by Peter Jackson (of *Lord Of The Rings* fame).

- *Ed and His Dead Mother* (1993). Starring Steve Buscemi, Ned Beatty, and John Glover, this is a horror comedy a la *Dead Alive*, but with its own twists.

- *Cemetery Man* (1994). This excellent blend of horror and quirky comedy was directed by Michele Soavi (a protégé of horror film auteur Dario Argento). It stars Rupert Everett and the stunning Anna Falchi in a bizarre live-after-death love story riddled with the walking dead. The story was adapted from a graphic novel of the same name by Dylan Dog. It is the only flesh-eating zombie flick to play in art houses, and deservedly so.

- *28 Days After* (2003). In this zombie film, a deadly virus sweeps London and within 28 days turns nearly everyone into insane flesh-eating zombies. The film was directed by Danny Boyle and stars Cillian Murphy, Naomi Harris, Megan Burns, and Brendan Gleeson.

Zombie. Artwork by Marie O'Brien.

VAMPIRES OF ARGENTINA

EL DIENTUDO

Throughout the rural areas of Argentina, especially in the dense forests surrounding Buenos Aires, there is the legend of a horrifying monster called El Dientudo, which translates as "The Big Teeth."

This aptly named creature is a flesh eating and blood drinking predator. It is vaguely manlike in appearance, covered completely in thick matted hair; stands seven or eight feet tall; and reeks like rotting flesh.

Even though there are relatively frequent sightings of Dientudos every year, there is very little else known about the monster beyond its vicious nature. Apparently it prefers to hunt animals, but there have been stories of humans dragged off into the jungle never to be see again, or to be found only as remnants of torn flesh and gnawed bone.

LOBIZÓN (also spelled Lobisón)

This fox-like shapeshifter is popularly believed to have traveled to South America with Portuguese settlers. It is a foul and disgusting beast that feeds on dead flesh, excrement, and un-baptized infants.

Like its Brazilian cousin the Lobishomen, the Lobizón can be warded off by Wolf's Bane. Though Wolf's Bane is not common to South America, it was imported by wise and cautious travelers who feared to be without the protective herb. Wolf's Bane seeds are sown into the soil of a freshly dug grave so that the herb's presence will forever keep the dead at rest.

The Lobizón can be killed by fire and steel, but it is very fast and powerful, and is seldom cornered.

RUNATURUNCO

Werebeasts (monsters who change from human into animal forms) are common throughout South America. The Runaturunco and its cousin, the Yaguareté Abá (*see* next entry) are both shapeshifters. But whereas the Yaguareté Abá uses sorcery to effect a transformation, the Runaturunco makes a pact with the Devil to acquire its powers.

The Runaturunco prefers to hunt at night and preys exclusively on those of Indian ancestry. It eschews anyone with predominantly Spanish or Caucasian blood.

The Runaturunco can only be killed by a bullet through the brain. Even then its carcass must be burned, and the ashes scattered for miles so that its powerful spirit cannot return from the dead.

A Runaturunco risen from its own ashes—luckily a very rare occurrence—cannot be killed again except by the father of a virgin. This slayer must be blessed by three priests and wear a charm containing hairs from the Runaturunco's first body. For this reason, if a Runaturunco is ever caught, some hairs from the creature are always kept.

YAGUARETÉ ABÁ

The Yaguareté Abá is an Indian who uses sorcery to transform himself into a jaguar that is even more ferocious than the common hunting cat. Human intelligence is diabolically combined with animal cunning and the lightning fast reflexes of a great hunting cat to create a powerful monster that hunts humans for food and sport. A fearsome opponent for any slayer.

The Yaguareté Abá can be killed with guns, swords or spears, but since it is faster, stronger, and smarter than a Siberian Tiger, killing one takes the combined efforts of several brave, experienced hunters.

The Yaguareté Abá. Artwork by Marie O'Brien.

WOLF'S BANE (ACONITE)

In werewolf fiction and, to a lesser degree, vampire fiction, Wolf's Bane has been held to be a protection against these creatures. It is a small, mildly poisonous plant, about a foot high with pale, divided green leaves and yellow flowers. The stem is firm, angular and hairy and the flowers, which are large and hooded, grow on top of the branches in spikes. The root is tuberous. There is a farina (fine mealy powder) in the flower which is caustic to the eyes. If the oil on the leaves is rubbed on the skin it will cause soreness and irritation.

The plant is widely used as a homeopathic remedy for treating the initial stages of fever and inflammation resulting from exposure to dry cold. It is also used for healing skin inflammation, coughing, dry skin, exposure to extreme weather, palpitations, panic attacks, and fear of dying.

A decoction of the root makes an effective lotion to wash body parts bitten by venomous creatures. This is the basis for the legend that it can ward off the bite of werewolves and vampires.

The genus of the plant is called *Anthora*, and various species of the plant have been given a variety of nicknames: Auld Wife's Huid, Blue Rocket, Friar's Cap, Helmet Flower, Monk's Hood, Mousebane, Soldier's Cap, Wolfbane, and Wolf's Bane.

However, to be precise, *Aconitum Septentrionale* is the true Wolf's Bane. *Aconitum Anthora* is Yellow Monkshood (not Wolf's Bane as is often reported), *Aconitum Orientale* is known as Drowsy Wolf's Bane, *Aconitum Lycoctonum* is Purple Wolf's Bane, and *Aconitum Vulparia* is Yellow Wolf's Bane.

VAMPIRES OF ARMENIA

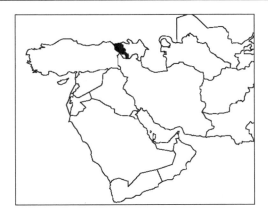

DAKHANAVAR (also called Dashnavar)

The Dakhanavar is a nasty mountain spirit that attacks weary travelers in the deep of night. The Dakhanavar stalks its victims and then waits until they've fallen asleep, then creeps into the camp, tent, or roadside inn and sucks blood from the soles of their feet.

The Dakhanavar is fiercely territorial and will attack anyone who tries to make a map of its lands, or even count the hills and valleys, fearing that knowledge of the local landscape will reveal all of its secret hiding places.

The Dakhanavar is not the brightest of the undead. One popular legend tells of two smart travelers who slept with their feet under each other's head. The Dakhanavar was unable to make sense of this and went mad, fleeing into the darkness never to be seen again.

Whereas confusing a vampire is a fairly popular theme throughout folklore, a good vampire slayer traveling in the land of the Dakhanavar should take certain precautions, such as placing garlic around each traveler and setting a nice, bright fire. Few vampires can tolerate garlic, and fire is a handy weapon against any foe, natural or otherwise.

Dakhanavar. Photo by Jason Lukridge.

VAMPIRES OF ASSYRIA

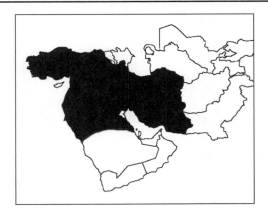

AKHKHARU (also Akakharu)

The plague of vampirism was not a threat that began in the Middle Ages. Vampiric creatures have tormented mankind since the days of antiquity. Ancient Babylon and Assyria, six thousand years ago, were victimized by several different kinds of vampires, each as fierce and terrible as the other.

The Akhkharu was an ancient Assyrian female vampire. It used seduction and sexual powers to overcome its victims, draining them of life force as well as blood. In some stories the Akhkharu did not drink blood at all, but essentially "loved" her prey to death, draining the victim of all physical essences through a long and rather heated affair. This affair restored the vampire's youth, leaving her strong while her prey became a dead and withered husk. The Succubus (*see* Vampires Of Various Cultures, p. 515) shares many similar characteristics with this older species .

Ekimmu. Photo by Jason Lukridge.

<u>EKIMMU</u>

The eerie Ekimmu is a ghostly creature that, if not properly buried, can rise from its unquiet grave to prey on the living. Those who have died sudden and violent deaths become Ekimmu, especially murder victims, women who died during childbirth or their stillborn children, those who have been poisoned or who ate spoiled food, those who were interred without proper burial rites, victims of drowning, victims of starvation, the unburied on battlefields. Even the recent dead who have perished without ever having been fulfilled in love—or who have been scorned and died lonely and bitter—can rise from the grave as an Ekimmu.

The Ekimmu is a tormented soul, caught in the twilight between this world and the next, unable to move on because of unresolved matters on earth, unable to sever the ties that bind it to this world. Bitter and angry, the Ekimmu takes out its wrath on the living, killing wantonly and wreaking havoc with anyone who lives near its burial place.

The Ekimmu is most often seen in the form of a rotting corpse staggering stiffly through the night. In other accounts it appears as a foul night wind, as a deadly shadow, or in the form of a shadowy phantom. But in whatever form it assumes, the Ekimmu is a vile and malicious monster.

Knives and swords are ineffective against the creature. Only wooden weapons have any effect against this monster. Yet it is not a stake that works best, but a long spear with a fire-hardened point. Men often work in groups with spears and clubs to fend off an Ekimmu, cornering it in a deserted space and pinning it to the wall or the ground. It must be trapped long enough for a ritual of exorcism to be performed by a priest. After lengthy prayers are incanted, the priest and his helpers force garlic into the Ekimmu's mouth, taking away the last of its supernatural powers and allowing it to be beheaded with an ordinary sword, axe, or woodsman's saw. The corpse, now rendered inert, is usually burned and the ashes re-buried in the grave of the person who had become the Ekimmu.

This is an elaborate process that requires nerve, muscle, and the coordinated efforts of lay-people and the clergy. As often as not, the Ekimmu escapes.

UTUKKU

Another unquiet Assyrian ghost-vampire is the Utukku. This is a spirit of vengeance who cannot abide the silence of the grave until it has risen and killed its own murderer.

There are also Babylonian stories of the Utukku, wherein the reasons for its resurrection from the grave are not always so noble. Sometimes the Utukku rises to simply prey on the living, satisfying nothing but its insatiable hunger for evil. It can also be invoked by ill will through curses or black magic spells.

VENGEFUL VAMPIRES

Many of the legends and accounts of vampires describe them as being vengeful spirits risen from the grave to redress wrongs so severe that they cannot rest until the scales have been balanced.

· The Assyrian and Babylonian Utukku is the spirit of a murdered person who cannot rest until it has killed its own murderer.

· The Farkaskoldus of Greece is usually the unnaturally resurrected spirit of a shepherd who has been abused or unfairly treated in life, and returns to seek revenge. It is resurrected as a species of blood-sucking werewolf.

· The Lamiai, named after Lamia, a Greek goddess who was the mistress of Zeus. Hera, Zeus' wife, was so enraged by the liaison that she killed any of the offspring that resulted from the union. Grieving and outraged over the death of her children, Lamia swore as revenge for this act of cruelty that she would kill as many other children as possible. She created the monstrous Lamiai for this purpose, creatures who prey upon newborns, drinking their blood and consuming their flesh.

· Pregnant Indian women who die during the Dewali festival are in danger of returning as blood-sucking Churel. Because they have died so unfairly--carrying new life--they are bitter and vengeful and return to take out their resentment on the living, often attacking whole families because they remind them of what they've lost. But their greatest enmity is directed toward their relatives, whom they blame for allowing them to die when their need for care was greatest.

· The Gayal of India returns from the dead to avenge itself when its family members have not adhered strictly to proper burial rites.

VAMPIRES OF AUSTRALIA

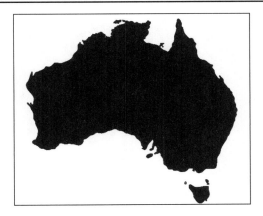

GARKAIN

The Aboriginal people of the Northern Territories of Australia have folktales about a variety of giant and smaller hominid races. Some of these creatures are considered to be leftovers from the days of the Neanderthal, and some of have a more supernatural origin. These creatures terrified the Aborigines in ages past.

Legends tell of giants, pygmies, ape-men (similar to Homo erectus, or the Java Man), and the bloodthirsty vampiric creatures called the Garkain. Garkains lived in remote areas, inhabiting caves and rock shelters on higher plateaus. They hunted in the swamps, hiding in the rushes and feeding on reptiles and insects.

The Garkains were not evolved creatures. They could not make fire or use tools, and had no weapons other than their own unnatural strength.

Some Aborigines still believe that Garkains inhabit the Liverpool River region. The Garkains lurk in the trees and swoop down on unsuspecting travelers, favoring the lost or the helpless.

But it is not the monster's size and strength which first overcomes its victim; rather their prey is rendered almost senseless by the creature's overwhelming stench, a reek so powerful that it works like a narcotic. Then the Garkain smothers its victim with its wings so that he is trapped by that awful stench. It is this that kills the victim. Once its prey has succumbed, the Garkain feasts on its flesh.

The hapless spirit of the Garkain's victim is then doomed to wander the forest, unable to find his way home to his tribe's final resting place.

The Garkain. Artwork by Robert Patrick O'Brien.

Though the Garkain can be killed by ordinary means (spears, knives, stones, fire), getting close enough to deliver the killing blow is difficult because the beast emits such a poisonous stench.

In more recent folklore the Garkains have become more clearly supernatural. They are now described as huge bat-like humanoids, as big as a man but with massive black wings, and a human torso topped with the dog-snouted head of a fruit bat.

THE YOWIE

According to the Aborigines, the Garkain was related to the Yowie, a more peaceful and ape-like creature of eastern Australian legend. The Yowies are also cousins to the North American Bigfoot. They are hairy, apelike creatures that vary in size, though most stories tend to tell of three separate sizes for the creatures. This suggests three different subspecies: the Yuuri species is described as being four feet tall; the Dooligah is six to eight feet tall, and the Giant Quinkin is over nine feet tall. The three sizes may also represent males, females, and children.

The Yowies can be aggressive, but are generally not so. They attack mostly in self-defense or to protect their territory.

There are scores of Yowie sightings every year in Australia.

Used with permission of Rex Gilroy and the Australian Yowie Institute, (c) Rex Gilroy 2001.

MART

Another night creature haunting Aboriginal folklore is the Mart, a vampire-like creature that haunts campsites in remote areas. The Mart will either sneak in and carry away someone sitting at the edge of a campfire's light, or it will wait until someone has left the fire and stepped into the darkness, perhaps to answer the call of nature, before it will attack them.

The Aborigines believe that a second soul exists in each person, a darker self. It is commonly believed that the Mart is the ghost of someone who has died under bad circumstances (such as murder or violence) so that the dark soul has taken control of the body, reviving it from the grave, and forcing it to do evil and appalling things. For this reason the wise men of Aboriginal villages use heavy rocks to weigh down a body during burial. Sometimes the villagers break the legs of a newly dead corpse to cripple it and keep it from rising and returning to plague the living.

When a person dies, his possessions are destroyed so as not to lure the Mart from the grave. That person's campsite is eradicated so it will not anchor the evil spirit to the world.

TALAMAUR

Off the coast of Australia are the Bank Islands, lovely in their way, but also an abode of darkness. The Talamaur dwell there.

The Talamaur are not traditional vampires inasmuch as they do not drink blood, but they are equally evil creatures who feed on the pain and despair of the people of their own village. They are Living Vampires who possess the ability to speak with the dead. Some natives go in fear of these dead spirits and wisely want no contact; others crave to speak with departed loved ones and would risk the dangers of the Talamaur to make that connection. The Talamaur deceive these trusting folks by claiming to act simply as mediums, but the Talamaur have a darker purpose. They do far more than contact the dead—they can control them, enslave them, make them into familiars. Then they use these servant ghosts to do all manner of evil in their communities, even sending them as agents of destruction against their own families.

Being a Talamaur is not a crime. It is even a profession that some advertise in order to make a living, and some Talamaurs may have good intentions (or hide their crimes behind occasional good deeds). But

A Talamaur. Artwork by Marie O'Brien.

when a village begins to feel the presence of evil and see the evidence at hand, the villagers will launch an investigation. Those within the community who understand the nature of such magic devise a method of reversing the evil of the Talamaur and its familiar. The evil Talamaur is taken by force to a sacred space and forced to smell the smoke of burning leaves until it confesses its evil nature and reveals the names of the creatures under its control. It also has to list all of its crimes and name all of its victims; past, present, and future. Once the crimes are confessed openly the spell is broken, the familiar is released back to the spirit world, and the reign of evil is ended. The Talamaur's life is often ended as well.

TARUNGA

Some Talamaurs from the Bank Islands are very powerful sorcerer-vampires who can go into a trance and separate their spirits from their bodies. The spirit—known as a Tarunga—consumes the lingering life essence of a person who has recently died.

Once this evil has begun to affect a village, the people begin looking for signs that a Tarunga is in their community. Some people begin having visions or vivid dreams which tell of the Tarunga. Watchers will be posted by newly dug graves, listening for the telltale sounds of a Tarunga's approach: a whisper-soft scratching sound, like cat claws on a door.

YARA-MA-YHA-WHO

On the Australian mainland there is a particularly nasty vampiric creature called the Yara-Ma-Yha-Who. This monster is not the typical tall, pale, dark-eyed vampire with long fangs; rather, the Yara-Ma-Yha-Who is only about four feet tall, with red skin and an oversized head. It has no teeth, but an enormous mouth with which it swallows its food whole. Each of its octopoid-like fingers and toes ends in a hook-like sucker that is used to drain the blood from the prey.

Like the tree-dwelling Asasabonsam of Africa, the Yara-Ma-Yha-Who lurks in fig trees, waiting for the unsuspecting to pass beneath. Then it seizes its victim with its tentacled hands and feet, drag their prey into the upper branches, and feeds on the victim's hot life blood.

Sometimes the Yara-Ma-Yha-Who kill their victims, first draining the blood and then swallowing the victims whole. More often than not they would feed and then release the victim, drained but not dead. Occasionally they return to feed on that same person again. If they do

Yara-Ma-Yha-Who. Artwork by Robert Patrick O'Brien.

this often enough the person begins to develop red skin and grow shorter, and his fingers and toes begin to resemble the tentacles of an octopus. Soon the victim will become a Yara-Ma-Yha-Who himself and the plague of terror will increase.

VAMPIRES OF AUSTRIA

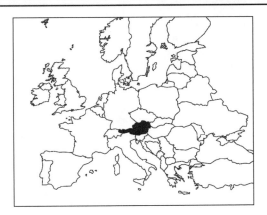

BLAUTSAUGER

The term Blautsauger ("blood sucker") is found throughout Austria, Germany and Bosnia-Herzegovina, referring to one or more vampire species. The Austrian Blautsauger appears to have more in common with its German cousins than with the Bosnian variety. (*See* Vampires Of Germany.)

The Austrian Blautsauger is a living-dead Revenant who has the typical pale skin, rotting flesh, and gaunt features of a zombie. The most common way to become a Blautsauger is to eat the flesh of any animal that has been killed by a wolf. Like the zombies of popular films, the Blautsauger is a flesh eater as well as a blood drinker.

Like many vampires of Eastern Europe, the Blautsauger sleeps in its grave during the day and rises at night to feed on the living. The

Blautsauger does not fear the sun, but prefers to hunt at night like other nocturnal predators, using darkness to help it sneak up on its prey. It is rarely merciful.

The Blautsauger can only be prevented from entering a house by smearing all doorways and windows with a paste made from mashed garlic and an attar of hawthorn flowers.

The Blautsauger can most easily be killed while it sleeps. To do this several people surround the coffin as it is opened. As soon as the lid is raised, baskets full of garlic are tipped into the coffin. The garlic acts like a neurotoxin that keeps the monster immobile. In case the garlic should not have the desired effect, a long stake of freshly cut hawthorn should be thrust through the abdomen, pinning the creature to the coffin so it cannot rise. Once it has been staked—a process that does not kill it but merely immobilizes it—the monster's head should be struck off with an axe or sword. Then its mouth is stuffed with garlic. This would end its unnatural life and free its body to decay according to the laws of nature.

(*See* also Vampires Of Bosnia-Herzegovina, p. 107, for a different perspective of this European vampire.)

Blautsauger. Used with permission (c) 2003 Breanne Levy.

AUTHENTIC AUSTRIAN VAMPIRES

Austria had more than its share of persons truly believed to be vampires. In the 1720s an Austrian named Peter Plogojowitz was thought to be a Blautsauger. Though Plogojowitz died at age 62, he was believed to have risen from his grave and was later reported to have visited his son numerous times asking for food. Plogo-jowitz's son and neighbors were found dead and drained of blood the next day. The man himself was never caught, but after the deaths of his son and neighbors he was not seen or heard from again. An official report of this incident was filed with the Austrian court in 1726. The name of the Austrian physician who wrote the report is no longer known, but it was in this report that the word *vanpir* was used in an official medical capacity. That brought the word into common usage among the mannered and educated, whereas previously the word and its many dialectic variations had been used almost exclusively by rural folk and the church. An abbreviated version of the report on Plogojowitz is as follows:

The Report 1725

And since with such people (which they call vanpir) various are to be seen that is, the body undecomposed, the skin, hair, beard, and nails growing—the subjects resolved unanimously to open the grave of Peter Plogojowitz and to see if such above-mentioned signs were really to be found on him. To this end they came here to me and, telling of these events, asked me and the local parish priest, to be present at the viewing. And although I at first disapproved, telling them that the praiseworthy administration should first be dutifully and humbly informed. And its exalted opinion about this should be heard, they did not want to accommodate themselves to this at all, but rather gave this short answer: I could do what I wanted, but if I did not accord them the viewing and the legal recognition to deal with the body according to their custom, they would have to leave house and home, because by the time a gracious resolution was received from Belgrade, perhaps the entire village— and this was already supposed to have happened in Turkish times—could be destroyed by such an evil spirit, and they did not want to wait for this,

Since I could not hold these people from the resolution they had made, either with good words or with threats, I went to the village of Kisilova, taking along the Gradisk priest, and viewed the body of Peter Plogojowitz, just exhumed, finding, in accordance with thorough truthfulness, that first of all I did not detect the slightest odor that is otherwise characteristic of the dead, and the body, except for the nose, which was somewhat fallen away, was completely fresh. The hair and beard—even the nails, of which the old ones had fallen away—had grown on him; the old skin, which was somewhat whitish, had peeled away, and a new one had emerged from it. The face, hands, and feet and the whole body were so constituted, that they could not have been more complete in his lifetime. Not without astonishment, I saw some fresh blood in his mouth, which, according to the common observation, he had sucked from the people killed by him.

In short, all the indications were present that such people (as remarked above) are said to have. After both the priest and I had seen this spectacle, while people grew more outraged than distressed, all the subjects, with great speed, sharpened a stake—in order to pierce the corpse of the deceased with it—and put this at his heart, whereupon, as he was pierced, not only did much blood, completely fresh, flow also through his ears and mouth, but still other wild signs (which I pass by out of high respect) took place. Finally, according to their usual practice, they burned the often mentioned body, in his case, to ashes of which I inform the most laudable Administration, and at the same time would like to request, obediently and humbly, that if a mistake was made in this matter, such is to be attributed not to me but to the rabble, who were beside themselves with fear.

One of the most famous documented cases of vampirism, both in Austria and in the world in general, was that of Arnod Paole and his many victims. Following is a translation of the 1732 official report by Regimental Field Surgeon Johannes Fluckinger:

> After it had been reported that in the village of Medvegia the so-called vampires had killed some people by sucking their blood, I was, by high degree of a local Honorable Supreme Command, sent there to investigate the matter thoroughly along with officers detailed for that purpose and two subordinate medical officers, and therefore carried out and heard the present inquiry in the company of the captain of the Stallath Company of haiduks*, Gorschiz Hadnack, the standard-bearer and the oldest haiduk of the village, as follows: who unanimously recount that about five years ago a local haiduk by the name of Arnold Paole broke his neck in a fall from a hay wagon. This man had during his lifetime often revealed that, near Gossowa in Turkish Serbia, he had been troubled by a vampire, wherefore he had eaten from the earth of the vampire's grave and had smeared himself with the vampire's blood, in order to be free from the vexation he had suffered.
>
> In 20 or 30 days after his death some people complained that they were being bothered by this same Arnod Paole; and in fact four people were killed by him. In order to end this evil, they dug up this Arnold Paole 40 days after his death—this on the advice of a soldier, who had been present at such events before; and they found that he was quite complete and un-decayed, and that fresh blood had flowed from his eyes, nose, mouth, and ears; that the shirt, the covering, and the coffin were completely bloody; that the old nails on his hands and feet, along with the skin, had fallen off, and that new ones had grown; and since they saw from this that he was a true vampire, they drove a stake through his heart, according to their custom, whereby he gave an audible groan and bled copiously. Thereupon they

---

*A haiduk was a type of soldier.

burned the body the same day to ashes and threw these into the grave. These people say further that all those who were tormented and killed by the vampire must themselves become vampires.

Therefore they disinterred the above-mentioned four people in the same way. Then they also add that this Arnod Paole attacked not only the people but also the cattle, and sucked out their blood. And since the people used the flesh of such cattle, it appears that some vampires are again present here, inasmuch as, in a period of three months, 17 young and old people died, among them some who, with no previous illness, died in two or at the most three days. In addition, the haiduk Jowiza reports that his step-daughter, by name of Stanacka, lay down to sleep 15 days ago, fresh and healthy, but at midnight she started up out of her sleep with a terrible cry, fearful and trembling, and complained that she had been throttled by the son of a haiduk by the name of Milloe, who had died nine weeks earlier, whereupon she had experienced a great pain in the chest and became worse hour by hour, until finally she died on the third day. At this we went the same afternoon to

Photo by Jason Lukridge.

the graveyard, along with the often-mentioned oldest haiduks of the village, in order to cause the suspicious graves to be opened and to examine the bodies in them, whereby, after all of them had been dissected, there was found:

1. A woman by the name of Stana, 20 years old, who had died in childbirth two months ago, after a three-day illness, and who had herself said, before her death, that she had painted herself with the blood of a vampire, wherefore both she and her child—which had died right after birth and because of a careless burial had been half eaten by the dogs—must also become vampires. She was quite complete and un-decayed. After the opening of the body there was found in the cavitate pectoris a quantity of fresh extravascular blood. The vessels of the arteries and veins, like the ventriculis ortis, were not, as is usual, filled with coagulated blood, and the whole viscera, that is, the lung, liver, stomach, spleen, and intestines were quite fresh as they would be in a healthy person.

   The uterus was however quite enlarged and very inflamed externally, for the placenta and lochia had remained in place, wherefore the same was in complete putredine. The skin on her hands and feet, along with the old nails, fell away on their own, but on the other hand completely new nails were evident, along with a fresh and vivid skin.

2. There was a woman by the name of Miliza (60 years old), who had died after a three-month sickness and had been buried 90-some days earlier. In the chest much liquid blood was found; and the other viscera were, like those mentioned before, in a good condition. During her dissection, all the haiduks who were standing around marveled greatly at her plumpness and perfect body, uniformly stating that they had known the woman well, from her youth, and that she had, throughout her life, looked and been very lean and dried up, and they emphasized that she had come to this surprising

plumpness in the grave. They also said that it was she who started the vampires this time, because she had eaten of the flesh of those sheep that had been killed by the previous vampires.

3. There was an eight-day-old child which had lain in the grave for 90 days and was similarly in a condition of vampirism.

4. The son of a haiduk, 16 years old, was dug up, having lain in the earth for nine weeks, after he had died from a three-day illness, and was found like the other vampires.

5. Joachim, also the son of a haiduk, 17 years old; had died after a three-day illness. He had been buried eight weeks and four days and, on being dissected; was found in similar condition.

6. A woman by the name of Ruscha who had died after a ten-day illness and had been buried six weeks previous, in whom there was much fresh blood not only in the chest but also in fundo ventriculi. The same showed itself in her child, which was 18 days old and had died five weeks previously.

Photo by Jason Lukridge.

7. No less did a girl ten years of age, who had died two months previously, find herself in the above-mentioned condition, quite complete and un-decayed; and had much fresh blood in her chest.

8. They caused the wife of the Hadnack to be dug up, along with her child. She had died seven weeks previously, her child—who was eight weeks old—21 days previously, and it was found that both mother and child were completely decomposed, although earth and grave were like those of the vampires lying nearby.

9. A servant of the local corporal of the haiduks, by the name of Rhade, 21 years old, died after a three-month-long illness, and after a five week burial was found completely decomposed.

10. The wife of the local bariactar, along with her child, having died five weeks previously, were also completely decomposed.

11. With Stanche, a local haiduk, 60 years old; who had died six weeks previously, I noticed a profuse liquid blood, like the others, in the chest and stomach. The entire body was in the oft-named condition of vampirism.

12. Milloe, a haiduk, 25 years old; who had lain for six weeks in the earth, also was found in the condition of vampirism mentioned.

13. Stanoika, the wife of a haiduk, 20 years old, died after a three-day illness and had been buried 18 days previously. In the dissection I found that she was in her countenance quite red and of a vivid color, and, as was mentioned above, she had been throttled, at midnight, by Milloe, the son of the haiduk, and there was also to be seen, on the right side under the ear, a bloodshot blue mark, the length of a finger. As she was being taken out

of the grave, a quantity of fresh blood flowed from her nose. With the dissection I found; as mentioned often already, a regular fragrant fresh bleeding, not only in the chest cavity, but also in ventriculo cordis.

14. All the viscera found themselves in a completely good and healthy condition. The hypodermis of the entire body, along with the fresh nails of hands and feet, was as though completely fresh. After the examination had taken place, the heads of the vampires were cut off by the local gypsies and burned along with the bodies, and then the ashes were thrown into the river Morava. The decomposed bodies, however, were laid back into their own graves.

Visum et Repertum

Seen and Discovered

1732

Regimental Field Surgeon Johannes Fluckinger

To the Emperor

In 1746, the noted scholar and physician to the Empress of Hungary, Dom Augustin Calmet published his treatise on vampires, *Dissertations sur les Apparitions des Ages des Demons et des Espits, et sur les Revenants, et Vampires de Hundrie, de Boheme, de Moravie, et de Silesie*. Despite the common belief in the undead, and numerous eyewitness accounts, Calmet concluded that the tales of vampires were spurious and that he found no evidence of any true existence of the creatures. Empress Marie Theresa than passed a law prohibiting the Austrians from digging up graves or destroying dead bodies.

The legends of vampire attacks, however, did not stop, and soon tales of vampiric activity spread throughout Europe.

VAMPIRES OF ANCIENT BABYLON

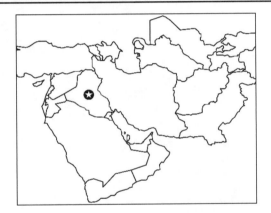

LIL

This creature is most often described as a female vampire (or at least one that adopts the form of a woman), although there are male versions of this creature (called Lilu). The plural of Lil is Lilitu.

The Lil is certainly a blood drinker; perhaps the very first recorded blood drinker, dating back to legends six thousand years old. These were evil beings that entered houses by night and drank the life blood of babies and young children.

In Sumerian cosmology the Lilitu were one of several demons spoken of in the *Epic Of Gilgamesh*. These demons inhabited the desert wastes and were seen as negative spiritual influences on sexuality and fertility, used primarily to curse someone else with barrenness. Either separately or together they were regarded as extremely dangerous to pregnancies and newborns. Their child, called Ardat-Lili ("Maiden Lilitu"), was seen as a spirit of sexual dysfunction and frustration, straying or abusive husbands, malevolent wives, and degeneracy in general.

Some historians believe that the mythology of these three demons formed the basis of the Lilith of Hebrew mythology. Lilith was the "first vampire" and, according to the Talmud, Adam's first wife, who was expelled from Eden and went to dwell in the "abode of demons." (*See* Vampires Of Israel, p. 286) for a different perspective on Lilith).

Used with permission, (c) Lilian Broca 2003.

VAMPIRES OF BENGAL

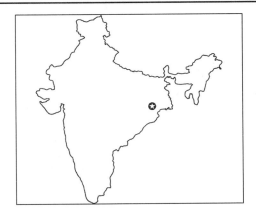

CHORDEWA

This peculiar creature is actually a witch and Essential Vampire, from among the Oraons caste of the hills of western Bengal. The Chordewa is capable of transforming her very soul into the shape of a large black cat. This cat ingratiates itself with potential victims, acting very friendly, eating the victims' food, and even showing "affection" by licking people on their lips. This lick, however, is a kiss of death. The cat gradually drains the victim's life force, which is absorbed by the Chordewa. The victim will soon die.

Other legends of the Chordewa hint that if the cat so much as licks a person's shadow, it is enough to doom them to a quick and certain death.

The Chordewa cat creature can be identified by its peculiar mewing, like that of a child in distress. Rather unsettling.

If the cat is harmed, the injury will be reflected on the Chordewa. Any Bengali wise in the ways of demon hunting will know how to identify the Chordewa in cat form, and how to attack it and kill it, in turn slaying the vampire-witch.

CAT SUPERSTITIONS

The Bengalese are certainly not the only people to have developed superstitions around cats.

American superstitions:

- A black cat crossing your path is considered bad luck.
- Seeing a white cat at night is bad luck, but seeing a white cat on the road is considered lucky.
- Good luck will come to you if you dream of a white cat.
- When you see a one-eyed cat, you can make a wish come true. Just spit on your thumb and stamp it in the palm of your hand while making the wish.
- When moving into a new home, have the cat enter through the window instead of the door so that it will never leave.
- A cat washing itself on your doorstep means that clergy will come calling.

Dutch superstition:

- In the Netherlands cats are believed to be gossips, so they aren't allowed in rooms where private conversations are occurring.

Egyptian superstition:

- In Egyptian mythology, cats are sacred to the goddess Isis. In honor of Isis, if a person killed a cat, he was put to death.

English superstitions:

- If a cat washes behind its ears, expect it to rain.
- If a cat is sleeping with all four paws tucked under its body, expect cold weather to come.
- When a cat's pupils get bigger, it will soon rain.

- Seeing a white cat is considered bad luck if the person is walking to school. To prevent bad luck, the person must spit or turn away and make the sign of the cross.

- A cat sitting atop a tombstone means that the person buried below has been possessed by the Devil.

- Two cats fighting near a dying person or over the grave of a recently deceased person are supposedly a devil and an angel fighting for possession of the soul.

- Illness will never leave a house if a cat deserts it.

- In the early sixteenth century, a visitor had to kiss the family cat for good luck.

French superstitions:

- It is considered bad luck to cross a stream while holding a cat.

- Accidental death follows after seeing a tortoiseshell cat.

Irish superstitions:

- If a black cat crosses a person's path by the light of the moon, a deadly epidemic will soon follow.

- Seventeen years bad luck is granted to a person who kills a cat.

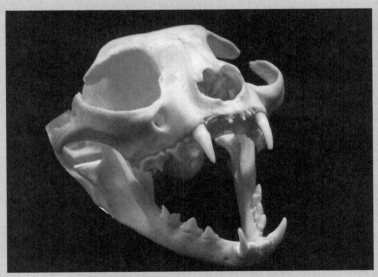

Photo by John West.

Italian superstitions:

- If you hear a cat sneezing, it means good luck.

- In sixteenth century Italy, a sick man who had a black cat lay on his bed would shortly die.

- If the family cat refuses to stay inside a house, it is a bad omen because it is believed cats won't stay where there is illness.

Scottish superstition:

- A strange black cat on your porch will lead to wealth.

Unknown or multi cultural origins:

- In the seventeenth century, if a cat was washing its face, a storm was brewing.

- If the cat washed its face in front of a group of people, then the first person the cat looked at would get married.

- Some cultures believe that a black cat crossing one's path is actually good luck.

- You can tell which direction a storm is coming from by the direction the cat's paw is pointing as it cleans its face.

- Seeing a white cat at night is not only bad luck, but can be considered a harbinger of death.

- Cats are thought to suck the breath from newborns.

- A cat's pupils dilate at low tide and contract at high tide.

- If a cat lays on its ear, it is a sign of rain.

- A kitten born in May is thought to become a witch's cat.

- A cat that has been bought with money instead of adopted will never be a good mouser.

- If a cat sneezes once, it is going to rain.

- If a cat sneezes three times, the family will catch a cold.

- Kicking a cat will cause you to develop rheumatism.

- Killing a cat is equal to sacrificing your soul to the Devil.

VAMPIRES OF BOHEMIA

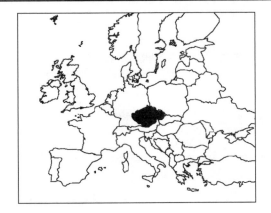

OGOLJEN

Bohemia shares many of its vampire legends with other Eastern European nations. Vampires are disturbingly common throughout this part of the world.

One vampire particular to Bohemia is the Ogoljen, a particularly bloodthirsty Revenant. The Ogoljen can be stopped by fire or beheading, and once brought down has to be properly buried to keep it from rising again. Dirt from its burial site is both a charm against it and a potent inhibiting magic which, when placed in the navel of the resting Ogoljen, will prevent it from rising.

A burial at a crossroads is a sure way of eliminating this fierce blood drinker. But before the creature is interred a thread must be taken from its shroud and stitched through the Ogoljen's navel. This will effectively bind the creature to its grave and stop its reign of terror.

DOWN AT THE CROSSROADS

Throughout history the intersections of roads have been key points for supernatural events. Here are just a few of the myths, legends, and facts tied into the crossroads:

- Burying a vampire at a crossroads was a widespread practice through Europe. Should the corpse rise as a vampire, the choice of four equally appealing directions would confuse it. Revenant vampires, especially those newly risen, are stupid and greedy. Stupidity prevents them from making a reasonable choice; and greed makes them want to go in all four directions, unable to let any choice slip past. In 1928, the noted occult scholar Reverend Montague Summers wrote: "... when the ghost of body issues forth from the grave and finds that there are four paths stretching in as many directions he will be puzzled to know which way to take and will stand debating until dawn compels him to return to the earth, but woe betide the unhappy being who happens to pass by when he is lingering there perplexed and confused."

- In Alsace-Lorraine it was believed that at least one direction in a crossroads would lead to hell. Vampires feared to take any road because they did not want to go to the land of the dead but rather remain among the living to feed.

- Hecate, the Greek Goddess of Witchcraft, was also the Goddess of the crossroads. It was said that Hecate appeared at crossroads at midnight with spirits and howling dogs. Offerings were left at the crossroads for her

- In many European countries, criminals were hung at crossroads because those intersections saw the most traffic. Therefore the object lesson of the execution could reach the largest number of people.

- Soil from a crossroads where a thief was hung was carried as good luck against theft.

- In Celtic Ireland and Wales it was traditional to sit at a crossroads and listen for the howling of winds that would prophesy the year to come. Crossroads also represented the intersection of positive, neutral, and negative forces.

- According to blues music legends, Robert Johnson was supposed to have made a deal with the Devil at the crossroads of Highway 61 and another street down near Clarksdale. The devil promised to fulfill his dreams, so Johnson traded his eternal soul for his extraordinary talents. Of course, the Devil wouldn't allow him to enjoy his success and the lord of the underworld soon claimed his prize: Johnson died young.

  I went to the crossroad
  Fell down on my knees
  I went to the crossroad
  Fell down on my knees
  Asked the Lord above "Have mercy now,
  Save poor Bob, if you please"

  - *"Crossroad Blues"* by Robert Johnson.

- Another blues singer, Tommy Johnson (no relation), made this often-repeated remark: "If you want to learn how to play anything you want to play, you take your guitar and you go to where a road crosses that way, where a crossroad is. Get there, be sure to get there just a little before 12:00 that night so you'll know you'll be there. You have your guitar and be playing a piece there by yourself. A big black man will walk up there and take your guitar, and he'll tune it. And then he'll play a piece and hand it back to you. That's the way I learned to play anything I want."

- In addition to the ultimately death of Robert Johnson, there has been a string of tragedies associated with musicians who recorded the song *Crossroad Blues* over the years. This includes musicians such as Eric Clapton, Lynyrd Skynyrd, and the Allman Brothers Band, who have experienced unusual or tragic losses of group members or loved ones.

- All over the world one will find folk tales and superstitions of fairies, goblins, ghosts and demons residing at desolate crossroads, awaiting the weary traveler.

- Suicides were buried at a crossroads because the act was a mortal sin and their souls were condemned to wander aimless throughout eternity.

• In Feudal Japan, if a *ronin* (a samurai without clan affiliation) was encountered at a crossroads it was popularly believed that he was a *kami* (demon) in human disguise. Even brave warriors would avoid arriving at a crossroads at the same time as a strange samurai.

• In Romania it was believed that crossroads—especially rural ones—somehow formed a link between this world and the world of ghosts and demons. Therefore travelers would never linger at a crossroads after dark; and vampires and witches met at crossroads because the energy there was more akin to their own unholy life essences.

• In his landmark 1922 book on the occult, *The Golden Bough*, Sir James G. Frazer wrote: "Here at a crossroads offerings are set out for the devils. After prayers have been recited by the priests, the blast of a horn summons the devils to partake of the meal which has been prepared for them. At the same time a number of men step forward and light their torches at the holy lamp which burns before the chief priest. Immediately afterwards, followed by the bystanders, they spread in all directions and march through the streets and lanes crying, 'Depart! Go away!'"

• In the Andes, crossroads were ritually swept by priests to allow the earth's energy to flow more smoothly and to create a sacred space. This was especially true along the energy lines (called ley lines) that many occultists believe connect all power centers on Earth. At Nazca in Peru these ley lines were always kept clean.

VAMPIRES OF BOSNIA-HERZEGOVINA

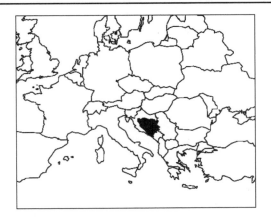

LAMPIRE

Bosnia-Herzegovina, that ancient land on the Adriatic caught between Croatia, Yugoslavia, and Serbia, has had its shares of supernatural woes as well as political troubles. Vampires have plagued Bosnia for centuries, both under the Slavic name of Lampire and the Croatian name of Vukodlak. No matter what name is used, the Bosnian vampire is a horrifying and destructive creature.

In 1878, when the Austrians seized control of this tempestuous country from the Ottoman Empire, they were shocked to learn that the villagers were still actively digging up the corpses of the newly dead and burning them as prevention against vampirism. The Austrians passed laws against this practice because they had "officially" stopped believing in the undead, or Blautsaugers as they had called them, for centuries; but the practice continued nonetheless. Anthropologists have recorded cases of suspected vampirism as late at the 1980s!

From the Austrian point of view the wave of suspicious deaths by wasting diseases was nothing more than an outbreak of plague; but to the Bosnians those diseases were the trademark of the Lampire, which spread pestilence wherever it went. The Bosnians believed that the first victim to die of a wasting disease was almost certainly the Lampire itself, and subsequent deaths were the work of his wicked will being worked on his own village. The plague of evil would continue and spread because anyone who died as a result of this vampiric disease was at risk for becoming a Lampire himself.

The only way to stop the spread of this supernatural plague was to disinter each victim and burn the corpse. The body must be completely incinerated and even the charred bones should be pounded to dust and cast back into a fresh fire. Thus the chain of evil would be broken.

PLAGUE

Plague has repeatedly cut deadly swaths through whole cultures, and pandemic plagues (those that spread over numerous regions) have destroyed much of mankind throughout history. In A.D. 541, the first great plague began in Egypt and swept like wildfire across the world during the next four years, killing between fifty and sixty percent of the world's population. In 1346, a second pandemic plague--the one known as the Black Death--began in the Middle East and spread into Europe. It killed more than 13 million people in China and a staggering 20-30 million in Europe (meaning that one third of the European population at the time died from the Plague).

The development of antibiotic therapy and improvements in living conditions, hygiene, public health, and medical care have combined to prevent a third pandemic plague.

The plague is not gone, however, and incidents of plague infection and death occur every year. But routine medical treatment and organizations like the Center for Disease Control keep this ancient terror in check.

BLAUTSAGER

This was a vampire legend partially adopted from the Austrians who occupied Bosnia from 1878 onward. Blautsager means "blood drinker" and it always lives up to its name. But the Bosnian Blautsager differs significantly from the Bavarian species of Blautsauger.

The Bosnia version of the Blautsager has no skeleton at all but holds its shape through supernatural will. Its body is covered in stiff hair, but otherwise looks more or less human. It had the power of transformation and can become a rat or a gray wolf.

The Blautsager is devious and tricky and in human form tricks people into eating a small clot of dirt from its own tomb. It holds the dirt behind its back and works its wiles on the unsuspecting, enticing them into believing it has a food treat or other goodie. But once the unfortunate person tastes the bit of dirt he will instantly begin to fade, his bones will begin to melt, and rough hair will begin growing all over him. He will become a Blautsager himself.

One of the few defenses against this powerful vampire is to scatter hawthorn flowers along the roads leading away from its grave or tomb. The hawthorn is a proof against many of the vampires of Eastern Europe. It will sicken the Blautsager, slowing his movements and clouding his thoughts. To destroy the beast, a vampire slayer will have to use fire or a sword. Burning and beheading are the two best methods of destruction, and generally both are used at the same time.

Blautsager. Artwork by Marie Elena O'Brien.

HAWTHORN

Hawthorn (*Crataegus* species) is a member of the rose family. It is a common thorny shrub that grows up to five feet tall on hillsides and in sunny wooded areas throughout the world. In May its flowers bloom, but even though hawthorn is in the same botanical family as roses, the flowers are not fragrant. They grow in small clusters and are white, red, or pink. Small berries, called haws, sprout after the flowers. They are usually red when ripe, but they may also be black. Hawthorn leaves are shiny and grow in a variety of shapes and sizes.

Archival photo.

Hawthorn has been used for centuries to prevent the entry of evil spirits into a house. It is generally hung over doorways or windows. In Eastern European folklore Hawthorn was used as a weapons against vampires, both to ward them off and to create stakes to immobilize the vampire during the ritual of exorcism.

Hawthorn also has a well-earned reputation in holistic and conventional medicine for its many health benefits. By the early 1800s, American physicians recognized the herb's medicinal properties and began using it to treat circulatory disorders and respiratory illnesses. Considered a "cardiotonic" herb (an herb that has a positive medical benefit for the heart), the flowers and berries of the hawthorn plant have been used in traditional medicine to treat irregular heartbeat, high blood pressure, chest pain, hardening of the arteries, and congestive heart failure.

VAMPIRES OF BRAZIL

JARACACAS

Around the world the vampire wears many disguises and takes many forms: wolf, bat, crow, moth, even cat. But in the steamy jungles of Brazil, the vampire known as the Jaracacas slithers in the shape of a serpent. Though the Jaracacas may be killed by any ordinary means, this evil monster is hard to recognize as anything other than an ordinary snake.

The Jaracacas drinks blood primarily from the breasts of female victims. It strikes when a woman is drowsing while she nurses her child, so that she is unaware of the serpent at her breast. To get its food the Jaracacas insinuates itself past a woman's nursing child. If the child cries or protests, the Jaracacas pushes its tail into the baby's mouth to silence it. This method of stifling the child's cries has also been known to suffocate a baby.

A few of the more horrifying tales relate how the Jaracacas sometimes does not stop at drinking the milk from the mother's breast, but often attacks and devours the breasts themselves, much like the evil Doppelsauger of Germanic legend.

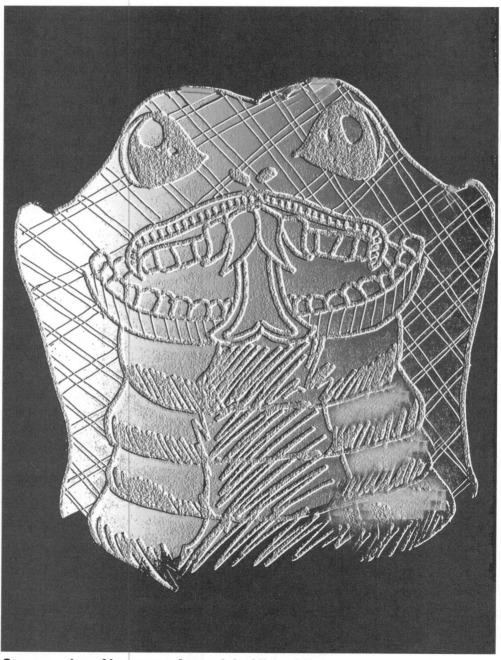

Stone carving of Jaracacas. Artwork by Michael Katz.

In many Brazilian households, especially those in rural areas, dogs and cats are kept as pets and trained to kill any snake they see just in case it is a Jaracacas. An ordinary house pet may often be the savior of the family without anyone knowing what heroic act it has performed.

LOBISHOMEN

The sinister Lobishomen is another Brazilian vampire that preys mainly on women. Like the Jaracacas, this creature seldom kills its victims. Instead it draws only enough blood to nourish itself. However, its bite creates a kind of infection that turns the woman into an insatiable nymphomaniac. As a result she often becomes a sexual vampire, preying on men other than her husband and destroying the sanctity of her marriage vows. In this way the Lobishomen accomplishes its evil purpose.

Portugal has a legend of a Lobishomen that is often overlapped with the legend of the Bruxa: vampire witches who attack children to suck their blood. In some areas where the Portuguese settled in Brazil, the Lobishomen is regarded more as a werewolf than a vampire.

In werewolf fiction, the herb Wolf's Bane is commonly cited as a protection against lycanthropes, much as garlic is used against vampires. The same holds true in the folklore of the Lobishomen. Wolf's Bane is planted on graves to keep the dead from rising as werewolves. In cases where a witch is suspected of being a werewolf, the herb is crushed into a paste with sweet onion and smeared around doors and windows.

Most sightings of the Lobishomen describe a small creature, hunchbacked and scampering on stumpy legs. Its face is horrifying, with pale and bloodless lips, jagged black teeth, jaundiced skin, and stiff bristling hair like that of a jungle ape.

Disposing of a Lobishomen is fairly tough because it is clever and elusive, but it has one often fatal weakness in that it has no head for alcoholic beverages. Leaving cups of strong wine will get it drunk, at which point it can be overcome by several strong men, crucified to a tree, and then stabbed to death. The corpse is then burned.

In centuries past it was believed that a knife or sword that had been used to kill a Lobishomen was tainted and had to be melted down or otherwise destroyed. But in the ninth century the belief sprang up that such weapons had become imbued with special powers and were kept as talismans, often hung over thresholds to send a clear message to other evil creatures: *Keep out!*

Lobishomen. Artwork by Robert Patrick O'Brien.

VAMPIRES OF BULGARIA

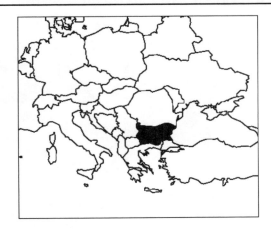

KRVOIJAC (also KRVOPIJAC)

Throughout the Balkans, vampirism is heavily linked with the spread and practices of Christianity. This is never more so than in the case of the Krvoijac of Bulgaria. All that is required of a person to become a Krvoijac is to smoke tobacco or drink alcohol during Lent, and the transformation is upon them. Fairly harsh punishment for breaking the vows of abstinence.

When a person is so cursed they die and are buried normally, but over the next forty days their skeleton melts to a gelatinous state and then is reformed as part of their unnatural immortal body. This new vampiric anatomy helps give the creature the strength necessary to tear apart its shroud, smash through the lid of its coffin, and claw its way up through the earth to escape the grave. When the Krvoijac rises it is a blood drinker and appears very much like a reanimated corpse, with pale rotting flesh, sunken eyes, and horrible breath.

The forty-day transformation of a blasphemer from human to Krvoijac represents the forty days Jesus wandered in the desert without food or drink. In Lent this was a purification process that helped the mortal Jesus prepare to accept the Holy Spirit and thereafter take up the mission for which He had been born. In the case of the Krvoijac the forty-day period is an unholy mockery of the forty days of Lent.

If a Krvoijac is suspected in an area, the preferred method of locating its grave is to ask a young virgin girl to remove all of her clothes, hop onto a black foal, and ride it through the graveyard. If there is any spot within the cemetery where the horse refuses to go, then that is

likely to be the Krvoijac's resting place. A Djadadjii (a vampire slayer, often a monk, with magical powers) is then called in to dispose of the creature by one of the ritual methods. One way is to scatter wild roses all around the grave. Wild roses have a powerful restraining effect on some species of vampires, like hawthorn and garlic flowers. In this case the presence of the flowers prevents the Krvoijac from rising. Planting wild rosebushes all around the grave will keep it in the earth as surely as bars will restrain a prisoner.

Krvoijac. Used with permission, (c) 2003 by Stefani Renee de Oliveira Silvia.

To actually destroy a Krvoijac, the Djadadjii must use his holy powers to invoke the creature's spirit, drawing it out of the ground through prayer, and then directing the spirit to enter a bottle that he has specifically prepared. The bottle is then taken to a great bonfire and hurled into the flames. Only in this manner can the evil soul be destroyed. Once this has been accomplished, the body, still in the grave, becomes nothing more than a lifeless corpse and troubles the village no longer.

OBUR (also UBOUR)

Another Bulgarian vampire is the Obur, a strange blend of vampire and poltergeist. The Obur is created when a person has died a sudden and violent death. Upon burial the spirit refuses to leave the body and either ascend to heaven or descend to hell. It is trapped and lingers on the mortal plane, creating havoc.

The Obur spirit is manifested inside a corpse during the forty days following burial. When that time has passed, it claws its way out of the grave and begins its mischief. The Obur possesses a strange static charge: when it is in the vicinity, sparks crackle in the air and it is the surrounded by the smell of ozone (often mistaken for brimstone).

The Obur acts primarily like a poltergeist, creating destruction, hurling things about, destroying furniture, and focusing most of its destructive attentions on its own family. The creature is fond of making loud, sudden noises, like firecrackers, and disturbing any peace its former family members might enjoy.

The Obur is a blood drinker but does not primarily do so. It prefers normal human food and will be satisfied with that until there is no more to be had. Only then will it turn on humans and attack them for their blood. When that happens the Obur will glut itself on blood.

The name Obur is actually an old Turkish word meaning "glutton," and considering the creature's insatiable hunger for food (and blood) is an apt choice. But its unnatural hungers were also often its downfall, because the Obur could be lured into a trap using rich food as bait. Some folk tales say that excrement could also attract it.

A Vampirdzhija generally handles the task of disposal, for the Vampirdzhija are trained vampire slayers as well as white sorcerers. The

Vampirdzhija have the ability to sense an Obur while it is still in its grave and forming its vampiric skeleton; but must wait until the creature has actually risen before undertaking its destruction. Like the Djadadjii who face the Krvoijac, the Vampirdzhija will summon the spirit of the Obur and consign it to a bottle, which is then burned.

BULGARIAN VAMPIRE SLAYERS

In the dense forests and rocky hills of Bulgaria, many monsters trouble the night. But the nation is not without its defenders. Unlike many countries, Bulgaria has not one but two types of vampire slayers, the Vampirdzhija and the Djadadjii.

Vampirdzhija translates as "vampire killer." This is a multi-purpose slayer, often hiring himself out to villages in need. The vampirdzhija is usually a sorcerer whose abilities include being able to see Ustrels, which were often invisible or which look like ordinary human children. The vampirdzhija can see through any disguise--often as a result of rituals and spells--and can use other spells to draw the creature into a specially prepared bottle which is then thrown on a fire.

The djadadjii work to accomplish the same goal of bottling and burning vampire spirits; but unlike the more mercenary vampirdzhija, the djadadjii is most often a monk or similar kind of cleric who either offers his services for free or in exchange for a donation to the church.

Whereas the vampirdzhija uses magic to overcome evil, the djadadjii relies on religious icons, which he holds in his hands as he walks through an infected town. When the djadadjii reaches an area frequented by a vampire, the holy icon will begin to shake in his hands. He then creates a trap for the vampire by placing the vampire's favorite food in a bottle, which lures the creature in. The bottle is then sealed and cast into the flames.

The Obur. Artwork by Marie O'Brien.

POLTERGEIST

There are many kinds of ghosts and spirits in the vast world of the supernatural, ranging from the most benign of house guests to pernicious creatures such as the vampire. At the midpoint between threat and nuisance is the poltergeist.

The poltergeist is a mischievous and occasionally malevolent spirit that manifests its presence by making noises, moving objects, breaking things, and in some cases even assaulting people and animals. The term "poltergeist" comes from the German words *poltern*, "to knock," and *geist*, "spirit;" hence a "noisy spirit."

During the twentieth century there were quite a few scientific investigations into the nature of poltergeist phenomena, often yielding non-supernatural causes such as houses settling on their foundations, seismic activities, sunspots, and other reasons. But many cases of suspected poltergeists remain unexplained despite extensive scientific investigation, and these may involve actual spirits.

The poltergeist goes by different names in different cultures, and often overlaps with different vampire species. In Bulgaria it is the Obur. In Dalmatia it is the Kozlak. In Romania the Strigoi sometimes manifests as a poltergeist. In Russia, poltergeists are called Elatomsk, or "door knockers."

USTREL

Aside from the consequences of failing to keep the abstinence of Lent, other religious missteps resulted in the spread of vampirism through Bulgaria. A child who was born on a Saturday but died before he could be baptized the following Sunday was doomed to become a type of vampire called an Ustrel.

The Ustrel is a strange kind of vampire, even for the Balkans. It dies as an infant, and upon rising it is usually the size of a small child. But it can continue to grow in size and strength, and it possesses intelligence and cunning on a par with adult predatory animals like foxes or wolves. The Ustrel will return to its grave after a night of feasting (on animals like cows or sheep), but unlike many similar kinds of

The Ustrel. Artwork by Marie O'Brien.

Revenants it can eventually outgrow the need to rest in the earth. If an Ustrel is able to glut itself for ten successive nights it becomes so powerful that it no longer needs to rest in its grave. From then on it lives secretly among the herd, sleeping after feasting all night, and returning to its grave before dawn. Sometimes it would sleep through the daylight hours between the horns of a ram or a young bull, or hidden between the hind legs of a cow.

The Ustrel stakes out a specific herd and works its way through the animals. Sometimes the Ustrel's appetites are not too ravenous and it goes undetected, the attacks on the animals being ascribed to wolves and other predators. But if the vampire becomes too greedy and attacks half a dozen sheep or cows in a single night, then the villagers know that an Ustrel is in their community. Immediately they call in a Vampirdzhija to set about tracking down the blood drinker because only a true Vampirdzhija can actually see an Ustrel and track it to its resting place.

The Vampirdzhija initiates a ritual called the "lighting of the need-fire" which begins the complicated procedure of defeating the Ustrel. On the first day (generally a Saturday, just after dawn), all of the livestock in town are gathered together into a central place and the villagers extinguish all fires in town. Then the villagers gather together and drive their herds toward the closest crossroads, where a pair of bonfires have been prepared. Once the herds approach, the bonfires are ignited by the old method of rubbing two sticks together. The shepherds, under the direction of the Vampirdzhija, drive the herds between the newly blazing bonfires. The passage between the flames makes the unseen Ustrel lose its grip on whatever animal it is resting upon, and the creature drops helpless to the road.

Though invisible, the Ustrel is still mortal in some ways, and its body can be felt and even touched. It can certainly be smelled, because the bonfires and the presence of the Ustrel attract the hungry forest wolves that come in once the herds and the villagers leave. They devour the Ustrel completely.

As they leave the crossroads, some of the villagers take brands lit in the fires and carry them back to the village to relight all of the home and cook fires. The bonfires are allowed to burn themselves out, and for several days afterward no one dares to approach the crossroads for fear that the Ustrel is still lingering and not yet devoured. If the Ustrel survives for a day or so before the wolves come, it may follow any person home and begin again its reign of terror.

NEED-FIRE

This was a special kind of bonfire, also known as a "living fire," lit to purify a town, its people, and their livestock. Once the need-fire was lit, the people and animals would either pass between burning mounds, through a veil of smoke, or over the ashes (particular methods vary from culture to culture). Generally all of the fires in town would have to be extinguished first and then rekindled with a brand from the need-fire, symbolizing new life and health for the village.

Effigies of witches and vampires are often thrown into a need-fire, to symbolize destroying them.

VAMPIR

This is a general term used to describe any of the various vampires of Bulgaria. Vampir is derived from *Opyr*, the ancient Slavic word for vampire. The term still exists in one form or another even today, though it may be spelled as Viper, Vepir, or Vapir. Vampir is the most common version, and happens to be the Russian spelling.

Another common variation, Vampyr, is the Magyar spelling for vampire. This spelling appears in many countries throughout that part of the world, including Bulgaria, Czechoslovakia, Hungary, Poland, Russia, and Serbia. There are even folktales in Sweden and Denmark that speak of the Vampyr.

MAGYARS

The Magyars are the dominant people of Hungary, but also live in Romania, Ukraine, Slovakia, and Yugoslavia. The terms Magyar and Hungarian identify the same body of people, but in non-Hungarian languages the word Magyar is frequently used to distinguish the Hungarian-speaking population of Hungary from the German, Slavic, and Romanian minorities. A nomadic people, the Magyars migrated from the Urals to the Northern Caucasus region in the mid-fifth century and remained there for about 400 years before moving westward across southern Russia and into present Romania. The Magyar-Hungarian language belongs to the Finno-Ugric family of languages.

Woodcut of Magyars hunting werewolves. Archival artwork.

VAMPIRES OF BURMA

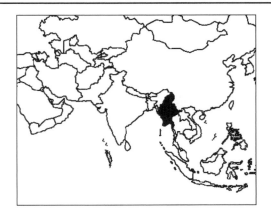

KEPHN

Throughout the world's many species of vampires there is a sub-species that are witches or sorcerers who are also vampires. The Obayifo of Ghana's Gold Coast, the Hebrew Striga, the Tlaciques vampire-witches of the Nahautl Indians of Mexico, the Serbian Vjestitiza, the Navajo Skinwalkers, the Russian Upyr, and the Adze of Togo are all part of this wicked sub-grouping. Along with them is the vicious Burmese vampire called the Kephn.

The Kephn is a hideous demon found among Burma's Karen tribe, a people descended from the same ancestors as the Mongolians. The Kephn appears as the floating head and stomach of a local sorcerer who has made a pact with evil spirits to gain enormous and vile super-natural powers.

The Kephn soul-vampire is a particularly unholy creature with quite an unsavory reputation. It attacks the unwary and consumes their souls.

The sorcerer Kephn, when not hunting the night in its monstrous form, can be killed the same way any ordinary person is killed, though cremation is mandatory to keep it from returning from the grave.

Native sorcerers also make a practice of stealing the souls of sleeping villagers and forcing them into recently dead corpses, thereby creating Revenants. These reanimated monsters are also called Kephn even though they lack the immense power of the true Kephn sorcerers, and are often used in battles between the wizards of villages. These Revenant Kephn are incredibly strong, feel no pain, and are nearly impossible for any single man to stop, so it is often a small party of armed men who heroically attack the monster and try to bring it down. The Revenant Kephn can be stopped by decapitation or amputation of arms and legs (thereby rendering them unable to move), but the entire corpse must be burned immediately.

There have been folk tales of Ghurkhas, the highly trained fighting men of Burma, returning home to their villages and, upon discovering the presence of a Kephn, using their military training to dispatch these beasts. The Ghurkhas were used mainly by the British as their front line troops, and though the Ghurkha ranks often included men from various peoples of South and East Asia, the bulk of their numbers were made up of Burmese men. Armed with their fierce curved Kukri knives, and highly skilled in the ancient Burmese martial art called Bando, the Ghurkhas were as formidable a human weapon as could be imagined. Only a Ghurkha could face a Kephn in single combat and be victorious.

DRACULA VS. THE KUKRI KNIFE

In the novel *Dracula*, the Count is actually not dispatched by a stake. He is instead slain by a Kukri knife in the hands of Jonathan Harker. Stoker writes:

> "We men are all in a fever of excitement, except Harker, who is calm. His hands are cold as ice, and an hour ago I found him whetting the edge of the great Ghoorka knife which he now always carries with him. It will be a bad lookout for the Count if the edge of that 'Kukri' ever touches his throat, driven by that stern, ice-cold hand!"

Close-up of the Kukri knife. Archival photo.

And then in an encounter with Dracula:

> "Harker evidently meant to try the matter, for he had ready his great Kukri knife and made a fierce and sudden cut at him. The blow was a powerful one. Only the diabolical quickness of the Count's leap back saved him. A second less and the trenchant blade had shorn through his coat, making a wide gap whence a bundle of bank notes and a stream of gold fell out. The expression of the Count's face was so hellish, that for a moment I feared for Harker, though I saw him throw the terrible knife aloft again for another stroke."

Dracula escapes that attack, though in the closing scenes he is again confronted by Harker with his Kukri as well as the American adventurer, Quincy Morris, armed with another fierce knife:

"But, on the instant, came the sweep and flash of Jonathan's great knife. I shrieked as I saw it shear through the throat. Whilst at the same moment Mr. Morris's Bowie knife plunged into the heart. It was like a miracle, but before our very eyes, and almost in the drawing of a breath, the whole body crumbled into dust and passed from our sight."

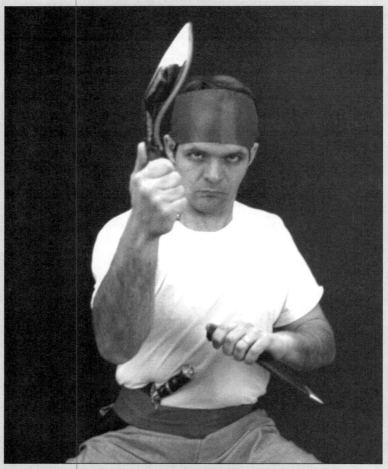

The Kukri knife. Archival photo by John J. Hyland, III.

TASE

In Burma the distinction between vampire and ghost is indistinct. In fact the vampire feared most by the Burmese is, technically, a blood-sucking ghost. The Tase is the disembodied spirit that lingers on earth to prey on the living for their blood and also to spread plague and other diseases.

There are three sub-species of Tase: Hminza Tase, Thabet Tase, and Thaye Tase, each one possessing their own evil and pernicious qualities:

- *Hminza Tase* are the most rare of the three sub-species. They are evil demons who enter and possess the bodies of animals such as crocodiles, dogs, hunting birds, owls, and tigers. Once they have inhabited the animals they slaughter all others of the animal's species in a given area, staking out a hunting ground. Once it has destroyed all competitors, the Hminza Tase begins using a combination of animal cunning and demonic intelligence to lure humans into remote spots in order to attack them. The attack of a Hminza Tase is savage and leaves the victim torn to pieces, which disguises the nearly total loss of blood.

- *Thabet Tase* are the vengeful spirits of women who have died during childbirth and return to the world of the living as Essential Vampires that feed on the sexual essence of men. They are skilled seducers and it is said that no man can resist their charms, especially while asleep and dreaming. It is the special delight of the Thabet Tase to disrupt a new marriage so severely that no child will be conceived between the newlyweds.

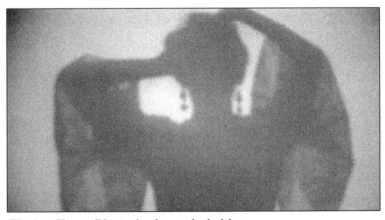

Thabet Tase. Photo by Jason Lukridge.

- *Thaye Tase* are hideous giants that appear near twilight to spread diseases such as cholera, typhus and smallpox. The Thaye Tase are the angry and confused spirits of people who died violently and are somehow caught between this world and the next. This feeling of being trapped apparently either drives them mad or brings out the worst qualities in them, because for amusement the Thaye Tase appear beside the beds of the dying and taunt the sufferers by mocking them for their helplessness and pain.

Proper burial rites help keep the Tase in their graves, but some folk-tales suggest that one custom was to forego using gravestones so that the risen spirit will not know who he is (or was) and will therefore be unable to locate his own village, family, and friends. Though not a prevention per se, this did keep Tase ghosts from visiting their old homes.

When a Tase is suspected, the only method of combating it is to drive it off by loud noises such as the beating of drums, clanging of pots, and firecrackers. The Tase, for all of their powers, cannot abide loud noise.

VAMPIRES OF BYELORUS

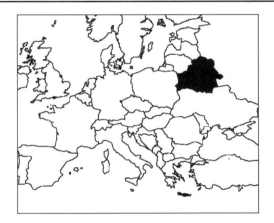

MJERTOVJEC

Sometimes the shadowy line between what is a vampire and what is a werewolf becomes all but impossible to distinguish, and in many cultures they are inextricably linked. The Mjertovjec is a prime example: when a werewolf (or, in some cases a witch) dies, it can be reincarnated as a strange kind of vampire called a Mjertovjec.

There are other ways in which a person can be cursed into becoming a Mjertovjec. If a person becomes an apostate (someone who has abandoned his faith or defied the church), or openly curses the Church or God, then doom is on them. Also, if a person merely acts like a werewolf—attacking people and biting them—then he suffers the same fate.

The Mjertovjec appears as a disembodied head and thorax, with a dark red or purple face and many sharp teeth. From the hour of midnight until the rooster has cried three times it holds sway over the hours of darkness, and will attack the unwary with great strength and a terrible thirst for blood.

To prevent a Mjertovjec from haunting the countryside, villagers spread poppy seeds on the road between the cemetery and the house where the creature dwelled while it was alive. Like many Slavic vampires, the Mjertovjec is compelled to stop and count the seeds, thus wasting the entire night. A wise vampire slayer would secretly follow the Mjertovjec back along the trail of seeds to its resting place.

In order to destroy the Mjertovjec, the vampire slayer has to wait until the disembodied head and thorax have left the grave again (or were busy counting seeds in the road). Only then can an iron shaft be driven through the creature's chest. Once transfixed, the spirit is cast loose from the body and destroyed. But even so the corpse itself has to be burned quickly or the Mjertovjec might somehow return.

APOSTATE: One who has forsaken the faith, principles, or party to which he before adhered; especially one who has forsaken his religion for another; a pervert; a renegade.

UPOR

Similar in most ways to the Upyr of Russia (*see* Vampires Of Russia, p. 444), the Upor is a vicious blood drinker that attacks children.

A shapeshifter by nature, the Upor can adopt many animal guises such as dogs, chickens, various small birds, insects, and rats. The Upor also possesses an empathic connection with different beasts and uses them as his spies and familiars.

In many Russian folk tales the Upor mentally controls a family dog to make it run off so the children who own it will go looking for it.

The Mjertovjec. Artwork by Robert Patrick O'Brien.

Naturally the dog leads them to the waiting vampire. At other times the Upor will use a kind of telepathy to call a household pet to him and then he will "return" it to the house as if he were a kind stranger who had stopped to do an act of kindness. Often the grateful family will invite him in for a drink and a bite, but not in the way they were expecting.

In human form the Upor is often seen riding a wild horse, or the horse of someone who has recently died through violence. In this guise he preys on travelers, shepherds, and other folks out alone and away from the lights and safety of town.

The Upor can only be killed using the standard European ritual of exorcism: disinterring it, staking the body to prevent it from rising, cutting off the head, and filling the mouth with garlic. Garlic cloves and flowers should be scattered inside the shroud or coffin when the body is reburied.

TELEPATHY

Telepathy is a psychic phenomenon by which two or more persons communicate through mind-to-mind contact rather than through speech, writing, or gestures. Telepathy may be as subtle as the communication of sensations or emotions, or as comples as an actual exchange of thoughts.

Many of the world's cultures have stories about telepathy. Some suggest that telepathy is a latent or potential human ability. Others believe it to be some celestial or supernatural gift.

In some cultures, such as among the Aborigines of Australia, telepathic communication is accepted as a normal human facility. In more modern societies, such as twenty-first century America, it is not openly accepted but is extensively studied by scientific researchers.

WEREWOLVES IN MOVIES

Werewolves have been the focus of films for nearly as long as vampires, resulting in movies ranging from the silly to the truly frightening. Among the better and more interesting werewolf films are:

- *The Werewolf* (1913). Early (and lost) silent Canadian film directed by Henry McRae in which a Navajo Witch Woman transforms her daughter into a wolf in order to attack invading white men. An actual wolf was used in the transformation sequence.

- *The Wolfman* (1915). A silent film from Reliance-Mutual studio. Sadly no print is still known to exist. Other silent werewolf films include *The Wolf* (1915), *Le Loup Garou* (France, 1923), and *The Wolf Man* (1924).

- *The Werewolf* (1932, Germany). Directed by Friedrich Feher, this was the first "talkie" featuring a werewolf. The film was based on the Alfred Machard novel *Der Schwarze Mann*.

- *The Werewolf of London* (1935). The first of Universal's werewolf films and one of the best of all time. Dr. Wilfrid Glendon (played by Henry Hull) is a botanist who is bitten by a werewolf (played by Warner Oland), and once back in England transforms into a monster himself. Intelligent, moody, and watchable even three quarters of a century later.

- *The Wolf Man* (1941). The most famous werewolf film of all. Lon Chaney, Jr. stars as the tragic Larry Talbot. He is bitten by a werewolf played by Bela Lugosi, and survives to carry the curse himself. This film introduces the link between werewolves and wolf's bane.

- *I Was a Teenage Werewolf* (1957). This teen angst film starred a nineteen year old Michael Landon as the unfortunate victim of the werewolf curse.

- *The Curse Of The Werewolf* (1961). Though campy and talky, this Hammer Films entry presents one of the more frightening werewolves in the form of the muscular Oliver Reed. In this film's mythology a person can become a werewolf as a result of being the offspring of a raped woman, apparently perpetuating the evil seed of the rapist father.

- *An American Werewolf In London* (1981). The first of the special effects werewolf extravaganzas, for which it set the standard. Blending black comedy with real shocks, this film explores the curse of werewolfism and its implications for both the werewolf and its victims.

- *The Howling* (1981). Made the same year as *An American Werewolf in London* and based on the excellent novel by Gary Brander, The Howling explored the concept of werewolves living in a structured community, much like a wolfpack. The transformation scenes are even more horrific than *American Werewolf*.

- *Wolfen* (1981). This thought-provoking film starred Albert Finney and Gregory Hines as a cop and a coroner investigating killings by wolflike creatures. Not truly a werewolf film (no humans transform) it instead deals with a different species of predatory wolf that has near human intelligence.

- *Silver Bullet* (1985). Stephen King's underrated and underappreciated werewolf film is a nice small town fable about good versus evil that explores issues such as the power of compulsion, the nature of inner strength, and the bonds of family. It is based on a limited edition graphic novel written by King and beautifully illustrated by comic book artist Bernie Wrightson.

- *The Howling III* (1987). A sequel to the first *Howling* film in name only, this odd but interesting entry deals with a species of marsupial werewolf in Australia. Worth catching mostly for its efforts to think outside the Hollywood box.

An American Werewolf In London. **Artwork by Robert Patrick O'Brien.**

- *Wolf* (1994). Starring Jack Nicholson as an aging doormat of a man who becomes a business and sexual tornado after getting bitten by a werewolf.

- *Ginger Snaps* (2000). Much like the film *Carrie*, this movie uses the plot device of a horrifying transformation as a metaphor for puberty. A Goth teenager named Ginger (played by Katharine Isabelle) is bitten by a wolf on the eve of her first period and then begins changing in extreme and dangerous ways.

- *Dog Soldiers* (2002). In one of the best werewolf films in decades, *Dog Soldiers* tells the story of a squad of British soldiers training in the lonesome Scottish hills who stumble upon a ferocious family of werewolves. Bloody, action-packed and entertaining.

- *Le Pacte des Loups (The Brotherhood of the Wolf)*. A 2002 action film based on the real events of over a hundred killings by a wolflike creature in Gevaudan, France between 1765 and 1767. The movie combines horror, court intrigue, and martial arts into a visually stunning film experience.

- *Underworld* (2003). This movie takes a twisted version of *Romeo And Juliet* and substitutes the Capulets with vampires and the Montagues with werewolves. Kate Beckinsale plays a vampire who falls for a werewolf while the clans of vampires and werewolves prepare for an all-out war.

VAMPIRES OF CANADA

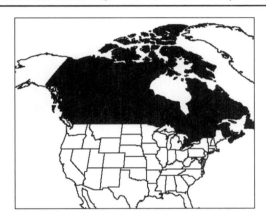

THE ADLET

Among the Inuit peoples of Canada and Alaska there is an ancient legend of a race of bloodthirsty were-dogs called the Adlet.

The Adlet race began as the hideous offspring of an unholy union of an Inuit woman and a monstrous red dog that was very likely possessed by a demon. This blasphemous sexual encounter bred creatures that were half human and half dog. The Inuit mother essentially gave birth to a "litter" of five of these creatures. Aghast at what she had brought into the world, she bundled them onto rafts made from whalebone and animal hides and set them adrift in the frozen artic waters.

The infant dog-creatures did not perish from the cold, however, but rather crossed the ocean and came ashore on the banks of one of the European countries (the legends don't specify which). According to the mythology of the Inuits it was this pack of vicious monsters became them the progenitors of all of the white races of Europe, which explains (according to the) why there are so many tales of monsters and shapeshifters in white European culture.

Either the tale of the mother setting them adrift is wrong or the Adlet somehow managed to return, but there have reports for centuries of Adlet attacks—monstrous doglike creatures who attack hunters or villagers and feast on their flesh and blood.

MARA

Many of the supernatural predators from "The Old World" traveled with settlers to the shores of North America. A Slavic vampire called the Mara was unknowingly brought to Canada in the eighteenth century by Kashube Slavs who had lived in West Prussia and in northeastern Pomerania.

The Mara is both frightening and tragic, a damned spirit created when a girl-child dies before she can be baptized or when a woman is unknowingly baptized by a corrupt priest. This spirit is then doomed to walk the earth until Judgment Day, and is so bitter that it seeks

Used with permission, (c)2003 by Bill Chancellor.

vengeance on the living. The Mara is a nightcomer, a fiend that exists only during the hours of darkness. Once the sun has set it takes human form and steals into the houses of the sleeping and crushes its victims to death.

The Mara's favorite victims are sleeping children upon whose blood it also feeds, robbing them of their life as a way of striking back at the world that denied it a life of its own.

Other tales tell of the Mara appearing as a more physically mature spirit, though no less deadly. In these accounts the adult Mara preys on sleeping men, often developing a dark sexual obsession with any adult man whose blood it drinks. Having tasted that man's blood, the Mara will return, night after night, drinking more and more from him until he wastes away and dies.

In both versions of the legend of the Mara, the victims die from what appears to be disease rather than the bite of a vampire because the Mara leaves no marks. The wounds of its bite heal before dawn, though the damage it has done never heals unless the victim is taken under the care of a physician skilled in medicine as well as more metaphysical cures.

The Mara has appeared in slightly different forms in different countries, including Germany, Poland, and most notably, Scandinavia.

NIGHTCOMER: A creature that travels only by night and generally cannot abide the light of day. Most vampires are Nightcomers in that they hunt at night, but only a few species are actually rendered powerless by the sun.

Many species of Essential Vampires are Nightcomers because they drain life essence or sexual vitality from their victims while they sleep, which is also when people are at their most vulnerable. The night is an excellent hunting time because people are off their guard, tired, often at home and isolated, and defenseless. Seductress Vampires, such as the Mara, are also Nightcomers because night is such a useful time for seduction.

SASQUATCH

All over the world there are stories, legends, and myths about strange manlike creatures living wild in the mountains and deep forests. From Russia to Australia, from China to the Pacific Northwest, there have been sightings of these ferocious wildmen every year. Some of these creatures appear to be benign (especially those living at higher altitudes) whereas others are bloodthirsty predators.

Perhaps the most famous of all of these humanoid monsters is Bigfoot, more formally known as Sasquatch. This creature roams the forests of Western Canada, all the way down to Northern California.

For centuries, Native Americans have told tales of hairy manlike predators. Sightings among the European-American population date back only to the 1960s. On October 20, 1967, Roger Patterson and Bob Gimlin shot footage of what was purported to be a "real" Bigfoot. Although the film has been analyzed thousands of times and generally discredited as a hoax, sightings persist.

The Sasquatch is often described as being about seven to ten feet tall, with a face similar to a Neanderthal, but markedly more simian. The creature has powerful sloped shoulders and long arms, and its body is completely covered with fur or hair that can be brown, black, red, or white. Casts have been made of supposed Bigfoot tracks, and these feet range from twelve to twenty inches. The creature's weight has been estimated at 500 pounds, half the weight of a grown horse.

Like most of the similar creatures around the world, the Sasquatch is supposed to emit a foul stench, described as either sulfurous or like rotting meat. But unlike most forest-dwelling wildmen, Bigfoot does not appear to be aggressive and is demonstrably shy of humans. Close cousins such as the Shampe of the Chocktaw Native Americans (*see* p. 380) or the Wendigo (*see* next entry) have grim reputations as predators, meat-eaters, and blood drinkers.

WENDIGO

According to folklore of Ontario, Canada (as well as Minnesota in the United States), the Wendigo is a fierce predatory monster created whenever a human resorts to cannibalism. The Wendigo is also known as the Cannibal Demon of the Northern Woods. Wendigo stories are thematically linked to both werewolves and vampires in that both of these creatures can also be created by committing sins, and cannibalism is certainly a taboo in nearly all human cultures.

During frontier days cannibalism was a bit more common (although still rare) because the heavy snows and brutal winters trapped settlers and Native Americans in the remote northern woods. Game was scarce and the will to survive strong, so a trapped and desperate person was sometimes forced to eat another human in order to survive. That was all it took for the Wendigo spirit to emerge from a man's deepest inner recesses and take total command of that person, body and soul.

Wendigo. Used with permission, (c)2003 by Jack Schrader.

The Inuit Indians have told tales of the Wendigo for centuries. They called the creature by various names, including Wendigo, Witigo, Witiko and Wee-Tee-Go, each of which translates roughly as "the evil spirit that devours mankind." European settlers in the region re-translated this simply to "cannibal," which is close enough.

The Wendigo is generally described as a transformed human who is over fifteen feet tall, with glowing eyes, long yellowed fangs, a lolling tongue, and a muscular body matted with coarse hair. The creature stalks through the woods, preferring to stick to the shadows beneath the boughs of trees during the daylight hours and most often hunting at night.

It has been also speculated that the Wendigo belongs to a race of beings who exist in some parallel dimension and who can emerge only one at a time when the circumstances are just right. If this fanciful concept is correct it suggests that human actions, such as the commission of mortal sins, are somehow linked to the substance that makes up the walls of these dimensions. By that reasoning the Wendigo, as described, could not exist in a universe that had no directing religious force. Perhaps the Wendigo is the ultimate expression of either human weakness or human evil made manifest in a monstrous form.

THE WENDIGO IN FICTION

The Wendigo seldom appears in films, with the exception of *Wendigo* (2002). Directed and written by Larry Fessenden and starring Patricia Clarkson, Jake Weber, and Eric Per Sullivan, this eclectic low-budget horror film blends Canadian mythology with elements of films like *Straw Dogs* and *Deliverance*.

A comic-book character called the Wendigo was introduced by Marvel Comics in *The Incredible Hulk* #162. Despite the usual prohibition of the Comics Authority code, the story dealt accurately with the origins of the creature, chronicling the fate of a man who was forced to eat a dead companion after being snowbound in Canada. The character recurs in various Marvel comics, including *The X-Men, Captain Marvel, Wolverine, Spider-Man,* and other books.

VAMPIRES OF CHILE

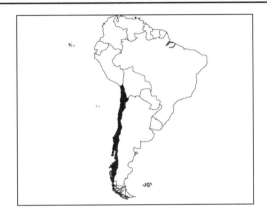

CHONCHON

The Mapuche Indians are one of the few tribes whose traditions have survived almost totally unchanged since pre-Columbian days. The Mapuche's religion is based on both animal and ancestor worship, and there is strong archeological evidence that their people have existed for 12,000 years.

The Mapuche people are very spiritual and upstanding and they have waged a war against evil for centuries. Their first line of defense is found in the Machi, female spiritual leaders and healers who train for most of their lifetimes to become doctors and vampire slayers for their people. Like the Greek Sabbatarian and his Fetch Dog, the Machi use their animal familiars as sources of power and allies in the fight against evil.

The creatures the Machi fight are the Wekufe, which are evil spirits summoned by Kalku (witches) that can manifest in several ways, particularly as vampires called Chonchon. The Chonchon is a vulture with the head of a Kalku witch. It swoops down on people as they walk through the jungles at night, knocks them to the ground, and savages their throats with wicked teeth. The Chonchon feeds on the victim's spurting blood.

Though the Chonchon can be driven off by spears, especially those with tips fire-hardened and blessed by the Machi, the creature can only be killed by a Machi's familiar. It is important for the Machi to pick a familiar that has great physical and spiritual power, such as a jungle snake or hunting bird.

WAILLEPEN

Another creature that preys on the Mapuche is the fierce and powerful shapeshifter called the Waillepen. These monsters are ghosts who manifest physical forms, usually that of a monster composed from different animal aspects. The Waillepen can also assume human form so they can intermingle with the living and sow discord, such as inspiring infidelity, poisoning water, stealing food, and damaging crops.

The Waillepen are bloodsuckers. The more they feed on human blood, the more powerful they become. When ravenous, the Waillepen transforms into its monster shape and hunts humans through the forests, delighting in the fear it inspires during the chase.

A Machi and her familiar are needed to create charms to protect each house in a village, and to fashion talismans for travelers, farmers, and shepherds. Confronting and defeating the Waillepen is immensely difficult, even for a Machi. Though the familiar can usually locate the creature, the Waillepen is already dead so no ordinary weapons can hurt it. Only prayers invoked to Ñenechen (the God-ruler of the Mapuchen deities) in the presence of the Waillepen can end the creature's unnatural life and send it back to the world of the dead.

VAMPIRES OF CHINA

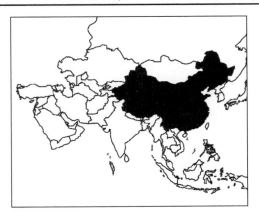

CHIANG-SHIH (also Kiang-Shi and Kuang-Shi)

There are as many ways in which a person can become a vampire as
there are vampires. In the case of the Chiang-Shih there are many
ways in which a person can become this particular kind of vampire.

Most commonly, it is demonic possession that transforms a helpless
victim into this terrible Chinese blood drinker. Usually it is a demon
that inhabits a newly dead corpse, especially of a person who died as a
result of suicide or a violent death such as murder, hanging, drowning,
or a death occurring during the commission of a crime. There are some
legends which hold that if a cat jumps over a corpse, the body will rise
as a Chiang-Shih. And there is another, even more metaphysical cause,
based on a Chinese belief that a body houses two separate souls: one
very strong and rational (called *hun*) and one weak and irrational (called

p'ai or *p'o*). It is the lesser soul which inhabits the body first in its fetal stage and then again at death. Normally, at the moment of death both souls will leave and move on; but sometimes the lesser soul does not want to leave the body and lingers, creating the aberrant and unnatural being called the Chiang-Shih.

The Chinese believe the body houses two souls. Artwork by Robert Patrick O'Brien.

The Chiang-Shih is a very violent vampire, driven by pure bloodlust and heedless of any consequences. They act insanely because they are the manifestations of the irrational aspects of the soul.

The Chiang-Shih have great difficulty walking due to the pain and stiffness of being a decaying corpse, so they hop instead. In fact, a series of horror-comedy-martial arts movies have been made about the hopping vampires of China. Whereas hopping scenes in the movies are largely shot for laughs, the creatures of legend are no laughing matter. They are vicious and sadistic and always hungry for blood. They are vastly strong and enjoy tearing their victims limb from limb. Some Chiang-Shih have been known to sexually assault female victims.

The most common Chiang-Shih looks quite human, even at a slight distance. It uses this deception to draw close to its victims before attacking.

A sub-species of Chiang-Shih are tall, gaunt, animated corpses with wild hair all over their bodies that is either green, white, or both. This particular sub-species has savage claws, jagged teeth, flaring red eyes, and breath so foul that they can kill with an exhalation. This Chiang-Shih seem to be the most dangerous because they can leap great distances and with great force, and some have even learned to fly on the night winds. Luckily this more dangerous species is also the most rare.

Another rare form of the Chiang-Shih is that of a ball of flickering light, which sometimes moves across the countryside as a frosty and bone-chilling mist.

Like some of the Slavic vampires of popular fiction, the Chiang-Shih shun sunlight, fear garlic, cannot cross running water, and can even shapeshift into wolves.

Luckily there are many ways to combat these deadly creatures. One quick way is to hold your breath if one draws near. The Chiang-Shih cannot see well and rely heavily on their sense of smell. If they cannot smell a person's breath, they cannot find them and will pass by.

As with many other kinds of vampires, the Chiang-Shih is compelled to stop and count seeds or grains of rice left out for it. If enough is left out the vampire will have to complete its task even if it takes all night. Leaving a stack of rice, a bunch of dried peas, or even tiny iron pellets on its grave will ensure that it does not stray far once it has risen. If it is still counting the grains at dawn, the sunlight will destroy it.

Although (despite what is shown in the movies) sunlight does not harm most vampires, it is fatal to the Chiang-Shih. Lightning is also fatal to the Chiang-Shih, but (obviously) hard to arrange.

Taoist monks have perfected many strategies against these creatures and are often called into villages to defeat Chiang-Shih. The priests

Chiang-Shih : The Hopping Vampire. Sculpture by Robert Patrick O'Brien.

prepare charms which they write with chicken blood on small pieces of yellow paper. The trick is then to affix these small paper charms to the Chiang-Shih's forehead, which is easier said than done with a monster that can kill with its breath or tear a man limb from limb. But once accomplished, the Chiang-Shih is instantly helpless. Of course, many Chiang-Shih movies contain at least one scene of the small pieces of paper accidentally falling off a Chiang-Shih's forehead.

HOPPING VAMPIRES IN FILM

The Hopping Vampire films of Hong Kong cinema are a bizarre blend of humor and fright. The vampires are dressed in Ching Dynasty garb, have pale green skin, yellow fangs, and long nails. They often hop around, arms outstretched, like sleepwalking kangaroos. According to Chinese legend, if a body is buried where the grave soil is too dry, the coffin blocks out soil humidity, and the body's preservatives won't absorb moisture. Sun and moon spirits then dry out the corpse and turn it into a vampire. Popular myth explains the "hopping" of these vampires by stating that their ankles are sometimes pierced by an iron bar, or that their bodies are so stiff from rigor mortis that they are forced to jump after their victims. Unable to bend over and bite, they must levitate, then float down to kill their prey by biting them on the neck.

Chiang-Shih. Sculpture by Robert Patrick O'Brien.

HIS-HSUE-KEUI

This is the general Chinese term for vampire and translates as "suck-blood demon."

YEREN

The Yeren is another of the world's many strange man-beasts. It lives in China's rocky northern territories, and sightings of this hairy creature have been so common for so long that in 1994 the Chinese government formed an organization to find them. The Committee for the Search for Strange and Rare Creatures is comprised of scientists in various fields (paleontology, cryptozoology, paleanathropology, etc.) and has sent a number of official expeditions into the hills.

Expeditions have returned with artifacts such as hair samples, feces, plaster casts of Yeren footprints, and so on. Extrapolating the creature's height from the size of it footprints (which range up to sixteen inches), the creature is believed to be an average of seven feet tall.

Repeated searches for the Yeren have not resulted in any captures or even video footage, but the search continues. Though not particularly harmful, the Yeren are a compelling mystery and possibly a link to the world of the supernatural or perhaps to man's own evolutionary past.

There is an interesting postscript to the various accounts of man-beasts found throughout the world. Creatures who dwell in the higher altitudes, such as the Yeren and the Yeti, tend to be shy and nonviolent. Similar creatures living at lower altitudes tend to be predatory. No one has been able to offer an explanation for this difference.

VAMPIRES OF CRETE

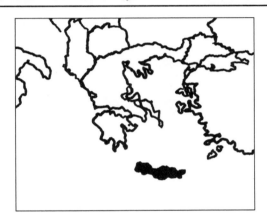

KATHAKANO

Never trust a smiling vampire. Though not a true aphorism, it is certainly good advice when in Crete. The native blood drinker of that island is the Kathakano, a Revenant who constantly grins. From a few yards away, on a darkened country road or badly lit city street, the Kathakano might appear to be nothing more than a friendly stranger, or at worst a happy drunk. But then it draws closer and spits tainted blood at its victims, burning them with some foul acid produced by its unnatural body. Blinded and in agony, the victims are helpless as the Kathakano rushes forward and bites them with its smiling mouth full of sharp, white teeth.

Like most vampires of Eastern Europe, the Kathakano can be tracked to its grave and it is helpless while sleeping. Once the grave has been opened the corpse should be impaled through each shoulder and each thigh with sharpened staves. Thus immobilizing the creature, the vampire slayer should quickly cut the head off and wrap it in a blouse once worn by a virgin girl (symbolizing purity). The head is then taken to a remote spot where a cauldron or large cooking pot has been specially prepared by the slayer's assistants. This large pot is filled with a mixture of one part vinegar and two parts water from melted snow. As soon as the mixture boils, the head should be unwrapped and lowered by tongs into the liquid.

The head is left to boil for one hour, the time kept according to a church clock tower or a priest's pocket watch.

After this process is complete, the head is carried back to the grave and the body is reburied. In some cases the head and corpse are cremated and the ashes poured back into the grave.

Kathakano. Artwork by Robert Patrick O'Brien.

VAMPIRES OF CROATIA

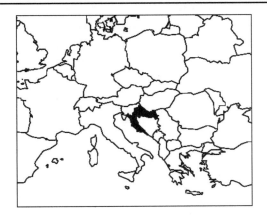

KUDLAK

Many Slavic countries share the same supernatural folklore concerning witches, demons, and vampires. The Kudlak from the Croatian peninsula of Istria is identical to the creature of the same name from Serbia, Bosnia, and Slovenia. Kudlak is likely an abbreviation of the southern Slavic word, Vorkudlak, a general term for vampires in that region.

The Kudlak is one of those unfortunate creatures that is doomed from birth to become a vampire. Any child born with a caul (a veil of skin covering the face) was thought to become either a Kudlak (an evil being) or a Kresnik (a force for good). Only Fate would decide.

The unfortunate whose path leads them to the dark ways of the Kudlak will grow up with evil alive in his heart and will do all manner of harm while still a living being. But at night the soul of this tainted being will leave the body and roam the night wind in the shape of a locust, night bird, or bat, or perhaps stalk the byways as a wolf; attacking the innocent, sometimes killing outright, sometimes amusing itself by merely maiming or tormenting. The Kudlak can also cast spells over the community, resulting in crop failures, bad weather, stillbirths, and other calamities.

When the living Kudlak finally dies (whether naturally or through violence), it will rise again as an undead Revenant, a true vampire. And then the real reign of terror will begin.

If Fate chooses to let a person born with a caul become a Kresnik, his destiny will be to become a champion and protector of his people. He, too, can leave his body and adopt the form of an animal or bird, but his sole purpose is to seek out the Kudlak and destroy it in any of its evil guises. The Kresnik is fierce and strong and can confront the Kudlak in either its living or undead form.

> **CAUL:** An amniotic membrane covering the face of some newborns. This is believed in many cultures to indicate either psychic abilities or the presence of an evil spirit. Many children born with cauls are believed to be fated to become vampires after their deaths.

There have been many ferocious battles between Kresniks and their evil counterparts, including the legend of the brothers Mutimirov who were both born with cauls over their faces. One brother, Matej, was born an hour before midnight on a Saturday. His twin, Dmitar, was born nearly three hours later, early Sunday morning. The boys looked identical, acted the same, and were both raised to be millers like their father, Mutimir. When they reached puberty, Matej began straying from his duties and constantly argued with the elders of the family. His aunts, both of whom were old and wise, believed that Matej was beginning to display signs of spiritual corruption and they feared that he would become a Kudlak. Eventually he became so wild that he was sent away to live with a relative, a harsh man named Ninoslav who was asked to put the fear of God into the boy.

Meanwhile Dmitar grew to be a very quiet and respectful young man. He worked hard alongside his father, fell in love, and married. His brother, Matej, was allowed to come home for the wedding, but was made to sleep in the barn rather than the main house.

A week after Dmitar was married his wife was found murdered, her body drained of blood and showing signs of great violence. Matej was immediately arrested for the crime and thrown into jail pending the arrival of a priest-exorcist.

But once the exorcist arrived and examined the young man he announced that Matej was the Kresnik and that his mannerly twin, Dmitar, was actually the Kudlak. The priest confronted Dmitar and his vampiric nature emerged. Dmitar attacked the priest and members of his own family. Only the timely arrival of Matej saved them from being killed.

Matej and Dmitar fought in the woods outside the village, and the fury of their battle uprooted trees and caused well water to boil. The battle lasted three nights, during which the moon was eclipsed three times and cows being milked yielded blood instead.

On the fourth day of battle, a few hours after midnight, Matej overcame Dmitar and staked him to the ground with a sharpened stave of hawthorn. The priest was able to perform the exorcism despite his injuries. It was completed just as Dmitar died, which meant that the young man's soul had been saved.

Matej became a hero to his people. His uncle Ninoslav was praised for having helped the boy find his true destiny, and together the uncle and the Kresnik traveled throughout the region seeking other vampires to destroy.

PIJAUICA

The Croatian blood drinker called the Pijauica is created by the unsavory union of incest between a mother and son, an act held by many Slavic Christians to be the ultimate perversion of the sanctity of birth demonstrated by Mary and Jesus. The offspring of such a union is born evil, and is eternally damned and doomed to be a vampire.

A blood drinker, the Pijauica's face is most luridly flushed after it has fed, and it likes to feed often and well. The entire six quarts of blood filling a healthy man's veins will just about satisfy it for a single night, but after the next sunset it is out hunting again, impelled by a truly terrible thirst.

The name Pijauica means "one who is red-faced with drink" and is often used as a harsh slang term for drunkards. But in the folk tales of Croatia the vampire of the same name is no staggering sot, but a vicious supernatural killer. The Pijauica will often pretend to be a drunken person, singing loud songs or making jokes and beckoning others of the village to accompany it to the next tavern or inn. Once someone joins the Pijauica, the Pijauica waits until they are both out of sight and then attacks with quick, efficient ferocity.

There are two kinds of Pijauicas. One is a Revenant that has risen from the grave of a damned person; and the other is a Living Vampire whose demonic nature has emerged during its mortal lifetime. For the latter to occur, the person must be exceptionally vile and corrupt, a worshipper of the devil, or a witch.

The Pijauica does not require darkness in order to hunt, but it prefers darkness in the way an owl or other nocturnal predator chooses to use the shadows for concealment and to confuse its prey. If it hungers enough, however, the Pijauica can easily hunt by day, even in the brightest sunlight.

In direct confrontation, the Pijauica is nearly unbeatable. It is extremely powerful and fast and has an animal's quick, ruthless, and efficient fighting instincts. When it is awake and hunting, ordinary weapons are of little use, partly because its body is supernaturally resistant to harm and partly because it is so formidable a fighter that it can defeat even a skilled swordsman or marksman.

The only means of stopping this creature is to wait until it is resting (in its grave if it is a Revenant Pijauica, or in its hiding place if it is a Living Vampire) and then, using a sword or axe, cut its head off with a single stroke. The head should be placed between the Pijauica's legs and the body sewn into a shroud and buried deep.

VAMPIRES OF CZECHOSLOVAKIA

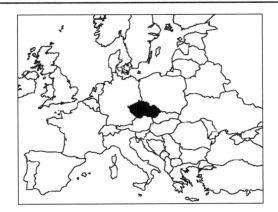

NELAPSI

The most dreaded vampire in Czechoslovakia is the deadly Nelapsi, a creature that delights in destroying entire villages. This vampire will invade a town, glut itself on the blood of humans and livestock, and leave the region a lifeless wasteland. The Nelapsi uses strong teeth to tear at its victims and often smothers them with a fierce strength. It is believed that the Nelapsi has two hearts and two separate souls, which makes killing the vampire far more difficult.

When confronted, the Nelapsi has the power to kill with a single fierce glance of its flaming red eyes. It generally brings with it a virulent plague that slays the few people that survive the vampire's blood thirst.

The villagers know that the best defense against the Nelapsi is to prevent its creation, and luckily have methods for insuring this. One way is to make sure to bump a coffin on the dead person's threshold while carrying the burden out to be buried. This "shakes loose" any bad luck clinging to the coffin so it will not attract any evil spirits.

Poppy seeds should be strewn along the road between the deceased's and the graveyard, all around the grave, and inside the open grave itself. More seeds, and perhaps some millet, should be used to fill the corpse's nose and mouth. Vampires like the Nelapsi are enthralled by seeds and will always stop to count them. With thousands of seeds scattered within and around the grave, the creature will feel compelled to count each one and won't have time to rise.

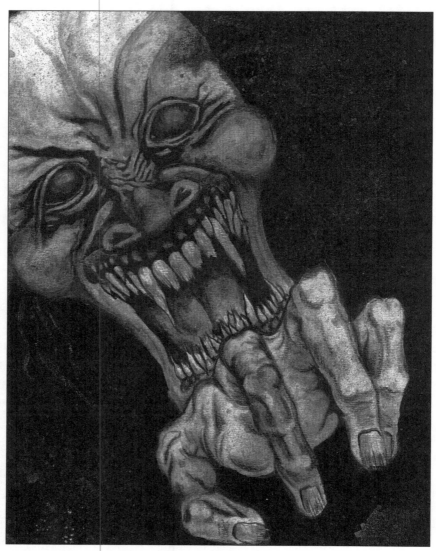

Nelapsi. Artwork by Marie O'Brien.

Some folktales suggest that it is not the seeds but the poppy flower that should be placed inside the grave. The belief is that the narcotic effect of the opium will keep the Revenant in a dreamlike state and therefore make it unwilling or unable to rise.

THE POPPY

The medicinal use of opium predates written history. Images have been preserved from the ancient Sumerians (4000 B.C.E) depicting the poppy. The powers of the opium poppy have been known since at least 3400 B.C., when the Sumerians called it *hul gil*, the "flower of joy." The use of poppies passed from the Assyrians to the Babylonians, who in turn passed it on to the Egyptians.

In the capital city of Thebes, Egyptians (1300 B.C.E.) cultivated opium (called "White Lotus") in their famous poppy fields. The opium trade flourished during the reign of Thutmose IV, Akhenaton, and King Tutankhamen (until 330 B.C.).

Alexander the Great introduced opium to the people of Persia and India. The resulting trade routes included the Phoenicians and Minoans, who shipped it across the Mediterranean Sea into Greece, Carthage, and Europe. By 300 B.C., opium was being used by Arabs, Greeks, and Romans as a sedative and soporific.

Through the centuries, the use of opium spread into Persia, India, China, Europe, and the Americas. In 1753 B.C.E., Linnaeus, the father of botany, first classified the poppy as "sleep-inducing" in his book *Genera Plantarum*.

The scientific name for the poppy is *Papaver somniferum*. The seeds of the poppy do not contain opium. It is the pods which contain an opium latex, and morphine is one of its alkaloids. It is this material from which heroin, codeine, moscapine, papaverine, and thebaine are made.

As an added precaution, iron nails should be deeply driven to pin the arms and legs of the corpse to the wood of the coffin. Smaller nails should be used to securely pin the hair and clothes of the body to the coffin. The arms and legs should also be bound to prevent it from moving within its coffin, and the jaw is often bound tightly to keep it from feeding on itself.

The final burial precaution is to pierce the corpse's heart or head with a long hat-pin, a thin iron spike, or a stake made from hawthorn, blackthorn, or oak.

BINDING A CORPSE

The practice of restricting a vampire's movements by tying a corpse's arms or legs to prevent it from rising and wandering is used by many cultures, especially among Eastern Europeans. Methods of binding vary according to local customs. Some cultures believe in tying the legs together, others the arms, and many wrap the entire corpse so that it could not move more than a finger. Often a binding was used to keep the corpse's jaw shut so that it could not feast on its own flesh. Garlic was often placed in the corpse's mouth to prevent unnatural life from returning to it, and coins were placed in the mouth to prevent it from chewing.

The Nelapsi is so feared that even when all of these precautions are taken with the utmost care, the villagers will go home and thoroughly wash their hands if they have touched either corpse, coffin, or grave dirt. Then as a final act they will light a need-fire, a special type of bonfire made from new wood. Effigies of evil things (witches, vampires, werewolves, etc.) are thrown into the fire, as well as any animal which may have come in contact with the Nelapsi and any creature suspected of being a familiar for the vampire. This type of animal sacrifice actually gave the bonfire its name, as the original expression was "bone fire."

Once the fire has burnt down, the villagers will quickly walk through the smoky ashes, purifying themselves of any taint of evil. The villagers will often herd their livestock through the smoke to keep them safe from attacks by any Nelapsi. Then they carry the embers or tapers to their homes to re-ignite their hearth-fires, and keep the extinguished brand in the house as a talisman against lightning, wild-fire, witchcraft, and the Nelapsi. The ashes are spread over fields and along roads as a final charm against evil.

With all these rites and rituals performed, the villagers believe that they are now safe from this most dreaded of vampires.

BONE FIRE

Also known as Bane Fire and, more commonly, Bonfire, a Bone Fire was used in purification rituals all through out Europe. Since the Bone Fire purified a village of evil, the association of celebrations with bonfires has become part of many cultures. But few people today are aware of the bonfire's connection to the battle against evil.

PIJAVICA

The Pijavica is another Czech vampire which, though not as over-whelmingly deadly as the Nelapsi, is still a vicious killer.

A blood drinking Revenant, the Pijavica was someone who either was deliberately evil in life and died unrepentant, who died during the commission of a sin, or who died after having been excommunicated from the church. A Pijavica can also be created from someone who had committed incest at any time during his life.

Often the Pijavica is resurrected by another evil person through a ceremony that involves animal sacrifices, a mixture of ashes from incense and candle wax, a child's urine, and the hairs of the deceased. This ceremony takes several hours and it can take several days before the flesh is reanimated and the creature rises. Once risen, the human who has invoked the creature must offer it a bowl of fresh blood (animal or human) within its first hour or the Pijavica will die again. After this point, no magic can restore it.

In other tales of the Pijavica, it rises on its own sometime between the date of its death and the anniversary of its birthday. Once risen it is weak and must feed on animals for the first twelve nights until it gains enough strength to begin hunting humans. Like many vampires, the Pijavica's bite can spread disease, both to humans and livestock

The Pijavica's favorite prey are the surviving members of its family. If it dies in a distant town, or if it does not have any living relatives, it will stake out any random family and begin killing their members one by one.

Spreading a paste made from garlic around the doors and windows of a house will keep it from entering. But the Pijavica is not stupid and can use a variety of tactics to gain access to its prey: anything from making a call in the night like a frightened child, to setting fire to a house and waiting to attack whomever rushes outside to flee the blaze.

Fortunately, the Pijavica is not difficult to kill. A sword, axe, or scythe can dismember or behead it. A bullet to the brain will render it immobile. After it has been brought down, the body must be burned and the ashes buried with a mixture of garlic and poppy flowers.

(*See* also Vampires Of Slovenia, p. 475.)

UPIR

General Slavic term for Vampire.

VAMPIRES OF DALMATIA

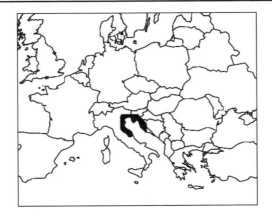

KOZLAK (also Kuzlak)

Spread along the edge of the Adriatic, between Croatia and Albania, is the nation of Dalmatia, home of the vampire-poltergeist called the Kozlak. If a child dies because it has not been properly breast-fed, there is a great risk that it will become a Kozlak, returning to haunt its neglectful mother and the whole community. The angry infant spirit smashes crockery and throws things around the house, and can even muster the strength to pull hay carts around a the yard, sometimes overturning them. Occasionally the creature manifests itself as a bat or other small predator and attacks the family's cattle, drinking blood and spreading disease.

If the creature's rage spills out of the house and into the village, the resulting destruction generally creates an outcry resulting in some quick and decisive action. Traditionally the villagers appeal to the

The Kozlak. Artwork by Robert Patrick O'Brien.

Franciscan Brothers for help, and a monk trained in fighting supernatural evil is dispatched to save the village.

The monk creates a special amulet to protect himself against the Kozlak by incanting prayers over the amulet. He must also obtain a thorn from a hawthorn bush that was grown high in the mountains and at a point where there is no view of the sea. With the amulet and the thorn, the monk goes to the graveyard where the Kozlak's mortal remains are buried. There he sits and prays until his chants summon the Kozlak spirit from its grave. Once the Kozlak has risen, the monk leaps up and transfixes it with a sharpened stick of hawthorn wood. This destroys the evil spirit, leaving the resting remains sanctified and harmless, and the village in peace.

There is an interesting historical oddity about the Kozlak: it is the only known vampire species that can be destroyed merely by a stake through the heart. Unlike the vampires in popular fiction, vampires of folklore are not generally destroyed by a stake, but simply held immobile so other methods of exorcism can be performed.

VAMPIRE BATS

Vampire bats (*Desmodus rotundus*) are far less fierce than fiction makes them seem. Unlike the huge bats that appear in vampire films, most of which seem to have a wingspan a few feet long, the true vampire bat has a wingspan of about eight inches and a body no larger than an adult man's thumb. If not for their gruesome diet, people would not even notice these diminutive predators. As a rule, vampire bats do not attack humans but rather feed on the blood of large birds, cattle, horses, and pigs. They do not suck their victims' blood, but instead use their sharp teeth to make tiny cuts in a sleeping animal's skin. Bat saliva contains several chemicals, including one that keeps blood from clotting and another that numbs the animal's skin and keeps it from waking up.

Scientists have discovered that vampire bat saliva is better at keeping blood from clotting than any known medicine. Vampire bats may one day help prevent heart attacks and strokes.

Because bat saliva can also transmit disease, vampire bats are one of the few bat species that are considered a pest. In many countries, particularly Latin America, bats are slaughtered wholesale. The attempt to limit vampire bat predation backfires because many other species of bats are likewise killed, particularly those that eat far more dangerous insect predators like mosquitoes.

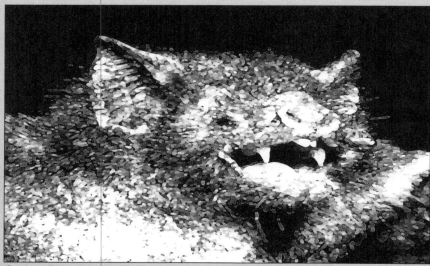

Artwork by Michael Katz.

VAMPIRES OF DOMINICA

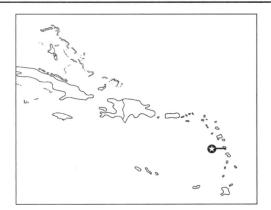

SOUCOUYAN

In the tiny island nation of Dominica (not to be confused with the Dominican Republic) in the Lesser Antilles, between Martinique and Guadalupe, there resides a vampiric creature called the Soucouyan. The Soucouyan looks like a wizened old woman, but this is merely a disguise. Like a serpent, the Soucouyan sheds its skin each night and rises into the air as a ball of fire that swoops down on the unsuspecting. The creature knocks its victim to the ground and feeds hungrily on their blood. The Soucouyan does not always kill, but when it does the drained corpse will as often as not become a vampire as well.

The Soucouyan must reclaim her skin by first light of morning. Discarded skins are often collected and used as powerful ingredients in some of the charms and potions of Obeah magic. Possession of a discarded Soucouyan skin also gives a magician great power over the vampire.

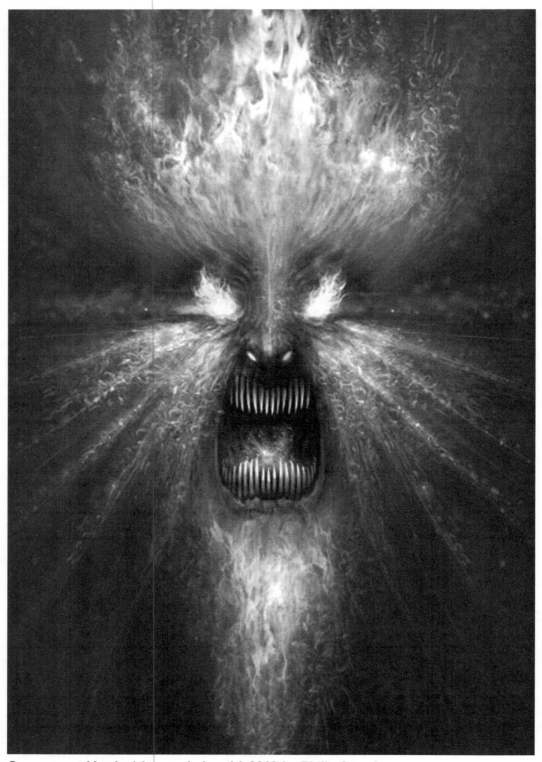

Soucouyan. Used with permission, (c) 2003 by Philip Straub.

VAMPIRES OF ENGLAND

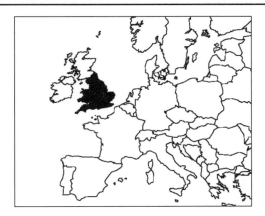

VAMPIRES OF THE MIDDLE AGES

There have been vampire legends among the British for over a thousand years, but it was during the twelfth century that widespread belief in the living dead flourished, as clearly chronicled in the writings of scholars of that age. Three scholars of the Middle Ages, Walter Map, William of Newburgh, and William of Malmesbury, penned accounts of vampirism in England that stand as the earliest British records of the undead.

WALTER MAP (1140-1210; also known in scholarly circles as Gualteri Mapes) was born into a Norman family from Herefordshire. After studying in Paris, the young scholar worked for Henry II as a clerk. Henry enjoyed Map's company and often took him on his travels throughout his kingdom.

In 1193, Walter Map published his *De Nugis Curialium; On The Trivialities Of Courtiers.* This book included a few early accounts of vampiric creatures in England. Map wrote several books, but only *De Nugis Curialium* (more commonly referred to as *Courtiers' Trifles*) has survived in its entirety.

WILLIAM OF NEWBURGH (1136– 1198; also known as Guillelmus Parvus), was an English chronicler and monk of Newburgh, Yorkshire. He wrote the *Historia Rerum Anglicarum* (*The History Of English Affairs*), a history and philosophical commentary on England from 1066 to 1198. The book's chief value lies in its commentary on contemporary events, particularly its analysis of the causes and effects of the anarchy under King Stephen. These writings are still considered of great value because they consist of more than a simple telling of events; they form a real history in which the connection of events is traced, a proper sense of proportion is observed, and men and their actions are judged from an intelligent and independent point of view.

Aside from its well-crafted accounts of history, *Historia Rerum Anglicarum* also prominently mentions vampires and their activities in England.

WILLIAM OF MALMESBURY (c.1096-c.1143) was born in Wiltshire. His father was a Norman and his mother came from England. William became a Benedictine monk at Malmesbury Abbey and, while working in its library, he became interested in history.

Malmesbury's books include *Gesta Regum Anglorum* (*Deeds Of The Kings Of England*) (449 to 1127) and *Historia Novella* (*Recent History*) (1128 to 1142). Malmesbury was a conscientious historian and linguist who searched for reliable (though often obscure) sources to verify his writings. His willingness to look critically at primary sources and his interest in cause and effect helped him become one of the most important historians of the medieval period. These qualities gave his accounts of vampires in *Gesta Regum Anglorum* serious weight.

REVENANT

The British version of the vampire is the one most commonly known in the Western world, thanks to the writings of Bram Stoker, Lord Byron, and others. Generally referred to simply as a "Revenant," England's vampire is a corpse that rises from the grave each night to prey on the living and drink blood.

It is generally believed that a Revenant is a corpse animated by a demon, and that no part of the original person remains within the decaying shell. Some writers have fancied that while inhabiting the body, the demon is able to access the memories stored in the dead person's brain and can use these memories to make the corpse act and speak like the person it once was, thereby deceiving its friends and loved ones.

Revenant. Used with permission, (c) 2003 by Krista McLean.

Folkloric accounts of how a person becomes a Revenant differ considerably from what is commonly found in movies and books. Legends used to most frequently suggest that only a person who leads a wicked or sinful life could be cursed to become a Revenant, and that this would automatically happen once the person dies and is buried. Popular culture has totally supplanted this concept of the vampiric transformation which had been passed down through the centuries.

The publication of *Dracula* led to the current popular belief, which is now that someone only becomes a vampire through an exchange of blood with a vampire.

The process that involves having the vampire bite the victim at least once and draining them of blood to the point of death. The vampire then wounds itself and forces the victim to drink from the vampire's own blood.

Before England used the word Revenant as the name for its vampires, William of Newburgh, in his account of the Red Knight of Ainswick, called the creature by the Latin term *sanguisuga*. This word means "leech" or "blood sucker" (from *sanguis* (blood) and *sugo* (to suck)). Very apt in this case.

Revenant. Artwork by Robert Patrick O'Brien.

THE RED KNIGHT

The story of the bloodthirsty Red Knight of Ainswick or Yorkshire sounds like the basis for a Hammer Films vampire movie. The Knight was in the service of the Lord of Ainswick Castle, but he was not a very noble knight. He led a life of wickedness and excess, of brawling and lewd behavior, and he died ignobly by falling from a rooftop (probably drunk at the time) while trying to spy on his adulterous wife. He was buried according to the standard Christian rituals of the day, but shortly afterward he was reported to be stalking the roads and streets, reeking of rotting flesh and carrying a highly contagious plague. The Knight attacked people with great violence, savaging them and drinking their blood. The plague swept like wildfire through the region and the townspeople believed that as long as the Knight still moved among them the plague would endure.

Arming themselves with pitchforks and torches, they hunted him down, chancing to find him at a time of rest in his grave. The corpse was florid and looked healthy, and his body was swollen with all of the blood he'd drunk from the villagers.

The villagers dragged the Red Knight's corpse out of his grave, threw him on a cart, and wheeled him out of town. They took him to a deserted place and burned the body to ashes. At once the plague began to fade away and was soon gone, and there were no further sightings of the Red Knight.

The Red Knight by Shane MacDougall.

LORD BYRON

The great Romantic poet George Gordon Lord Byron is largely responsible for the change in the public perception of vampire from a shambling monster to an urbane and aristocratic sexual predator. Though he only wrote about vampires in passing (in *The Giaour*, 1813), his vision influenced his friend and physician, Dr. John Polidori. Polidori in turn wrote a very powerful story called *"The Vampire,"* which introduced the evil seducer Lord Ruthven. This vampire character was almost certainly a major inspiration for Bram Stoker's *Dracula* in 1897.

Archival artwork.

THE GIAOUR

George Gordon Lord Byron

No breath of air to break the wave
That rolls below the Athenian's grave,
That tomb which, gleaming o'er the cliff
First greets the homeward-veering skiff
High o'er the land he saved in vain;
When shall such Hero live again?

Fair clime! where every season smiles
Benignant o'er those blesséd isles,
Which, seen from far Colonna's height,
Make glad the heart that hails the sight,
And lend to loneliness delight.
There mildly dimpling, Ocean's cheek
Reflects the tints of many a peak
Caught by the laughing tides that lave
These Edens of the Eastern wave:
And if at times a transient breeze

Break the blue crystal of the seas,
Or sweep one blossom from the trees,
How welcome is each gentle air
That waves and wafts the odours there!
For there the Rose, o'er crag or vale,
Sultana of the Nightingale,
The maid for whom his melody,
His thousand songs are heard on high,
Blooms blushing to her lover's tale:
His queen, the garden queen, his Rose,
Unbent by winds, unchilled by snows,
Far from winters of the west,
By every breeze and season blest,
Returns the sweets by Nature given
In soft incense back to Heaven;
And grateful yields that smiling sky
Her fairest hue and fragrant sigh.
And many a summer flower is there,
And many a shade that Love might share,
And many a grotto, meant by rest,
That holds the pirate for a guest;
Whose bark in sheltering cove below
Lurks for the passing peaceful prow,
Till the gay mariner's guitar
Is heard, and seen the Evening Star;
Then stealing with the muffled oar,
Far shaded by the rocky shore,
Rush the night-prowlers on the prey,
And turns to groan his roudelay.
Strande—that where Nature loved to trace,
As if for Gods, a dwelling place,
And every charm and grace hath mixed
Within the Paradise she fixed,
There man, enarmoured of distress,
Shoul mar it into wilderness,
And trample, brute-like, o'er each flower
That tasks not one labourious hour;
Nor claims the culture of his hand

To blood along the fairy land,
But springs as to preclude his care,
And sweetly woos him—but to spare!
Strange—that where all is Peace beside,
There Passion riots in her pride,
And Lust and Rapine wildly reign
To darken o'er the fair domain.
It is as though the Fiends prevailed
Against the Seraphs they assailed,
And, fixed on heavenly thrones, should dwell
The freed inheritors of Hell;
So soft the scene, so formed for joy,
So curst the tyrants that destroy!
He who hath bent him o'er the dead
Ere the first day of Death is fled,
The first dark day of Nothingness,
The last of Danger and Distress,
(Before Decay's effacing fingers
Have swept the lines where Beauty lingers,)
And marked the mild angelic air,
The rapture of Repose that's there,
The fixed yet tender thraits that streak
The languor of the placid cheek,
And—but for that sad shrouded eye,
That fires not, wins not, weeps not, now,
And but for that chill, changeless brow,

Where cold Obstruction's apathy
Appals the gazing mourner's heart,
As if to him it could impart
The doom he dreads, yet dwells upon;
Yes, but for these and these alone,
Some moments, aye, one treacherous hour,
He still might doubt the Tyrant's power;
So fair, so calm, so softly sealed,
The first, last look by Death revealed!
Such is the aspect of his shore;

'T is Greece, but living Greece no more!
So coldly sweet, so deadly fair,
We start, for Soul is wanting there.
Hers is the loveliness in death,
That parts not quite with parting breath;
But beauty with that fearful bloom,
That hue which haunts it to the tomb,
Expression's last receding ray,
A gilded Halo hovering round decay,
The farewell beam of Feeling past away!
Spark of that flame, perchance of heavenly birth,
Which gleams, but warms no more its cherished earth!
Clime of the unforgotten brave!
Whose land from plain to mountain-cave
Was Freedom's home or Glory's grave!
Shrine of the mighty! can it be,
That this is all remains of thee?
Approach, thou craven crouching slave:
Say, is this not Thermopylæ?
These waters blue that round you lave,—
Of servile offspring of the free—
Pronounce what sea, what shore is this?
The gulf, the rock of Salamis!
These scenes, their story yet unknown;
Arise, and make again your own;
Snatch from the ashes of your Sires
The embers of their former fires;
And he who in the strife expires
Will add to theirs a name of fear
That Tyranny shall quake to hear,
And leave his sons a hope, a fame,
They too will rather die than shame:
For Freedom's battle once begun,
Bequeathed by bleeding Sire to Son,
Though baffled oft is ever won.
Bear witness, Greece, thy living page!

Attest it many a deathless age!
While Kings, in dusty darkness hid,
Have left a nameless pyramid,
Thy Heroes, though the general doom
Hath swept the column from their tomb,
A mightier monument command,
The mountains of thy native land!
There points thy Muse to stranger's eye
The graves of those that cannot die!
'T were long to tell, and sad to trace,
Each step from Splendour to Disgrace;
Enough—no foreign foe could quell
Thy soul, till from itself it fell;
Yet! Self-abasement paved the way
To villain-bonds and despot sway.
What can he tell who tread thy shore?
No legend of thine olden time,
No theme on which the Muse might soar
High as thine own days of yore,
When man was worthy of thy clime.
The hearts within thy valleys bred,
The fiery souls that might have led
Thy sons to deeds sublime,
Now crawl from cradle to the Grave,
Slaves—nay, the bondsmen of a Slave,
And callous, save to crime.
Stained with each evil that pollutes
Mankind, where least above the brutes;
Without even savage virtue blest,
Without one free or valiant breast,
Still to the neighbouring ports they waft
Proverbial wiles, and ancient craft;
In this subtle Greek is found,
For this, and this alown, renowned.
In vain might Liberty invoke
The spirit to its bondage broke
Or raise the neck that courts the yoke:

No more her sorrows I bewail,
Yet this will be a mournful tale,
And they who listen may believe,
Who heard it first had cause to grieve.

Far, dark, along the blue sea glancing,
The shadows of the rocks advancing
Start on the fisher's eye like boat
Of island-pirate or Mainote;
And fearful for his light caïque,
He shuns the near but doubtful creek:
Though worn and weary with his toil,
And cumbered with his scaly spoil,
Slowly, yet strongly, plies the oar,
Till Port Leone's safer shore
Receives him by the lovely light
That best becomes an Eastern night.
Who thundering comes on blackest steed,
With slackened bit and hoof of speed?
Beneath the clattering iron's sound
The caverned Echoes wake around
In lash for lash, and bound for bound;
The foam that streaks the courser's side
Seems gathered from the Ocean-tide:
Though weary waves are sunk to rest,
There's none within his rider's breast;
And though to-morrow's tempest lower,
'T is calmer than thy heart, young Giaour!
I know thee not, I loathe thy race,
But in thy lineaments I trace
What Time shall strengthen, not efface:
Though young and pale, that sallow front
Is scathed by fiery Passion's brunt;
Though bent on the earth thine evil eye,
As meteor-like thou glidest by,
Right well I view and deem thee one
Whom Othman's sons should slay or shun.

On—on he hastened, and he drew
My gaze of wonder as he flew:
Though like a Demon of the night
He passed, and vanished from my sight,
His aspect and his air impressed
A troubled memory of my breast,
And long upon my startled ear
Rung his dark courser's hoofs of fear.
He spurs his steed; he nears the steep,
That, jutting, shadows o'er the deep;
He winds around; he hurries by;
The rock relieves him from mine eye;
For, well I ween, unwelcome he
Whose glance is fixed on those that flee;
And not a star but shines too bright
On him who takes such timeless flight.
He wound along; but ere he passed
One glance he snatched, as if his last,
A moment checked his wheeling steed,
A moment breathed him from his speed,
A moment on his stirrup stood—
Why looks he o'er the olive wood?
The Crescent glimmers on the hill,
The Mosque's high lamps are quivering still
Though too remote for sound to wake
In echoes of the far tophaike,
The flashes of each joyous peal
Are seen to prove the Moslem's zeal.
To-night, set Rhamzani's sun;
To-night, the bairam feast's begun;
To-night—but who and what art thou
Of foreign garb and fearful brow?
And what are these to thine or thee,
That thou shouldst either pause or flee?

WEREWOLF AND WOLFMAN

Some linguists believe that the term "werewolf" is of Old English origin. Certainly there have been tales of werewolves in England for centuries.

The English werewolf comes in two varieties: the natural and the supernatural. Natural werewolves are those persons so mentally disturbed that they adopt the ferocious and predatory traits of wolves and attack other people, often biting and savaging them. Although these werewolves are people who are clearly insane, during the Middle Ages the common man had no understanding of psychosis and ascribed supernatural elements to this form of werewolf. The concept of mental illness was only grudgingly accepted in rural England prior to the twentieth century.

Werewolf. Artwork by Robert Patrick O'Brien.

Similarly, the idea of transformations occurring only on a lunar cycle is a relatively recent development, probably an outgrowth of the documented effects of the full moon on mental illness. It is almost certainly more closely related to the natural werewolves than the supernatural.

Supernatural werewolves are, like vampires, people who have fallen under the curse of werewolfism and are doomed to become monsters. According to older folktales, a werewolf may transform from man to monster at any time, day or night.

Among the supernatural werewolves there are two additional subgroups: Wolfman and the true Werewolf. The true (and far more common) Werewolf completely transforms into a wolf. It possesses the natural speed, cunning, strength, and ferocity of that animal, but only in those levels typical of a natural wolf. The Wolfman is a creature that possesses qualities of man and wolf: generally walking upright, wearing human clothing, and possessing some degree of human intelligence. It is the Wolfman which is endowed with unnatural power, not the Werewolf.

Most of the Werewolves seen in movies tend to be of the Wolfman variety, though in the film *An American Werewolf in London* the creature was a little of both: a gigantic wolf, larger than any normal wolf and far more powerful.

The method by which someone becomes a Werewolf (of either species) varies from folktale to folktale. Many stories influenced by the early Christian church hold that a person may become a Werewolf when his ability to keep his sinful nature in check has failed and the animal that lurks inside all men is released. In other tales, it is a curse that brings out the wolf. Beginning in the early 1800s, the story changed so that it was the bite of another Werewolf that began the transformation. This theme is now endemic to all werewolf film and fiction.

Two of the earliest fictional treatments of werewolves were Sutherland Menzies Hughes's *The Wer-wolf*, serialized in the 1850s; and W.M. Reynolds 1857 novel *Wagner The Wehrwolf*. A better and more enduring story was Guy Endore's 1934 classic *The Werewolf Of Paris*, which was actually largely based on a true story of a ghoul (not a werewolf) in the person of a French army officer named Francois Bertrand who was arrested for digging up and eating corpses. A year after the book was published it was made into a film, *The Werewolf Of London*, but with such significant story changes that it bore little resemblance to the novel.

In 1941, Lon Chaney, Jr. created the classic role of the tortured Lawrence Talbot in the film *The Wolf Man*. Film and fiction have changed the folkloric beliefs so radically that the pervasive beliefs nowadays come almost exclusively from pop culture, and *The Wolf Man* set several standards for what has become the new werewolf folklore: the werewolf sees a pentagram in the palm of its next victim; it is vulnerable to silver (and is in fact beaten to death by a silver-headed walking stick); it is the werewolf's bite that transmits the curse; and only the death of the last werewolf breaks the bloodline. These themes have all been picked up and used by other films in much the same way that the crosses and other trappings of the novel and movie *Dracula* have been adopted.

According to folklore, the werewolf is not particularly hard to kill, no more difficult than an ordinary wolf. It cannot pass on its curse through a bite or a scratch. However, the bite can cause a lingering sickness much like that of a poisonous snake, and death is the most common result.

There are two links from the past that have carried over into fiction that may have more solid connections to the ancient beliefs: Wolf's Bane and silver.

In medieval times, silver was considered the purest of metals, although this speaks more to its color rather than any knowledge of metallurgy. Something so essentially pure was believed to be a proof against evil, and it apparently severed the connection between the physical body and the demonic spirit inhabiting it.

Theoretically, silver should have worked like an antidote to werewolfism, but there are no reported cases of it being a benign cure. Instead, a person had to be killed by silver—or silver had to be involved in the killing—for the demonic possession to be broken. Although this did little to help the cursed person while they were alive, it did prevent them from being damned in death.

Wolf's Bane has been used for centuries in herbal medicines, and it exists in a variety of species. It is used to treat bites from poisonous animals and this is very likely the basis for the belief that it cures a person of the poison from a werewolf's bite. Unlike garlic, Wolf's Bane does not drive off a werewolf, as is suggested by the movies. *See* also Wolf's Bane, p. 70.

One fact never touched on in the movies is that in many cultures, werewolves and vampires are not only linked, but are overlapping creatures that possess similar qualities. And in quite a few cultures, when a werewolf dies it can come back from its grave as a vampire, which is a truly terrifying thought.

WEREWOLVES AND THE MOON

Most popular fiction has it that a person cursed with werewolfism will only transform into a monster during the three days of the full moon, and that the transformation is totally outside of their control.

Folklore differs from this in most cases. Transformation is not generally believed to be beyond the werewolf's control, but rather a deliberate act. In most legends around the world, a person may become a wolf or a wolf-man (depending on the species of werewolf) by deliberate choice. Most often, this choice is based upon an evil nature and a desire to do great harm.

The concept of a werewolf transformation occurring only during the full moon most likely dates back to 1250 C.E.. It can be traced to the writings of a Norseman named Kongs Skuggsjo, who related the tale of how St. Patrick prayed to God to punish some men who heckled him, or "howled" him down, when he attempted to convert them to Christianity. God bestowed an ironic punishment: the men were condemned to howl like wolves at each full moon. Skuggsjo's story does not say that the men actually became wolves or engaged in werewolf predation, but it is the most likely link between werewolfism and the full moon.

Most legends to mention that werewolves often hunt by moonlight, not necessarily the light of the full moon. The Venerable Bede wrote of this, in 731 C.E. as did Gervaise of Tilbury in 1214. This does not mean that daylight keeps a person safe from werewolf attacks, as the creatures can also transform and hunt by the bright light of the sun.

VAMPIRES OF FRANCE

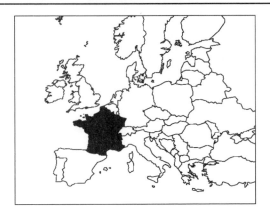

CRAQUEUHHE

Like most European countries, France has had its share of vampires. In some cases, such as the Alouby of Aquitaine, few accounts exist to provide vampire slayers with useful knowledge. But in the case of the Craqueuhhe of Lorraine, much is known.

The Craqueuhhe is one of Europe's most savage monsters, a true anthropophagous Vampire, which means that it is not just a blood drinker but a flesh eater as well.

ANTHROPOPHAGOUS: From Greek *anthropophagos* meaning "man-eating"; a generic term for a cannibal.

The Craqueuhhe is a Revenant, a corpse animated from dead flesh, and it rises from the grave of a person who has died in sin or who was never baptized. This creature is more Zombie in appearance than vampire, like a decaying corpse with sunken eyes, greasy hair clotted with dirt, fingernails broken from having clawed its way out of its coffin, and the stench of decay about it. Maggots and other insects crawl through tears in its flesh and infest its clothing.

One thing that makes the Craqueuhhe so horrible to behold is that it will rise from its grave and walk no matter how badly it was injured at the time of death. Accounts of Craqueuhhe shambling along on shattered legs, with arms torn out, or with other massively disfiguring injuries are very common.

By the same token, the creature's complete disregard for concepts like pain or crippling injury make it difficult to fight and even more difficult to kill. Gunshots pass right through it and knives are useless. And despite its decaying and wretched appearance, the Craqueuhhe is extremely fast and very powerful.

Only fire and beheading will stop the creature. It requires either a skilled warrior protected by holy relics or a group of people with fire, sharpened staves, and scythes to bring it down and lay it to final rest. Once it has been defeated, even if it was beheaded, the reanimated flesh will cling stubbornly to unnatural life. The Craqueuhhe must be burned to keep it from rising again or tainting the soil of the entire graveyard, thereby creating a host of these hideous monsters.

The modern Zombie films, such as *Night Of The Living Dead* and its followers and imitators, depict creatures more in keeping with the Craqueuhhe than with any version of the traditional Zombie.

Craqueuhhe. Artwork by Robert Patrick O'Brien.

DAMES BLANCHE (WHITE LADIES OF FAU)

In the Jura region of France there is a legend of beautiful faerie folk who live in the woods, the White Ladies of Fau. Despite their innocent-sounding name, these alluring faerie-women do not flit around on moonbeams and sprinkle pixie dust. Instead they use their physical charms and magical charisma to lure young men from the towns and farm fields and bring the willing lad to some nice private place. Once alone, they fall upon their victim, drinking his blood and eating his flesh.

The White Ladies of Fau. Photo by Breanne Levy.

The most famous of the White Ladies was named Melusina, of whom much has been written. The legend of Melusina became very popular during the Middle Ages, especially in France, but her stories reach well into Germany. Most of them were collected by the scholar Jean d'Arras in the sixteenth century and presented in two volumes, *Chronique de Melusine* and *Le Liure de Melusine en Fracoys* (the latter of which was published posthumously). D'Arras' research had drawn heavily on earlier research by William de Portenach, but de Portenach's writings were sadly lost, though both of D'Arras' works still exist.

These tales differ as to Melusina's exact nature. In various legends Melusina is either a tragic heroine under a curse, a monster trying to pass as a human, or a demon living among humans in order to sew discord. In each legend there is one constant: Melusina always requests that her lover respect her wish that one day a month she could be sequestered away where no one could see her. Such promises never last and each doomed lover invariably spies on her (usually because he could not bear to be parted from her for even a single night). When Melusina is seen in her hiding place she is caught in some state of transformation: in the nicer stories Melusina would be bathing in a tub with her mermaid's tail flopped over the rim, but in other tales she would be in a hidden forest pool feasting on human flesh.

THE GREEN OGRESSES

Another species of regional France's evil sirens are the nasty Green Ogresses. These are watery vampires, like Naiads but far more destructive. Despite their name, the Green Ogresses are usually intensely beautiful women whose sexual appeal is too powerful for any but the purest of souls to resist. Since there are few truly pure souls, the Ogresses seldom go hungry. They lure men into lakes and streams and drink their blood before devouring them.

The Green Ogresses are similar to the White Ladies in many regards, except that they do not try to live among humans. They prefer to live on the fringes of society and lure men into their ponds or swamps.

The Green Ogresses. Artwork by Marie O'Brien.

SIRENS

The White Ladies and Green Ogresses can be traced back to the Sirens of Greek mythology. A Siren had a woman's head on a bird's body. The most notable Sirens lived on an island surrounded by dangerous rocks, and they sang beautiful, enchanting songs to lure mariners to their deaths.

The Sirens were confronted by Odysseus and by Jason and the Argonauts. When Jason set sail to seek the Golden Fleece, he was told by the seer Chiron that he needed to take Orpheus on his journey to help him combat the Sirens. When the Argo approached the island, Orpheus began to play his lyre. His music was more beautiful than that of the Sirens and drowned out their singing.

As Odysseus and his crew approached their island, Odysseus ordered all of his men to plug their ears with wax so they could not hear the Sirens. But Odysseus wanted to hear them for himself, so he had his crew tie him to the ship's mast. He thrashed around like a madman while he could hear the Sirens, then calmed down as the ship passed.

Ovid wrote that the Sirens were Nymphs, a large class of female spirits found in nature and bound to a particular piece of land or body of water. Specifically, the Sirens were nymphs who were Persephone's playmates. When Persephone was kidnapped by Hades, Persephone's mother, Demeter, punished them for not stopping the abduction by turning them into bird-like monsters.

There were many different species of nymph in Greek mythology. They are broken into land and water categories:

Land Nymphs
  Alseids (groves)
  Auloniads (pastures)
  Dryads (woods)
  Hamadryads (trees)
  Ieimakids (meadows)
  Meliae (manna ash trees)
  Napaeae (mountain valleys)
  Oreads (mountains)

Water Nymphs
  Crinaeae (fountains)
  Eleionomae (marshes)
  Limnades or Limnatides (lakes)
  Naiads (rivers, brooks, streams)
  Nereids (the Mediterranean Sea)
  Oceanids (salt water)
  Pegaeae (springs)
  Potameides (rivers)

Naiad. Used with permission, (c) 2003 by Adam Garland.

·PART THREE·

BECOMING UNDEAD

"Der Vampire"
My dearest little girl believes
Constant, firm, and steady
In the old teachings
Of her devout mother,
As people of the Theyse
Have always believed
In deadly vampires.

Now wait, little Christina,
You don't want to love me;
I will have revenge on you,
And drinking the Tokay wine,
I will become a vampire.

And when you are softly sleeping,
Then I will suck up
The fresh crimson of your cheeks.

And if you are afraid
When I kiss you,
And kiss you as a vampire,
And if you are trembling
And faint in my arms,
Feebly sinking into death,
Then I will ask you,
Is my teaching better
Than your good mother

Heinrich August Ossenfelder,
1748

Every culture has a different pathway to darkness.

For some it is a deliberate choice, such as with the vampire-witches of the Nahautl Indians of Mexico, the Brujas of Spain, and the Lobishomen of Portugal. These twisted creatures make pacts with dark forces, sacrificing their humanity in order to gain vast magical powers.

Some vampires were created by the ancient Gods, such as the Empusae and the Mormo, who were blood drinking demons in the service of Hecate; the Lamiai who were the creations of the scorned goddess Lamia; and the Rakshasa of India. These powerful creatures were created to serve the will of bloodthirsty or vengeful gods and goddesses.

There are even vampires who were considered gods themselves, such as the Hindu deity Kali, the Aztec Xipe Totec, the blood drinking god Yama from Nepal, and the Fifty-Eight Wrathful Deities of Tibet.

Most vampires, however, are the result of either a life lived in sin or a bad death.

Used with permission, (c) 2003 by Matej Jan.

Being born with a caul covering the face is a common sign of a child who will become a vampire after death. This is seen in the Ohyn and the Upier of Poland, the Romanian Strigoi, the Kudlak of Austria, and the German Nachzehrer.

Children born with teeth are likewise a sign of impending vampirism, again seen with the Ohyn and the Upier, as well as the Neuntoter of Germany.

According to some beliefs, a child born from incest is doomed to unlife, such as in the case of the Pijavica of Czechoslovakia and its close cousin, the Croatian Pijauica.

Also, a child born out of wedlock may become a vampire after death, as seen in cases of the Strigoi, and (in essence) most of the Slavic vampires.

Children born on certain holy days may likewise be damned, such as the Strigoi (if born between Christmas and New Year's Day) and the Callicantzaros of Greece.

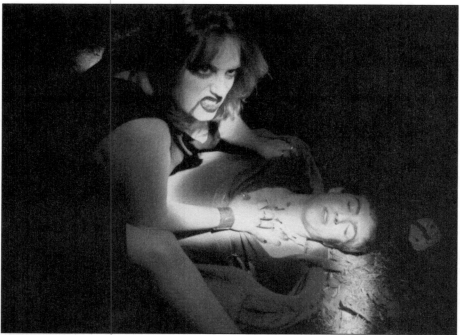

Photo by Jason Lukridge.

The bite of a vampire can, of course, create another vampire, but this is far less common than popularly believed. Actually, the most common cause of vampirism is a bad death. Stillbirths, death during childbirth,

Photo by Breanne Levy.

suicide, death by violence or murder, death on a battlefield, and accidental deaths account for most of the undead around the world.

Also, anyone who dies unrepentant of his sins (as seen in the legend of the Czech Pijavica), or who was excommunicated from the church (as with the Greek Brukulaco), is sure to return as a blood drinker.

Many of the world's vampires are created when an animal chances to jump over a corpse. Most of the Slavic vampire legends mention this, as do the Chinese tales of the Chiang-Shih. Cats, tigers, black hens, even dogs can somehow prompt a demonic spirit to enter a corpse, just by jumping over the corpse as it lays in preparation of the burial rites.

Finally, if a person is buried and the funeral rites are not adhered to in every detail, then there is a good chance the corpse will rise as a vampire. This is seen with the Gypsy Mullo, the Gayal of India, the Japanese Kasha, the Tlahuelpuchi of the ancient Aztecs of Mexico, the Babylonian Ekimmu, and Czechoslovakia's deadly Nelapsi, among others.

There are a lot of vampires out there, and there are a frightening number of ways they can return from their graves to feast on the blood of the living.

Beware!

EXCOMMUNICATION

Excommunication is an ecclesiastical censure whereby the person against whom it is pronounced is, for the time, cast out of the communication of the church and excluded from fellowship in all things spiritual. There are two kinds of excommunication, the lesser and the greater; the lesser excommunication is a separation or suspension from partaking of the Eucharist; the greater is an absolute execution of the offender from the church and all its rights and advantages, even from social intercourse with the faithful.

Scottish cemetery. Used with permission, (c) 2003 by Alan Wilson

In his *The Present State of the Greek and Armenian Churches, Anno Christi 1678*, the British Consul at Smyrna, Paul Ricaut, wrote this report on the Church's beliefs on the effects of excommunication:

"The effect of this dreadful Sentence is reported by the Greek Priests to have been in several instances so evident, that none doubts or disbelieves the consequences of all those maledictions repeated therein; and particularly, that the body of an excommunicated person is not capable of returning to its first Principles until the Sentence of Excommunication is taken off.

"It would be esteemed no Curse amongst us to have our bodies remain uncorrupted and entire in the Grave, who endeavour by Art, and Aromatic spices, and Gums, to preserve them from Corruption: And it is also accounted amongst the Greeks themselves, as a miracle and particular grace and favour of God to the Bodies of such whom they have Canonized for Saints to continue unconsumed, and in the moist damps of a Vault, to dry and desiccate like the Mummies in Egypt, or in the Hot sands of Arabia. But they believe that the Bodies of the Excommunicated are possessed in the Grave by some evil spirit, which actuates and preserves them from Corruption, in the same manner as the soul informes and animates the living body; and that they feed in the night, walk, digest, and are nourished, and have been found ruddy in Complexion, and their Veins, after forty days Burial, extended with Blood, which, being opened with a Lancet, have yielded a gore as plentiful, fresh, and quick, as that which issues from the Vessels of young and sanguine persons.

"This is so generally believed and discoursed of amongst the Greeks, that there is scarce one of their Country Villages but what can witness and recount several instances of this nature, both by the relation of their Parents, and Nurses, as well as of their own knowledge, which they tell with as much variety as we do the Tales of Witches and Enchantments, of which it is observed in Conversation, that scarce one story is ended before another begins of like wonder."

FUNERAL CUSTOMS

There are as many funeral customs as there are religions and cultures. Every culture and civilization attends to the proper care of their dead. Almost everywhere there are three primary concerns for proper burial:

1. Some type of funeral rites, rituals, and ceremonies
2. A sacred place for the dead
3. Memorialization of the dead

Photo by Breanne Levy.

The methods of fulfilling these three concerns vary greatly.

•   Researchers have found burial grounds of Neanderthal man dating to 60,000 BC with animal antlers on the body and flower fragments next to the corpse indicating some type of ritual and gifts of remembrance.

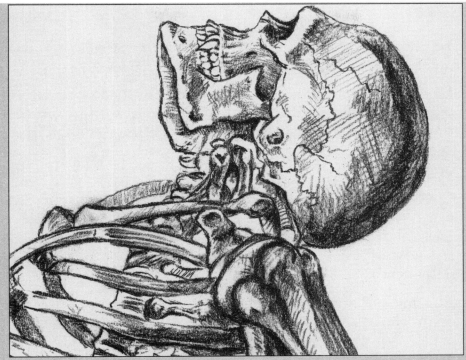

Artwork by Shane MacDougall.

- In Buddhism, death is prepared for through meditation, and death itself is viewed as a rebirth. Once dead, the body is washed, rituals are performed over it, a wake is held, and then it is typically cremated.

- Christian custom has changed from an earlier period where a funeral was treated as a joyous occasion to one where it is a time for mourning (usual form) or cremation.

- Hindu ceremonies are closely tied to a belief in reincarnation. Thus an elaborate set of rituals is conducted, mostly by relatives, to ensure a proper rebirth.

- Islamic ceremonies include washing and preparing the body, prayers, reading from the Qur'an, and placing the body on the right side facing Mecca for burial (cremation is not practiced).

- Early Judaism, with perhaps the simplest of all ceremonies, included a prayer service, washing the body, and wrapping it in linen, followed by a funeral banquet.

Even modern Western funeral customs are ritualized and are often outgrowths of much older customs:

- Modern mourning clothing came from the custom of wearing special clothing as a disguise to hide identity from returning spirits. Pagans believed that returning spirits would fail to recognize them in their new attire and would be confused and overlook them.

- Covering the face of the deceased with a sheet stems from pagan tribes who believed that the spirit of the deceased escaped through the mouth. They would often hold the mouth and nose of a sick person shut, hoping to retain the spirits and delay death.

- Feasting and gatherings associated with the funeral began as an essential part of the primitive funeral where food offerings were made.

- Wakes held today come from ancient customs of keeping watch over the deceased hoping that life would return.

- The lighting of candles comes from the use of fire mentioned earlier in attempts to protect the living from the spirits.

- The practice of ringing bells comes from the common medieval belief that the spirits would be kept at bay by the ringing of a consecrated bell.

- The firing of a rifle volley over the deceased mirrors the tribal practice of throwing spears into the air to ward off spirits hovering over the deceased.

- Originally, holy water was sprinkled on the body to protect it from the demons.

- Floral offerings were originally intended to gain favor with the spirit of the deceased.

- Funeral music had its origins in the ancient chants designed to placate spirits.

·PART FOUR·

VAMPIRES AROUND THE WORLD

G–L

"The Vampire"

A fool there was and he made his prayer
(Even as you and I!)
To a rag and a bone and a hunk of hair
(We called her the woman who did not care)
But the fool he called her his lady fair
(Even as you and I!)

Rudyard Kipling
1897

VAMPIRES OF GERMANY

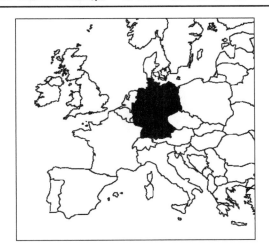

ALP

Sometimes the distinction between vampire, ghost, and demon seems blurred. In many cases it overlaps, as in the case of the deadly German vampire, the Alp. The world Alp means "shining white one." Some legends hold that the Alp is the returning spirit of a man who has died under bad circumstances. Others suggest that it is the vampiric ghost of a child who died before he could be baptized. There are also those who believe that the Alp is a demon and not a ghost at all. Whichever version of its origin is correct, they all agree that the Alp is a blood drinker and that it is nearly impossible to kill one.

Like the Incubus, the Alp preys mostly on women, appearing first in dreams and then manifesting in the physical world to drink their blood or, in some cases, nurse at their breasts to drink their breast milk. Sometimes it drinks both milk and blood from its victim's nipples. It may also attack men and young boys for blood, likewise feeding at the nipple. In all cases when the Alp has fed but left its prey alive, the victims have suffered from horrific nightmares.

The Alp. Artwork by Robert Patrick O'Brien.

In all of its many unnatural manifestations, the Alp wears a *tarnkappe* ("cap of concealment") which gives it various magical powers, including invisibility. If the hat is stolen, the Alp loses this power of concealment and its powers are reduced. The Alp's main weapon against humanity is its "evil eye" with which the Alp can trouble the dreams of the living.

The Alp is also a shapeshifter. It most often appears as a moth or butterfly, but is able to assume a variety of animal forms, including birds, dogs, and wolves, and in some cases it can transform into a cold mist. Some folktales link the Alp to tales of werewolves because of its shapeshifting ability.

The Alp is nearly impossible to destroy, so various methods have been devised to try to deter this creature. Women are instructed to sleep with their shoes placed by the side of the bed with the toes facing outward toward the door. Scissors can also placed under one's pillow with the points facing toward the head of the bed. Either method will deter the Alp because for some reason it will become confused, turn away from the sleeper, and back out the door. Another popular deterrent is to take a large sack of seed and pour some in the center of a crossroads with thin trails of seeds laid along the center of each of the four offshooting ways. Like many vampires, the Alp will feel compelled to count them; but because the seeds go off in all directions the Alp will get thoroughly confused and sit there weeping in frustration until dawn when it must slink away to seek a resting place. In those rare times when an Alp can be cornered, or better yet caught sleeping, it can only be deterred by filling its mouth with lemons.

Sunlight does not kill the Alp, but it weakens the effectiveness of its concealing tarnkappe, and the Alp does not like to be seen.

BLAUTSAUGER

The folk tales of Bavaria, in Southern Germany, have been filled with tales of the Blautsauger, which means "blood drinker." Like the Austrian Blautsauger, the German Blautsauger is a Revenant with pale skin, rotting flesh, and gaunt features.

One way of becoming a Blautsauger is to eat the flesh of any animal that has been killed by a wolf. Another is to be unlucky enough to have a nun step over your grave. This unlikely cause amounts to religious carelessness: a nun should know and respect sanctified burial spots and should never be so careless as to walk over someone's sacred grave. This carelessness is tantamount to straying into sloth, which is a sin. Apparently a nun who strays into sloth commits a bigger sin than an ordinary person.

In many ways typical of the European vampire, the Blautsauger sleeps in its grave, rises to feed on the living, and is generally unmerciful. Aside from its thirst for blood, from which it gets its name, the Blautsauger is also a cannibal and will feast on human flesh.

Although the myth that a vampire cannot enter a house unless it has been invited is not found in folklore (that was made up for books and movies), there are methods of barring a vampire from entering one's home. Smearing all doorways and windows with a paste made from mashed garlic and hawthorn is sure proof against unwanted night visitors. Also, like the Alp, the Blautsauger will not attack a sleeping person who has placed scissors beneath his pillow with the points facing toward the head of the bed.

To kill a Blautsauger, it has to be caught sleeping in its grave. A long stake, particularly of ash or hawthorn, is driven through its chest—not

Blautsauger. Used with permission, (c) 2003 by Vinesh V. George.

to kill it, but to weaken it and pin it to the ground. The creature's head must be cut off and its mouth stuffed with garlic. This will effectively end its un-life.

(*See* also Vampires Of Bosnia-Herzegovina, p. 107, for a different perspective of this European vampire).

DOPPELSAUGER

Breast-feeding vampires seem fairly common in Europe, especially in Germany. Aside from the Alp there is also the Doppelsauger of Hanoverian legend. Not content with drinking blood from the breasts of its victims, the Doppelsauger actually consumes the breasts as well.

Folklore suggests that the Doppelsauger is created when a mother has allowed a child who has been weaned to begin breast-feeding again. Hence the name Doppelsauger, which means "double-sucker." If that child were to die it would be condemned to return to haunt the living as a Doppelsauger. First, while still in its grave—and once its unnatural hunger awakens—it will eat its own breast. Once it has consumed that, it rises from the grave as a fearsome Revenant to feed on the breasts of its family members. The Doppelsauger typically attacks only its own relatives, but it will attack others out of need.

Various preventative strategies are open to the family of the dead child to reduce the risk of becoming a Doppelsauger. The key is to make sure it cannot begin eating itself while in the grave. Denied this initial and unwholesome meal, the Doppelsauger will lack the strength necessary to break free of its coffin and rise from the grave. Blocks are put in place to prevent the jaws from working, such as a metal coin wedged between its teeth or a semi-circular wooden board placed under its chin to make it impossible for the corpse to bite at itself. Wrappings are often wound around the body to deny it the use of its hands, and care is taken to make sure cloth from the shroud or burial garments does not come into close contact with the mouth.

MARA

See Vampires Of Canada (p. 140) or Vampires Of Scandinavia (p. 461).

MANDUCATION

The term given to the act of a reawakened vampire eating its own flesh while still trapped in its coffin. In many vampire legends, disinterred corpses show signs of having been partially self-devoured. Some scientists hold that this is proof of premature burial and the resulting starvation and mania. Vampire slayers disagree and believe that a reawakening vampire feeds on itself to gain strength so it can rise from its grave.

The Nachzehrer. Sculpture by Robert Patrick O'Brien.

NACHZEHRER

The Nachzehrer is a Germanic vampire that shares much in common with the Doppelsauger. It begins feeding on its own clothing and flesh while still in the grave and then rises to attack its living relatives. The Nachzehrer leaves its grave at the cold stroke of midnight to go in search of its relatives and begin its ritual feeding.

Nachzehrers are created when a child born with a caul dies, or when someone has drowned. Upon first awakening, the Nachzehrer lies in its grave with its left eye open and slowly gnaws upon its shroud or its flesh. Family members can often tell that a recently buried relative has become a Nachzehrer because they will begin to sicken and die as soon as the vampire awakens in its grave and begins feeding on itself. Eventually the creature has fed enough on itself to have the strength to rise. Then it turns to blood by attacking the living.

The Nachzehrer has a reputation for spreading various plagues, and throughout German history has reappeared in times of famine and disease, a dark pestilential presence.

The best protection against this dreaded vampire is placing scissors beneath one's pillow with the points facing toward the head of the bed. This charm also works well against the Alp and the Blautsauger.

Garlic is the standard proof against it, but that is just for protection. To kill the vampire, the Nachzehrer has to be disinterred, its head cut off with an axe, and its mouth stuffed with garlic bulbs.

NEUNTOTER

Vampires and the spread of plague are two concepts often linked in German folklore, never more so than in the legend of the Neuntoter. Very similar to the Nachzehrer, the Neuntoter is believed to be a great carrier of plague and pestilence—a quality that is feared more than its blood drinking. It is rare, in fact, for a folktale of the Neuntoter not to include a reference to a local plague. The Neuntoter's body is covered with open sores and bloody wounds, which spread the plague.

The name Neuntoter means "killer of nine." It refers to the popular belief that it took nine days from when the creature was buried for its supernatural body to fully form.

Many believe that a child born with teeth is destined to become a Neuntoter after its own natural death. These children will be carefully watched, and when they eventually die—even as older adults—their birth "defect" will be remembered and the appropriate actions will be taken.

To destroy the Neuntoter, its grave should be opened in the late evening between eleven o'clock and midnight, the hour when it typically rises. As soon as the body is uncovered, before it can rise, the creature should be quickly decapitated with a sword or axe. Fresh lemons must be placed in its mouth and it should be quickly buried again.

THE CHEWING DEAD

In 1679, the theologian Philip Rohr wrote *Dissertatio Historico-Philosophica de Masticatione Mortuorum* (*A Dissertation Of The History And Philosophies Concerning The Chewing Dead*). This treatise discusses common folklore that some corpses return to life via a process known as manducation: eating their funeral shrouds and any nearby bodies, preferably fresh corpses in adjacent graves. No specific name was given to this species of flesh eating vampire, but they were nicknamed "chewing dead." In truth quite a few vampire species around the world are reported to be flesh eaters.

Eighteenth century German writer Michael Ranft, in his work titled *De Masticacione Mortuarum in Atumulus Liber* (*Book Of The Chewing Dead In Their Tombs*), essentially refuted everything Rohr written. It was his assertion, based on his understanding of medicine and science, that the dead were quite simply incapable of chewing.

VAMPIRES OF GHANA

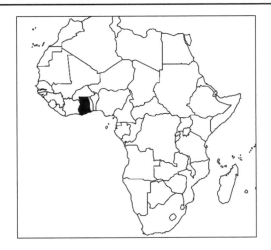

ASASABONSAM

The Asasabonsam originated among the Ashanti people. It is also featured in legends from Togo and the Ivory Coast.

The Asasabonsam favor the deeper reaches of the forests of West Africa. They lurk in dense shrubs or hide among the leaves of trees, and leap out to attack passersby. Those that dwell in trees will often lean down, snatch their prey up into the branches, and kill them there. Asasabonsam that favor the ground will carry their victims off to a quiet spot in the woods, a secluded ravine or gully, then kill the victims and leave the remains for the animals.

The Asasabonsam are sadistic monsters and will often taunt travelers, spooking them into frightened flight so they can hunt them down. They are also tricksters, and will mimic the sounds of a child in distress or a friendly voice in order to lure campers away from their protective fires.

Unlike traditional vampires, the Asasabonsam do not grow extra-long canines. Instead they develop a set of powerful iron teeth with which they rip open the flesh of their prey to drink the fresh blood. In addition to the fearsome dental hardware, the Asasabonsam also have strange hook-like legs, much like those of a praying mantis, with which they clutch their victims. Aside from these two fearsome attributes, the Asasabonsam are otherwise human in appearance.

Some legends say that an Asasabonsam bites its victims on the thumb, others that it favors the throat. In either case, steel teeth make dreadful armament for one of the Undead, and when victims are discovered they show signs of having been savaged.

There is a zoological link to the Asasabonsam that bites its victims on the thumb: this is actually in keeping with reports of bites by real vampire bats. In the rare cases where a vampire bat has bitten someone (and the cases are very rare), it was more often than not on the thumb. This may explain why some legends of the Asasabonsam mention biting victims on the thumb. It may also be a link between vampire bites and disease, because bites from actual vampire bats have been directly associated with the spread of rabies.

ASIMAN

Less common name for the Obayifo. *See* following entry.

OBAYIFO (also called ASIMAN)

The Ashanti of the Gold Coast of Africa (now called Ghana) have their own vampire, one linked to the practice of witchcraft. The Obayifo is the supernatural spirit of a living person (always a witch or sorcerer) who is able to leave his/her body and flit through the air as a malicious spirit in the form of a ball of light.

The Asasabonsam. Artwork by Robert Patrick O'Brien.

The Obayifo preys primarily on infants and young children, drinking blood and sometimes leaving the victim alive but horribly diseased. When it is unable to get human blood, the Obayifo will feed on the juices of fruits and vegetables. In places where it feeds on crops it often causes blight, and if the Obayifo is fraught with great hunger it may wind up destroying an entire field, leaving the fruits withered to dry husks and the plants diseased and inedible.

Though the Obayifo is an Ashanti creation, its legend either has spread to other areas, or it has close relatives elsewhere. In the legends of the Dahomean it is known as the Asiman, and by other names in nearby places. But wherever it appears, blight and death follow.

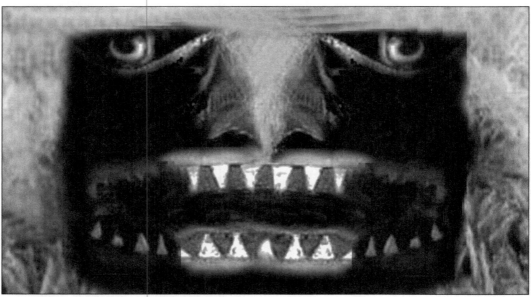

Obayifo. Artwork by Michael Katz.

AFRICAN VAMPIRES IN FILM

Though many vampire films feature African-American actors and actresses, there have been only a handful of films dealing with vampires of African origin or (more often) Africans who have become vampires.

- The first American film of this kind was *Blacula* (1972), starring William Marshall as noble African Prince Mamuwalde who is turned into a vampire by Count Dracula. Though the film was of the "blaxploitation" genre, Marshall managed to give the character gravity and dignity. Marshall returned in *Scream, Blacula, Scream* (1973), co-starring Pam Grier as a voodoo priestess. Neither film discussed any of the vampires native to Africa, but rather perpetuated the Dracula mythos.

- *Ganja & Hess* (Also known as *Black Vampire*, *Possession*, *Black Evil*, and *Black Out*). This is a 1972 horror film that deals with vampirism as a metaphor for addiction. The main character, Dr. Hess Green (Duane Jones, better known as the hero of *Night of the Living Dead*) acquires the "addiction" from a ceremony while traveling in Africa and becomes a kind of vampire. Unlike other film vampires, Hess walks in the daylight, sleeps in a bed, goes to church, and does not have fangs. The movie is a confusing mess, unfortunately, wasting the opportunity to bring both an interesting view of African culture and a different slant to vampire storytelling to film.

Cover art to the DVD edition of Ganja & Hess. Artwork by Bill Chancellor. Used with permission of David Kalat, (c) 2003 All Day Entertainment. (www.alldayentertainment.com).

- *Alabama's Ghost* (1972) starred Christopher Brooks, Lani Freeman, Pierre LePage, and the Turk Murphy Jazz Band. This obscure blaxploitation film tells the story of Alabama (Christopher Brooks) who discovers a dead magician's secret stash and instantly turns himself into a master magician. What he doesn't know is that he is the pawn of a pack of space vampires who are planning a super seaside concert where the audience will be slaughtered for their blood. This ultra low-budget film comes complete with purple faced vampire zombies, an evil wheelchair-bound concert promoter, lots of dancing hippy chicks, and tons of gore.

- *Vampire In Brooklyn* (1995). Eddie Murphy plays Maximillian, the last surviving vampire of the African branch of the "Nosferatus", which is a screenwriter's attempt to describe a species of vampires by simply using a word common to vampire fiction. The movie, though often comedic, has a dark edge to it that makes it highly watchable even if there is no trace at all of genuine African culture.

- *The Young Ones: Nasty*. An episode of this over-the-top British sitcom featured the lads engaged in an all-night viewing of a porn video called *Nasty* while being interrupted by a visit from a South African vampire. The bit was played entirely for laughs (which it earned) with no attempt to even nod in the direction of folklore.

- *Queen of the Damned* (2002), based on the Anne Rice novel, featured an ancient Egyptian creature (Akasha) who was the mother of all vampires on earth. Akasha was immensely powerful and her life was linked directly with all other vampires on earth. The movie failed to capture the grandeur and complexity of the vampire mythology Rice had constructed, instead going for corny dialogue and mediocre special effects. The role of Akasha was played by the young hip-hop singer Aaliyah, who tragically died in a plane crash prior to the release of the film.

Archival photo.

THE RELIGION OF VODOUN (VOODOO)

The Africans had a number of belief systems, including Akan, Ifa, Orisha, La Reglas de Congo, and Mami Wata. Some were even Muslims. These collective religions have become popularly known today as "Voodoo," although they are more appropriately named Vodoun.

The name Vodoun is traceable to an African word for "spirit." The roots of Vodoun may go back 6,000 years.

When Africans were taken as slaves and brought from Dahomey, Ewe, Nigeria, Senegal, Ghana, the Congo, and other West African nations to America, they did not automatically become Christians as history books and stereotyped movies would suggest. During the slave era the Africans did not allow themselves to worship as Christians, though many made a show of doing so as a way of ingratiating themselves with their so-called masters. The slavers fell for this begrudging "acceptance" of Christian worship because it appeared to sever yet another tie to the slaves' native land, and held the promise of reducing rebelliousness.

However, many Africans continued to believe in their own religions. They gave their Gods the names of Christian saints for protective coloration. Their religious beliefs were very strong, and deeply entrenched.

Today, there are two virtually unrelated forms of the religion:

- The actual religion Vodoun is practiced in Benin, Dominican Republic, Ghana, Haiti, Togo, and various centers in the United States. Vodoun is a positive religion, stressing ethical behavior, family values, and deep religious devotion to God.

- The imaginary "evil" religion which is more often called Voodoo was created for Hollywood movies, complete with "voodoo dolls," violence, bizarre rituals, etc. This version of voodoo only exists in fiction and is a racist slander on what is actually a very positive religion.

Vodoun and the fictional Voodoo both use the *gris-gris*, a fetish, charm, or talisman kept for good luck or to ward off evil. Gris-gris probably started out as dolls or images of the Vodoun gods, but nowadays most gris-gris are small cloth bags containing herbs, oils, stones, small bones, hair, nails, pieces of cloth soaked with perspiration, and/or other personal items gathered under the directions of a god for the protection of the owner.

A gris-gris is ritually made at an altar containing the four elements of earth (salt), air (incense), water, and fire (a candle flame). The number of ingredients placed in the gris-gris is always one, three, five, seven, nine, or thirteen. Ingredients are never an even number or more than thirteen.

The word gris-gris comes from the West African term *grou-grou*, which is a general term that refers to any sacred object. Since many fetishes were fashioned into doll shape, early European explorers in Africa began to associate the word grou-grou with any doll made for a spiritual purpose, hence the origin of the expression "voodoo doll."

The gris-gris have always been popular in New Orleans, America's center for Vodoun. They are used for various things such as attracting money and love, stopping gossip, protecting the home, maintaining good health, and achieving innumerable other ends. In the early to mid-twentieth century, even police officers were known to carry gris-gris for protection.

VAMPIRES OF GREECE

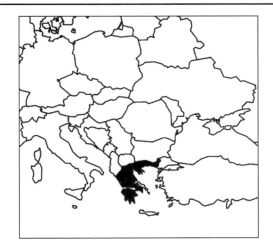

BRUKULACO (also Bruculaco)

The regions of Thessaly and Epirus in Greece have long been haunted by the spirits of the undead, including the Brukulaco. This vampire is created when a person is excommunicated from the church, effectively severing the person from the grace and protection of God. In some cases the curse can be passed on to the son of an excommunicate.

After death the corpse transforms into a swollen, monstrous shape with skin as hard as tree bark. It smashes its way out of its grave and lopes off into the night, body hunched and head held low, teeth bared, very similar to the interpretations of werewolves seen in films like *The Howling* and *Dog Soldiers*. The beast has a barrel chest that, when struck, booms like a drum. Its arms are packed with muscles and each long finger tapers into a razor-sharp claw as long as a steak knife.

Once the Brukulaco has set out to feed it will utter a strange plaintive cry. If someone comes to investigate the sound, the Brukulaco will slaughter him and feast on his blood and flesh.

Like the vampires of Germany, the Brukulaco also spreads the plague. This kills more people than its nightly attacks.

In the region of Thessaloniki there is a somewhat different version of the Brukulaco legend. There it is believed that when a person suffering

The Brukulaco. Artwork by Robert Patrick O'Brien.

from catalepsy lapses into a fit, his soul leaves the body and enters that of any nearby wolf. At once the wolf becomes a killer and will hunt down livestock and human alike.

The only sure way to destroy a Brukulaco is to cut off its head and burn both head and corpse. In the case of the Brukulaco from Milo, the severed head should be boiled first and then reburied with the corpse.

CALLICANTZARO (also Kallikantzaros)

According to the folklore of Christian Greeks, any child born between Christmas and New Year's Day (or, in some tales, between Christmas and the Epiphany, January 6th) is at risk for becoming the vampire called a Callicantzaro (plural is Callicantzaros or Callicantzaroi).

The Callicantzaros are very vicious beasts, actually closer to were-wolves than vampires. They exhibit insanely violent behavior, but only during the span of days between Christmas and New Year. They have powerful clawlike fingernails with which they rip their victims to shreds. Some scientists have postulated that the legend of the Callicantzaro is a way of explaining the rare and extreme aberrant psychological condition of necrophagism, where a person eats the body parts of someone who was recently murdered.

During the period of time when the Callicantzaro is active, it will hide in caves by day and venture out to attack wanderers, merchants, travelers, shepherds, and anyone else caught on the roads at night. The remainder of the year, the Callicantzaro is consigned to the Netherworld where it is trapped with other demons and creatures of darkness. Sometimes a male Callicantzaro will capture a woman and bring her down to the Netherworld with him, forcing her to bear his children. The children would be born as Callicantzaros.

If a child is born during this holy period, precautions have to be taken to prevent it. The infant must be lowered feet-first into a fire, held just above the flames until the baby's toenails are singed black. The toenails must then be eaten to secure the reincarnation of the deceased.

The Callicantzaro. Artwork by Robert Patrick O'Brien.

NECROPHAGISM AND CANNIBALISM

Necrophagy is a term used in clinical psychology to describe the consumption of pieces of the corpse of someone who has been terribly mutilated. Often done while in a state of high agitation or frenzy, this deviant act is differentiated from true cannibalism in that it is most often directed toward a specific organ or body part, usually of a victim who was murdered only moments before. Necrophagy is common among various vampire species as they often eat the flesh of humans.

This condition is often confused with Necrophilia, which is an erotic attraction to the dead sometimes resulting in sexual acts committed on corpses.

It also differs from cannibalism in that cannibalism is the practice of eating members of one's own species for ritual purposes or for survival. The fictional character Hannibal Lecter, from *Silence Of The Lambs* by Thomas Harris, displays characteristics of cannibalism rather than necrophagism as one of his many horrific traits,. The ugly habits of the real-world maniac, Jack the Ripper, were also cannibalistic in nature.

Cannibalism is also part of the customs of various Native American peoples, particularly the Kwakiutl Indians of British Columbia and the Haida Indians of the Queen Charlotte Islands, for whom the custom is acceptable and not linked to evil or vampirism.

In ancient Mexico, when a young man was sacrificed to the god Tetzcatlipoca, the body was then chopped up and distributed amongst the priests and nobles as a sacred food. In Australia, the Biblinga tribesmen chop up the bodies of their beloved relatives.

EMPUSA (also called Mormolykiai; plural Empusae)

Ancient Greek mythology contained many fantastic creatures, including were vampires called the Empusae. The Empusae were blood drinking demons in the service of Hecate, Goddess of the Crossroads and one of the most powerful Goddesses in all of the ancient religions. The Empusae often went about in human form, but that was just a disguise. Their true forms were reportedly very hideous, and they were believed to have one leg of brass and one like that of a donkey.

These vile vampires have been written about in stories, histories, folktales, and plays for thousands of years, but the most famous and important account was that by Philostratus in his *Life Of Apollonius Of Tyana*. Philostratus wrote of the handsome youth Menippus, who was enticed by an Empusa disguised as a Phoenician woman. Apollonius confronted the Empusa, and the Empusa revealed itself and admitted to fattening up Menippus so that she might devour him.

THE FROGS, A PLAY BY ARISTOPHANES

The Empusae were also mentioned by Aristophanes in his play, *The Frogs*, where Dionysus and his servant Xanthias encounter the monster:

XANTHIAS:	And now I see the most ferocious monster.
DIONYSUS:	O, what's it like?
XANTHIAS:	Like everything by turns. Now it's a bull: now it's a mule: and now the loveliest girl.
DIONYSUS:	O, where? I'll go and meet her.
XANTHIAS:	It's ceased to be a girl: it's a dog now.
DIONYSUS:	It is Empusa!
XANTHIAS:	Well, its face is all Ablaze with fire.
DIONYSUS:	Has it a copper leg?
XANTHIAS:	A copper leg? yes, one; and one of cow dung.
DIONYSUS:	O, whither shall I flee?
XANTHIAS:	O, whither I?
DIONYSUS:	My priest, protect me, and we'll sup together.

FARKASKOLDUS

The Farkaskoldus is an interesting twist (and blend) of the vampire-werewolf relationship. Resisting classification as either vampire or werewolf, and embracing characteristics of both, the Farkaskoldus is usually an unnaturally resurrected spirit that returns to seek revenge. When a wronged person dies (usually a shepherd who has been abused or unfairly treated in life) he is resurrected as a blood drinker; not a thirsty vampire but instead a blood sucking werewolf.

The majority of legends hold that once the Farkaskoldus has gotten whatever justice is desired, its spirit will be able to rest and it will return to the grave, never to rise again. In some folktales the Farkaskoldus, once freed of its compulsion to seek redress, will begin attacking anyone until it is hunted down and killed.

The Farkaskoldus can be killed by ordinary means—a sword, gun, or even clubs—but it is a fierce fighter and cannot easily be overcome. The safest method for disposing of the monster is to have a large group of armed men with torches and hunting dogs herd it toward a

The Farkaskoldus. Sculpture by Robert Patrick O'Brien.

clearing where a bonfire has been prepared. Once in the clearing the men can overpower it using nets, ropes, or sheer numbers, then bind the creature to a stake and light the bonfire.

KERES (also called KER)

Another of Greece's grim vampires from the days of the old gods, the Keres, were the personification of violent death—either in battle, by accident, or by murder. These literal "children of the night" appeared as women clothed in bloody garments, but with long fangs and wicked talons. They were in the service of the Fates, who measured the length of a man's life on the day of his birth and who represented the inevitability of death.

The Keres typically hovered over battlefields, waiting to feed. They descended to dying men and ripped souls free from wounded bodies, sometimes as the injury was being inflicted, sometimes after the event. Once a soul was freed to begin its journey to Hades, the body was theirs to consume with great hunger and relish. Thousands of these creatures would flock like vultures to each battlefield, and would fight viciously among themselves for the bloody spoils of war.

The Greek poet Hesiod wrote of the origins of the Keres in his classic *Theogony*, an account of the origins of the Gods: "And Nyx (the goddess of Night) bore hateful Moros and black Kera . . . and again the goddess murky Nyx, though she lay with none . . . bare the . . . ruthless, avenging Kerai . . . they pursue the transgressions of men and of gods: and these goddesses never cease from their dread anger until they punish the sinner with a sore penalty."

The Keres. Archival artwork.

THE KERES IN GREEK LITERATURE

The monstrous Keres is mentioned frequently in Homer's *Iliad* and other masterworks of Greek literature and history. Following are a few excerpted quotes:

- "[Sarpedon:] But now, seeing that the Keres (Spirits of Death) stand close about us in their thousands, no man can turn aside nor escape them, let us go on and win glory for ourselves, or yield it to others." -*Iliad* 12.326

- "And [he] tried to prevent his two sons from going into the battle where men die. Yet these would not listen, for the dark Keres were driving them onwards." -*Iliad* 2.834

- "Yet the reading of birds could not keep off dark Keres (Destruction) but he went down under the hands of swift-running Aiakides [Akhilleus]." -*Iliad* 2.859

- "Since he was hated among them all as dark Ker (Death) is hated." -*Iliad* 3.454

- "[Hektor:] I pray to Zeus and the other immortals that we may drive from our place these dogs [the Akhaians] swept into destruction whom the Keres (Spirits of Death) have carried here on their black ships." -*Iliad* 8.528

- "[He] was not destined to evade the evil Keres (Spirits of Destruction) nor ever to make his way back to windy Ilion." -*Iliad* 12.114

- "[Telemakhos:] So now I will strive as best I may to set the Keres (Spirits of Doom) upon you." -*Odyssey* 2.316

- "But the Keres (Death Spirits) carried him down to Hades' house." -*Odyssey* 14.207

- "[The men were] fighting their battle, and where they were the Keres, dark-colored, and clattering their white teeth, deadly faced, grim-glaring, bloody and unapproachable, were fighting over the fallen men, all of them rushing forward to drink of the black blood, and each, as soon as she had snatched a man, down already or just dropping from a wound, would hook her great claws around his body, while his soul went down to the realm of Hades and cold Tartaros. Then when the Keres had sated their senses on the blood of men's slaughter, they would throw what was left behind them and go storming back into the battle-clamor and the struggle." -*Shield of Heracles* 248

- "These [men] stood their ground and fought a battle . . . and Eris (Hate) was there with Kydoimos (Confusion) among them, and Ker (Death) the destructive; she [Eris] was holding a live man with a new wound, and [Kydoimos] another one unhurt, and [Ker] dragged a dead man by the feet through the carnage. The clothing upon her shoulders showed strong red with the men's blood as she glared horribly and gnashed her teeth till they echoed. All [the Keres] closed together like living men and fought with each other and dragged away from each other the corpses of those who had fallen." -*Iliad* 18.535 & *Shield of Heracles* 156

- "And all of these were [Keres] were making a grisly fight over one man, glaring horribly at each other with eyes full of anger, and making an equal fight of it with claws and bold hands." -*Shield of Heracles* 261.

- "Penthesileia in her goodlihead left the tall palaces of Troy behind. And ever were the ghastly-visaged Keres (Fates) thrusting her on into the battle, doomed to be her first against the Greeks." -*Quietus Smyrnaeus* 1.171

- "For round him now hovered the unrelenting Keres (Fates)." -*Quietus Smyrnaeus* 3.44

- "And there [depicted on the shield of Akhilleus] were man-devouring wars, and all horrors of fight . . . Phobos (Panic) was there, and Deimos (Dread), and ghastly Enyo with limbs all gore-bespattered hideously, and deadly Eris (Strife) ... Around them hovered the relentless Keres (Fates); beside them Hysminai (Battles) incarnate onward pressed yelling, and from their limbs streamed blood and sweat." -*Quietus Smyrnaeus* 5.25

- "The dark Keres (Spirits of Doom) stand beside us, one holding grievous old age as the outcome, the other death." –*Mimnermus Frag* 2 (from *Stobaeus, Anthology*)

- "Artemis . . . give ear to my prayers and ward off the evil Keres (Death-Spirits). For you, goddess, this is no small thing, but for me it is critical." –*Theognis* 1.11

- "Megistias, whom once the Medes killed when they crossed the river Sperkheios: he was a seer, who recognised clearly that the Keres (Spirits of Death) were approaching then, but could not bring himself to desert." -Greek Lyric III *Simonides Frag* 7 (from *Herodotus, Histories* 7.228.3)

- "[Depicted on the chest of Cypselus at Olympia] Polyneikes, the son of Oidipous, has fallen on his knee, and Eteokles, the other son of Oidipous, is rushing on him. Behind Polyneikes stands a woman with teeth as cruel as those of a beast, and her fingernails are bent like talons. An inscription by her calls her Ker (Doom), implying that Polyneikes has been carried off by fate, and that Eteokles fully deserved his end." –*Pausanias* 5.19.4

- "Ker: Spirit (*psykhe*); also death-bringing fate (*moira thanatephoros*). Also [in the plural] Keres, death-bringing fates. Those who bring on burning (*kaenai*) .... The spirit [is] a Ker, because it consists of fire. For that which [is] inborn warmth [is] a spirit. 'I am a tomb-haunting Ker, and Koroibos killed me [Poine].'" -*Suidas 'Ker'*

- "Anamplaketoi (Unerring): The [Keres, goddesses of death and doom] who miss nothing, but overcome everything. Alternatively inescapable, inexorable, unfailing, invisible, they who cannot be fled. Sophokles [writes]: 'dread Keres are following [him], unerring.' That is, those of Laios." -*Suidas 'Anamplaketoi'*

LAMIAI

Though not true vampires by accepted standards, the Lamiai of ancient Greece nonetheless share many of the same qualities. The Lamiai are considered evil birth demons that prey upon newborns, drinking their blood and consuming their flesh.

The Lamiai are named after Lamia, a Greek goddess who was one of Zeus' mistresses. Zeus's wife, Hera, was so enraged by the liaison that she killed any offspring that resulted from the union. Lamia was naturally outraged and swore that in revenge for this act of cruelty she would kill as many other children as possible.

She created the Lamiai for this purpose. They were female demons with deformed lower limbs (like snakes or other animals), talons, and wicked teeth. The Lamiai can assume the shapes of various birds and do so at night as they hunt the countryside for victims. Once they spy their prey they attack, and once again assume their regular hideous forms. They tear out their victim's entrails, devour the flesh, suck out any milk, and drink the blood. Sometimes the Lamiai even seek out pregnant victims and slaughter both mother and child.

The Lamiai do not confine their bloodlust to women and children, however. Sometimes they seduce young men, have sex with them, and attack them at the peak of orgasm by tearing out their throats and drinking their blood.

Though the Lamiai are supernaturally strong, they do need to rest once in a while. When they do so they find a quiet place and remove their eyes. This reduces them to a slumbering state, and it is only in this condition that they can be killed by fire, sword, or spear.

The Lamiai are one of the oldest known vampire legends. Various ancient Greek writings tell of the Lamiai, and the creature appears in quite a lot of modern fiction, even in song. The Progressive Rock band, Genesis, recorded a song called *"The Lamia"* for their 1974 album *The Lamb Lies Down On Broadway*; and songs about the Lamiai have been recorded by Odwalla, Lord Belial, and Enten Eller. The noted horror writer, Clark Ashton Smith, wrote a brilliant poem called "Lamia" which was collected with his other poetical works in *The Dark Chateau And Other Poems*. Other poets have written of these creatures, and the most famous and influential poet to write about this ancient evil was John Keats in his 1819 epic masterpiece, "The Lamia."

The Lamiai. Artwork by Robert Patrick O'Brien.

MORMO

Like the monstrous Empusa, the Greek Mormo is an ancient slayer of children. Also a servant of the goddess Hecate, the Mormo is one of the few demons of the truly ancient world that has survived into the 21st Century. Nowadays it is generally considered as a kind of bogey-man used to scare naughty children into being good, but the original Mormo was no scary story for kids.

The Mormos were female demons that attacked sleeping children for their blood, leaving them cold and dead for their parents to find. Some scholars speculate that this was the way the ancient Greeks tried to rationalize the otherwise inexplicable tragedy of SIDS (Sudden Infant Death Syndrome).

Oddly, among the many world cultures that tell of a child-killing demon, that creature is almost always female. It is like an anti-mother, a demon who demonstrates the exact opposite of the nurturing and protective actions of a true mother: it kills instead of nurtures, feeds upon rather than nurses. These she-demons are also frequently portrayed as seductresses, preying wantonly on young men as well as children. In short, they are (by the standard of the day) the worst examples of what a woman should be: evil mothers, unfaithful wives, sexually promiscuous, and immoral. Freudian psychologists could spend years working through the legends of the Mormo and the Empusae, as well as the two other female child-killing demons of Greek myth, the Gelloudes and the Stringla.

SUDDEN INFANT DEATH SYNDROME (SIDS)

This is the sudden death of an infant under one year of age which remains unexplained after a thorough case investigation, including performance of a complete autopsy, examination of the death scene, and review of the clinical history. SIDS is often believed to be caused by putting infants to bed on their stomachs. Many cultures throughout history have blamed vampirism for SIDS.

MONSTERS OF GREEK MYTH

There are many creatures of Greek myth. Here are just a few of the strange creatures that populated the mythology of that ancient island:

Argus was a monster with multiple sets of eyes. He could see nearly everything, and so became a guardian creature. In Greek myths there are stories of Argus subduing a wild bull that was destroying the Arcadian countryside. He also defeated a malicious cattle-stealing satyr.

Cerberus was the guardian of the Underworld, and a devoted servant of Hades, lord of that fiery realm. Cerberus was a gigantic and enormously powerful three-headed dog (although the poet Hesiod claims that Cerberus had fifty heads) with the thrashing tail of a serpent. It was the offspring of Echidna (a half-woman, half-serpent) and Typhon (a beast with a hundred heads), and brother to the Hydra and the Chimera.

Chimera: This was a savage fire-breathing monster said to be made from three different creatures: lion, she-goat and serpent. The Chimera was a destroyer, reveling in slaughter. It devastated the Greek farmlands until the hero Bellerophon, riding the hippogriff Pegasus, slew it.

Geryon was the ruler of a distant land called Erythia, and he was a powerful monster with three heads and three bodies. He ruled Erythia with a savage iron fist and with the aid of his herdsman, Eurytion, and his savage hound, Orthrus. One of the labors assigned to the demi-god Herakles (Hercules) was to kill Geryon and drive his vast herd of cattle back to Greece. Herakles accomplished this as his tenth labor, ending Geryon's rule of terror.

Gorgon (sometimes called a "gorgo"). This was a female monster with a writhing mass of serpents for hair and a face so hideous that any mortal who looked at it would be so horrified that he would be turned instantly to stone. There were many Gorgons throughout the Greek Isles, but by far the most famous were Medusa and her sisters Stheno and Eluryah. They were the daughters of the sea gods, Ceto and Phorcys. Though her sisters were immortal, Medusa was not. Once she had been a woman of unsurpassed beauty, noted for her long and luxuriant hair. But she boasted of being more beautiful even than the goddess Athena. Visiting Athena's temple, Medusa was overpowered and ravished by another of the sea gods, Neptune. Athena was outraged by this carnal act in her temple, and blamed Medusa's beauty for the rape. The idea of blaming the rape on the rapist, Neptune, was never brought forth, making Medusa doubly a victim. Her only crime was vanity. The Greek Gods were seldom fair-minded or moral.

Athena cursed Medusa and turned her into a monstrous parody of her former self. Her beauty became a lethal ugliness and her long silky hair became a tangle of venomous snakes. In time Medusa, embittered by her curse, became a monster in nature as well as form and took delight in the destruction of handsome men whom she could not possess and who were repulsed by her.

Medusa's undoing came by at hands of the heroic Perseus while he was on a quest to rescue his mother Danae from King Polydectes. He was forced to complete a quest, and one of the tasks assigned to him was to retrieve Medusa's head. Perseus was able to do so with help from Athena (who was still bitter and spiteful) and Hermes. Perseus was given a mirrored shield and a magical sword. He used the mirror to gaze only at Medusa's reflection (which apparently was not as lethal as a direct line of sight); thus more or less able to confront Medusa, he used the sword to behead her.

The likeness of the Gorgon had been a staple of artwork through-out ancient Greece, and it was used as a charm or proof against evil. The faces of Gorgons were painted on warrior's shields to

Gorgon. Archival photo.

fend off evil spirits such as the Keres, and Gorgon plaques were hung above doorways or archways to prevent evil from entering homes and public places.

Hydra: The Lernean Hydra lived in a swamp and terrorized everyone in the area. With its poisonous venom and many heads (the exact number of which varies in different versions of the story), the creature appeared to be invincible. Herakles confronted the beast and started cutting off the hydra's heads, but each time he removed one head, two other heads immediately grew from the stump. Realizing that Herakles was losing the fight, his nephew Iolaus grabbed a torch. As Herakles cut off a head Iolaus dashed in to cauterize the stump, preventing any additional heads from growing. With the other heads gone, Hercules cut off the middle, immortal head, and the monster died. Herakles toppled a massive boulder over its corpse and that became its grave.

In films such as *Jason And The Argonauts* (1963), the slaying of the Hydra is ascribed to Jason, but in mythology Jason fought a fire-breathing dragon in order to obtain the fleece, not a Hydra.

Minotaur: The dreaded Minotaur appears in the legends of the Labyrinth. The Minotaur was a brutish creature with the head of a bull atop the body of a powerful man, the offspring of a bizarre mating between Queen Pasiphae of Crete and a bull.

The bull had been given to Minos, King of Crete and Pasiphae's husband, by the sea god Poseidon as an intended sacrifice, but the greedy Minos decided to keep it. Poseidon (or in some accounts, Aphrodite) became furious at Minos and punished him by making Pasiphae fall madly in love with the bull. She coerced the royal architect and engineer, Daedalus, to construct a cow-like device that she could enter so that she could mate with the bull. The resulting unholy union produced a hybrid of human and bovine. Minos confined the creature in a labyrinth that he ordered Daedalus to build at Cnossus, from which escape was impossible.

Every nine years, seven young men and seven maidens were sent from Athens to be devoured by the Minotaur. With the assistance of King Minos' daughter Ariadne, Athens' hero, Theseus, made his way to the heart of the labyrinth, killed the Minotaur, and made his way safely back out.

VRYKOLAKA (also called Upirina)

Legends of the fierce Vrykolaka are well documented in the folklore of both Greece and Macedonia, with echoes of these superstitions lingering well into the mid-nineteenth century, and possibly later. The Vrykolaka is a vampire created when a person has either committed suicide (a mortal sin resulting in damnation), or dies a violent death (resulting in an unquiet spirit filled with rage and confusion). A grossly immoral—or amoral—person was also a likely candidate for becoming this species of vampire.

The name Vrykolaka can be variously translated as "wolf-pelt" or "werewolf," which is odd since this species of vampire does not share any qualities with werewolves.

The Vrykolaka gains vast powers as it grows older. It is very hard to identify, and few methods of destroying it are known.

Although popular fiction provides that vampires cannot enter a house unless invited, this rarely holds true in vampire folklore. The Vrykolaka is a rare exception, as it cannot enter any house where it is not invited. The creature will stand outside and call the name of its desired victim, hoping either to be invited inside or for the person to come out.

Once it can approach its prey, the Vrykolaka will leap onto the victim, bear him to the ground, and smother him with its body. In some accounts the Vrykolaka is invisible and the victim merely feels a crushing weight on his chest. People who have escaped the vampire's attack describe symptoms very much like those of a heart attack: a great weight on the chest, shortness of breath, and pain.

The people of the island of Chios in the Aegean Sea (reported to be the birthplace of the poet Homer) believe that placing a cross made from wax or cotton (or both) on the lips of a corpse can help prevent the corpse from becoming a Vrykolaka. A priest can increase the odds of preventing the creation of a Vrykolaka by taking a shard of pottery, preferably from a bowl belonging either to the family of the deceased or to the local church, inscribing "Jesus Christ Conquers" on it, and burying it with the corpse.

Greek scholar and theologian Leone Allacci, also known as Leo Allatius, (1586-1669), wrote extensively about the Vrykolakas in his treatise, *De Graecorum Hodie Quorundam Opinationibus, Cologne 1645*:

"The Vrykolaka is the body of a man of wicked and debauched life, very often one who has been excommunicated by his bishop. Such bodies do not, like other corpses, suffer decomposition after burial nor fall to dust, but having, so it seems, a skin of extreme toughness becomes swollen and distended all over, so that the joints can scarcely be bent; the skin becomes stretched like the parchment of a drum, and when struck gives out the same sound.

"This monster is said to be so fearfully destructive to men that it actually makes its appearance in the daytime, even at high noon, nor does it then confine its visits to houses, but even in the fields and in hedged vineyards and upon the open highway it will suddenly advance upon persons who are labouring, or travelers as they walk along, and by the horror of its hideous aspect it will slay them without laying hold on them or even speaking a word."

Photo by Jason Lukridge.

Sabbatarian and Fetch Dog. Art by M. Katz.

SABBATARIAN

The enemies of the Vrykolaka are the Sabbatarian and his Fetch Dog. A Sabbatarian is a person born on a Saturday (the Greek term is *Sabbatianoi*). Persons born on this holy day often exhibit supernatural powers such as the ability to see invisible monsters like the Vrykolaka and other pernicious specters. The Sabbatarian is accompanied by a kind of white magic familiar called a Fetch Dog that travels with him and can chase away ghosts and vampires.

In some legends the Sabbatarian is invisible and only the Fetch Dog can see him, hence strange dogs walking alone are regarded as potential Fetch Dogs accompanying an unseen Sabbatarian. These dogs are often treated kindly and given food because it is possible they are helping to save the village or town from an unseen monster such as a Vrykolaka.

VAMPIRES OF GUINEA

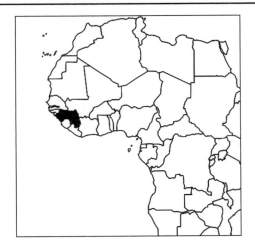

OWENGA

In the North African nation of Guinea the ghosts of dead sorcerers or people who had lived evil and corrupt lives often return to earth in physical form as vampires called Owengas. The Owengas prey upon the people from their own villages. The creatures cannot be killed by any means but they can be appeased by blood offerings. Animal blood is most often used, especially the blood of female animals that have never mated. The blood is usually placed in wooden bowls and left outside of huts at night.

Sometimes an Owenga will accept the blood offerings and leave the village in peace. But if it is angered by the quality or quantity of the offering it will return and spread deadly disease throughout the village.

If blood is spilled by accident and not cleaned up, the Owenga will return even stronger. This has instilled in the natives of Guinea a custom of immediately cleaning up all spilled blood and burning any object that is stained with blood. A village that adheres strictly to this will often be free from an Owenga for generations.

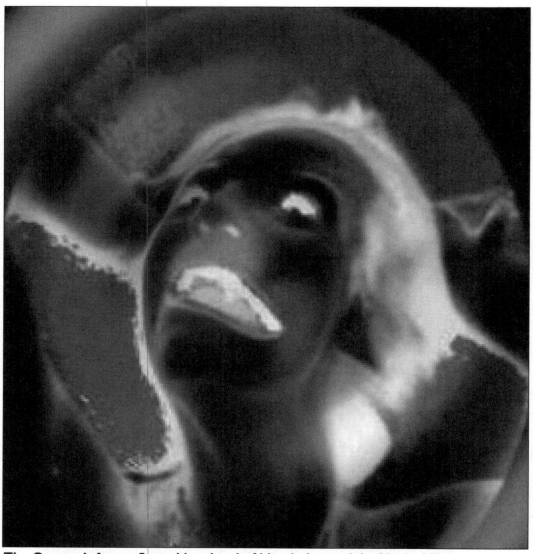

The Owenga's face reflected in a bowl of blood. Artwork by Marie O'Brien.

VAMPIRES AMONG THE GYPSIES

MULLO

For long centuries there has been a strong link between Gypsies and vampires. Despite some fictional references to the contrary, the Gypsies are not friends to the vampire. Like every other culture, the Romani hate and fear these creatures of evil.

One such vampire is the Mullo. These creatures are Revenants that rise from the graves of those who have died from sudden death, violence, improperly performed burial rites, or other unnatural causes. A death at the hands of one's relatives can create a Mullo, especially where a relative keeps the deceased person's possessions instead of passing them on as in the typical Romani custom.

Many Gypsies are wise enough to take measures to prevent a dead person from becoming a Mullo. At the time of burial they will place small pieces of steel in the newly deceased person's mouth, over the eyes and ears, and between the fingers. Then a stake made from newly cut hawthorn will be driven through the legs or hawthorn splinters will

The Gypsy Mullo. Photo by Jason Lukridge.

be placed in the socks. Even if the Mullo comes to life it would be unable to stand or walk, and would soon perish again from lack of nourishment.

Literally meaning "one who is dead," the Mullo is sometimes depicted as a ghost and sometimes a vampire. In either case it is a predator who attacks the living and drinks blood. But accounts of what a Mullo looks like and what powers it possesses vary from region to region. In many areas Mullo are invisible or can become invisible at will. In some countries they are half-human and half-animal in appearance. Others believe that the Mullo appear as mutilated corpses. Gypsy Mullo from Sweden are reported to have shape-shifting abilities. Mullo from India have flaming hair. Often a person missing fingers or toes is suspected of being a Mullo.

These vampires have an enormous sexual appetite. Once it has risen, the Mullo often seeks out its mate in life and attempts to seduce that person. Failing that, they will sexually prey on anyone at hand.

Other tales suggest that a Mullo can lead a fairly normal life as a human being, even to the point of marrying (usually a Mullo of the opposite sex). But their sexual hungers will soon exhaust their mates, sometimes to the point of death.

Destroying a Mullo usually requires contracting the services of a professional vampire slayer called a Dhampir (also Dhampire, Dhampyr, etc.). The Dhampir is the human son of a vampire, and therefore possesses special powers that enable him to sense a vampire's presence and location, including a Mullo. If a Mullo has not yet risen from its grave, or is resting in a coffin or tomb, the Dhampir will open the grave and quickly drive long iron needles into the corpse's heart. Then the body will be decapitated and sometimes burned. Another method involves pouring boiling water over the corpse before beginning the work with the needle.

Oddly, even animals such as dogs, cats, or farm animals can become Mullo; and in some rare cases, plants as well. Pumpkins and other kinds of gourds or melons kept in the house too long might actually start to move about, make strange noises, and leak blood.

For information on a similar species of Mullo *see* Vampires Of Serbia (p. 469).

For more on the Dhampir, *see* Part 5: Fighting The Undead (p. 323).

ANIMAL VAMPIRES

The Gypsy Mullo is one of only a few vampire species that can arise from an animal. Mother Nature, however, has created a host of naturally occurring animal vampires:

- **Leech:** Leeches are brown or black worm-like creatures with suckers on each end. They live just about anywhere there is water. They can range in size from one centimeter to over twenty-five centimeters long. Some leeches feed on decaying plant material while others are parasites, feeding on animal blood and tissue. Blood-sucking leeches use a proboscis to puncture their quarry's skin, or use their three mouths and millions of little teeth. Leeches find their prey by detecting skin oils, blood, heat, or even exhaled carbon dioxide.

- **Mosquito:** These diminutive but annoying (and often dangerous) pests are found all over the world, particularly in warm, moist climates. Some 2,700 species of mosquitoes exist. Mosquitoes attack at will, but their predation increases 500% on the nights of a full moon (science is still trying to determine why). Only female mosquitoes bite. A mosquito can detect a moving target at 18 feet away. The average life span of a female is 3 to 100 days; whereas the male lives 10 to 20 days. Mosquitoes prefer children to adults, and blondes to brunettes. Though the average mosquito only drinks about 5 millionths of a liter, they can carry a variety of diseases, including malaria and West Nile virus. The mosquito is responsible for more human deaths worldwide than any other animal, which means that mosquitoes have killed more people than all species of supernatural vampires combined!

- **Vampire Bat:** Vampire bats need about two tablespoons of blood each day. If they go two days without blood, they will starve to death. They have chemicals in their saliva that prevent their victim's blood from clotting, so they can feed longer. Bats are not carriers of rabies. The chances of coming into contact with a rabid bat are very low because if they get the disease, they usually die from it. Most states do not allow bats to be kept as pets. Responsible bat organizations, such as the Organization for Bat Conservation, strongly discourage taking wild bats as pets.

- **Tick:** These arthropods attach themselves to humans or animals and burrow their heads into their victim's flesh. They feed on blood, stopping only when glutted. A tick can have serious or even deadly affect when its bite introduces a disease-causing microbe into its victim's blood.

VAMPIRES OF HAITI

LOOGAROO

The Haitian vampire called the Loogaroo sheds its skin each night, like the Soucouyan of Dominica and the Asema of Surinam. The Loogaroo goes to a "Devil Tree" and removes its skin, then flies off in the form of a sulfurous ball.

In the folklore of Haiti and other islands of the West Indies, Loogaroos are often depicted as old women who have made an unholy pact with the Devil. They collect fresh human blood each night and offer this up to the Devil. In return the Evil One grants them magical powers.

The word Loogaroo is a slurring of the French word *Loup-garou* (were-wolf), and is used in various places where French-based dialects have developed, including Haiti, Grenada, Louisiana, and elsewhere.

The Loogaroo can enter freely into any house and attack whomever it pleases, but it can be foiled by spreading uncooked rice (in some cases, sand) in front of the doors. Like many vampires around the world, the Loogaroos are compelled to stop and count every single grain before entering. With enough rice left out, the Loogaroo might waste the entire evening and then have to return to its skin before sunrise, unfed and unhappy.

Some folk-tales suggest that the Loogaroo is the male of this species and the Soucouyan is the female (*see* Dominica, p. 169), but opinions seem to differ substantially on this point.

The Loogaroo. Artwork by Marie O'Brien.

VAMPIRES OF HUNGARY

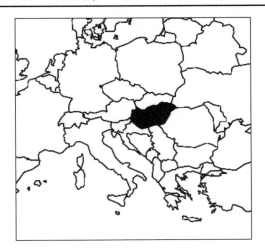

LIDÉRC NADALY

The Lidérc Nadaly is one of the many vampires around the world that are sexual predators as well as hunters of fresh blood. This breed may be related to the legends of the Incubus and Succubus in that it essentially loves its victims to death.

Death through sexual exhaustion is its trademark, and the Lidérc Nadaly is very hard to defend against because it does not adopt a standard vampiric form. No shambling hulk of a dead body, no fiery-eyed monster, no flitting moth; the Lidérc Nadaly has the magical ability to appear as a different thing to each viewer. Sometimes it even chooses to appear as a ball of light. So its victims will not see a monster, but rather behold some desired person—wife, husband, or secret lover.

Should someone discover that their lover is, in fact, a Lidérc Nadaly, the only defense is to kill it by driving an iron nail through its temple.

THE VAMPIRES OF HIADAM

In 1720, investigators from the Holy Roman Empire were sent to a village on the border of Hungary called Hiadam (also spelled Haidam), to investigate reports of vampirism. This investigation stands as one of the best-documented cases of vampirism of all time. Stories tell of a stranger who came uninvited into a house where a soldier was billeted with a peasant family. The stranger silently joined the meal and would answer no questions about himself. Next morning the head of the household, a farmer, was found dead. The family appealed to the soldier to protect them from the stranger, whom they believed was the killer. The soldier told his comrades about it and eventually the story reached their commanding officer, Count De Cadreras, a general in the army. The Count began a formal investigation, deposing everyone concerned, and even exhuming the farmer's corpse. When the corpse was disinterred--weeks after its death--it was perfectly fresh and flushed with apparent life.

Reports of vampiric attacks began flooding in and the body count rose quickly. At the same time there were reports of another farmer, dead for sixteen years, who had risen from his grave and consumed the lifeblood from his two sons. Then a third vampire began troubling the town.

Count De Cadreras took decisive action. He had one "dead" farmer decapitated, cremated a second, and drove an iron spike into the brain of a third. This stopped the plague of vampirism in its tracks.

The Count sent a full account of these events to Emperor Charles VI. The Emperor was appalled at the spread of evil and ordered another investigation, this time by lawyers, surgeons, and theologians, to make sure the evil had been stopped. But it seemed the Count had done his job well and there were no further vampiric attacks in Hiadam.

<u>NORA</u>

Part evil imp and part vampire, the Hungarian Nora is a small hairless creature that is otherwise human in appearance. It runs on all fours like an animal. Often making itself invisible, the Nora generally attacks women who are immoral or who speak and act irreverently, biting them on the breasts and drinking their supposedly "tainted"

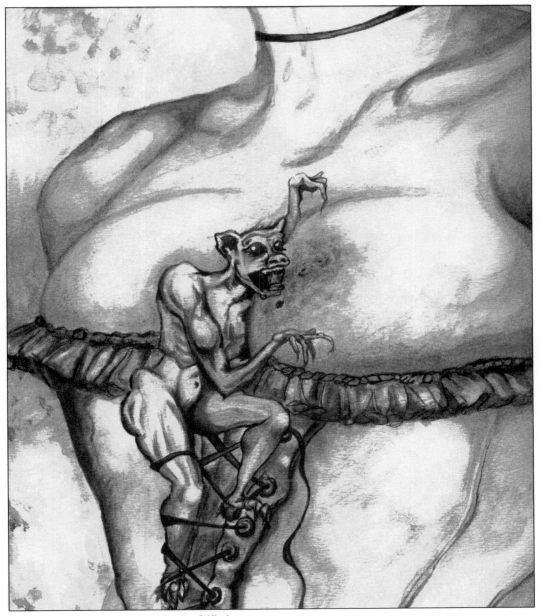

The Nora. Artwork by Marie O'Brien.

blood. The creature's bite causes an allergic reaction which makes the victim's breasts swell to startling size, thus revealing both her shame and the fact that the woman has been the victim of this sprite.

The cure for the Nora's bite is an ointment or poultice made from crushed garlic, applied liberally to the breasts. This helps reduce the swelling and prevents further attacks.

THE BLOOD COUNTESS

Elizabeth Bathory (1560-1614) was a Hungarian noblewoman who became known as the "Blood Countess" because of her practice of murdering young women and bathing in their blood. Elizabeth feared aging and developed an obsession with preserving her youth and beauty. She was also a sexual predator and would engage in lavish orgies with young women before slaying them and draining their blood into her bathtub. It is believed she also drank their blood as well as bathed in it.

Some historians calculate the number of her murders to be as few as fifty or as many as six hundred. Her lieutenants were her co-conspirators in both the debauchery and the butchery. When her crimes became known she and her accomplices were arrested and convicted. Her lieutenants were executed and she was walled up inside her bedroom at Castle Csejthe, where she eventually died.

The Blood Countess has been the subject of a number of films, often depicted as a true vampire and immortal being. These movies range from very bad to very good. In order of release, they include: *I Vampiri* (1959), *The Blood Countess* (1970), *Daughters Of Darkness* (1971), *The Legend Of Blood Castle* (1972), *The Devil's Wedding Night* (1973), *Three Immortal Women* (1974), *Mama Dracula* (1979), and *The Mysterious Death Of Nina Chereau* (1988).

Archival artwork.

VAMPIRES OF ICELAND

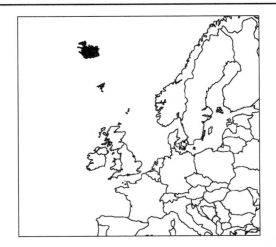

ALFEMOE

See Alp (Vampires Of Germany, p. 201).

DEARG-DUL

See Vampires Of Ireland (p. 279).

DRAUGR

The Draugr are strange Norse vampires (also found in Norway) that live in the graves of dead Vikings, sometimes inhabiting the Vikings'

The Draugr. Sculpture by Robert Patrick O'Brien.

bodies and reanimating them. As Vikings are often buried along with stores of great wealth, the Draugr will jealously guard its horde, attacking and killing anyone who tries to take so much as a silver penny.

Sometimes the Draugr will venture out of its grave in the dead of night—when it thinks it safe to leave its treasure unguarded for a short time—and attack sleeping humans. The Draugr's attack is terrible and it leaves behind much death and destruction, tearing its victims apart and feeding on their blood and flesh. The Draugr will then hurry home to check on its treasure.

Some legends suggest that the Draugr has the power to control the weather, and will call fogs and storms to shroud the region so that it can safely leave its cairn and go hunting. Other tales say that the Draugr is a shapeshifter and can become a wolf or hunting bird at will.

The Draugr has little trouble defending its treasure since it possesses tremendous supernatural strength and is immune to weapons. Only a true hero will dare to engage the Draugr in single combat (either to steal the treasure or, more commonly, to free a village of this creature).

Monolithic burial chamber. Used with permission, (c) Andy Burnham.

The monster can only be overcome with wrestling alone: bare hands and a noble heart are the only weapons that can defeat this monster.

HAUGBUI

The Haugbui (translated as "mound dweller") was another form of the undead in Norse mythology of Iceland and Norway. Similar to the Draugr, the Haugbui was an animated corpse. However, the Haugbui rarely strayed from its burial mound (or "barrow"), staying to guard its treasures. Grave robbers had to be wary of Haugbui residing in the burial plots that they targeted. Haugbui would fight viciously, wrestling, clawing and biting. It was also said that the Haugbui could use trollskap, a form of black magic.

Having a Haugbui dwell within a burial mound on its family's property was believed to be beneficial, as the Haugbui would look after its property and, consequently, its family. But the Haugbui could be temperamental, becoming upset at children playing nearby or animals grazing near its barrow and attacking them.

VAMPIRES OF INDIA

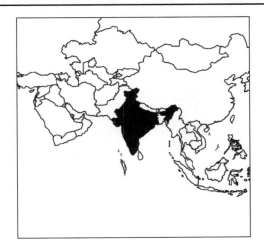

BAITAL

India has more vampire legends than nearly any country on earth. Some are steeped in its ancient religions and some dwell only in regional folktales.

One of the most well known Indian vampires is the creature called the Baital. This strange monster is half-man, half-bat and stands about four feet tall. It is written about in the *Baital-Pachisi*, or *Twenty-five Tales Of A Baital*, an ancient Hindu text written in Sanskrit. The *Baital-Pachisi* tells of this evil vampire, or evil spirit, which possesses and reanimates dead bodies and served as inspiration for one of the *Thousand And One Nights*. It also inspired the "Golden Ass" of Apuleius, as well as Boccacio's "Decamerone."

The *Baital-Pachisi* tells of how King Vikram (the Hindu equivalent of Britain's King Arthur) promised a Jogi (a magician, also known as a Yogi) that he would bring the Jogi one of the Baital. King Vikram found a Baital hanging from a tree, and much of the story relates the many troubles the king and his son had in capturing the vampire and bringing it to the Jogi. Many of King Vikram's adventures are humorous, but the story also has serious aspects in that it is meant to convey important information about Hindu culture and honor.

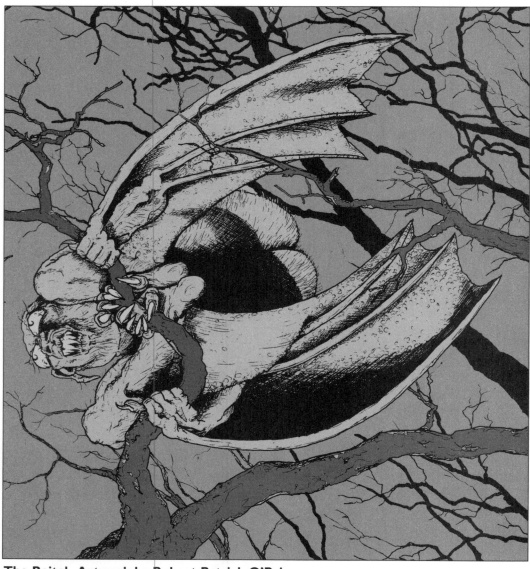

The Baital. Artwork by Robert Patrick O'Brien.

The story also relates that Hindu yogis are able to lapse into such a deep meditative state that they appear dead—kind of a self-induced catalepsy. Some even make arrangements for their followers to bury them alive for weeks at a time and then dig them up, just to demonstrate their powers.

BHUTA (also Bhuts, Bhut or Vetala)

In many cultures, those who are not physically "normal" are feared or shunned. Often it is held that deformity, illness, or mental instability is a sign of demonic possession. In the case of the Bhuta of India, it is popularly believed that any person who is disabled, has birth defects, is insane, or is suicidal is fated to become a vampire after their death. Grim punishment for a life lived in pain and torment.

The Bhuta haunts graveyards, ruins, cremation sites, and desert wastelands. It often appears in the form of a ghostly apparition or will-o'-the-wisp. The Bhuta are also shapeshifters and can take the form of owls, bats, or other night-flying creatures.

The Bhuta are bringers of sickness and plague, but that is not their preferred method of killing; they are also ghouls that feed on the intestines and excrement of the recently buried. They have also been known to possess living people and use these borrowed host bodies to attack newly fed infants, in an attempt to get the milk the babies have just drunk.

Like many of the demons of India, there are some who worship the Bhuta. These devotees erect *bhandara*, or small shrines, which are used both as a place of worship and also as a sanctuary where the vampires can dwell in safety. The bhandara are built on poles or stilts or other forms of elevation so that the Bhuta does not touch the ground, the earth being sacred and therefore denied to the unholy demons. Sometimes a bhandara is constructed to placate a vampire, rather than as a service to the creature.

CATALEPSY

Catalepsy is a frightening condition characterized by sudden loss of consciousness and a fierce rigidity of muscles that essentially freezes the person's limbs in whatever position they were in at the moment the seizure occurred. However, the limbs can be moved in much the same way as an articulated doll's, and will remain in any new pose.

Cataleptic seizures can last for minutes, hours, or even days. Catalepsy is often a symptom of some other clinical syndrome, most frequently in schizophrenia, epilepsy, and hysteria.

Symptoms include the complete loss of voluntary motion, rigidity of the muscles, and a decreased sensitivity to pain and heat. Someone suffering from catalepsy can may be able to see and hear, but cannot move. Breathing, pulse, and other regulatory functions slow down to the extent that, to an untrained eye (such as a villager in the Middle Ages), it would seem as though they were dead.

This condition can last from minutes to days. Many people have been buried alive as a result of this condition, which may account for some reported cases of misdiagnosed vampirism. When the coffin of such a victim was opened, there would be clear evidence that the "corpse" had awakened post-burial. Signs of extreme agitation were often present, and even signs that the buried person had torn at his own skin and clothes and even tried to feed on himself.

It is a rather horrible thought to consider how many cases of catalepsy went undiagnosed in the days before modern medicine reached rural villages. Even now there are remote spots on earth where science has yet to shed light on the darkness of superstition.

In the chancel of St. Giles, Cripplegate, there is a carving in memory of Constance Whitney. Ms. Whitney was buried alive, her cataleptic state mistaken for death. This horrible mistake was discovered when the church sexton opened the coffin to steal the "corpse's" jewelry. The carving shows her rising from her coffin.

BRAHMAPARUSH (also Brahmaparusha)

One of the more ferocious Indian vampires is the Brahmaparush, a creature that not only attacks and kills for blood, but goes as far as to consume its prey completely.

The Brahmaparush takes particular delight in its own rituals of slaughter. First it will punch a hole in its victim's skull, and will drink every drop of blood. Then it will suck out the entire brain. Next it rends the body limb from limb, devouring it entirely, bones and all. Saved for last are the intestines, which the Brahmaparush winds around itself as it dances in the moonlight. Often it will wear the circled intestines like a turban, and that is how it is depicted in ancient paintings.

Wall painting of the Brahmaparush. Artwork by Michael Katz.

Killing a Brahmaparush is difficult and often requires a strong warrior who has not sinned (even a little) for ninety days, has prepared himself with a fast, and has visited nine temples. Once the warrior has been purified, he takes a sword that has been blessed and passed nine times through incense smoke, then goes hunting for the creature. Even then the Brahmaparush may still triumph, but at least these rituals give the warrior an edge.

CHEDIPE

In Indian folklore there are a number of different types of vampire prostitutes. The Chedipe is a perfect example because the name even means "prostitute." In folklore and various old paintings, the Chedipe is depicted as a vulgar prostitute, riding a huge male tiger under a moonlit sky.

This powerful female vampire will cast a spell over an entire household and then enter while all are in a trance. There it will select a strong male to be the victim and suck his blood through his toes. Sometimes the Chedipe will sexually attack the man while he sleeps, polluting the sanctity of the household. It delights her to destroy a family's love, trust, and marital purity, because the Chedipe also feeds on sorrow and misery.

The vampire's bite is rarely fatal, but the Chedipe may return again and again, taking more blood before the body can replenish what has previously been stolen. The victim soon weakens and begins to waste away, and if he does not seek treatment he will die.

The surest way to defeat a Chedipe is to sanctify the house with incense and holy icons. The incense must be renewed every hour, meaning someone stay awake all night. The presence of an awake person maintaining the rites of religious protection will frighten off the Chedipe, but she will search out another household in the vicinity and begin the destruction of another family.

CHORDEWA

See Vampires Of Bengal (p. 99).

CHUREL

Pregnant Indian women who die during the festival of *Divali* (the Hindu Festival of Light) are in danger of returning as blood sucking Revenants called Churel. These Churel are hideous vampires with lolling black tongues, thick coarse lips caked with rouge, wild and tangled hair, heavy sagging breasts, and feet that are twisted around backwards.

Because they have died so unfairly—carrying new life—they are bitter and vengeful and return to take out their resentment on the living. The Churel attack young families, handsome men, and anything else which would remind them of what they have lost. But their greatest enmity is directed toward their relatives, whom they blame for allowing them to die when their need for care was greatest.

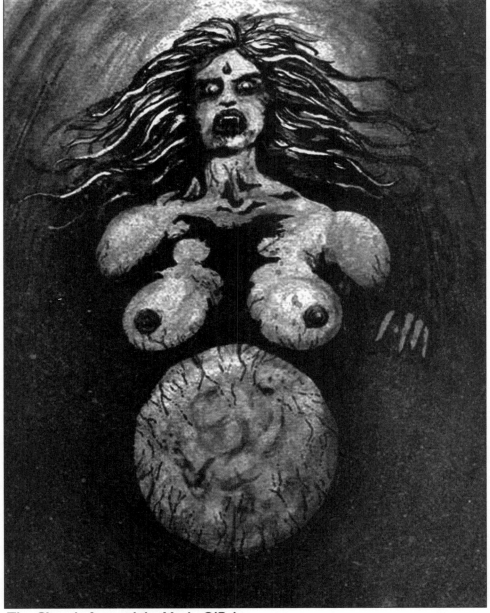

The Churel. Artwork by Marie O'Brien.

The best way to defeat a Churel is to prevent its creation, either by attending a pregnant woman and providing the best possible care; or by burying her with absolute attention to every detail of the sacred burial rites, and celebrating her life in song and prayer.

If a Churel comes into existence, only a Hindu Pundit (priest) can drive it out using prayer and incense and offerings. But this is difficult, and often the Churel is driven away for a time, only to return again months or years later.

THE PUNDIT

A Hindu Pundit is a priest who carries out all religious ceremonies as prescribed in the sacred texts of the religion he follows.

On every auspicious occasion, it is the Pundit's moral responsibility to invoke the mighty spirits to bless the ceremonial function, be it a marriage, entering a newly built house, the opening ceremony of a shop or a factory, or the driving away of an evil sprit.

Pundits play a very important role in community activities. No individual household can manage without one. On the death of an elder in the family, only a Pundit knows all the rituals and requisite procedures required by the religious manuals.

GAYAL (also called Ut)

Improper burial rites have always been dangerous. The dead who are not properly interred do not lie quiet, as with the case of the Gayal. This Indian ghost-vampire is an angry male spirit that cannot rest because the burial rites have not been properly adhered to. It rises to take its anger out on the members of its family in revenge for their religious negligence.

A spiteful vampire, the Gayal will also vent its wrath on other families by killing their sons, preferably while they sleep.

JIGARKHWAR

The Jigarkhwar is a vampire-sorceress from the Sind region of south-west India. She has a piercing and lethal stare that will instantly transfix her prey. Then the Jigarkhwar mystically removes the hapless victim's liver, leaving him alive for the moment. Once she is back in her lair, the Jigarkhwar takes a pomegranate seed, specially prepared in advance with magic spells, and throws in onto her cooking fire. In the heat of the fire the seed expands and is quickly removed from the flames. The seed is allowed to cool before it is eaten by the Jigarkhwar. Only after the vampire has eaten the seed will her prey finally die. Once she has performed this ritual, the Jigarkhwar sits down to a more satisfying meal of human liver.

There is some hope for the Jigarkhwar's victim. Despite his missing liver, he cannot die until the magical pomegranate seed has been cooked and eaten. If some brave soul were to discover the Jigarkhwar's lair, find her cache of ensorcelled seeds and steal them, he could then get the victim to swallow one of the seeds. Once swallowed, the pomegranate seed magically transforms into a new and healthy liver.

A variation on this legend suggests that the Jigarkhwar uses magic to make her victim's liver turn into a pomegranate seed while still in his body. He then vomits up the seed, and she in turn steals it, cooks it, and eats it.

In either case, the method of saving the victim is the same. A successful rescue has a second benefit: identifying the Jigarkhwar and uncovering her hiding place. All that remains now is to brand the creature on both sides of her head, fill her eyes with salt, and then imprison the monster in an underground chamber for forty days. Of course, this is a lot easier said than done, and usually requires a team of highly trained and very courageous vampire slayers. But folktales tell of it being accomplished. Once this process has been completed the Jigarkhwar becomes human. A person cured of being a Jigarkhwar then has the power to detect her own kind and is often used to assist vampire slayers.

THE POMEGRANATE

The pomegranate, often called the "jewel of winter," is about the size of an orange or an apple and has a tough dark red or brownish rind. Its seeds and juicy translucent scarlet red pulp are edible, although only the pulp has any flavor. Encased within a bitter-tasting, white, spongy, inedible membrane, the seeds can be gently pried out and eaten.

The pomegranate is one of the earliest cultivated fruits. Historical evidence suggests that man first began planting pomegranate trees sometime between 4000 B.C.E and 3000 B.C.E. In ancient Egypt, pomegranates adorned the treasures placed inside King Tutankhamen's tomb, insuring safe passage and rebirth.

Many Biblical scholars now suggest that it was a pomegranate, not an apple, that was depicted in the biblical Garden of Eden. This theory is given further support throughout ancient and medieval times. In the mythical tale of the unicorn, pomegranate seeds "bleeding" from its horn symbolized the suffering of Christ. The pomegranate tree to which the unicorn was bound represented eternal life. This theme also occurs in the Greek myth of Persephone, when Hades abducts the beautiful daughter of Zeus and Demeter and carries her to the Underworld. Hades tempts her with the luscious fruit, and once Persephone eats its seeds she becomes his eternal queen, only able to return above ground during springtime.

With these ties to immortality, it is not so strange that the Indian Jigarkhwar vampire requires them to sustain her eternal existence.

Of course, modern science also treasures the pomegranate for its health benefits, in particular its disease-fighting antioxidant potential. Recent medical studies indicate that pomegranate juice may contain almost three times as much antioxidant ability as similar quantities of green tea or red wine. It also provides a substantial amount of potassium, is high in fiber, and contains vitamin C and niacin. It has been used for centuries in the folk medicine of the Middle East, India, and Iran to treat inflammation, sore throats, and rheumatism.

KALI

The most dreaded of all Indian vampires is the blood drinking goddess, Kali. This bloody immortal appears during times of violent warfare, hovering above the scenes of the greatest slaughter.

Kali is almost always described as having a terrible, frightening appearance. She is black or dark, usually naked, and has long, disheveled hair. She adorns herself with a girdle made from severed arms, wears a necklace of freshly cut heads, children's corpses as earrings, and serpents as bracelets. She has long, sharp fangs, is depicted as having claw-like hands with long nails, and is often said to have blood smeared on her lips.

Her favorite haunts heighten her fearsome nature. In most paintings she is usually shown on the battlefield as a furious combatant who gets drunk on her victim's hot blood. She is also depicted on a cremation ground, sitting on a corpse, surrounded by jackals and goblins.

Kali is a malevolent representation of the great Hindu goddess Maha Devi. In this form, she is the Dark Goddess bringing widespread death and destruction. Kali means *black* but it is also used as the word for *time*.

Many texts and contexts treat Kali as an independent deity, for the most part not associated with any male deity. When she is associated with a god it is almost always Lord Shiva, taking the role of his consort, wife, or associate. A mischievous goddess by nature, Kali's actions seem aimed at enticing Shiva to take part in dangerous, destructive behavior that threatens the stability of the cosmos.

Kali embodies the destructive characteristics of power and energy. It is believed that in order to appease her, blood sacrifices must be offered. Some theories suggest that Kali emerged as an explanation for the outbreak of plagues in India, which would certainly be in keeping with the legends of other vampires who are known to be plague carriers.

Unlike most vampires, Kali can also be a powerful force for good. She will protect her worshipers, visiting on their oppressors a terrible vengeance.

Kali is still worshiped today. The Kaligat temple in the Indian city of Calcutta (the name of the city itself is an anglicized version of the word *Kaligat*) is dedicated to the goddess Kali. She requires blood sacrifices daily to satisfy her thirst, so every morning goats are sacrificed on its altar.

Other vampire gods include the Aztec Xipe Totec, the blood drinking god Yama from Nepal, and the Fifty-Eight Wrathful Deities of Tibet. Blood-drinking Demigods include the Empusae, Lamiai, and Keres of ancient Greece. And of course, there is Lilith, Adam's first wife and the mother of all vampires according to Hebraic lore.

Kali. Artwork by Robert Patrick O'Brien.

VIKRAM AND THE VAMPIRE

In Sir Richard Burton's translation of the classic Indian folk tale, *Vikram And The Vampire*, Kali is described as follows:

> "There stood Smashana-Kali, the Goddess, in her most horrible form. She was a naked and a very black woman, with half severed head, partly cut and partly painted, resting on her shoulder; and her tongue lolled out from her wide yawning mouth; her eyes were red like those of a drunkard; and her eyebrows were of the same color; her thick coarse hair hung like a mantle to her knees."

Kali herself tells of her powers and destructive desires in this Hindu poem (whose authorship is lost to time):

I am the dance of death that is
Behind all life
The ultimate horror
The ultimate ecstasy
I am existence
I am the dance of destruction that
Will end this world
The timeless void
The formless devouring mouth
I am rebirth
Let me dance you to death
Let me dance you to life
Will you walk through your fears to dance with me?
Will you let me cut off your head
And drink your blood?
Then will you cut off mine?
Will you face all the horror
All the pain
All the sorrow
and say "yes?"
I am all that you dread
All that terrifies
I am your fear
Will you meet me?

HINDU DEATH RITUAL

Every culture around the world has its own very specific burial customs. Since death is such an overwhelming mystery, linking the mortal world with unknown planes of existence, care is given to avoid an affront to the deceased or an invitation for some otherworldly entity to enter the now vacant corpse. Improper burial rites are tied to the creation of many species of vampires. For this and other reasons, burial procedures are laid down very precisely and followed to the letter for fear of some dreadful repercussion.

The ancient scripture of Garuda Purana describes the sacred rituals that will help a soul attain eternal peace. The most important burial ritual is that of Pinda Dhana (the gift of the Pinda). A Pinda is a funeral cake made of cooked rice or rice flour. The spirit of the dead relative (called a Pret) is invoked into the Pinda. It is believed that the Pret is around for ten days, so five Pindas are given on the day of death and then one each is given for the next nine days.

The deceased's family then goes to Haridwar, which means Gate of God and is supposed to have been the place where the great god Shiva released the Ganges River to Earth. It has been one of India's most sacred places of pilgrimage since time immemorial. The deceased's mortal remains are immersed in the holy Ganges, and Pindas are given to the deceased over the course of a number of days.

Photo of Hindu burial ritual. Used with permission, (c) 2003 by University of Pennsylvania.

Lord Shiva.

MASAN (also known as MASAND)

One of the more tragic (yet horrifying) Hindu vampires of India is the Masan. This blood drinker is the ghost of a child who, usually due to improper burial rituals, has not passed on to the afterlife or a new incarnation. The ghost becomes trapped on earth as an immortal monster, naturally filled with rage at being damned. It seeks to inflict as much vengeful harm as it can on the living.

Wicked and spiteful in its unholy afterlife, the Masan delights in torture and murder. Because it died as a child, it vents its fury on the world by preying on living children. The Masan takes human form, often that of a child, though not always the child it was before it died. It befriends other children and lures them into secluded spots where it then attacks and kills them, feeding on their blood.

The Masan has vast magical powers and is known for casting hypnotic spells or laying curses. It is so vile and peevish that it will even curse a child that chances to walk in its shadow.

One way the Masan selects its prey is to loiter on a public street and follow any woman whose gown happens to drag across its shadow. Once it reaches her home, the creature will prey upon any children therein, either attacking them as soon as the mother is not watching, or luring them outside to "play" and murdering them in quiet.

The predatory habits of the female Masan are somewhat different. She sleeps by day in the cold ashes of a funeral pyre and rises at night to attack unwary travelers passing by the burial grounds. Completely covered in black ashes from the funeral pyre, the Masani blends in with the night. She will attack anyone—man, woman, child, even livestock.

PISACHA

These hideous flesh-eating ghouls are similar to the Yatu-Dhana (*see* entry later in this chapter), in that both of them eat the flesh left behind when the fierce Rakshasa (*see* entry next page) slaughters a victim. Unlike the Yatu-Dhana, who cook the flesh they scavenge, the Pisachas eat raw flesh.

These monsters are ghostlike beings who rise from the grave to feast on the newly dead. Despite their horrible nature, they are pitiable creatures. They are trapped in a hell between life and true death, so they are in deep spiritual torment at all times.

The creatures can be killed by swords, but their greatest fear is fire. They cannot abide even a small torch, and can be easily driven off by someone wielding a brand. There are also a number of spells and charms that keep them at bay; these should be utilized following any burial because the Pisachas are not above digging up a freshly buried corpse to make a dreadful meal. To properly dispel them, however, one should have a holy man perform proper burial rites. If the holy man can state the Pisacha's true human name during the ceremony, the creature's link to the material world will be severed and it can move on to its next (and much cleaner) incarnation.

Since these creatures live in a ghost world, they are not subject to the normal laws of time and space, and this gives them great knowledge of the past, present and future. They are often captured by sorcerers and enslaved, and must then reveal any secrets they possess.

The Pisachas are also linked to the spread of disease throughout India, hardly surprising since their diet consists of raw and spoiling flesh.

PRET

In general terms, a Pret is a person's ghost that lingers for ten days following death. Normally a spirit passes on peacefully after certain post-mortem rituals are performed by the deceased's family, but in certain unfortunate circumstances the Pret can linger and even become pernicious.

One of India's more tragic and heartbreaking vampire legends concerns the Pret of a stillborn child, or one who was born deformed and later died as a result of the birth defects. This Pret is doomed to wander the earth for one full year following its burial. A tiny creature, only the size of a man's thumb, the Pret is generally harmless as long as it is left alone and given occasional food offerings. But crossed, cornered, or denied, it becomes violent and will attack the human offender for blood.

An angry Pret will come back time and again to drain its victim's blood, and can eventually weaken a person to the point of death. An angry Pret can also carry disease.

Pret is the masculine term for this Revenant; Paret and Pretni are both used for the females of this tragic and accursed species.

RAKSHASA

One of the most well known vampiric creatures from India is the dreaded and powerful Rakshasa. They often appear as beautiful and seductive women, and use their unnatural sexual charms to lure men to their deaths. But the Rakshasa's appetites are not confined to male flesh; they will also prey on pregnant women and even babies, slaughtering them and drinking their blood.

These creatures are also shapeshifters, and select whatever appearance —human, demon, or animal—will help deceive their prey. Sometimes a Rakshasa will appear as an aggregate of various kinds of beasts, sprouting teeth and claws, wings, and slitted eyes all at once. In more recent centuries, beliefs in the Rakshasa suggest that the creatures have become wandering flesh eating and blood drinking versions of elves, with batlike fangs.

The Hindus believe that the Rakshasa were originally created by Brahma (the Supreme Deity) to protect the sea from those who

The Rakshasa. Used with permission, (c) 2003 by Alberto Moreno.

desired to steal the elixir of immortality from it. While the Rakshasa were servants of Brahma, they lived in Sri Lanka (Ceylon) and were ruled by King Rawana. As Hindu culture and religion changed, the Rakshasa became known less as celestial protectors in the service of a god or king, and more as purely demonic creatures who killed to suit their own desires and hungers.

The legends of the Rakshasa have undergone great change over the years, and in later centuries it has been more popularly believed that a Rakshasa is created if a child is forced to eat human brains. A curse is another way of bringing this monster into being.

In whatever form they appear, the Rakshasa have haunted the dreams and troubled the waking thoughts of Hindus for many centuries. Accounts of their ghastly attacks can be found in the *Vedas*, the sacred teachings of India.

Though the Rakshasa are clever and very powerful, they can be defeated and destroyed. A good hearty torching will destroy them as easily as it does most other species of vampire around the world. They are among the very few vampires against whom sunlight is an effective weapon, although forcing the creature out into the light of day is another (and far more difficult) matter. A last resort is exorcism, but the Rakshasa has to be identified first and the exorcist needs to be highly trained and very brave. Improper rites of exorcism lead to certain bloody demise for all parties involved.

THE RAKSHASA IN POPULAR FICTION

An episode of the television series *Kolchak: The Night Stalker* featured the Rakshasa as a flesh eating demon from Hindu legend that would take the form of a person trusted by the victim, then lure the victim into its clutches and eat them. The episode (titled "Horror In The Heights") first aired in 1974.

The novel *The Tomb* by F. Paul Wilson pits the hero nicknamed Repairman Jack against Rakshasas (called Rakoshi in the book) under the control of an Indian sorcerer. Though a work of fiction, *The Tomb* is a very powerful image of the savagery of these ancient monsters.

YATU-DHANA (also spelled Yatudhana, Hatu-Dhana)

The Rakshasa has a sordid spiritual connection with a breed of sorcerers called the Yatu-Dhana. These dwarfish wizards are impish, intelligent, cowardly, and very dangerous. Among their vast collection of unsavory and unnatural practices, they eat the grisly leavings of the Rakshasas, roasting flesh and organs on special fires and feasting with great relish.

The Yatu-Dhana worship the fierce Rakshasa and are sometimes thought to be a lesser species of those monsters. Unlike the Rakshasa, however, a human can become a Yatu-Dhana.

Anyone who acts out of character, especially by displaying an unwholesome lust (for flesh, power, whatever) could be suspected of being a Yatu-Dhana in disguise. Because suspicion used to be very high, an oath came into common usage when a person wanted to establish his humanity, generosity, or other virtuous qualities: "May I die today, if I am a Yatu-Dhana."

Yatu-Dhana. Artwork by Shane MacDougall.

VAMPIRES OF IRELAND

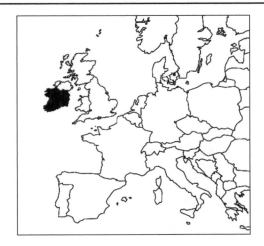

DEARG-DUL (also known as Dearg-Due)

Ireland, home of many ghost tales and legends of faerie folk, is also home to the deadly Dearg-Dul. This is an ancient vampire whose name means "red blood sucker" and whose bloody crimes date back to druidic times.

Unlike other Revenants, the Dearg-Dul do not appear as moldering corpses. In fact, stories tell of male and female Dearg-Dul appearing as beautiful and sexually appealing specters that lure their victims to trysting places—and then kill them.

The druids—wise in the ways of the supernatural world—have fought these creatures for a thousand years and have devised ways of stopping them. Once the grave of a suspected Dearg-Dul is identified, the druids erect a heavy cairn of stones over it. Even with their unnatural strength, the Dearg-Dul cannot dislodge thousands of pounds of rock. Trapped in their graves, the vampires will eventually degenerate into dust.

The legends of the Dearg-Dul mingle with those of the Icelandic vampire, the Dearg-Due. It is likely that the creature either migrated to Ireland along with the Norse invaders, or went to Iceland and other countries with them. The creature has also spread to the Isle of Man, the Orkney Isles, and other places around the United Kingdom, moving outward like a bloodthirsty plague.

LEANHAUN-SIDHE (also called Lianhaun Shee)

Countless times the undead have used beauty and seduction to entice and trap their human prey. Faerie folk often use the same ploy, and to

the same end. Though not strictly a vampire, the Leanhaun-Sidhe kills in much the same way as the Dearg-Dul.

The Leanhaun-Sidhe appears as a lovely faerie woman—beautiful and ethereal—and lures willing men to her with her looks, song and laughter, and promises of pleasures beyond human understanding. But once alone with her prey, she draws away his life force, leaving him cold and dead.

In some tales the Leanhaun-Sidhe keeps her prey alive for a time, striking a bargain with him that she will become his Muse in exchange for his life essence (or, as some would have it, his immortal soul). In such cases the victim has time to recognize his folly and attempt to escape, but the only defense against this doom is for the poor fellow to find another man to be the creature's slave in death. This is a difficult choice because it is tantamount to murder.

Leanhaun-Sidhe. Artwork by Marie O'Brien.

LEANHAUN-SIDHE IN POETRY

The poem "La Belle Dame Sans Merci" by John Keats tells of a Leanhaun-Sidhe:

LA BELLE DAME

O what can ail thee, knight at arms,
Alone and palely loitering?
The sedge is wither'd from the lake,
And no birds sing.

O what can ail thee, knight at arms,
So haggard and so woe-begone?
The squirrel's granary is full,
And the harvest's done.

I see a lily on thy brow
With anguish moist and fever dew,
And on thy cheeks a fading rose
Fast withereth too.

I met a lady in the meads
Full beautiful, a faerie's child;
Her hair was long, her foot was light,
And her eyes were wild.

I made a garland for her head,
And bracelets too, and fragrant zone;
She look'd at me as she did love,
And made sweet moan.

I set her on my pacing steed,
And nothing else saw all day long,
For sidelong would she bend, and sing
A faerie's song.

She found me roots of relish sweet,
And honey wild, and manna dew,
And sure in language strange she said-
I love thee true.

She took me to her elfin grot,
And there she wept, and sigh'd full sore,
And there I shut her wild wild eyes
With kisses four.

And there she lulled me asleep,
And there I dream'd-Ah! woe betide!
The latest dream I ever dream'd
On the cold hill's side.

I saw pale kings, and princes too,
Pale warriors, death-pale were they all;
They cried-"La belle dame sans merci
Hath thee in thrall!"

I saw their starv'd lips in the gloam
With horrid warning gaped wide,
And I awoke, and found me here
On the cold hill's side.

And this is why I sojourn here,
Alone and palely loitering,
Though the sedge is wither'd from the lake,
And no birds sing.

VAMPIRES OF THE ISLE OF MAN

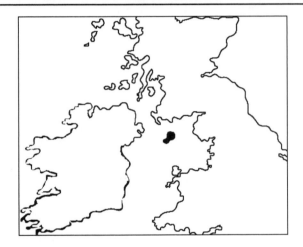

DEARG-DUE

On the Isle of Man, the Irish legends of the Leanhaun-Sidhe and the Dearg-Dul have become blended into a single creature, the Dearg-Due. Like her Irish cousins, the Dearg-Due is a beautiful female vampire faerie. She makes an unholy pact with a mortal man to provide him with artistic inspiration in exchange for his "love." But to the Dearg-Due "love" means life essence. The Dearg-Due holds her mate captive in her kingdom beneath the waves of the Irish Sea, off the eastern tip of Ireland. She drains her lover's life essence over a period of time, until he is dead

The Dearg-Due does also take blood from her victims, but not to drink. Rather she drains it off and boils it in a crimson cauldron in which she brews her special magics.

The ancient Celtic Crone Goddesses were those who presided over the great cauldron of life, death, and rebirth. They are very similar to the Dearg-Due, so they may have been the source of the Dearg-Due legend.

To defeat the Dearg-Due, a potential victim has to invoke the protection of Manann, the great god of the sea. His presence alone will overthrow her power.

Dearg Due. Used with permission, (c) 2003 by Krista McLean.

VAMPIRES OF ISRAEL

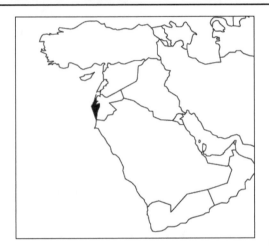

ALUKA (also ALUGA)

One of the most ancient blood drinkers is the demonic "king of the vampires" known as the Aluka. The name itself has the same root origin as the Algul of Arabia, and means "horse leech." The Latin translation of Aluka is "sanguisuga," which means "blood sucker." The reference is not to some mere parasitic insect but rather a demon of great power with an unquenchable thirst for blood.

The term "horse leech" first appears in Proverbs 30:15. The reference is unclear, but the comment does seem to refer to some kind of vampiric creature: "The horse-leech had three dearly-beloved daughters; and these three did not satisfy her; and the fourth was not contented so as to say, Enough."

ESTRIE

One of the most fearsome (and feared) vampires in Hebrew folklore is the Estrie. These are a kind of female witch-vampire that has the sole purpose of attacking humans for blood. An Estrie will attack any person at will, but favors the blood of children above all.

The Estrie are shapeshifters, capable of adopting various forms to deceive their prey. When an Estrie takes to the night air to fly above villages and farms it will revert back to its horrific demonic shape.

Killing an Estrie does not require magical weapons; ordinary swords and spears will work, and fire is always useful. Should a human injure an Estrie, the creature will die unless it somehow contrives to steal some salt and bread from the house of its enemy. Consuming these things will restore the Estrie to health, and by the next evening it will be able to hunt again.

LILITH

Vampires have been part of Jewish history since the Creation. According to the various interpretations of the Hebrew Bible, and from such sacred writings as the *Talmud* (the Hebrew sacred writings on holy matters), Lilith is often regarded as the mother of all vampires. One school of thought is that Lilith is the translation into Hebrew culture of the Lilitu of ancient Sumer and Babylon. (*See* Vampires of Ancient Babylon, p. 91.)

According to the *Talmud*, Lilith was created to be Adam's first wife. But she had such an evil spirit that she left Adam to reside in the abode of demons.

Another ancient story tells that God had originally created Adam and Lilith as twins joined together at the back. Lilith wanted complete equality with Adam but was denied, so she fled from him in anger. Legend has it that she went to the abode of demons and there mated with evil creatures and gave birth to thousands of demons.

There is a Muslim legend that after leaving Adam, Lilith slept with Satan. Their unholy union was the demonic Djinn.

Yet another variation of this tale has it that Adam married Lilith because he was tired of having sex only with animals, a common

Middle-Eastern herdsmen practice even though the Old Testament declared it a sin (Deuteronomy 27:21). Adam tried to establish sexual dominance over Lilith by making her lie beneath him during sex. Lilith did not accept this as her lot, and wanted to be the one on top. This resulted in the first divorce due to irreconcilable differences in history. Lilith left and went to live by the Red Sea, where she became the lover of demons and began producing children at the rate of one hundred per day.

The legend goes on to say that Adam appealed to God, who sent three angels, Sansanvi, Sanvi, and Semangelaf, to fetch Lilith back to Eden. Lilith cursed the angels and refused to go. The angels warned her that God would take these demon children away from her unless she returned to Adam and submitted to his will. Lilith refused and was punished by God, and her children were scattered across the world and

Used with permission, (c) Lilian Broca 2003.

cast into demon dimensions. Adam was then placated by the creation of Eve, who was far more docile.

None of the Lilith tales appear in the canonical Bible, but the legends have been passed down through the millennia. Though openly refuted by Hebraic scholars, even as late as the Middle Ages there were Jews wearing amulets to ward off the Lilim—the vampiric children of Lilith.

Many of the legends of the Lilim are very similar to those of the Succubi (*See* Vampires of Various Cultures, p. 515). The Greek Lamiae and Empusae are interpretations of the legend of the Lilim.

Though the Lilim act more like Succubi, Lilith herself is said to favor the blood of children, perhaps as revenge for God having scattered her own offspring. Folktales say that Lilith enjoys plaguing children as well as women in childbirth, and has a particular enmity toward male children. Those same folktales insist that the three Angels who came to her at the Red Sea forced her to swear an unbreakable oath that she would not harm any mother or child who wore an amulet bearing the name or image of one of the Angels. Magic circles of protection are sometimes drawn around a male baby's crib, inscribed with the name of one of the angels, or sometimes Adam's name.

The *Zohar*, the principal text of the Jewish mystical work known as the *Kabbalah*, suggests that Lilith's unholy powers are at their height during the waning of the moon.

To the ancient Canaanites, Lilith was known as Baalat, the "Divine Lady." On a tablet from Ur, circa 2000 B.C., she was called Lillake.

(*See* Vampires Of Assyria, p. 75, and Vampires Of Ancient Babylon, p. 91, for more on alternate origins of Lilith.)

MOTETZDAM

A generic Hebrew word for "bloodsucker," used to describe any species of vampire.

LILITH (For a Picture)

by Dante Gabriel Rossetti

Of Adam's first wife, Lilith, it is told
(The witch he loved before the gift of Eve,)
That, ere the snake's, her sweet tongue could deceive,
And her enchanted hair was the first gold.
And still she sits, young while the earth is old,
And, subtly of herself contemplative,
Draws men to watch the bright net she can weave,
Till heart and body and life are in its hold.

The rose and poppy are her flowers; for where
Is he not found, O Lilith, whom shed scent
And soft-shed kisses and soft sleep shall snare?
Lo! as that youth's eyes burned at thine, so went
Thy spell through him, and left his straight neck bent,
And round his heart one strangling golden hair.

Lilith Visiting Adam. Used with permission, (c) Lilian Broca 2003.

STRIGA

The Striga was another ancient Hebrew witch-vampire, similar to the Estrie. It was able to transform into a large black crow and attacked the unwary, pecking at them to tear their flesh, then hastily drinking their blood.

The creature is apparently a version or sub-species of the vampire that was called the Strix in ancient Rome and the Striges in Greece. In Albanian it is spelled *Shtriga* and in Romanian, as in Hebrew, it is *Striga*. The name Striges is a variation on the Italian word *Strega*, which means "witch." In Italy, especially during the Middle Ages, it was widely believed that witches could shapeshift into a variety of birds, and that in these transformed shapes they fed on the blood of infants.

The Roman writer Publius Ovidius Naso, better known as Ovid (author of *The Metamorphoses*) wrote in his book, *Fasti*, that the Striges used their beaks to tear wounds in the chests of infants and then feasted on the blood that welled from the gashes. These bird-like vampires would return night after night to feed on the same child until the infant's parents prayed to the demi-goddess Crane for intercession. Crane would appear and go through the entire house, casting potent spells and performing rituals to prevent the Striges from returning. Her final protective act would be to place a branch of white thorn (a species of hawthorn which is used throughout Europe as a weapon against vampires) in the window of the infant's room. Thereafter the Striges could not enter.

Charms can be used to keep the Striga away, such as this early sixteenth century incantation:

> *Black Striga, black and black*
> *Blood shall eat and blood shall drink*
> *Like an ox she shall bellow*
> *Like a bear she shall growl*
> *Like a wolf she shall crush.*

Striga is also the name of an herb commonly called Witchweed. It is a flowering parasitic plant that has a devastating effect on crop production wherever it springs up. Species of striga are able to attack crops, including all of the important tropical cereals (maize, sorghum, pearl millet, finger millet, upland rice, and sugar cane) and many grasses grown for fodder.

VAMPIRES OF ITALY

BENANDANTI

Benandanti, which means "good walkers," were theriomorphs, meaning they could change readily from human to animal and back again. When preparing to fight evil, they most often took the form of a wolf. Perhaps because the change was deliberate the Benandanti were able to channel the better qualities of the natural wolf: loyalty, intelligence, and a desire to kill only in defense. The Benandanti who chose to assume wolf form adopted the nickname the "hounds of God."

The Benandanti possessed the ability to sense evil spirits--witches, evil werewolves, vampires, even ghosts--and could sometimes harness the forces of nature to combat them. In a pitched battle between a Benandanti and an evil werewolf, the Benandanti might summon fierce winds, driving rain, earthquakes, and even lightning strikes.

Some Benandanti engaged in battles only on the astral plane, entering into coma-like sleep states that allowed them to astrally project their spirits into other dimensions to seek out and combat the supernatural. They envisioned their astral forms riding into battle on strangely mutated goats, giant cats, or fire breathing horses. Their astral selves were armed with sticks from fennel, a plant that is widely held to have many wholesome curative properties. The Benandanti were most active in agricultural areas, largely because they possessed a special talent for defeating those supernatural forces that cause crop blight, plagues, and famine. The Benandanti themselves were believed to have potent healing powers as well.

These intrepid hunters lived in secret for untold centuries before coming to the attention of the Inquisition in the sixteenth century. Unfortunately the Inquisition saw them not as doers of good but as witches or werewolves themselves. Many people were executed because they were avowed (or suspected) Benandanti.

One trial had a different outcome. In 1692 an 80-year-old resident of Jurgenburg, Livonia named Theiss claimed to be a Benandanti. He told the Court that he and a band of other shapeshifters descended into Hell to fight a coven of witches that were causing famine in the area. The judges were astounded by the story of Theiss and his fellow "hounds of God," and though church law demanded that any supernatural beings be punished, they sentenced him to a mere ten lashes.

Those Benandanti who survived the Inquisition went into hiding until the latter part of the twentieth and early twenty-first centuries. The advent of New Age mentality created a more accepting climate for the Benandanti. They have become regarded as being similar to Wiccans, part of the Earth's natural healing process. Though no modern Benandanti claim to fight werewolves and vampires, they still bless crops and claim to be able to turn aside blight and plague.

Persons destined to become Benandanti were born with a caul over their face, an event that heralds supernatural qualities of many kinds in various cultures. There is one longstanding custom of the Benandanti that still lingers: mothers of children born with a caul often save that amniotic membrane. When the child grows up and accepts the task of being a Benandanti, she wears the caul in a charm around her neck.

ASTRAL PROJECTION

For thousands of years people of all cultures have been experiencing a psychic event called astral projection, also called out-of-body experiences (OBEs). These are experiences in which one's consciousness actually seems to separate from the physical body in some kind of cohesive (if invisible) form.

Photo by Jason Lukridge.

There seem to be two major kinds of Astral Projection: the intentional projection of one's spirit from the physical body, and the accidental projection caused by trauma such as a near-death experience (NDE).

Astral projection has been used (or perhaps misused) by various sorcerers and vampires over the centuries. In recent years it has come to be used as a tool for spiritual refinement and growth. Many yogic systems and similar spiritual disciplines teach astral projection as both a learning experience and a method of cleansing the spirit of the material trappings in everyday life.

Though Astral Projection has not been proven to the satisfaction of the scientific community, it has been under study for many years. The frequency of NDEs has brought many scientists to the very brink of belief. It has recently been postulated that Astral Projection may someday be explained by the emerging science of Quantum Physics, a field that is constantly revamping what have been the "accepted" laws of the universe.

STREGONI BENEFICI

Throughout the world there are several different kinds of vampire slayer, including the Dhampir of the Gypsies, the Djadadjii and Vampirdzhija of Bulgaria, the reformed vampire Jigarkhwar of India, and the Kresnik of Dalmatia. Standing proudly in that company is the Stregoni Benefici of Italy.

But unlike his slayer brethren, the Stregoni Benefici is himself (or herself) a vampire—one fighting on the side of good and a mortal enemy of all evil vampires. The term Stregoni Benefici essentially means "beneficial vampire."

There are a number of ways someone can become a Stregoni Benefici. Dying from a vampire's attack is the most common. Perhaps having died at the hands of a monster creates some kind of spiritual outrage

that cannot be satisfied until some manner of redress is sought. Many folk tales suggest that there may be beings like the Stregoni Benefici that were created by vampires all over the world, hinting that this is the reason mankind has not been overwhelmed by the undead.

Another theory regarding the creation of a Stregoni Benefici is that it is a vampire who performs great acts of contrition and is officially forgiven by the church. Though still trapped in a kind of undead limbo, the vampire is at least on the side of righteousness.

Stregoni Benefici. Artwork by Marie O'Brien.

STREGONI BENEFICI ON TELEVISION

In the TV shows *Angel* and *Buffy the Vampire Slayer*, created by writer-director Joss Whedon, there are two characters who fit the description of the Stregoni Benefici. One is the heroic Angel, as played by David Boreanaz. Angel was an old and very evil Irish vampire. He was punished by Gypsies for his monstrous deeds by being "cursed" with the return of his soul, and his humanity took over the demonic vampire spirit that had inhabited his body since his unnatural death. At first, appalled by the horror he had done, Angel went mad with despair and clung to the fringes of society. An agent of a higher power rescued him from this dissolution and set him on a different path. He emerged as a true champion, striving with other supernatural and human allies to destroy evil and stop an impending apocalypse.

Spike (played by James Marsters) was a second vampire from the *Buffy* mythology to have regained his soul. He did so by way of a more painful yet ultimately admirable transformation. Spike was captured by a secret military cadre working to control supernatural beings for possible bio-weapons development. A pain-inducing chip was implanted in Spike's head, making it impossible for him to attack humans. Buffy (the Vampire Slayer) began using the disempowered Spike to provide assistance and information in her fight against vampires and demons. Spike began to develop deep emotional feelings for her, became part of Buffy's small group of vampire fighters, and even had a short and very torrid affair with Buffy. Spike eventually left town on a quest to have his soul restored and, after suffering great torment, was granted this wish. The restoration of his soul was accompanied by the sudden return of feelings, especially remorse, which drove him insane for a time. But he emerged as one of the Slayer's most powerful allies in her last battle against a vast, ancient evil. Although Buffy survived the conflict, Spike apparently sacrificed himself to save the world, ending his life as a true hero who perhaps atoned for all the harm he had done as a vampire.

In the TV series *Forever Knight*, the lead character (played by Geraint Wyn Davies) was an eleventh century vampire who had gone by many names over the centuries. Now reformed and helping to protect humans against others of his kind, by day he was officially Nick Knight, a homicide detective, and by night he was secretly a crime-fighting (and evil-fighting) hero. With the help of a medical examiner friend he sought a cure for his vampirism while continuously facing his past.

VAMPIRO

Most of Italy's vampire legends date back to the days of ancient Rome (*see* Vampires Of Rome, p. 437), but in the seventeenth century many vampire legends and tales began springing up. Most reports of these new creatures were dismissed by the church as figments of the imagination, the product of uneducated and rustic villagers. But some scholars, even among the clergy, took quite another view.

The Franciscan monk Ludovico Maria Sinistrari (1622-1701) of Pavia wrote about vampires in his study of demons and their practices, *De Aemonialitate, En Incubus Et Succubus.* In that timeless work he postulated that vampires were not actually reanimated corpses (which was the popular belief of the day), but another race of beings entirely: the Vampiro. Set apart from the descendants of Adam and Eve, but just as old, the race of vampires had grown up with their own culture. They did not have as many numbers as humans and lingered on the fringes of human society, preying on humans for food. Sinistrari believed that vampires even had immortal souls, much the same as humans, but that their physical bodies were different and, in his view, perfect, whereas the human form is flawed.

This is an odd view, especially for a monk, since the vampires of the day were seen as moldering, decaying corpses with gaunt features, rotting flesh, and fetid breath; hardly anyone's idea of perfection. Nevertheless, in Sinistrari's view the Vampiro was perfect, but mankind was apparently unable to perceive that.

Vampiro, believed to be perfect in form. Artwork by M. Katz.

VAMPIRES OF JAPAN

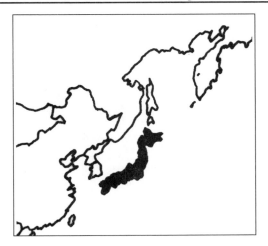

GAKI (also Ga-ki)

"Hungry ghosts" have haunted the countryside of rural Japan for hundreds of years. Called "Gaki," these monsters love the darkness and lure victims by uttering lonely wails that sound like an injured child or the cry of someone lost and desperate. Travelers coming to help the lost and wailing "waif" instead encounter a pale-skinned, shambling Revenant with wickedly sharp teeth, enormous strength, and a thirst for blood.

Aside from being condemned to Hell, a Gaki is further cursed with a hunger so fierce that no matter how much it feeds it always feels as if it is starving. Driven by this desperation it feeds and feeds, never satisfied, always killing to slake the impossible thirst.

Reports of the supernatural Gaki suggest that it is a theriomorph, a shapeshifter capable of adopting any guise in order to deceive its prey. Even if the Gaki successfully impersonates a living person, its true nature can be found out by a single touch: its skin is bloodless and cold.

Weapons have little effect on the Gaki. They can be driven off by prayers and rituals performed by Buddhist Monks; and by the placement of sacred scrolls and icons of Buddha set in precise locations around the house.

In colloquial Japanese speech, the term "gaki" has come to be used to describe someone who is extremely stingy and greedy. This can also mean greedy for attention.

Thirteenth century Gaki images provided courtesy of Saint Xavier University of Chicago (www.sxu.edu)

Thirteenth century Gaki images provided courtesy of Saint Xavier University of Chicago (www.sxu.edu)

HANNYA

Legends of many countries hold that dying badly while afflicted with physical or mental deformities is a cause of vampirism. The simple folk who lived in rural villages and towns feared deformity because they misunderstood it to be a sign of demonic possession, or at the very least a demon's taint.

The Japanese Hannya is such a creature. These vampires had once been beautiful women who fell into mental illness and later died. Some legends have it that the Hannyas were women whose lives had been tormented by insane jealousy—a psychosis so deep that it twisted their souls into ugly and unholy shapes. While in their graves, their corpses become possessed by demons, and they rose from the dead as blood drinking monsters. The creatures they become after death were physically ugly, a manifestation of the ugliness of their souls while alive.

The undead Hannyas have grotesque faces marked with evil: wicked fangs, knobby chins, and sharp horns on their heads. Their eyes burn with an icy blue light.

The Hannyas attack with their long powerful claws, catching and rending their prey. Then they gore the hapless victim with their horns.

The Hannyas also use the power of their voices to inflict terror and actual physical harm. Masters of the Japanese martial arts teach the use of the *ki-ai*, or spirit shout, to unnerve their opponents; but the Hannyas use *kiai-jutsu* (the art of the spirit shout) to actually harm their prey. Their intense sound waves can shatter bone, tear flesh, and reduce victims to cringing helplessness, leaving them totally vulnerable to the Hannyas' murderous physical assault.

Though the Hannyas spend most of their unnatural lives in *Jigoku* (Hell), they venture into this world to hunt and kill. Their preferred prey are unfaithful men. Perhaps they are invoked by the prayers of the men's slighted lovers, or perhaps the Hannyas merely enjoy the

taste of philanderer's flesh. In either case, they are spirits of retribution ever hungry for the kill.

A different take on the Hannya, as related in folk tales from the Japanese countryside, suggests that the predominantly female creature may sometimes manifest itself as a male. In these tales, both male and female Hannyas favor infants and young children for their unholy meals.

The Hannya is a frequent figure in Japanese folk art, and is generally depicted as a truly horrifying being.

Hannya. Archival artwork.

THE SPIRIT SHOUT

The Japanese word *Ki-ai* is defined as "spirit meeting" or the "spirit shout." In Japanese martial arts the Ki-ai is used to clear the mind, give confidence, and also frighten an opponent. It tightens up the body, especially in the abdominal region, thereby protecting one from blows.

It was believed that some martial arts masters in feudal Japan were able to use the martial shout to both injure and heal others. This was known as *Kiai-jutsu*, "the art of ki-ai." Kiai-jutsu masters could stun a person, or even animals, with a powerful yell. Conversely, they could revive unconscious people or perform such feats as stopping nosebleeds with a Ki-ai.

When a martial artist utters a Ki-ai, the sound or vibration may momentarily paralyze an opponent and render him or her more susceptible to an attack. The Ki-ai purifies the mind of extraneous thought, enabling the warrior to channel their pure energy (*Ki*) to full intensity. Certain martial arts masters maintain that there are three or four kinds of Ki-ai: low and weighty at moments of action; high and piercing with a cry of victory; normal for the purposes of resuscitation; and silent (*Kensei*) in certain meditative exercises.

KAPPA

The infamous Japanese demon called the Kappa is just one of the many Yôkai, or supernatural beings of Japanese folklore, and it has a centuries-long history of murder and mayhem. Other supernatural creatures from Japan's rich religious culture include the Oni (a host of different species of demons), Oiwa (ghosts of various kinds), and various imps (such as the Kappa). Scholars differ as to whether the Kappa is actually a vampire. Most say that the creature is an evil water sprite, but others insist that it is a vampire-ghoul.

The Kappa is vaguely humanoid, about the size of a child, and it is extremely strong. It is amphibious in appearance, with yellow-green skin, a frog-like mouth, webbed feet, and large bulbous eyes. The Kappa have crusty tortoise-like shells and they smell like rotting fish. Each carries a concave bowl on its head that holds water. If the water is spilled, the Kappa will lose its strength.

Kappas lurk by the edges of streams and ponds, waiting for an unsuspecting person to happen by. Then they leap out and grapple with the unfortunate, pulling them into the water, biting them, and sucking their blood. Sometimes they steal their prey's liver then take it into the water to eat.

Kappas are very warlike. When they spot a potential victim who looks fit and strong, they try to Sumo wrestle with the person. Despite their diminutive size they possess enormous strength, so they seldom lose.

Kappas have also been known to attack horses by dragging them into lakes and rivers and drowning them.

The Kappa. Artwork by Robert Patrick O'Brien.

KASHA

The Kasha is a simpler, less complex, but no less horrifying monster. This Japanese ghoul feeds by stealing recently buried corpses from their graves, or taking bodies laid out in preparation for cremation. It is a small creature, about the size of a large dog, but immensely strong. It can easily run at full speed while carrying a corpse.

The Kasha are unpleasant, smell like rotting fish, and are exceedingly foul tempered. They have just enough human intelligence to take offense at the slightest insult, and sometimes listen at doors to see if someone is speaking ill of them. If so, they will intentionally despoil the graves of that person's family.

The creature can be defeated by fire, and various Shinto tales featuring Samurai suggest that steel can harm the Kasha, as described in . It is not known whether gunfire will harm them, although it seems likely.

The surest way to defeat the Kasha is to adhere to proper burial rites so it cannot obtain any sustenance. With the proper religious rituals used, and the body guarded before burial and then protected by a strongly sealed coffin, the Kasha will become frustrated and skulk off in search of easier prey.

The Kasha. Archival artwork.

The Nobusama (seen through a keyhole). Artwork by Marie O'Brien.

NOBUSUMA

According to Japanese folklore, a bat that lives to be a thousand years old will evolve into a form somewhere between animal and human, called a Nobusuma (Japanese for "most ancient"). The Nobusuma has a body like that of a flying squirrel, with wings that attach to the ankles of each of its four limbs.

The Nobusuma is not a blood drinker. Instead it comes out at night and sucks the breath out of sleeping victims while tapping on their chests.

Oddly, if another person witnesses a Nobusuma's attack, the victim will survive and live a long and healthy life. But if there are no human witnesses, the victim will die within three days.

NODEPPO

An even older bat-like creature is the Nodeppo. There are no accurate accounts of Nodeppo sightings because anyone who has seen it has died. There are tales, however, of people who saw the creature's horrific face reflected in mirrors or pools of water. Though these people survived the immediate encounter, many became ill and died within a few months.

The Nodeppo swoops down and wraps its victims in its great dark wings, then sucks all of the breath out of them, instantly killing them. Travelers most often fall prey to this beast, but a wise traveler can protect himself by carrying a few nanomani leaves close to his skin.

O TOYO

The legend of the cat vampire named O Toyo has been the basis for many Japanese tales, songs, operas, and plays. O Toyo was a beautiful courtesan to Prince Hizen, and the apple of his eye. But unbeknownst to the prince, O Toyo was attacked and smothered to death by an unnaturally large cat. The cat hid her corpse and assumed her appearance. Over the next few weeks it began coming to the prince as he slept, leeching off his life essence.

O Toyo. Artwork by Robert Patrick O'Brien.

The court physicians tried every cure they could think of, but the prince wasted away day by day. Only the combined wisdom and strength of a priest, Ruiten, and a young samurai, Ito Soda, could discover the source of the prince's malady and drive off the cat demon.

Once free of her spell, the prince quickly recovered. When the cat demon began terrorizing the local villagers, he ordered it be hunted down. Along with Ruiten and Ito Soda, Prince Hizen tracked the beast down and destroyed it.

Prince Hizen and his courtesans. Archival artwork.

The tale of O Toyo explains why it is so hard to identify the kind of vampire who craves life force, not blood. The involvement of such creatures is difficult to diagnose because there are no wounds to account for the victim's failing health.

TSUTSUGA

In the sixth and seventh centuries, Japanese villagers were plagued by a fierce shapeshifter called a Tsutsuga. These creatures could assume nearly any shape, including animals, insects, birds, balls of light, mist, and even likenesses of holy people. But no matter what face they adopt, the Tsutsugas were completely evil.

At night, a Tsutsuga would enter a house using trickery or deception and then feed off the blood of the sleeping humans, usually not killing them but weakening them and spreading sickness. They delighted in causing misery; if someone died, so much the better. It was not uncommon for victims of these monsters to commit suicide in order to escape their predations.

Tsutsuga attacks eventually attracted the Royal Court's attention. During the mid-seventh Century, the Empress Saimei Tenno (655-661) sent for a wise sage and commanded that he put an end to the Tsutsuga's evil reign of terror and sickness. The sage prayed day after day for the power to defeat the monsters, and cast many complicated and dangerous spells. When he had gathered sufficient strength he drove the Tsutsugas into a remote area of the wilderness and trapped them there forever.

Thirteen hundred years later these creatures are still remembered. A common expression is *tsutsuga nashi*, meaning "without tsutsuga," used to suggest that someone is free from sickness.

Samurai demon hunter. Archival artwork.

HEROIC VAMPIRES IN JAPANESE POP CULTURE

Japanese *Anime* (action cartoons on television and in movies) and Japanese *Manga* (action comic books) have been filled with just about every kind of diabolical monster imaginable, from supernatural earth spirits to multi-dimensional alien invaders. These forms of storytelling are often very complex, possessing surprising subtlety of character and plot. Often the lines between good and evil, hero and villain, are blurred. This is especially the case in stories dealing with vampires. Three series in particular feature vampires in major roles, both as heroes and villains.

In the series of films starring *Vampire Hunter D*, vampires have emerged from the ashes of a global nuclear holocaust and rule the earth in feudal states. A lone swordsman called simply "D" is a Dhampir (a half-human, half-vampire) who takes a rather violent stand against his evil father's reign of vampiric terror. The movie was followed by a sequel, *Vampire Hunter D: Bloodlust*.

Another series, *Vampire Princess Miyu*, features a teenage vampire who patrols the dimensional pathways between the human world and the world of demons. She uses her prodigious powers to keep humanity safe from demonic invaders.

A third series is *Blood: The Last Vampire*. The series begins during the Vietnam war and focuses on a young woman named Saya, a mysterious savior sent by an even more mysterious "organization" to stop an invasion of blood sucking parasites.

Anime vampire. Artwork by Michael Katz.

In each series the action is constant and the characters are well-drawn (both in terms of art and developmental storytelling).

Anime vampire. Used with permission, (c) 2003 Pedro Lara.

VAMPIRES OF JAVA

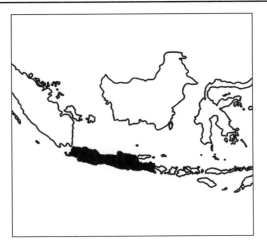

PONTIANAK

Java shares many of its folktales with Malaysia. One of the most terrifying legends is that of the bloodthirsty Pontianak.

Like the Kudlak of Croatia, the Babylonian Ekimmu, and the Cihuateteo of Mexico, the Pontianak is created from a stillbirth or a woman who dies while giving birth. This tragedy breeds a monster of particularly violent appetite. It takes the form of a beautiful woman who entices men, or mimics the cry of a lost child to lure concerned adults into dark places. What waits for them there is a creature with wicked talons and sharp fangs. The Pontianak slashes and rends its victims' stomachs with its teeth and claws, drinking the welling blood and feasting on the flesh.

Since destroying the Pontianak is so difficult (they are even more fierce when cornered), the best tactic is to prevent their creation in the first place. Proper medical attention for pregnant women is vital to prevent birth catastrophes. If a woman or a child dies during delivery, the corpse's mouth will be filled with glass beads to prevent a Pontianak from uttering its plaintive and irresistible cry. Eggs are placed in the armpits and steel needles thrust through the palms, essentially crippling the Pontianak's ability to fly.

SUNDAL BOLONG

The Javanese Sundal Bolong is a seductress vampire that attacks only the bravest and most handsome men of a village. The Sundal Bolong assumes human form and dresses all in white (very much like the French White Ladies of Fau), luring men to secret places such as a hut in the woods, a cleared space in the forest, a grotto, or some other remote and secluded spot. After using them sexually (presumably to feed off their potent sexual energy), it transforms back into its hideous natural shape and attacks the depleted victims, tearing them apart and feasting on flesh and blood.

But the Sundal Bolong does not always kill quickly. It is one of the cruelest of the vampire species and enjoys the torment and suffering of its victims. It may curse a victim with a painful and wasting disease—something particularly dreaded by strong warriors—or inflict injuries while stranding the victim deep in the forest, harassing him as he struggles to make it back to his village. Should the victim actually make it all the way back to his village despite the injuries and indignities he has suffered, the Sundal Bolong will wait until help is actually moments away and then kill him with a flick of her claws across his throat.

In some versions of the Sundal Bolong legend, it possesses similar qualities to the Polong of Malaysia in that it is a diminutive creature that sneaks into bedrooms at night and drinks blood from the thumbs of the sleepers. In this variation of the Sundal Bolong tale, the vampires can be captured and placed in bottles specially prepared by priests.

VAMPIRES OF KENYA

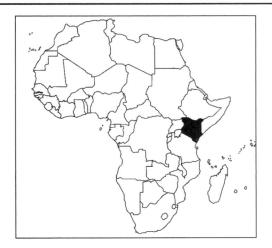

ILIMU

Among the Kikuyu tribe of Kenya there is an enduring legend of a shapeshifting monster called the Ilimu. It is not a human being cursed to be a monster, like the European werewolf, but a demon that possesses animals and shapeshifts into the likeness of a man.

The Ilimu can possess any animal. Once in control of its host, it can transform into any human from whom it has managed to obtain a strand of hair, a drop of blood, or some other body part. Perhaps it somehow samples the person's DNA and can replicate their body or the sham of one; or perhaps there is a residual spiritual essence in the body part that they utilize.

The exact nature of the demonic force that drives the Ilimu is unknown, but it does seem to have great intelligence. It also keeps the feral hunting qualities of the animal it has possessed.

Once it adopts human form, the Ilimu insinuates itself into a village to seek its prey. Often it will finagle an invitation into a home and slaughter all of the occupants; or it might come into a strange village in the guise of a traveler or beggar, then attack the first person it is alone with. Other times it will lure victims to a secluded spot and attack them

The Ilimu generally picks a human form that looks frail or harmless, so the finger of suspicion is seldom pointed in the right direction. Only a village medicine man or witch doctor can ferret out an Ilimu's presence in the community. Once discovered, the Ilimu usually transforms back into its original animal shape and try to flee, but the witch doctor will send brave and wise hunters after it.

This creature appears in one form or another in legends from many African nations, including Ghana and Uganda. In 1898, two lions in Uganda were suspected of being Ilimu, and were responsible for the deaths of over 130 people involved in the building of a bridge across the river Tsavo. The lions hunted together using deceptive tactics and trickery uncommon to animals, and over the course of their two month reign of terror everyone—even the Europeans supervising the construction—came to believe that there was something supernatural about them. Big game hunters eventually brought the lions down, but only after the lions had foiled their traps time and again.

The incident was made into a movie in 1996, *The Ghost And The Darkness*, starring Michael Douglas and Val Kilmer.

Artwork by Shane MacDougall.

VAMPIRES OF KOREA

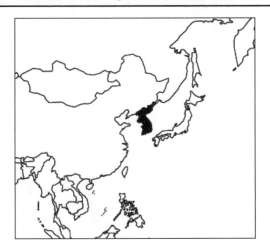

KUMIHO

The folkloric entity called the "cunning fox" appears in various forms throughout Southeast Asia. In Japan the fox is presented mostly as a benevolent creature, but in Korea it is a darker and very evil monster known as the Kumiho ("nine-tailed fox"). The Kumiho is apparently what an ordinary fox will turn into after it has lived one thousand years. Several tales are found in *Hanguk Kubimunhak Taegye*, the ency-clopedic compendium of Korean oral literature.

The Kumiho is a shapeshifter that can transform into, among other things, a bewitchingly beautiful woman that seduces men. In the tale, "Transformation Of The Kumiho" ("*KumihoUi Pyeonshin*"), the creatures transforms into the likeness of a bride at her wedding. Not even the

Kumiho. Artwork by Marie O'Brien.

bride's mother can tell them apart. The Kumiho is finally discovered when her clothes are removed, revealing a hideous animal body.

In "The King And The Kumiho" ("*Wanggwa Kumiho*") an unlucky king meets a girl in the woods at night, and talks her into having sex with him by promising to help her financially stricken father. Unfortunately for him their resulting dalliance takes place in the dark and he is unable to see the creature's animal body. His mating with the monster drains him of life and vigor. This suggests that the Kumiho is some species of Essential Vampire.

This belief is supported by the legend of "The Emperor's Kumiho Daughter-in-Law" in which a Kumiho living in secret among the Emperor's household begins draining life energy from court retainers. Only when a heroic monster slayer kills the Kumiho are the remaining courtiers saved.

In a similar tale, "Pak Munsu And The Kumiho " ("*Pakmunsuwa Kumiho*") the famous folk hero Pak Munsu meets a girl who lives in the woods and has a distinctly fox-like appearance. She is later revealed as a treacherous Kumiho, and Pak Munsu only narrowly escapes the encounter.

Though the Kumiho can change its shape, it apparently still maintains some essence of the fox about it. This is demonstrated in the legend called "The Maiden Who Discovered A Kumiho Through A Chinese Poem" ("*Hansiro Kumiho Reul Aranaen Ch'eonyeo*"), where the creature was revealed when a hunting dog caught the scent of the fox and attacked. Though the Kumiho most often transforms into the likeness of a woman, it can assume any shape, and in "The Maiden Who Discovered A Kumiho Through A Chinese Poem" it also shapeshifts into the appearance of a young man. This is a very rare account, however.

Fighting the Kumiho is not particularly difficult, although identifying and catching it are. Aside from using a hunting dog to sniff out a suspected Kumiho there are few other ways of discovering one. One extreme method is to strike a suspected woman very forcefully on the cheek; the blow shakes the creature's concentration and it shifts back to its normal form. But if the suspect is actually an innocent woman, then the blow will obviously cause great unnecessary harm.

THE MYTH OF THE SHAPESHIFTING TIGER

A long time ago a woman was walking home from her work at a nobleman's house, carrying a basket of buckwheat puddings to feed her two children. A monstrous tiger leaped out of the woods and demanded that she give him one of the puddings or he would eat her. The woman complied and continued her long trek home, but the tiger was greedy and he kept harassing the woman until he had devoured all of the puddings intended for her hungry children.

The woman fled, knowing that the tiger's insatiable hunger could never be satisfied by just the puddings. The tiger chased her, tormenting her the way a cat would torment a mouse. Finally he tired of the game and killed her. He removed all of her clothing and devoured the woman whole.

But the tiger was no ordinary tiger. He was magical and could change his form. He transformed himself into the likeness of the woman he'd just devoured, put on her clothes, and went home to her children. His appetite was still keen and the thought of tender young children made his mouth water.

The dead woman's children, a boy and girl, were very clever and highly suspicious and could see through the tiger's disguise. As the tiger came in the front door they fled out the back and climbed a tree to hide. The tiger discovered their hiding place in the morning, but the tree was too tall and narrow for him to climb.

Using a cajoling voice and still pretending to be their mother, the tiger asked them to tell him how to climb the tree. The children first told him that coating the tree with sesame oil would help him climb, but when the tiger tried that it proved to be more of a hindrance than a help. All day the tiger tried to get them to tell him how to climb up, and all day the children told him different incorrect ways, foiling him time and again. Finally, careless from exhaustion, the children told him to use an axe to split the tree. The tiger did so, and the two halves of the tree leaned down toward the hungry tiger.

Immediately the children cried out for help from the Heavenly King. After repeated cries the great Heavenly King answered them and lowered a chain to the children. With the tiger's claws scratching at their feet, the brother and sister hastily climbed the chain to Heaven.

The tiger quickly devised a plan and, using the dead woman's voice, he also cried out to the Heavenly King for help. This time the Heavenly King lowered the end of an old, frayed rope. The tiger grabbed it and started to climb, but when he was halfway to heaven the rope broke and he fell to his death.

After the orphans rested awhile in the Heavenly Kingdom, they were brought before the Heavenly King. He told them that everyone in the Heavenly Kingdom must do special tasks and that he had special jobs for them. He made the brother the Moon and the sister the Sun.

Legend has it that when the Sun rises in the sky and people gaze upon her, the girl's modesty makes her blush so intensely that she shines more and more brightly, to the point that no one can look upon her directly.

In the skies of Korea, Brother Moon and Sister Sun live forever, happy in the Heavenly Kingdom.

Artwork by Robert Patrick O'Brien.

FAMILIAR ANIMALS MAKE ANIMAL FAMILIARS

Familiars are a link between the supernatural realms and the natural world. They are used to carry out spells and bewitchments. They are generally believed to be low-ranking demons under the control of a witch, warlock, or other kind of sorcerer. Familiars can take the form of an animal such as a cat, toad, owl, mouse, dog, hen, or other creature, including insects. In some cases Familiars are called Imps and are thought to be servants given to a witch by the Devil. In the Middle Ages cats were commonly considered familiars, so feared and reviled that there were several mass slaughters of cats.

In European witchcraft trials, if even so much as a housefly entered the court while someone was being tried as a witch, it was suspected of being that person's familiar and often sealed the accused's fate.

In Czechoslovakia, any animal that has come into contact with the fierce Nelapsi species of vampire is immediately suspected of having become its familiar. The animal is either slaughtered outright or purified in the smoke of a "bone fire" (*see* the entry on the Czechoslovakian Nelapsi, p. 159,k 162) for more on this).

The Bajang of Malaysia is a creature that assumes the shape of a hungry polecat and goes hunting for children. It is often brought under the magical control of a witch or warlock and thereafter becomes that sorcerer's familiar. It is even handed down from one generation to the next.

The Machi of Chile and the Sabbatarian of Greece are vampire slayers who use their familiars to fight evil.

Photo by Jason Lukridge.

VAMPIRES OF LATVIA

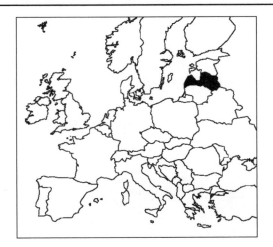

VILKACIS

The Vilkacis (translated as "wolf's eyes") is a malicious Latvian creature whose nature combines elements of werewolf and vampire. Latvian folklore is uncertain how a person is transformed into such a monster, but curses and sinning against the gods of the Latvian pantheon play a major role. Quite a few folk tales suggest that when a person sleeps, the darker side of his personality sometimes "escapes" as a Vilkacis and goes running free in the dark, often taking nightmarish shape. In Latvia this kind of astral projection is called "running with the wolf."

Luckily it is no more difficult to kill a Vilkacis than an ordinary wolf, though this creature is smarter and more cunning. If the Vilkacis is killed then the sleeping person dies as well.

When the Vilkacis appears it hunts randomly in the forests around its own home or village. If a person catches the Vilkacis while sleeping and encircles it with rose petals, the Vilkacis is then subject to that person's will and can be made to sniff out buried treasure. In some stories the Vilkacis will lead someone to treasure without being forced to do so, but will take pleasure in the corruption this sudden wealth often brings to the villager's life.

The Vilkacis belongs to the same lower level of Latvian mythological beings as Dievini, Ragana, Pukis, and the shapeshifting and devious Vadatajs.

VADATAJS

The name Vadatajs means "leading to nowhere." These creatures are demons that trick people into losing their way in forests or send people the wrong way at crossroads, so that the victim's soul loses its way as well. The Vadatajs often assume the shape of an animal, but can also appear as a human being.

Photo by Jason Lukridge.

·PART FIVE·

FIGHTING THE UNDEAD

"Metamorphosis of the Vampire"

Thou who abruptly as a knife
Didst come into my heart; thou who,
A demon horde into my life,
Didst enter, wildly dancing, through

The doorways of my sense unlatched
To make my spirit thy domain--
Harlot to whom I am attached
As convicts to the ball and chain,

As gamblers to the wheel's bright spell,
As drunkards to their raging thirst,
As corpses to their worms--accurst
Be thou! Oh, be thou damned to hell!

I have entreated the swift sword
To strike, that I at once be freed;
The poisoned phial I have implored
To plot with me a ruthless deed.

Alas! the phial and the blade
Do cry aloud and laugh at me:
"Thou art not worthy of our aid;
Thou art not worthy to be free.

"Though one of us should be the tool
To save thee from thy wretched fate,
Thy kisses would resuscitate
The body of thy vampire, fool!"

Charles Baudelaire
From <u>Flowers of Evil</u>
1857

Imagine being born for the sole purpose of fighting vampires.
Imagine learning that you have special powers but are cursed by destiny to face deadly supernatural danger over and over again, and that you probably won't live very long.

No, that is not a description of *Buffy The Vampire Slayer*. That is the tragic destiny of the Dhampir, the offspring of an unholy union between a human being and a vampire.

The Dhampir is one of several vampire slayers found throughout folklore of the battle against the undead. Unlike most slayers, the Dhampir is born to the task and has no other choice in life. Legend has it that the Dhampir's skeleton is weak, almost gelatinous, and because of this he will have a limited life span filled with pain and discomfort. But the Dhampir possesses special powers, and during his brief span of years he will have the ability to detect vampires such as the invisible Mullo (a deadly creature much feared by the Romani) and battle them to the death.

Photo by Robert Patrick O'Brien.

Most Dhampirs make this a true profession instead of a cultural obligation, charging stiff fees in order to seek out and destroy the undead. Once they have been engaged they use their psychic powers to locate the unseen monsters, then begin a strange ritual punctuated with sharp whistles and strange body movements, ending in a deadly struggle with an invisible Mullo.

Dhampirs have been active even into the twentieth century. The last known professional killing by a Dhampir was reported in 1959, in the Yugoslavian province of Kosovo.

Another natural born vampire killer is the Kresnik of Croatia. Like the vampiric Kudlak of the same country, the Kresnik is born with a caul covering his face. Any Croatian child born with this amniotic membrane is destined to some supernatural future. Such children are watched closely because it is rarely clear which path in life they will take: good (Kresnik) or evil (Kudlak).

Both Kudlak and Kresnik possess vast supernatural powers: they can shapeshift into various beasts, and even become birds and fly. The term Kresnik is drawn from the root-word *krat*, meaning "cross;" this is suggestive of which side of the line between light and darkness is favored by this noble creature.

Photo by Robert Patrick O'Brien.

The Stregoni Benefici of Italy is very much like the Kresnik, in that it is a "good vampire" who loathes the evil undead and will do anything in his (or her) considerable power to destroy them.

In India can be found the vampire known as the Jigarkhwar. This vampire can be conquered, tamed, and cured of vampirism through magical rituals. It then becomes human again, but possesses the power to detect other vampires. It is then often used to assist vampire slayers.

In the real world, vampire slayers are usually priests or sorcerers who are steeped in the religious rites of their culture and have spent their lives learning everything they can about combating vampires. One such sorcerer vampire slayer is the Bulgarian Vampirdzhija, often a monk who is learned in magic. The Vampirdzhija is able to perform certain spells that enable him to see and detect vampires.

A similar sorcerer is the Djadadjii, also from Bulgaria and neighboring lands. The Djadadjii is basically a subset of the Vampirdzhija, and specializes in vampires who take the form of spirits or poltergeists. The Djadadjii baits a trap for a spirit-vampire by placing the vampire's favorite food in a bottle to lure it in, then uses religious icons and casting spells to draw the vampire's spirit into the bottle. Once the vampire is trapped therein, the Djadadjii will throw the bottle into a fire to destroy the creature.

In Sumatra, priests known as Bataks are a combination of witch doctor and vampire slayer. They possess the ability to reclaim the human spirit of a person who has been cast out of his body by a vampiric demon, usually the vampire called the Pontianak. The Bataks use garlic to attract the human's soul, then urge it to return to its body, thereby forcing out the demonic inhabitant.

In Greece, a Sabbatarian is a person born on a Saturday who has the power to cure illness as well as detect—and defeat—supernatural creatures such as vampires. The Sabbatarian is often accompanied by a Fetch Dog, a spirit that acts like a supernatural hunting hound.

Aside from these supernatural vampire slayers and those steeped in sorcery, there are a number of ordinary humans who take up the cause of fighting the undead. The image of the vampire slayer which usually springs to mind—based on pop culture—is probably that of Abraham Van Helsing with his Gladstone bag filled with stakes and hammers, huddled into a greatcoat and trudging up to the castle in search of Dracula's coffin. Heroic, yes; but unrealistic. For the most part, vampire slayers have been ordinary people—villagers, local priests, shamans, medicine men, village elders, warriors, even family members—who have been called upon by their friends and neighbors to combat a local evil. Relying on faith, strength of will, and love for their friends and families, they have stood up to the forces of darkness without supernatural powers, magic spells, or sacred weapons. Many have died, but the fight goes on, century after century; and as long as need demands it they will continue to slay the undead, one vampire at a time.

Vampire Hunter. Artwork by Marie Elena O'Brien.

THE DHAMPIR IN FICTION

The concept of the supernatural offspring of a human and a vampire has intrigued the imaginations of modern storytellers for decades. Beginning with the introduction of the Marvel Comics character Blade in issue #10 of *Tomb of Dracula* (1973), half-breed Dhampirs have cut a bloody swath through the world of the undead. Following are just a few of the Dhampirs (also spelled Dhampyrs) found in recent popular fiction, films, and games.

- *Blade The Daywalker*. Blade was originally introduced as a hard-edged near-vampire whose pregnant mother was bitten (and infected) by vampire Deacon Frost just moments before Blade was born. The resulting infection gave Blade virtually all of a vampire's strengths with none of their weaknesses. He could move around in daylight, was stronger than an ordinary human, his reflexes and senses were extraordinary, and he could heal from virtually any wound. In the series of action-horror films starring Wesley Snipes, Blade rose from the relative obscurity of a supporting comic book character to the star of a high-grossing franchise.

- *Vampire Hunter D*. In this post-apocalyptic Japanese anime movie, the man known simply as "D" is a Dhampir using Kenjutsu (Samurai swordplay), as well as his own superhuman abilities, to overthrow his evil vampire sire. The original movie was followed by a sequel, *Vampire Hunter D: Bloodlust*.

- *Half-Damned: Dhampyr* by Hal Mangold (White Wolf, 2002). The gaming company, White Wolf, is famous for its wonderful *Vampire: The Masquerade* role-playing game. The company publishes a number of books that tie into that and other gaming storylines to give players a good sense of the scope and history of the supernatural worlds in which they play. *Half-Damned* is part of White Wolf's modern-day Storyteller line and deals with a Dhampyr and his struggles against other and more powerful supernatural enemies.

- *Dhampir* by Barb & J.C. Hendee Magiere (Roc, 2003). This novel contains a twist within a twist. The hero of the piece is

Magiere, who claims to be a vampire hunter while her companion Leesil plays the role of a vampire. They run a confidence game where Magiere slays Leesil in town after town, collecting hefty sums for cleansing each town of evil. But Magiere eventually discovers that she actually is a Dhampir, and that she is fated to encounter a vampire of tremendous power and evil.

- *Dhampir, Child of the Blood* by V. M. Johnson (Mystic Rose Books, 1996). Author V. M. Johnson discusses the mating and offspring of vampires from the perspective that all of it is real. Neither campy nor tongue in cheek, the vampyre lifestyle is explained from a believer's point of view, discussing hunting, psychology and vampire culture, specifically that of the Clan of Lilith.

- *Dhampir* by Robyn D. Swaim (iUniverse, 2001). This novel takes place during the late 1800s in the English Midlands. It blends the original Gypsy legends of the Dhampyr with the heroics of Blade and similar characters.

Photo by Robert Patrick O'Brien.

·PART SIX·

VAMPIRES AROUND THE WORLD

M–R

"Oil and Blood"

In tombs of gold and lapis lazuli
Bodies of holy men and women exude
Miraculous oil, odour of violet.
But under heavy loads of trampled clay
Lie bodies of the vampires full of blood;
Their shrouds are bloody and their lips are wet.

William Butler Yeats
The Winding Stair and Other Poems
1933

VAMPIRES OF MACEDONIA

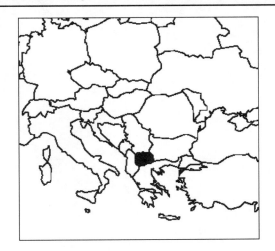

VRYKOLAKA

Like the Vrykolaka from nearby Greece, the Macedonian vampire of the same name is a blood drinking Revenant. The vampire is active during the long darkness from ten at night until just before the first cock crow of morning, and during that time it is a gluttonous monster.

Strong and dangerous as it is, the Vrykolaka can be killed by dousing it with boiling water, a tactic that destroys its hunting senses of smell, touch, and sight. This method is used most often when trying to keep the creature from breaking into a house, or if one happens to discover the monster's resting place. The creature can also be crippled by driving a long nail through its stomach while it sleeps (attempting this method while it is awake is generally fatal to the would-be slayer). The nails must pierce the spine as well as the internal organs so the creature cannot rise to feed. If the coffin is weighted down with rocks the creature will soon starve to death and the evil demonic spirit will depart, leaving only a regular corpse behind.

Like many vampires of the Adriatic and the Balkans, the Vrykolaka can be foiled by spreading birdseed outside of one's door, or (better yet) on the vampire's grave. This vampire would be compelled to stop and count each seed, at the rate of one per century!

Vrykolaka. Used with permission, (c) 2003 by Krista McLean.

VAMPIRES OF MADAGASCAR

RAMANGA

One of the strangest vampires in the world is the Ramanga of Madagascar. Ramangas (which means "blue blood") are living men who are employed by village elders and nobles to eat discarded nail parings or spilled blood.

It is the pervading belief in Macedonia that items like nail clippings and blood possess vast magical powers and, should they fall into the wrong hands, can be used to work evil magic against the person from whom they came. Since some people believe that a person's soul resides in their blood, this extreme custom can somewhat be under-stood.

Nobles maintain one or more Ramangas to collect and ingest these items so that no one else can gain access to them. Nobles who can afford it utilize a traveling Ramanga to accompany them on every journey so this grisly task will always be handled quickly and efficiently, keeping them safe from sorcery.

SIN EATERS

Throughout the world there are other kinds of creatures related, however distantly, to the Ramanga; people or supernatural beings who feed on discarded parts of the body or soul. Unlike the Ramanga, most of these beings do not eat blood or fingernail parings; instead they symbolically eat some aspects of another person's spiritual essence. The Sin Eater is a prime example of an ordinary human who feeds on the spiritual excesses of a newly deceased person.

In England, from the Middle Ages until the late nineteenth century, when a person died a professional Sin Eater would be called in to cleanse the departed's soul before it could ascend to heaven. The Sin Eater would be hired to appear at the wake. He would place a loaf of bread atop the corpse's chest, then perform an incantation that would transfer the deceased's sins into the bread. The Sin Eater would then eat the bread and take those sins into himself.

Similar customs were common throughout Ireland. and Wales. In Wales, an entire meal would be prepared over a corpse. However, an itinerant outcast would be offered the meal, often not being told that his meal contained the sins of a recently deceased person.

The custom crossed the Atlantic with immigrants from Britain, Scotland, Wales, and Ireland and rooted itself in the practices of people in the Appalachian Mountains.

VAMPIRES OF MALAWI

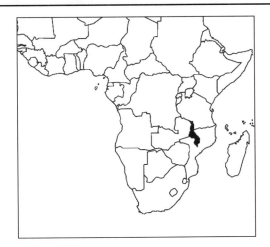

HUMAN VAMPIRES

Rumors of vampirism have risen sharply in the tiny Southern African nation of Malawi during the early twenty-first century. Fear of the spread of vampires has sparked attacks on people suspected of being bloodsuckers. The problem has been exacerbated by widespread rumors that Malawi's government has been colluding with vampires to collect human blood. In 2002, a man accused of helping vampires was stoned to death and three Roman Catholic priests were savagely beaten by villagers who suspected them of being monsters.

This crisis seems to stem from cultural and educational misunderstandings rather than from supernatural forces. Several international aid agencies have worked with the Malawi government for the last few years, attempting to collect clean blood for use in medical research and for humanitarian aid to other parts of Africa decimated by AIDS and warfare. But the Malawi people have a cultural taboo against the taking and sharing of blood, because this is their definition of vampirism.

The country is also desperately poor and the agreement to buy blood was made as part of an attempt to help the crippled economy. The United Nations World Food Program estimates that more than three million people in Malawi need emergency food aid. Officially, Malawian President Bakili Muluzi consistently dismissed allegations of government collaboration with international aid organizations to take blood from famished villagers in exchange for food. President Muluzi accused opposition politicians of spreading the vampire stories to try to undermine his government.

The whole issue seems clouded in allegations and counter-allegations, and claims that Malawi blood is being collected and sold are somewhat suspect because international medical organizations aver that a large percentage of Malawi's population is HIV positive, which makes all blood from that country suspect.

VAMPIRES OF MALAYSIA

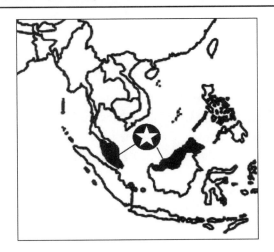

BAJANG

Japan is not the only country that has legends of feline vampires. The Bajang of Malaysia assumes the shape of a hungry polecat and goes hunting for children, stalking them on silent cat feet through the humid tropical nights.

Sometimes the Bajang is an independent monster, working according to its own wicked agenda. It can sometimes be more or less tamed by a witch or warlock into being their familiar. Bajang familiars will then be handed down from one generation to the next as a protector of the family and a weapon to be used against rivals. The enslaved Bajang is kept in a bamboo vessel called a tabong, is protected by various spells and charms and closed by a stopper made from special leaves. While the Bajang is imprisoned it is fed with eggs, and even though it is a slave, the Bajang will turn on its owner if it is given enough food.

When used as a weapon against its master's enemies, the Bajang does not rend and tear; rather it infects the master's enemies with a terrible wasting illness that, if not diagnosed and treated correctly, is fatal.

Many folktales have it that the Bajang is another of those tragic creatures that inhabit the corpse of a stillborn child. Unlike child vampires of Mexico and Croatia, the Bajang is brought into being through incantations.

Some folktales suggest that the Bajang is the male version of the female Langsuir. (*See* entry later in this section.)

BAS

The Chewong people of Malaysia believe in a vampiric being called the Bas. Not a blood drinker, the Bas hunts swine (its preferred prey) or humans (when animals are not conveniently at hand) to drain away their *ruwai*, loosely translated as soul, vitality, or life.

A woodland creature, the Bas will not venture into any town or village. It can even be frightened off by a simple campfire if the Bas takes it as a sign of civilization.

There are numerous tales by native Malaysians, ranging back hundreds of years, that claim that the Bas is a real monster. Some scholars and medical professionals believe that the Bas legend grew out of an attempt to explain plagues or the spread of other communicable diseases. But some modern believers refute these claims by saying that it is the bite of the Bas that spreads the disease.

ENG BANKA

Another soul-vampire in animal form is the Malaysian Eng Banka, a fierce dog creature that steals a person's soul, resulting in death within a few days. Though the Eng Banka is quick and clever, it is no more powerful than an ordinary dog and can be killed by any conventional method. However, the corpse of a slain Eng Banka should be burned and the ashes scattered to prevent the spirit from returning to the region.

Because the Eng Banka appears as a dog, or a dog-like creature, many rural Malaysians fear dogs that they do not know. They often carry charms to protect them against being approached by strange dogs.

The Bas. Artwork by Michael Katz.

CANINE SUPERSTITIONS

The Malaysians are by no means the only people who have superstitions concerning dogs. Here are many common beliefs tying dogs to the world of the supernatural:

- A howling dog at night means bad luck.

- A black dog is considered unlucky in some parts of the world.

- If a dog licks a newborn, the baby will always be a fast healer.

- Dogs are thought to be guides to the afterlife in both Egyptian and Eskimo cultures.

- Romans used "healer" dogs to lick the diseases out of people.

- If a dog howls by an open door, it is considered an omen of death.

- A dog howling during a child's birth is supposed to signal an unhappy life for the child.

- Some cultures believe that dogs are witches who took animal form and that they howl when other witches are nearby.

- A dog that howls three times in a row and then stops is supposed to signal the moment of a death.

- Hearing a dog barking first thing in the morning is thought to be a sign of misfortune.

- In Ireland, a strange dog digging up your garden means illness or death is on the way.

- If a dog sleeps with its tail straight out and its paws turned up, bad news is on the way. The direction the tail is pointing indicates the direction from which the bad news will come.

- In England it is a sure sign of good luck to have a strange dog follow you.

- A black and white dog crossing your path while you are on the way to a meeting means good luck at the meeting.

- A dog running between two newlyweds is an indication of many fights between them to come.

- If a dog runs between a woman's legs, the husband should have reason to doubt her fidelity.

- If a dog runs and hides under a table, expect a strong thunderstorm to occur.

- If a dog eats grass, it is supposed to rain.

- A dog scratching for a long period also means rain will come.

- A dog rolling on the ground is yet another reason to expect rain.

- A person bitten by a wild dog should eat a sandwich consisting of hairs from the dog and rosemary, leading to the cure for hangovers known as "the hair of the dog that bit you."

- Black poodles are placed on gravestones of German clergy who did not follow their religion too closely.

- The Greek Goddess of the hunt, Diana, was thought to ride with spectral hounds who would locate lost souls.

- Greeks thought dogs could foresee evil.

- Some black dogs are thought to be embodiments of unquiet souls, whereas others are thought to be protective guides to travelers.

- England has tales of packs of ghost hounds roaming the countryside. These hounds foretell death or disaster. To avoid spotting them, a person should drop face down onto the ground when they hear the dogs coming.

- The black spectral dog of Britain is called the Barghest, and is considered to be a harbinger of death.

- In Scotland, a new friendship will follow a strange dog coming to your house.

- Seeing three white dogs together is considered good luck.

- A black dog that follows a person and cannot be chased away is considered bad luck.

- Fishermen usually regard dogs as unlucky--so much so that they won't even mention the word "dog" while out at sea.

- Meeting a new dog, especially a Dalmatian, is thought to be good luck.

- A greyhound with a white spot on its forehead is considered good luck.

- A dog howling for no reason is thought to be howling at ghosts.

KAKLI BESAR

Tales of brutish, hairy monsters like Bigfoot appear all over the world, varying from the timid Yeti to the bloodthirsty Shampe. One of the most vicious of these predatory monsters is the Kakli Besar.

The Kakli Besar is a fearsome brute that stands well over eight feet tall. Its four-toed feet are at least eighteen inches long. The Malaysian tribespeople of the Johor believe this monster to be the direct creation of demonic forces.

The creature has haunted the region for years, preying on humans and livestock. In 1995, a massive hunt was conducted through the Tanjung Piai forests of Johor. Police and armed civilians scoured the woods, hoping to capture one of these monsters so that more could be learned about them. But the monsters eluded them.

Though nothing is known for sure about the nature of the Kakli Besar, the tribespeople have figured out various ways to keep it away. Smoky fires have driven them off in the past, as have loud metallic noises. Knowing this, villagers often burn leaves and grasses to keep the woods around their homes safe, and they hang empty tin cans on wires. In emergencies, they use gongs to drive away the Kakli Besar.

LANGSUIR (also Lansuyar)

Malaysia and Java share a number of cultural similarities, not the least of which are their troubles with vampires created from stillbirths and deaths of women during childbirth. The Malaysian Langsuir is a female vampire of overwhelming beauty who died from grief when her child was stillborn. Forty days after her burial she will rise from her grave as a vampire and fly away into the trees, forever haunting the region and hunting humans for their blood.

Though she has changed into a spirit of heart-rending beauty, the Langsuir can be identified as something other than human by her unnaturally long nails, green robes, and long silky black hair that hangs so low it swirls about her ankles. The long hair hides a second mouth that has formed at the back of her neck, and it is through this second mouth that she drinks the blood of children.

The Langsuir is also a flesh-eater and she will hunt, alone or in packs, eating raw fish caught in streams or attacking livestock.

The Langsuir. Artworkk by Robert Patrick O'Brien.

Like the Javanese vampires, the Langsuir can be crippled by burying it with its mouth filled with glass beads (in order to prevent it from making its hunting call or using its seductive voice to lure prey). Similarly, hens' eggs are placed in the vampire's armpits and long needles are driven through the hands to disable its ability to fly.

A Langsuir can even be cured and restored to normal humanity (a very rare turn of events in the world of vampires). To accomplish this, the Langsuir has to be captured and restrained. Her long hair must be shorn off and stuffed into the unnatural mouth at the back of her neck, and her fingernails should be cut all the way down to the skin. If these things are done correctly, the Langsuir will be restored to normalcy. She can even marry, have children, and live a normal life except in one regard: if she were to make merry and feel intense emotions, she would revert back to her vampiric self. Therefore the Langsuir must be sure to live a dour, somber life.

The stillborn child of a Langsuir is reborn as a Pontianak (*see* Vampires Of Java, p. 311, for more on this creature).

<u>MANEDEN</u>

One of the stranger animal vampires in Malaysia is the Maneden. These are small creatures that dwell in pandan trees and fiercely defend their territory. If a human disturbs its tree or cuts off the leaves, the Maneden will leap out and affix itself leech-like to the offender, sucking blood from the elbows of men and the nipples of women.

Once riled, the Maneden can only be appeased by an acceptable offering, such as a nut or choice tuber. Then it will take the offering and return, rather sulkily, to its tree. But like many animals (or animal-like creatures), the Maneden is likely to come prowling again once it gets hungry.

The creature can be killed by fire, but it is so fast and elusive that it is extraordinarily difficult to catch one or corner it long enough to burn the Maneden. Usually the Maneden will escape and thereafter become vengeful, preying exclusively on whoever tried to kill it.

MATI-ANAK

Another name for the Pontianak species of vampire (*see* Langsuir in this section and Pontianak in Vampires Of Java).

PELESIT

Vampires take many forms around the world, and quite a few are found in Malaysia, from animal vampires to the troubled ghosts of children to one of the strangest of all: symbiotic vampires. The Pelesit and the Polong are two blood drinkers that team up to overwhelm and destroy a victim from within.

The Pelesit arrives first, usually in the form of a house cricket. It burrows into a victim's head and begins to feed on the blood of the host. At the same time, it causes erratic behavior and madness in the victim, causing the person to rant and rave (often, for some inexplicable reason, about cats).

Once thus entrenched, the Pelesit invites a second creature, a bottle-imp called a Polong. This second creature is even stranger, appearing as a one-inch tall woman.

These two creatures are fashioned by a witch when the witch murders a man and fills a bottle with his blood. The witch then casts various spells over the bottle, and when the enchantment is done the creatures are manifested in the physical world.

Often these creatures are sent to a specific victim at the witch's direction. The terms of the witch's bargain are simple: the Polong, with the aid of the Pelesit, attacks the victim in exchange for being allowed to feed on the victim's living blood. When they are not feeding on an enemy, the imps must be fed by the witch with his or her own blood. If the Pelesit and Polong are not properly they will turn on their creator.

PENANGGALAN

The Penanggalan is one of the most gruesome vampires in the entire world. These bizarre creatures are created when women are startled during deep prayer. The shock causes their heads to leap off their bodies, dragging along their entrails and a twisted spine. These women become vampires and remain in this disgusting form throughout their immortal lives.

The Penanggalan generally dwell in trees and possess the ability to fly. The creature's flapping entrails drip a noxious fluid that spreads pestilence and disease. Should a Penanggalan linger too long in one place, the pooling fluids from its entrails will transform into a thorny, bioluminescent plant.

The Penanggalan preys on the blood of newborn babies or pregnant women. Sometimes it will force a pregnant woman to give birth so it can devour the newborn child.

Penanggalan are also thought to drain a mother's breasts of milk, or pollute the milk so that the nursing child will grow sick. To combat this, mothers should be given milk thistle. Milk thistle is a plant that has a variety of curative powers, including stimulating the production of breast milk.

All pregnant women and young children are kept inside at night to keep them safe from a Penanggalan's attack. A hunting Penanggalan will flit from house to house, looking for children or pregnant women in homes that are not properly protected. Malaysian women who fear the coming of a Penanggalan will strew dried thistle along their windowsills. The vampire will not come near these sharp thorns, fearing to get them caught in her entrails.

There are also rare cases where a witch will become a Penanggalan by choice. When a witch-Penanggalan returns to her secret lair she can immerse herself in a vat of vinegar and shrink her distorted self into a size that can be squeezed back into her body. Thereafter, during daylight hours, she will look and act normal; but come sunset the monster will emerge once more.

POLONG

See Pelesit.

PONTIANAK

See Vampires Of Java; as well as the listing for the Langsuir in this section.

MILK THISTLE

Milk Thistle (also known as Holy Thistle, Lady's Thistle, Marian Thistle, Mary Thistle, St. Mary Thistle, and Silybum) is a tall plant with large, prickly, glossy leaves and a reddish-purple, thistle-like flower. It has ancient curative powers that have been used as herbal medicines and proofs against evil. The plant protects the liver from chemical and biological toxins and is generally helpful for all liver disorders, including jaundice, cirrhosis, and hepatitis. It also helps stimulate the production of mother's milk, something that is considered a powerful natural magic by many cultures.

Milk Thistle is also thought to have antioxidant properties, positive effects on blood and immunity, and (in the case of Silymarin), may also decrease cholesterol levels.

SANTU SANKAI

The Santu Sankai (translated as "Mouth Men") are savage monsters from the dense forests near Kuala Lumpor. These hideous creatures appear to be a kind of werewolf and, like wolves, they often attack in packs. They are fierce predators, hunting animal and human alike for blood and fresh meat.

The Santu Sankai are very much like movie werewolves, particularly those in films like *The Howling* and *Dog Soldiers*. They are as tall as men, but with deformed bodies. They stand on two wolf-like legs, but have well-muscled human torsos and human arms that end in great clawed hands. Their most striking features, however, are their hideous faces and wolf snouts that gape wide to reveal savage fangs.

Though the more urban and modern residents of Malaysia tend to discount stories of the Santu Sankai, sightings in rural areas persist. In 1967, Henri Van Heerdan, a hunter on a trip to Kuala Lumpor, reported to the police that a pair of the monsters attacked him. Though his truck was damaged and he looked like he had been knocked about, the civilian authorities failed to take his claim seriously. He led them back to the scene and showed them splashes of blood from his encounter, as well as a scattering of footprints that seemed to be a strange mixture of human and animal. No further traces of these creatures have since been found.

Santu Sankai. Artwork by Robert Patrick O'Brien.

VAMPIRES OF MEXICO

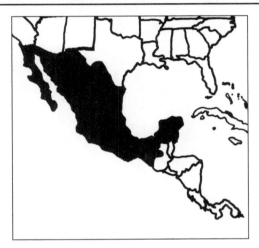

CAMAZOTZ

Camazotz is a religious figure found in Mayan tales. He is depicted as half-man and half-bat and, despite his appearance, is a kindly spirit who presides over crops and health. He lives deep in the caves and comes out at the behest of supplicants in order to bless their fields, their livestock, and the health of whole villages.

Though humble and quiet, Camazotz can be riled to great violence in defense of his worshipers. Folktales tell of him destroying demons and overthrowing monsters who tried to bring crop blight and plague to regions under his protection.

Stone carving of Camazotz. Artwork by Michael Katz.

CHUPACABRA

The Chupacabra (translated as "sucker of goats") is a strange bestial vampire that attacks animals for their blood. Though primarily a Mexican vampire, the Chupacabra has been reported all over lower North America, and even recently in South America. In recent years, sightings have increased and photos have been produced, purportedly showing an authentic flesh-and-blood creature.

The Chupacabra has three powerful claws on each "hand," a bristling line of tall spines running from skull to tailbone, and mottled skin. Many reports suggest that it has a face very much like that of a baboon; others say that it is more like a mutated rat. Some reports also claim it has wings.

The Chupacabra is shy of people, preferring to attack goats and other livestock for fresh blood. This bizarre creature may either be another of the world's many vampires, or a species of a mortal creature not currently identified and cataloged. There are many theories as to its origin.

Chupacabra wall painting. Artwork by Michael Katz.

Many UFO researchers have noted that sightings of the Chupacabra began shortly after a large number of UFOs were reported in the Mexican skies, leading some to speculate that the creature may be an extraterrestrial vampire.

Another theory is that the creature (or creatures) is something that escaped from a genetics testing lab somewhere in Texas, and that the reason there have been no official statements despite abundant evidence of the creature's existence is that there is a massive government cover-up in progress.

Yet another take is that the Chupacabra is some ancient and possibly prehistoric subterranean species driven to the surface by oil and natural gas mining.

Skeptics frequently bring up the wild tales of the Vampire of Moca, a creature that attacked livestock in Puerto Rico back in 1975. It turned out that the "vampire" was actually some crocodiles that had gone wandering far from their swamp and were eating everything in sight. The link between the Vampire of Moca and the Chupacabra was actually first made by Chupacabra believers, because both events began shortly after a rash of UFO sightings.

Whatever the Chupacabra may actually be, sightings continue and increase with each passing year.

CIHUATETEO (also Civatateo)

It is very curious that vampiric manifestations in different parts of the world, even in Pre-Columbian days, are so very similar. One case in point is the Cihuateteo of the Aztec people of old Mexico. Like the Kudlak of Croatia, the Babylonian Ekimmu, the Pontianak of Java, and the Langsuir of Malaysia, this Aztec vampire is a Revenant of a woman who died in childbirth. Unique among these similar vampires, however, the Cihuateteo's child is also a vampire.

The undead mother and child haunt the night and attack children, crippling them with a dreadful paralysis or infecting them with a wasting sickness. Sometimes the Cihuateteo and her child drink their victims' blood, but most often they feed on the essence of fear, and on the life force discharged as a person wastes away and dies of a lingering disease.

The Cihuateteo have pale faces and pasty skin. They dress in costumes like those worn by Tlazolteotl, the goddess of sorcery, lust, and evil. Fending off a Cihuateteo is very difficult and usually requires holy charms that were sacred to the ancient Aztecs. Modern crosses will not work, even if the Cihuateteo was a Christian in life.

Only the adult Cihuateteo is vulnerable to Aztec charms; her child, who never knew the rites and rituals of any religion, is immune to them. The only weapon known to work against both creatures is fire, and even then it will merely drive them off. No known method of totally destroying this vampiric pair is yet known.

TLAHUELPUCHI

Another Aztec vampire that attacks infants and young children for their blood is the Tlahuelpuchi. This creature is a shapeshifter that can adopt any form: cat, dog, bird. Their preferred shape is that of a turkey. While in animal guise, the Tlahuelpuchi glow with an unholy light. This allows the creature to easily be spotted and pursued (although pursuit should only be done in armed groups, never by a single person). To avoid pursuit, the Tlahuelpuchi will shapeshift into very fast animals such as cats, elusive animals such as birds, or, more often, nearly invisible creatures such as ticks or fleas.

For the most part the Tlahuelpuchi is not a Revenant but a person born under a curse, doomed to be a Living Vampire. Though the Tlahuelpuchi can be male or female, the females are far more common and much more powerful. The Tlahuelpuchi do not reside in trees or graves, but pass as ordinary humans during the daytime.

These creatures cannot escape their doom, though some are unaware of it and live contented lives during the day, not knowing that they transform into monsters at night. Other Tlahuelpuchi know what they are, and dwell with their human families, hiding their true evil natures. A Tlahuel-puchi residing with its family will seldom be turned in for its crimes, no matter how extreme or heinous. This is not due to familial love, but because if a Tlahuelpuchi is caught and killed, its curse will instantly pass to the betrayer.

It is also possible for the victim of a Tlahuelpuchi to rise from the grave as one of these foul creatures. To prevent victims from becoming

Tlahuelpuchi, a village shaman must use precise burial rites to establish an air of sanctity around both the corpse and the grave.

Unlike most vampires, the Tlahuelpuchi only needs to feed once a month. It may feed more often if possible, but should it miss its monthly feeding it will die. At night, when everyone is asleep, a Tlahuelpuchi will shapeshift into one of its chosen forms and go hunting for innocent blood. Like other predators, the Tlahuelpuchi are fiercely territorial and will violently defend their hunting grounds.

Mexican "Lust Mask" created by El 7 Coldivar of Tonala, Jalisco. The transformation of man into a cat-like beast is known in many regions, including Mexico. The pictured mask represents the Father of a family. The Mother is painted on the mask's forehead. The small cats around the neck are the Children. The mask is also known by the name Nahual. Used with permission of GoBamba USA, Inc., (c) 2003. See www.anymask.com, www.gobamba.com, and www.mayapan.com..

Though the Tlahuelpuchi may enter any house without invitation they are bound by strange rituals. Before entering they must assume bird shape and fly over the house from north to south then east to west, forming a cross pattern. This casts an enchantment that allows them entry. To save the victim's soul, a local shaman must disenchant the victim by "uncrossing" them.

Proper precautions include placing garlic and onions around doors, windows, and an infant's bed. The Tlahuelpuchi fears sharp metal, so an open pair of scissors left on a night stand near a crib is often enough of a deterrent to keep the child safe. Protective spells and charms can deny the creature its food and starve it to death. Some villagers pin small religious medallions and icons to their children's clothing as further protection, and it is believed that mirrors can sometimes scare this monster off.

TLACIQUE

The Tlaciques are vampire-witches among Mexico's Nahautl Indians. They possess a variety of supernatural powers that help them attack their prey and elude capture, including the ability to transform into blazing balls of flame. They can fly like fireballs across the sky, or dance through the woods like a Will-o'-the-Wisp, and often attack their prey in these fiery shapes. For some unknown reason their touch does not burn their victims, but mesmerizes them. The victims then slip into a stupor while the Tlacique drinks their blood.

If pursued, Tlaciques sometimes turn into ordinary animals, most usually fowl like turkeys. In this innocuous form they can blend in with farm animals, going unnoticed while feeding a bit here and there from animals as well as farmers.

XIPE-TOTEC

The name Xipe-Totec means "Our Lord the Flayed One." Less a vampire and more of a blood drinking god of the Nahuatl Aztecs, Xipe-Totec was the pre-Columbian Mexican god of spring (the beginning of the rainy season) and of new vegetation. His statues and stone masks always show him wearing a freshly flayed human skin, symbolizing the "new skin" (vegetation) that covered the Earth in the spring.

However, this flaying of skin was not just a mythological incident. During the second month of the Aztec year (*Tlacaxipehualiztli*, which translates as "Flaying of Men"), Aztec priests would kill human victims by removing their hearts. They would then flay the bodies and wear the skins, which were dyed yellow and called *teocuitlaquemitl* ("golden clothes"). Other victims would be fastened to a frame and put to death by arrows. Their blood dripping down was believed to symbolize fertile spring rains.

Xipe-Totec was actually considered a "gentle god" by Aztec standards. But he was by no means a passive one, and is upheld as the Aztec god of war.

Xipe-Totec. Artwork by Michael Katz.

VAMPIRES OF MOLDAVIA

DRAKUL

The novel *Dracula* by Bram Stoker does have some basis in vampire lore, even though it takes great license in its presentation of vampire powers and defenses. Aside from basing Count Dracula on Vlad Tepes (a native of Turkey), much of Stoker's information on vampires can be found in the legend of the Moldavian Drakul. The name actually means "devil" (or, according to some sources, "dragon") and is a common, and rather harsh, expletive. Fighting words, in any country.

The Drakul is a blood drinking Revenant, pale of skin and hollow-eyed —much like the common image of the vampire on film, but without the tuxedo and opera cloak. The Drakul keeps the name it had while it was alive.

Similar to the Vampiro of Moravia, the Drakul maintains a strange symbiotic relationship with a demon. They are essentially two parts of a single unnatural being. The Drakul requires the demon's assistance to move around at night and find victims upon which to feed.

Like the fictitious Dracula, the Drakul cannot be separated from its coffin for long or it will perish. But unlike the famous Count, the Drakul carries its coffin around on its head.

Since the Drakul must sleep by day in its coffin, the most direct way to kill it is to steal the coffin. Direct, perhaps, but not easy, because the Drakul is vicious and fast, and very powerful. The demon acts as a watchdog and will warn of any attack.

Disinterring a sleeping Drakul and stealing its coffin is marginally safer. It is generally helpful to bring along lots of garlic, a headsman's axe, a few torches, and a priest on any such outing.

Photo by Robert Patrick O'Brien.

VAMPIRES OF FACT AND FICTION

Dracula was not the only fictional vampire to be based on an actual person (in his case, Vlad III of Wallachia). Nineteenth century novelist Joris-Karl Husyman, writer of the 1891 novel *La Bas* ("*Down There*", a reference to Hell), based his fictional vampire on French Marshal Gilles de Rais. de Rais served for years as a soldier of Christ, and fought alongside Joan D'Arc in the fifteenth century. But de Rais later went mad, and he tortured and murdered close to 300 children.

ZMEU

The Zmeu is a Will-o'-the-Wisp creature, able to transform into a ball of flame. Girls and young women are its favorite prey, and once it has entered their bedchambers it will transform into a handsome young man with supernatural charismatic powers. In this form the vampire will seduce its victims and either drain them of blood or life essence.

In nearby Transylvania, stories of Zmeu are switched around: the creature adopts the form of a lovely young woman who seduces and feeds upon young male shepherds.

Going further back into the legends of various Balkan cultures, there was another and wholly different monster bearing the name Zmeu. These elder creatures were gigantic ogres covered in scales, like armor plating. They had several hearts, making them harder to kill and incapable of tiring. They also rode horses.

Like the more modern Zmeu, the ogres were shapeshifters who could trick their prey by appearing as friends, lovers, animals, and even birds of the sky. Perhaps these older monsters were the ancestors of the bloody creatures who have so long haunted the long cold Moldavian nights.

WILL-O'-THE-WISP

Will-o'-the-Wisp is the common name given to mysterious lights that are believed to lead travelers from well-trodden paths into treacherous marshes, quicksand, or other dangers and dooms. The Latin name for Will-o'-the-Wisp is *Ignis Fatuus*, which means "foolish fire." It is also often referred to as a "corpse candle."

Folklorists have always disagreed on the nature of the Will-o'-the-Wisp, arguing that it is a ghost, a faerie, a demon, or even a vampire. It is commonly agreed, however, that the Will-o'-the-Wisp is not a cute little forest sprite, but rather a malevolent spirit. The Will-o'-the-Wisp is also commonly believed to be a spirit (or somehow connected to a spirit) of a person who could not enter either heaven or hell, and is forever doomed to wander the earth. It is also frequently linked to funerals, or ghostly repetitions of funerals.

Scientists believe that the Will-o'-the-Wisp is an illusion formed by marsh gases. Under the right kinds of weather and environmental conditions, pockets of methane created by rotting vegetation can spontaneously ignite to form standing flames. Ball lightning is another natural phenomenon often blamed for sightings of the Will-o'-the-Wisp.

UFO-logists claim that the Will-o'-the-Wisp is a form of intelligent alien life or an alien ship here to observe us. In recent reports of crop circles, glowing balls of light have been frequently filmed and reported.

The Will-o'-the-Wisp is called by scores of different names across Europe. Here are just a handful:
  • Cornwall and Somerset: Joan the Wad
  • East Anglia: The Lantern Man
  • Hertfordshire and East Anglia: The Hobby Lantern
  • Lancashire: Peg-a-Lantern
  • Lowland Scotland: Spunkies
  • Norfolk: Will-o'-the-Wikes
  • North Yorkshire and Northumberland: Jenny with the Lantern
  • Shropshire: Will the Smith
  • Somerset and Devon: Hinky Punk
  • The West Country: Jacky Lantern; Jack a Lantern
  • Wales: Pwca and the Ellylldan
  • Warwickshire Gloucestershire: Hobbedy's Lantern
  • Worcestershire: Pinket

VAMPIRES OF MONTENEGRO

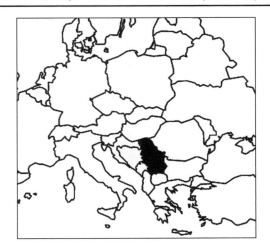

TENATZ

The legend of the Tenatz might explain how some vampires are able to rise from and return to their graves without churning the soil. These vampires can shapeshift into mice, and then burrow down through the earth.

The Tenatz are Revenants, reanimated through post-mortem demonic possession. Once freed of their graves, they transform back into their true corpse-like forms and roam the countryside looking for victims. The Tenatz are thirsty blood drinkers but not overly brave, preferring to attack sleeping victims rather than those who are wide-awake and potentially difficult prey.

A Tenatz can be destroyed by fire and decapitation, and staking it will render it helpless and unable to rise from its coffin. Severing the creature's hamstrings is also a common custom for limiting its activities.

Tenatz. Artwork by Robert Patrick O'Brien.

VJESTITIZA

In Montenegro and nearby Serbia there is a female witch-vampire who (along with so many of her kind) preys mainly on children. This beast, the Vjestitiza, is generally described as an old crone who undergoes a transformation when she settles down to sleep each night: her vampiric soul, in the form of a glowing ball of light, leaves her physical body and hunts for young blood. The Vjestitiza can also transform into animals, such as a hen, a black moth, or a fly. The Vjestitiza's fireball state may merely be a transitional stage between woman and animal.

Vjestitiza. Artwork by Michael Katz.

The transformed Vjestitiza enters the house of her prey and feeds on her victim's blood. Sometimes she will even cut out the heart and take it with her.

On some nights, several Vjestitiza will hold coven meetings in beast shape. They discuss evil spells and ancient lore, and occasionally share hearts they have stolen from sleeping children. An old woman wishing to join the coven and gain supernatural powers must first swear a blood oath to uphold the rules and defend the coven's secrecy. Breaking faith with her dark sisters will result in a horrible death.

A Vjestitiza is at the very peak of her powers during the first cold week of March. Knowing this, the wise folk of the village perform rituals of protection to deny a Vjestitiza access to their houses. The prescribed method is to stir the ashes in a home's hearth with two horns, then stick the horns into the pile of ashes.

If a woman is suspected of being a Vjestitiza, she will be arrested by the villagers and put on trial. However, the "trial" is very much like those held in Eastern and Western Europe. It is popularly believed that no witch can drown, so they tie the suspect up and throw her into the river. If she floats, then she is clearly guilty. If she drowns, she is innocent. Such rough justice makes it dicey to be a suspected Vjestitiza, inasmuch as the result is the same for the innocent and the guilty.

VAMPIRES OF MORAVIA

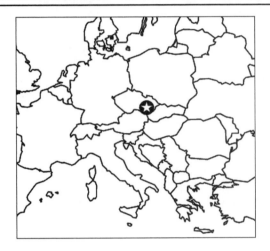

OUPIRE

The Oupire is a typical Slovonic Revenant in that it is a human who returned from the dead to prey on its family and village. Oupires attack livestock as well as humans, depending on their hunger. Oupires spread throughout Moravia, Hungary, Poland, and Silesia during the mid- to late-seventeenth century, and the number of Oupire attacks increased to nearly plague proportions. The Oupires also spread disease, so in effect they had the effect of an actual plague.

Vampire slayers who know their business rely on tried and true methods of disposal. Once an Oupire's grave is identified, the Oupire is disinterred. A long stake is driven through the creature's chest to pin it in place in its coffin. Its head is cut off and its heart removed, then the entire creature—body, head, heart, and coffin—is burned to ashes.

DISSERTATION ON SLAVIC MONSTERS

Dom Augustin Calmet was a revered French cleric, scholar, and occult researcher, born in Lorraine in 1672. He wrote one of the most famous and influential works on Slavic vampires: *Dissertations Sur Les Apparitions Des Anges Des Demons Et Des Espits, Et Sur Les Revenants, Et Vampires De Hundrie, De Boheme, De Moravic, Et De Silesie.*

In the book's preface, Dom Calmet cited the frequency with which vampires infested Slavonic countries, and suggested that vampires may not have spread to Western Europe until the end of the seventeenth century. He wrote:

> "In this present age and for about sixty years past, we have been the hearers and the witnesses of a new series of extraordinary incidents and occurrences. Hungary, Moravia, Silesia, Poland, are the principal theatre of these happenings. For here we are told that dead men, men who have been dead for several months, I say, return from the tomb, are heard to speak, walk about, infest hamlets and villages, injure both men and animals, whose blood they drain thereby making them sick and ill, and at length actually causing death. Nor can men deliver themselves from these terrible visitations, nor secure themselves from these horrid attacks, unless they dig the corpses up from the graves, drive a sharp stake through these bodies, cut off the heads, tear out the hearts; or else they burn the bodies to ashes.

> "The name given to these ghosts is Oupires, or Vampires, that is to say blood-suckers, and the particulars which are related of them are so singular, so detailed, accompanied with circumstances so probable and so likely, as well as with the most weighty and well-attested legal deposition that it seems impossible not to subscribe to the belief which prevails in those countries that these Apparitions do actually come forth from their graves and that they are able to produce the terrible effects which are so widely and so positively attributed to them."

VAMPIRES OF MOROCCO

BOUDA

The Bouda is a Living Vampire found in Morocco (as well as in Tanzania and Ethiopia). It uses sorcery to transform itself into a were-hyena. This creature loosely fits into the categories of vampire and werewolf, blurring the line of distinction between the two. It is alive, but is a shapeshifter, eats flesh, and drinks human blood. The Bouda is also very strong and deeply cunning.

Most Boudas are blacksmiths by trade, and use their skills to make powerful dark magic charms designed to enhance their supernatural powers of sorcery and shapeshifting. When it is in animal form, the Bouda looks every bit like a normal hyena. But in order to transform back to human after a hunt, the Bouda must wear a charm or object that it normally wears while it is human. This link to its humanity saves it from eventually turning into a normal (and spiritually benign) hyena; but it is also the only way in which vampire slayers can identify the creature and hunt it down.

While in its hyena form, it can be killed by any method that would kill an ordinary animal. When it is human it is as vulnerable as any man. But in both forms it is wicked and cunning. The Bouda is a master of trickery and deception. It uses various forms of chicanery to confuse its prey and foil the pursuit of slayers who want to end its reign of terror.

Hyena. Artwork by Shane MacDougall.

VAMPIRES OF NAMIBIA

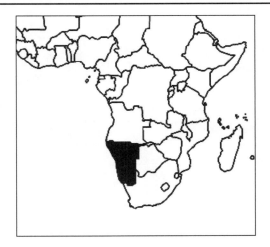

OTGIRURU

The Herero people of Namibia are plagued by a species of vampire called an Otgiruru, which is the demonic reincarnation of a dead medicine man or sorcerer. Unable, or more often, unwilling to depart into the afterlife, the ghost looks for some way to create a new body. But unlike Revenant vampires, the Otgiruru uses its supernatural will to construct a new body composed of dirt and offal from the earth. This new form is usually shaped like a dog or some hulking dog-like creature, but the mind and will within is that of the dead sorcerer.

In its dog-like guise, the Otgiruru lures victims with its plaintive and compelling howl, then attacks the inquisitive tribesmen and drinks their blood. Often it pretends to be a family pet or familiar village dog that has been injured, playing off the sympathies of kind hearts who can't stand to see or hear an animal suffer.

The Otgiruru is a vicious monster but it will only confront people one at a time. It flees from groups of two or more, unless they are young and vulnerable.

A spear can pierce it but will not kill the creature. Tribesmen use a spear to pin it to the ground so that it can be hacked to pieces and then burned.

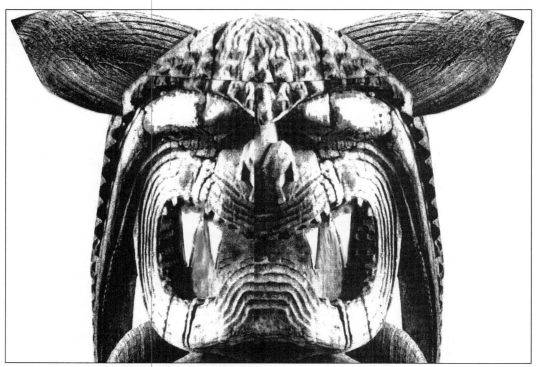

Otgiruru carving. Artwork by Michael Katz.

VAMPIRES OF NATIVE AMERICAN CULTURES

Among the many Native American nations there are thousands of tales of supernatural creatures, both evil and holy. Though few of these resemble vampires as defined by popular fiction, there are several creatures that have preyed on the flesh, blood, and souls of the peoples who populated pre-Columbian North and South America.

The following sections present just a few of the beings that are most closely akin to vampires or werewolves.

Photo by Jason Lukridge.

ATAKAPA (Choctaw)

The Atakapa (Attakapa, Attacapa) nation of Native Americans, including the subgroups Akokisas and Deadoses, occupied the coastal and bayou areas of southwestern Louisiana and southeastern Texas until the early 1800s. Atakapa means "eaters of men" in Choctaw, but the question has been raised whether the Atakapas were cannibals for subsistence or ritual. Some legends have it that the Atakapa were not merely cannibalistic humans but some species of supernatural predator, possibly a ghoul or a type of flesh-eating vampire. Unfortunately most of what is known of the Atakapa comes from European accounts which were rarely accurate nor sympathetic to any Native American peoples of the time.

LOFA (Chickasaw)

Many of the blood drinking or flesh-eating monsters of North America, especially those whose sightings continue into modern day, seem to be variations of what most people would refer to as Bigfoot. Among the Chickasaw of Oklahoma (the reservation to which they were transplanted), and their ancestors in what is now Mississippi, there is a story of a race of intelligent beast men called the Lofa.

Stories vary as to whether these creatures were evil, but most accounts relate that they were certainly hostile. They raided Chickasaw camps, killed the men, and took the women to mate and breed with them. In many stories the Lofas not only killed braves who were trying to protect their women, but tore their throats out and drank their blood as well.

Like the Sasquatch and the Shampe, the Lofa exuded a horrible body odor that was so pungent it could actually kill.

Although the Lofa was very strong and highly intelligent (even to the point of being capable of human speech), it could be killed. However, it was fiercely clannish and no Lofa clan would ever allow the body of one of their dead to be kept by humans.

MAI-COH (Skinwalkers) (Navajo)

The Mai-Coh are more commonly known as Skinwalkers or Navajo Witches. They are shapeshifting tricksters who prey on their own people.

The Navajos are the largest Native American tribe in North America. There are over 170,000 tribal members. As with any culture there are some members that do not follow the laws of their people. In the beliefs of the *Diné* (the correct term for Navajo), each person is required to follow the strict teachings of the Gods in order to achieve *Hózhó*, which is a state of harmony with all things. Though many Diné who stray from their culture are not evil, those who are evil are considered witches. To the Diné, witchcraft is evil magic that a person uses to do harm to another person.

Some of these witches are called "Skinwalkers" because they stalk the night wearing animal skins, looking for unsuspecting victims. Through ancient native spiritual abilities and powers, these Skinwalkers have the ability to imitate the animal whose skin they are wearing. For example, the witch will wear the skin of a wolf in order to be infused with that predator's power and qualities. The Skinwalkers can mimic any animal they choose, including a cat, coyote, dog, or bear. They pick different skins for different purposes. The coyote skin is for high speed, accurate sense of smell, and acute agility; the bearskin is for brute strength; and so on.

The Skinwalker is a very powerful creature. It can run faster than a galloping horse and jump mesa cliffs without any effort at all.

Unlike the theatrical werewolf that becomes a monster only during the full moon, real werewolves around the world, including the Skinwalkers, are not so limited. They can become an animal at any time they choose.

In animal form the Skinwalkers do not lose their ability to think and plot. They plan out the best ways to cause misery and suffering. Skinwalkers possess the power of mind control and use it to make their victims hurt or even kill themselves. Skinwalkers have also been known to place objects in their victims' bodies, such as tiny pieces of bone, to pollute the victims' health and cause pain, illness, even death.

Skinwalkers can be killed by ordinary means, but locating them is by no means easy.

Skinwalkers do not actually consume the flesh or blood of their victims. In many respects they are more like Psychic Vampires (such as the Succubus and Incubus) in that they feed off the disharmony they cause. They also cause sickness and death like the plague-spreading vampires such as the Asasabonsam, Impundulu, and Sampiro. One method of creating illness is by taking dust made from burned corpses and blowing it down through the smoke hole at the top of a *Hogan* (Navajo house). This dust is called "Corpse Powder" and anyone who breathes it becomes physically and spiritually ill. The disease is generally diagnosed by a Crystal Gazer or a Hand Trembler (*Ndilniihii*), who determines which ritual curing ceremony must be performed by a Singer (*Hatáálii*) to defeat this evil disease. Unfortunately, in the twenty-first century few *Hatáálii* know the full curing rituals.

Ritual Sings can be used to weaken the Skinwalker's powers and turn his own evil back on himself. Once the Skinwalker is defeated, everyone involved in the matter must do what their custom requires to return themselves to *Hózhó*, or harmony.

Wolf wood carving. Artwork by Michael Katz.

HARMONY AND BALANCE

The *Diné* (Navajo) believe that everything in nature and the universe has a male and a female aspect. Consider the weather, for example: male rains are hard and full of wind and lightning, whereas female rains are gentle and soaking. This philosophy is similar in many ways to China's Yin and Yang concepts.

By extension, the Diné believe that all people have a male and female aspect. Male energy is logical, courageous, ambitious, unemotional, and assertive. Female energy is creative, intuitive, psychic, loving, and nurturing. For any person to maintain good health and prosperity these two aspects must be kept in perfect harmony.

Hózhó symbolizes the basic Diné belief in harmony and balance. To the Diné, being in perfect emotional balance and in harmony with the universe is fundamental and is the basis for all Diné spirituality. To "step outside of Hózhó" is to step into a state of sickness or evil, because it means being out of balance with the universe.

OLD WOMAN BAT (Apache)

The Chiricahua Apaches of New Mexico have a legend of a supernatural batlike creature named Old Woman Bat, the mother of all bats. Old Woman Bat was not evil, and came to the aid of one of the younger Apache heroes, Killer of Enemies.

In the great tale of the Monster Eagles, Killer of Enemies set out to save his people from gigantic predatory birds that dominated the skies and carried off children. The mighty young warrior allowed himself to be captured so the Monster Eagles would carry him up to their lofty nest. There he slew all of the creatures, including their young. But he soon realized that he was trapped hundreds of feet above the ground with no way down.

After some time, he spotted a gigantic bat flying past and recognized it as Old Woman Bat. Killer of Enemies appealed to her for help and, grateful that he had killed the evil Monster Eagles, she agreed to carry him down.

On her back she wore a basket, affixed with straps made of spider's silk. Killer of Enemies was positive the basket wouldn't hold him, but Old

KILLER OF ENEMIES, THE MONSTER SLAYER

Killer of Enemies appears in various stories in Chiricahua and Mescalero mythology, and makes frequent appearances, usually as a hero, in the cultural histories of the Navajo, Western Apache, Lipan, and Jicarilla tribes. In the Navajo stories he is Monster Slayer, brother to Born for Water, and a Herculean hero of a great many epic tales.

Among the Chiricahua and Mescalero, Killer of Enemies often plays a lesser role. He is still heroic, but has a tendency to get into trouble.

Killer of Enemies has not always been regarded as a hero. In many cultures, even among some parts of the Apache culture, he is regarded as a vicious prankster. Anthropologists have recorded several cases where parents and grandparents would not allow children to utter the name Killer of Enemies, telling them that it is the name of the "devil" or an "evil one."

Killer of Enemies. Artwork by Michael Katz.

Woman Bat insisted he climb in. She knew she was unable to fly with his weight, so she decided that she would crawl down the cliff's rocky wall with Killer of Enemies on her back. Before they set out she warned him that he had to keep his eyes closed, and that if he opened them even for a moment they would both fall. Killer of Enemies squeezed his eyes shut and Old Woman Bat set off climbing down, with Killer of Enemies clinging to her in stark terror. As they descended, Old Woman Bat sang an ancient song in a high, exotic voice.

Though Old Woman Bat was powerful, Killer of Enemies' weight was oppressive and made her wobble from side to side. Convinced that they were about to fall, Killer of Enemies opened his eyes to look. Immediately, whatever spell Old Woman Bat had been using (presumably related to her song) was broken and they fell.

Old Woman Bat landed first and broke her legs, then Killer of Enemies fell hard atop her, smashing her legs even further. According to the Apaches, this mishap is the reason bats have short and stunted legs.

SHÍTA (Hopi)

The Hopi people of the Southwest tell of a cannibalistic creature called a Shíta. This monster preyed on the village of Oraíbi, attacking and devouring any children it could catch. When it could not catch a child it would turn and attack any person, young or old, slaughtering and feasting on them.

Frightened and frustrated, the villagers appealed to two magical brothers from a nearby village, Pöokónghoya and his younger brother Balö'ngahoya. The brothers asked the villagers to make each of them a special arrow, and then they went hunting. They ambushed the Shíta and allowed themselves to be swallowed whole by this enormous beast. Once inside the creature the brothers shot their magical arrows into its heart, slaying it.

This method of slaying of the creature—a wooden shaft through the heart—ties the Shíta legend to vampire legends from many other cultures. Although the Shíta never returned to earth to again trouble the living, the story is still told how Pöokónghoya and Balö'ngahoya defeated it . . . just in case the knowledge will ever come in handy again.

SHAMPE (Chocktaw)

The Choctaws have always had legends of great monsters and demons, and the most terrifying of all is the gigantic bloodthirsty beast called the Shampe.

This creature lives deep in the forests of western North America, and only emerges from his secret lair to hunt at night. The Shampe is one of only a handful of blood drinkers who actually fear and shun sunlight, but this is one of the creature's few weaknesses.

Shampe. Used with permission, (c) 2003 by Jack Schrader.

The Shampe has supernaturally acute senses, particularly those of sight and smell. It has a shark's ability to smell blood miles away and will relentlessly stalk anyone who is injured or carrying freshly killed game. Once on the track of its prey it is nearly impossible to shake loose. One trick is for the person to drop his bloody game and leave it behind for the Shampe. Another option is to shoot something else and leave its dead or dying body behind to distract the beast.

Fortunately there are qualities about this monster that have helped some of its intended victims survive. The Shampe has a particularly pungent odor, similar to that of a skunk, but sharper. It is so powerful that it can be smelled miles away. Some tales claim that the smell alone can kill, especially when the creature is very close. The Shampe also makes a high-pitched whistling sound, particularly when it is hunting, and this has always been a clear signal for the Chocktaw to flee the vicinity.

Like the Sasquatch and Wendigo—two other brutes from the North American forests—the Shampe is generally described as being covered in with coarse brown hair. But there are some reports that the creature is entirely hairless, suggesting either a different species of the creature, or perhaps the existence of males and females.

The creature is so fearsome and hard to kill that for centuries Choctaws would not live in any part of the forest where a Shampe had been spotted, even if the forest was rife with game and food.

Reports of the Shampe have all but disappeared in the last half of the twentieth century, but in recent years the Choctaw people have reported hearing its eerie whistling cry in their woods.

SKIN SHIFTING OLD WOMAN (Wichita)

A story from the Wichita Nation of Native Americans tells of an old woman who was a different kind of vampire: one who stole beauty rather than lifeblood. She did it by actually stealing another person's skin, hence the name "Skin Shifting Old Woman."

In the tale, a young woman often helped an older woman named Little Old Woman with the tiring task of gathering wood. Each day they would go deeper and deeper into the forest to collect great bundles of firewood. The younger woman was kind and very beautiful and did as much as she could to ease Little Old Woman's burden; and each night when they returned to their village, the younger woman was greeted by her handsome and loving husband (known in the legends as Healthy Flint Stone Man), who also happened to be the chief of the village. Little Old Woman began to envy the younger woman's youth and beauty, and the attention that the woman's husband lavished on her. Little Old Woman made a pact with dark forces, then waited for an opportunity to strike.

One day while they were deep in the woods, Little Old Woman helped the younger woman load a heavy burden of sticks onto her back. But instead of adjusting the straps, the older woman wrapped them around her rival's throat and choked her to death.

Using magical powers she acquired from her unholy pact with dark forces, Little Old Woman blew on the top of her victim's head, and the young woman's hair and skin came right off. Then the old woman put on the wife's skin, but because the dead woman had been smaller, the skin had to be stretched to fit. Little Old Woman then smoothed down the skin until it fitted her nicely. Next, she took the skinless corpse and threw it in a nearby stream. Finally, she took her pile of wood and carried it back to the village.

Once back in the village, Little Old Woman began to fear that her disguise would not work, especially because she had stretched the skin. She pretended to be ill, but this proved to be a mistake. She was put under the care of a healer named Buffalo Crow Man, who proved to be extremely perceptive and schooled in the supernatural. During the course of her supposed convalescence he deduced that she was not the lovely young wife of Healthy Flint Stone Man, but some kind of vampiric parasite that had taken over her body.

Buffalo Crow Man bound the woman to her bed and immediately began an exorcism using a sacred curing ceremony. This ritual subdued the woman and revealed her true face, and the chief ordered that the evil creature be slain.

Healthy Flint Stone Man was torn apart by grief and wandered through the woods, eventually coming across the spot where the murder had taken place. He sat by his wife's bundle of sticks and wept bitterly for his lost love. Although he did not know it, by chance he sat down facing east, in the direction of

Skin shifting old woman. Used with permission, (c) 2003 by Bill Chancellor.

the flowing stream where Little Old Woman had disposed of his wife's body. After spending hours alone with his heartache, he heard a voice singing:

Woman-having-Powers-in-the-Water,
Woman-having-Powers-in-the-Water,
I am the one you seek,
I am here in the water.

He knew at once that the voice was that of his wife. Healthy Flint Stone Man rushed to the water's edge and there he saw his wife—his real wife—standing whole and alive. The exorcism performed by Buffalo Crow Man had not only led to the vampire's destruction, but had somehow restored both flesh and life to the chief's lovely young wife.

TOAD WOMAN (Penobscot)

Among the Penobscot tribes of the Algonquin nation (in Maine) there is a legend of a creature called the Toad Woman (no relation to the Horned Toad Woman of Hopi legends). Toad Woman, wearing only green moss and a cedar bark belt, would assume the form of a seductive woman and lure unwary men into her embrace. This creature would also enter villages crying that she lost her child, in order to trick people into letting her hold an infant. In some stories she then soothes the child into sleeping, but this is a sleep from which the child will never awake. Other stories report Toad Woman carrying off her victims and killing them in a more violent manner.

Toad Woman. Artwork by Robert O'Brien.

U`TLÛÑ'TÄ (Cherokee)

A Cherokee legend tells of a terrible bloodthirsty ogress who slaughters people and eats their livers. Known as the U`tlûñ'tä, this she-creature can adopt any shape or appearance to suit her purpose. In her normal form she looks very much like an old woman, except that her whole body is covered with skin as hard as rock that no weapon can penetrate. On her right hand she has a long, stony forefinger made from hard bone, shaped like an awl or the head of a spear. She uses this ghastly weapon to stab whomever she encounters. This fearsome weapon is the source for her name, U`tlûñ'tä, which means "Spear-finger." Some people call her Nûñ'yunu'ï, or "Stone-dress," because of her stony skin. By whatever name she is called, this vengeful and bloodthirsty creature is to be deeply feared.

WENDIGO (Inuit)

See Vampires Of Canada, p. 142.

YÉ'IITSOH (Navajo)

Changing Woman, the great lawgiver of the *Diné* (Navajo), had twin sons named Monster Slayer (another name for the hero called Killer of Enemies) and Born for Water. The brothers' destiny was to rid Earth of monsters. As the story has it, the twins' father was the Sun, and it was the sun who sired all of Earth's monsters, meaning Monster Slayer and Born for Water were destined to fight their own kin.

The twins were imbued with enormous supernatural powers, including the ability to ride lightning and change shape to resemble creatures and natural phenomena like storm clouds. Their first encounter was with a powerful monster called Yé'iitsoh that had slaughtered nearly every human being on earth. Yé'iitsoh was a cunning creature and made himself nearly invulnerable by removing his heart, nerves, and breath and hiding them in a cave.

The young warrior gods battled the Yé'iitsoh fiercely, hurling lightning bolts at him with such force that the Yé'iitsoh's body began to spew a river of blood. A second torrent rushed forth from the mouth of the creature's cave. These rivers of blood became hot torrents of gore as

U`tlûñ'tä. Artwork by Robert Patrick O'Brien.

deadly as lava and they cut through the landscape in the direction of each other. The twins knew that if those two rivers of blood ever joined, the Yé'iitsoh would rise again, so they used their lightning bolts to disfigure the entire landscape so the streams could not meet. They took the creature's scalp as a trophy, and to prove to their skeptical mother that they were indeed victorious over so powerful a monster.

Visitors to Mt. Taylor in New Mexico can still see the spot where this battle took place, and the two long-since solidified rivers of lava that flowed around the mountain and very nearly connected.

SACRED MOUNTAIN

Mount Taylor is located on the southwestern part of the San Mateo Mountains, between Albuquerque and Gallup, New Mexico. The mountain itself was originally called "San Mateo," but was later renamed in honor of General Zachary Taylor, who had distinguished himself during the Mexican War and later became the twelfth President of the United States.

Mount Taylor's peak has an elevation of 11,389 feet. Projecting to the south and northeast are large lava flows which sheer off from their forested tops in irregular and ragged escarpments.

The *Diné* (Navajos) refer to Mount Taylor as their "Sacred Mountain of the South." Mount Taylor is linked to many ancient Diné beliefs, and figures into several sacred ceremonies, such as the Blessing Way and the Enemy Way. It is also called the "Turquoise Mountain," fastened from the sky to the earth with a great flint knife and decorated with turquoise, dark mist, female rain, and all species of animals and birds. It is home to Dootl'izhii 'Ashkii (Turquoise Boy) and Naadá'áltsoii 'Át'ééd (Yellow Corn Girl).

The other mountains that form the sacred land of the Diné are the San Francisco Peaks (Dook'o'oslííd), Mt. Hesperus (Dibé Ntsaa) in the La Plata Mountains, and Sierra Blanca Peak (Tsisnaasjini').

VAMPIRES OF NEPAL

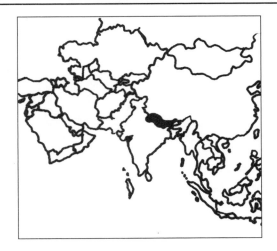

CHUDEL

Less common name for the Mashan. *See* below.

MASHAN (also called Chudel)

Mashan are vampiric demons that haunt Nepal and parts of India.
They exist almost entirely on another dimensional plane and seldom
come into contact with the human dimension. The Mashan are always
searching for places where the veils between the dimensions are weak
so they can try to break through into this world.

There are many theories as to how these weak spots are created, but
some folk tales suggest that corrupt sorcerers intentionally locate them

through a divination process called geomancy. Though these sorcerers seldom intend to invite the Mashan into this dimension, it is an acceptable risk because creating a dimensional rift imbues them with tremendous mystical powers. If the correct protection spells are not used, the Mashan's first meal will be the blood of an unwise sorcerer.

When a Mashan does enter our world it will prey on humans by causing madness, drinking blood, and sometimes even eating human flesh.

The Mashan can be defeated only by prayers to the god Shiva, who benevolently "encourages" the Mashan to return to its own place. Shiva will then seal the dimensional rift behind the Mashan.

GEOMANCY

Geomancy is a method of divination that is used to locate favorable sites for cities, residences, and burial grounds. The basic theory stems from the belief that the Earth is the mother of all things, so the Earth's energy in any particular location exercises a decisive influence over those who use the land. Heaven is the male aspect of life and Earth the female, and where male and female energies or qualities are in harmony, life will grow. Inner energy will blossom outward and outer energy will ferment, thereby producing wind and water. Geomancy is the method by which these sites can be located.

This ancient belief holds that happiness and prosperity will prevail over a house built on an ideal site. The site of an ancestral grave must be ideal as well, as the location is believed to exert a lasting and decisive influence over the destinies of all family members.

In darker magic, geomancy is used to find weaknesses in the walls between dimensions and to access negative energies stored in the earth.

YAMA

Vampire legends in Nepal, India, and Tibet date back over five thousand years. Wall paintings found in the Indus River Valley show beings that were blood drinking gods, depicted with greenish faces and pale blue bodies, and sporting terrible long fangs.

In one of the paintings, Yama, the Nepalese Lord of Death, is shown drinking blood from a skull cup as he stands on a mound of skeletons surrounded by a sea of blood. Many of the greatest paintings in Hindu art have depicted worshipers praying to Shiva for protection against this Lord of Death and other destructive forces.

Yama, the Lord of Death. Artwork by Robert Patrick O'Brien.

THE FESTIVAL OF LIGHTS

Yama is not always a deity to be feared. As a member of the vast Hindu pantheon of gods, Yama plays an important role as the God of Death. There are even cheerful festivals in his honor, such as Tihar, "The Festival of Lights." This festival honors both Yama, the Lord of Death, and Lakshmi, Goddess of Prosperity.

For five days Nepal is covered by tiny lamps and candles decorating homes, temples, and streets. Each day has a different ritual , each with a different meaning behind it.

The first day sees the appeasing of crows, associated with the underworld and the god of death. Each family leaves part of their meal outside their house to feed the birds and keep them happy.

The next day is for dogs, much beloved by Nepalis and kept as household pets more so than in India, although strays on the street are a common enough sight. On this day dogs are decorated with *tikas* (red colored marks on their foreheads) which is a privilege normally reserved for humans.

The third day is for cows, the Hindu's favorite holy beast. Cows are ceremoniously decorated and worshiped.

On the fourth day it is the family's turn, when households turn to each other and feast together in the Newari villages (the Newaris were the original inhabitants of the Kathmandu Valley).

The fifth day is for creating happy homes and celebrating filial ties. Devoted brothers and sisters swap presents and tikas.

Himalayan Vampire mask. Used with permission, (c) 2003 by University of Pennsylvania.

VAMPIRES OF NORWAY

HAMRAMMR

One of the most powerful monsters in all of folklore is the shapeshifter called the Hamrammr, frequently mentioned in Norse legends of Norway and Iceland such as the *Völsunga Saga*. This creature is unique among shapeshifters in that it shifts into the likeness of whichever animal it has just eaten. Its strength grows at an alarming rate, so if it has eaten ten wolves it becomes as strong as ten wolves.

Eventually the Hamrammr can become so powerful that nothing can kill it except fire. Even then the blaze must be white hot.

In a way, the Hamrammr's sheer viciousness is also its greatest weakness. As it grows in strength it quickly becomes drunk on its own power, and becomes so convinced of its invulnerability that it attacks without fear or caution. Unless it has actually reached that rare state where it is truly invulnerable, the Hamrammr's open and undisguised attack allows for its prey to deliver blows that would never land on a more cautious predator.

But that is often a marginal vulnerability unless the person facing the Hamrammr is a skilled fighter and armed to the teeth.

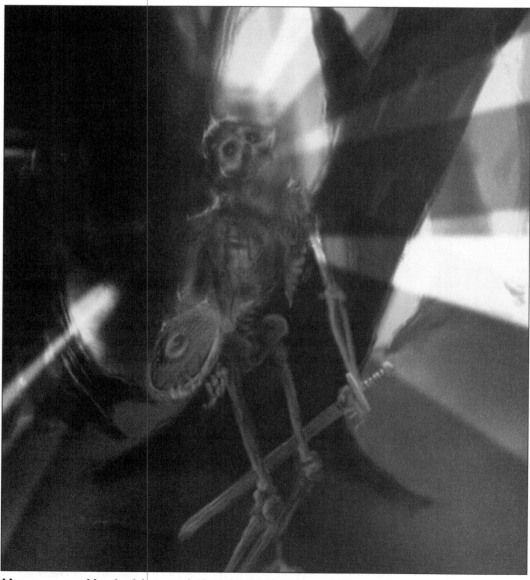

Hamrammr. Used with permission, (c) 2003 by Adam Garland.

BERSERKIR (also Berserker and Berserkr)

During the Middle Ages, it was customary for Norse warriors to cover themselves in the skins of animals they'd hunted and killed, especially bears and wolves. These Vikings believed that the skins of these fierce creatures imbued them with some of the animals' ferocity and power. These men, called Berserkirs, were mentioned frequently in the epic Sagas of Norway and Iceland, such as this reference from the great *Vatnsdæla Saga*: "Those Berserkir who were called ulfhednir, had got wolf-skins over their mail coats."

The method by which a man became a Berserkir was, apparently, voluntary, which speaks somewhat either to a preexisting mental condition or an actual evil nature. The aspiring Berserkir would drape himself in animal skins and then, essentially, open himself up to whatever violent spirits wished to inhabit his body and use it as a weapon to strike at the living.

While wrapped in their skins they could not be harmed by sword or fire. Their eyes glared through the eye sockets of the animal skins, flaring with real fire and emanating actual heat. Only a wooden club, wielded with great force, could hurt them by smashing their bones or crushing their skulls. When they attacked they howled like wolves. This combative fury became known as the Berserkir rage, an expression that still lingers in common usage today.

Used with permission, (c) 2003 by Adam Garland.

Berserkir mask. Metal sculpture by Steve Belden. Used with permission of The Hammered Wombat, (c) Copyright 2003. www.hammeredwombat.com

The Berserkirs were terrifying warriors capable of great savagery, and they would often drink the blood of their enemies in order to acquire their power as well.

Even though the Berserkirs were unmatched in combat and typically defeated their enemies, the Berserkirs were not always well received by their own people. Though champions by nature, they also had a reputation for evil deeds. If a Berserkir challenged another Viking to a fight and the other declined (knowing he could not defeat a potentially superhuman opponent), the Berserkir had the other man at his mercy. On one hand, if the Berserkir killed the man, everything that man owned was forfeited to the killer. But if the man declined to fight, then he lost any rights to any wealth or property he might inherit from his own family. It was a no-win situation for the ordinary man, and the Berserkir took as much delight in the misery his challenge caused as in the killing he so enjoyed.

The only way to defeat a Berserkir was to steal his animal skins while he slept, and then challenge the now human warrior to a battle. Though defeating the Berserkir was by no means a certainty, the match would at least be man against man, rather than man against a supernaturally powerful blood drinking demon. The *Völsunga Saga* tells of a Berserkir being defeated in just this manner.

In the early days of the Christian influence in Norway the number of men who willingly submitted to the Berserkir rage began to diminish. This apparently caused an outrage (or perhaps desperation) among the evil spirits ready to inhabit these warriors, because tales began to spring up of men succumbing to the rage against their wills. The famous *Saga of Thorir* contains this tragic quote by the afflicted title character, as Thorir appeals to his brother, Thorsteinn, for help: "I am the least worthy of us brothers, because the Berserkir fits come over me, quite against my will, and I wish that you, my brother, with your shrewdness, would devise some help for me." Thorir begged his brother for some method of releasing him from the demonic possession. The wise Thorsteinn replied, "Now will I make a vow to Him who created the sun, for I ween that he is most able to take the ban of you." Through prayers and sacrifices, Thorsteinn was able to help Thorir free himself of the possession.

Suggestions that Berserkir rages might be linked to werewolfism have been suggested for decades by scholars, largely based on a quote from the *Aigla Saga* which describes a man named Ulf (the name means wolf) who became savage at night:

> There was a man, Ulf by name, son of Bjálfi and Hallbera. Ulf was a man so tall and strong that the like of him was not to be seen in the land at that time. And when he was young he was out viking expeditions and harrying . . . . He was a great landed proprietor. It was his wont to rise early, and to go about the men's work, or to the smithies, and inspect all his goods and his acres; and sometimes he talked with those men who wanted his advice; for he was a good adviser, he was so clear-headed; however, every day, when it drew towards dusk, he became so savage that few dared exchange a word with him, for he was given to dozing in the afternoon. People said that he was much given to changing form, so he was called the evening-wolf, Kveldulfr.

Used with permission, (c) 2003 by Adam Garland.

VAMPIRES OF PERU

CANCHU (also called Pumapmicuc)

Pre-Columbian Peru suffered from an infestation of Canchus, a kind of bloodsucker that attacked only the young and strong. Their favorite meal was the hot blood of powerful warriors in the full flush of youthful vigor. Not daring to attack these stalwarts while awake, Canchus would sneak in to feed while a warrior was fast asleep. Sometimes they would kill the warriors by draining them dry of blood. Other times they would leave the man alive and allow him to regain his strength, then return again and again in order to feed on the powerful blood.

Rural stories in more recent times hold that the Canchus—lacking a warrior class to prey upon—will now attack any healthy person. Mountain passes are their favorite hunting grounds, especially during moonless nights or snowstorms.

UKUMAR

In the jungles and mountains of Peru there is a bloodthirsty creature called the Ukumar. Much like the Sasquatch and the Shampe, the Ukumar is massive, easily as big and strong as a bear, though more manlike in shape. The creature hunts the Andes of Peru and sometimes even in Bolivia. It has also been seen frequently in Argentina.

Like most predators—both natural and supernatural—the Ukumar tends to feed on the weak and generally attacks children, women, or the elderly. Though it seldom attacks a strong man, it can nevertheless put up a tremendous fight if necessary. Usually it requires several well-armed men to bring one down. Apparently the Ukumar can be killed by ordinary means, much like the bear it resembles.

The great writer Pedro Cieza de Leon wrote of an Ukumar being killed after a fierce battle near the town of Charcas in Bolivia. Sightings of the Ukumar continue, though reports of them attacking humans have dwindled. Perhaps they have learned to fear the efficiency of modern human weapons.

Photo by Jason Lukridge.

VAMPIRE SONGS

Over the last few decades a number of folk songs have been written about the mountain vampires, including *"Canchu, Canchu"*, which is often performed by Peruvian folk bands. In the song, a wise traveler protects his two lamebrained sons from the vampire's clutches by making them sing heroic songs all night, thus tricking the Canchus into believing they are all stalwart warriors.

"Canchu, Canchu" is something of a rarity in songs about vampires, because it tells of a vampire's defeat. There are many other songs around the world written about vampires and most (though not all) present vampires as romantic, misunderstood, tragic, or heroic. Rarely are they presented as monsters. Following is a list of vampire-related songs and the artists who recorded them.

- *"Do the Vampire"* by Superdrag
- *"Flight Of The Vampyre"* by Phantom Of The Organ
- *"Living Vampyre"* by Screaming Tribe
- *"No Vampire"* by Yarni Bolo
- *"Vampire"* by Amber Asylum, Yanmti Arafin, Astro Zombies, Barathrum, Bel Airs, Beto and the Fairla, Black Uhuru, Blue System, Bluetones, Yami Bolo, Richie Booker, Arthur Brown, Buppy, the Catholic Girls, Challengers, Chastain, Deadly Nightshades, Eddy Detroit, DJ Kirsh, Eight Ball Grifter, Elephant Man, Elijah's Mantle, Jad Fair, Ricky General, David Greenberger, Half Japanese, Hawkwind, Heavy Water Factory, Bap Kennedy, Steven Kowalczyk, Lucid Nation, Masochistic Religio, Mister Big, Lee Perry, Buffy Sainte-Marie, Claudia Schmidt, Sebadoh, Selecter, Settie, Michael Smith, Tory Voodoo, Peter Tosh, and the Upsetters
- *"Vampire II"* by Theory Music
- *"Vampire Babies"* by Victor Lams
- *"Vampire Baby"* by Branice McKenzie and Scaree Tales
- *"Vampire Bat"* by Benjamin Cone and Wesley Willis
- *"Vampire Black"* by Grave Danger
- *"Vampire Blues"* by Eric Ambel, Family Jewels, Russ Gilman, Mercury Rev, Loudon Wainwright, and Neil Young have each recorded versions

- *"Vampire Brown"* by Lee Russell
- *"Vampire Circus"* by Gary Lucas, Phillip Martell, Philharmonia Orchestra, and the Prague Philharmonic
- *"Vampire Club"* by Voltaire
- *"Vampire Crush"* by Narcotic Kisses
- *"Vampire Daddy"* by Jerry Bryan, Them Wranch
- *"Vampire Dance"* by Dave Miller
- *"Vampire Dating"* by The Ruiners
- *"Vampire Empire"* by Beyond, Two Witches
- *"Vampire Eyes"* by Goddo
- *"Vampire Girl"* by Devil's Brigade, Jonathan Richman
- *"Vampire In The Sun"* by Betty Already
- *"Vampire Kiss"* by Stun Gun
- *"Vampire Line"* by Bunny Plasm
- *"Vampirella"* by Deeper Listening, Kryptonix, Sciacalli, Brian Tarquin, and Teen Appeal
- *"Vampire Love"* by Pentagram, Phantom Rockers

Used with permission, (c) 2003 by Breanne Levy.

- *"Vampire Party"* by Crimony
- *"Vampire Rock"* by The Fabulous Poodles
- *"Vampires"* by Adam Ant, Atmosphere, Ray DeLaPaz, Fastball, Thee Flatliners, Godflesh, Godsmack, Kid Spatula, Mains Ignition, Meat Puppets, Pet Shop Boys, Radiorama, Settie, Paul Simon, Stars as Eyes, Steady Earnest, Billie Trix, and Twintone
- *"Vampire Ska"* by Horny Toad
- *"Vampire Slayer"* by Leather Strip
- *"Vampire Smile"* by Furtips
- *"Vampire Song"* by Concrete Blonde, Dave Miller, Shield, and Toxic Pets
- *"Vampiress"* by Funhouse
- *"Vampire Suite"* by Captain Beefheart & the Magic Band
- *"Vampire Sun"* by Cathedral of Tears
- *"Vampire Sushi"* by Old Time Relijun
- *"Vampire Vamp"* by Rah Band
- *"Vampire Walk"* by Jet Sound Inc
- *"Vampire War"* by The Bronx Casket Co.
- *"Vampire Woman"* by Hot Tuna, Jorma Kaukonen, Spark Plug Smith
- *"Vampyre"* by Wolverton Brothers
- *"The Vampyre"* by Tyla
- *"Vampyre Hunter K"* by Bile
- *"Vampyre Love"* by Pentagram
- *"Vampyres Cry"* by Nosferatu
- *"Vampyres Of The Day"* by Mephisto Waltz
- *"Vampyre Song"* by Kevin Book
- *"Vampyre With A Healthy Appetite"* by Steve Hackett

Quite a few bands have released albums with "vampire" in the title:

- *Return Of The Vampire* by Mercyful Fate
- *Vampire* by Shere Khan
- *Vampire* by the Fireballs
- *Vampire Of Tehran* by Muslimgauze
- *Vampire On Titus* by Guided by Voices

- *Vampire Rituals* (various Goth artists)
- *Vampire Rock* by Shakin' Street
- *Vampires* by Thee Flatliners
- *Vampiresongs* by Shield
- *Vampire State* by Kaylyn
- *Vampire Woman* by Eddie Burks
- *Vikram The Vampire* by Talvin Singh

There are also a number of performers or bands with the word "vampire" in their names: The Vampire, Vampire Slave, Vampire Slayers, Vampire Rodents, Vampire Nation, Kung-fu Vampires, Curse of the Golden Vampire, Vampire State Building, Vampyre Vyrgins, and Last Vampire.

Used with permission, (c) 2003 by Breanne Levy.

VAMPIRES OF THE PHILIPPINES

ASWANG (also Asuang)

The Aswang is easily the most fearsome and feared creature of Filipino folklore. It can take a variety of forms—dog, horse, bull, swine—and in beast shape roams the darkened roads at night. Its favorite prey are the old, the sick, or pregnant women.

The Aswang can fly through the night skies, assuming the shape of a large bird. The creature can also revert to a vaguely humanoid, all-black body, then wrench its head and intestines free from the rest of its body and take to the air. This is much like the Kephn of Burma, the Mjertovjec of Byelorus, and the gruesome Penanggalan of India.

The Aswang utters a compelling cry as it flies, "Kikik," which draws its victims to it by some supernatural compulsion.

The word "Aswang" is commonly translated as "sorcerer" but that isn't very accurate, considering the nature of the beast. As a rule, sorcerers are human beings who have chosen to do what they do of their own free will. A person becomes an Aswang because of some spiritual sickness. Once he has been so doomed, the afflicted person has no control at all over what he does, no more so

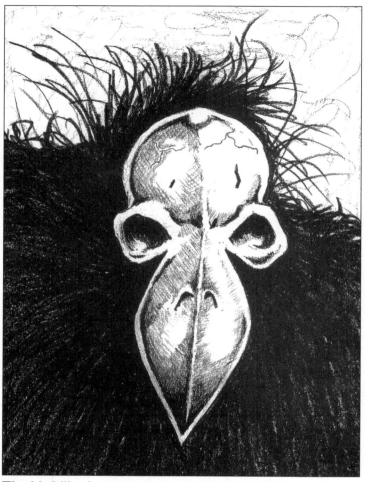

The bird-like Aswang. Artwork by Shane MacDougall.

than a hunting cat or bird of prey has any control over its nature. A person can also be made into an Aswang by another Aswang blowing air down the person's neck.

By day the Aswang looks as human as anyone else in the village, works at a job, even has a family and friends. It is clever and deceptive, and it maintains an excellent disguise that can fool people for decades. The Aswang is also smart enough to never hunt in its own village, and travels many miles at night to neighboring villages to hunt. However, the day after it has fed, the Aswang looks almost pregnant, its belly bloated and distended with consumed blood.

When the Aswang attacks it will stand upside down and then belch forth an odor so powerful and overwhelming that the victim will be rendered as helpless as if subjected to nerve gas. Then, while the victim is paralyzed—though not necessarily unconscious—the Aswang will begin to feed, starting with the heart and working down to the intestines.

The Aswang has earned its reputation as a loathsome monster, and has a number of other ghastly feeding practices. The Aswang can use birds to lead it to the homes of its prospective victims, where it will perch by a chimney or perhaps tear a hole in the roof. It will then send down its long pointy tongue, and use it to prick a victim's jugular vein, sucking their blood through its hollowed tongue. Possessing the ability to sniff out an unborn child, the monster can also extend its mouth like a feeding tube and extract the baby from its mother's womb.

Those in the know sleep with their stomachs covered lest the creature rip them open and steal their intestines. Children are protected from the Aswang by being made to sleep on the edge of their mats or pallets, because those sleeping in the center of their mats are vulnerable to attack.

While resting, the Aswang may look like nothing more innocuous than a cobweb dangling from the branch of a tree, but only the very unwary would dare touch such a seemingly harmless thing. There is too great a risk that it is an Aswang merely dozing, or perhaps lolling out its tongue, waiting for a victim to happen by.

If a person were to be confronted by an Aswang (in any of its guises), it is best to stand fast and give up all hope of running. Making direct eye contact is actually a reliable tactic, because an Aswang can be stared down after only a few minutes, at which point it will slink away and not attack. But if the person staring at the creature blinks or looks away, then he is doomed.

Garlic can act as a temporary protection. It should be rubbed liberally under the armpits, where body heat will release the herb's aroma.

One method of detecting an Aswang is to use a special oil that is carefully prepared using complex rituals and spells which can only be performed on Good Fridays. A vampire slayer, priest, or brave villager will then carry the oil in an open container and walk by as many people as possible. When passing an ordinary human, the oil will remain inert. But when passing near an Aswang the oil will instantly begin to boil.

A person can, in some cases, be cured of being an Aswang by having the curse removed. A mananambal, or healer, can create a curative potion and force the Aswang to drink it. If the potion has been properly prepared, the Aswang will instantly begin to vomit up a variety of strange things (everything from an egg to an entire bird!).

Belief in the Aswang is still common throughout the Philippines today. Even educated parents take precautions when a baby is on the way!

BEBARLANG

Vampirism takes many forms in the Philippines, from the drinking of blood to the taking of life essence. In the rural jungles of the Philippines there is a tribe of Essential Vampires called the Bebarlangs.

The Bebarlangs are advanced psychics who have developed astral projection to a high degree. While their bodies remain safe in their village, guarded by servants and protective spells, their spirits leave their physical forms and rise into the night air. Once free of their bodies they roam the skies, searching for other villages or, more often, target a specific village. Singly or in packs, they descend on the village and seek out victims, settling over them like an invisible blanket and immediately draining them of their life essence.

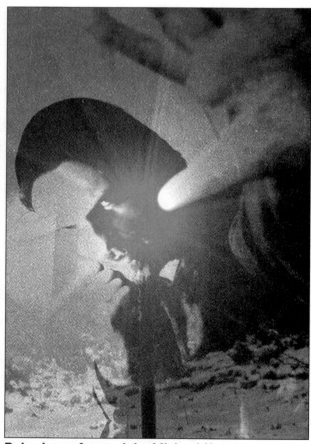

More advanced Bebarlangs can also intrude into a sleeping person's mind and steal his secrets as well as his life force.

Only potent magical charms can keep the Bebarlangs out. Each charm is made from drops of blood, bits of hair, and fingernail pairings mixed with wax and mud

Bebarlang. Artwork by Michael Katz.

taken from just outside the person's front door. These materials are fashioned into a small icon of a holy person or angel, then hung over one's person's bed or worn around the neck on a cord. Only then will the person safe from this psychic attack.

DANAG

Centuries ago the natives of the Philippines had forged an agreement with a group of spirits called the Danag. These otherworldly spirits were benign and friendly, and had such a deep knowledge of how to work the earth that they helped the Filipinos become excellent farmers. For generations the arrangement was idyllic, but then a simple accident and an act of kindness changed everything for the worst.

One day, a woman cut her finger while farming. One of the Danag tried to comfort her and help dress the wound. In an attempt to soothe the wound, the Danag licked it. But the taste of the blood—something totally new to these ethereal creatures—was overwhelmingly appealing. The Danag kept licking the wound, then started sucking it, and before anyone could do anything the Danag had drained every last drop of blood from the woman's body.

Everything changed. Suddenly the Danag were not interested in helping the natives farm the land; now the only thing any of them wanted was fresh human blood. It was worse than any addiction, it became an undying obsession. The Danag have plagued and haunted the Filipinos ever since.

MANDURUGO

A more traditional Filipino vampire is the Mandurugo, whose name literally means "bloodsucker." The Mandurugo is most active in the province of Capiz, in the northern region of Panay Island. Legends of it have spread throughout the Philippines.

These creatures appear in the form of beautiful and seductive women during daylight hours, but at night they transform into flying monsters.

Mandurugo can live ordinary lives and use their beauty to land a healthy young husband, but it is not out of love that they marry. A Mandurugo will enchant her husband into a deep sleep and feed from him by drinking a little blood each night. When a Mandurugo is hungry for fresh blood or blood in greater quantities, she takes to the night winds and hunts down a fresh quarry.

Fire is one of the few things that can destroy the Mandurugo. Knives and swords will only cause injury. Bullets have little effect beyond causing momentary pain: they may slow the Mandurugo down, but they will not stop this monster.

Mandurugo. Used with permission, (c) 2003 by Adam Garland.

VAMPIRES OF POLAND

MARA

See Vampires Of Canada or Vampires Of Scandinavia.

OHYN

In Poland, as in many other nations, birth defects are frequently blamed for creating vampires. The Polish vampire named the Ohyn is the result of being born with teeth and a caul (an amniotic membrane attached to the top of the head and covering the face). Though the person will not become an Ohyn until after their mortal life has ended, it is generally believed that such a person is to be "watched." Very carefully.

Some villagers feel that it is better to be safe (and harsh) now than sorry later, so they remove the caul and extract the teeth from any newborn, especially in the case of stillbirths. The villagers are particularly afraid that a stillborn infant will reawaken as a Revenant and use its milk teeth to chew at its own flesh and bones until it is strong enough to break free from its coffin, then begin feeding on the flesh and blood of its living relatives. If the newborn lives, it is believed that removing the caul and withdrawing its birth teeth will save it from a life doomed to a taint of corruption and an afterlife damned to eternal evil.

SRIZ

Opinions differ as to whether the Sriz is a vampire, ghost, demon, or some other unidentified species of supernatural creature. The Sriz is a ritualistic killer who climbs to the top of a church steeple and calls out the names of his victims. The victims invariably die, some from heart failure, others in violent accidents, still others of various wasting diseases.

The creature does not feed on flesh or blood, but is a kind of emotional vampire, gaining sustenance from the discharge of pure terror released by those who succumb to its call.

The surest way to defend against the creature is to ring church bells, especially during times of prayer. The Sriz cannot abide "holy music" of any kind and will be driven off.

If a church has been desanctified, it is important for the villagers to cover the rooftop with bits of jagged metal or broken glass so the Sriz cannot perch atop it. In some mid-eighteenth century folk tales, the Sriz was attracted to the sound of bells rung in a desanctified church, so removal of the bells became an important part of officially abandoning a church.

UPIER (plural UPIERCZI)

Also known as the Wampir or Viesczy in Russia, the Upier of Poland is almost more serpentine than batlike. Instead of fangs, the Upier has a vicious barbed stinger under its tongue. When it attacks it gluts itself on blood, draining every last drop it can find.

The Upierczi are not born as monsters but are Revenants that rise from the graves of certain kinds of recently dead humans, typically those born with teeth (a sign in many cultures of an unnatural hunger) or with a caul. During its human life the Upier is often hyperactive and agitated and shows a constantly flushed and intense face. After its death (by whatever natural means), the Revenant rises to become one of the Upierczi.

The Upier. Artwork by Marie O'Brien.

Like an animal, the Upier makes a nest for itself, usually in a stone crypt or some other enduring and moderately watertight vessel. Either it picks a suitable place and then constructs (or carries in) a nesting basin, or it finds a very remote spot where such an item already exists and then stakes out that spot as its own. Any creatures venturing into the area are doomed to a quick but painful death.

The Upier is primarily a daylight vampire, actively hunting during the hours of noon to midnight. When it finally returns to its resting place it fills its nesting basin with blood and sleeps immersed in the liquid.

The Upier will sometimes ring a church bell, and anyone who hears it—or heeds it—is doomed to die by its fell hand.

The single best way to prevent a corpse from rising as one of the Upierczi is to bury it face down. It will become confused and will consume its own flesh until it is too wasted to move.

Another protection against the Upier is called "Blood Bread." This unsavory but potent item is made by locating the coffin of a vampire that has already been destroyed and gathering up some of its blood. This blood is mixed with water and flour and baked into a loaf, which is then shared among a family. Anyone eating the blood bread will be safe from the Upier's bite.

These precautions are adhered to with great care because tales of revenge by an Upier would freeze the blood of even the most stalwart slayer.

There is only one way to destroy an Upier: fire. The creature must be thoroughly incinerated. Even in the midst of its fiery death, however, the Upier has one last power: as it burns, its body will burst open and out will pour thousands of vermin—rats, maggots, roaches, centipedes, and other equally base creatures. If any of these escape, then the spirit of the Upier will likewise escape to seek revenge. So the vampire slayers must build a huge bonfire, make sure that the Upier is in the center, and that all of the fuel is thoroughly doused with oil before torches are put to the wood.

VAMPIRES OF PORTUGAL

BRUXSA (also spelled BRUXA)

One of the most dangerous vampires on earth is Portugal's Bruxsa. This is a vampire who becomes so by choice, having been a witch who cast an evil enchantment on herself.

By the light of day the Bruxsa leads a normal life, appearing as a human (though extremely beautiful) woman. She can marry, bear children, attend church, and essentially pass unnoticed among her prey. But by night she transforms into a bird and flies into the darkness to seek her unnatural amusements. The Bruxsa loves to torment lost travelers, leading them astray, confusing them to the point of despair, then attacking them.

Her meal of choice, like that of many vampires, is the blood of children. Some legends hint that she even bears her own children for the sole purpose of having food at hand.

The Bruxsa has vast sorcerous powers. Immortal and invulnerable, the Bruxsa can also cast spells that cause drought and sickness, and bring rains that drown fields at just the wrong time in the growing cycle. Though there are no known methods of slaying the Bruxsa at this time, there are ways to protect a child against her attack. Various magical amulets can be obtained from priests or mystics (and sometimes from Gypsies, who have no love for the undead). These charms are made of soil from a shrine of the Virgin Mary, mixed with hairs from the child's head and seven drops of the mother's tears. The items are mixed together, put into a small ceramic or carved wood amulet, and worn on a silver chain.

Used with permission, (c) 2003 by Breanne Levy.

VAMPIRES OF PRUSSIA

GIERACH

Much like the Upier of Poland, the Gierach of Prussia kills with the power of pronouncement: once it climbs to the top of a house, a steeple, or a bell tower and speaks the name of its victim, that person will surely die. Generally only the victim can hear the Gierach speak, or at least can understand what it says. To everyone else, the vampire's call may sound like that of a night bird such as a crow, raven, or owl. Because of this, many rural Prussians consider owls to be evil, vampires in disguise, or at very least omens of ill fortune.

The Gierach can be foiled using one of the tried and true methods for thwarting Balkan vampires. Scatter poppy seeds on its grave and it will be compelled to stop and count them all. Another trick is to leave a stocking, woven mat, or a fishing net atop the grave. The vampire will not be able to go hunting until it has unraveled every thread.

THE OWL

Note: Much of the information in this section was generously provided by Deane P. Lewis of The Owl Pages (http://www. owl-pages.com).

Owls are night hunters of great antiquity and variety, ranging from the tiny elf owl (*Micrathene whitneyi*), to the large and powerful Eurasian eagle-owl (*Bubo bubo*). Their austere countenances and eerie calls have served to work them into folklore, mythology, and superstitions of nearly every country around the globe. On the average, the birds live more than twenty years (some considerably longer). Though they have sometimes been domesticated as pets they are always predators and are to be respected for their sharp talons, powerful beaks, and deep cunning.

Owl superstitions are many and varied. Here are just a few:

Abyssinia: The Hamites held the Owl to be sacred.

Afghanistan: The Owl gave Man flint and iron to make fire. In exchange, Man gave the Owl his feathers.

Africa, Central: The Owl is the familiar of Bantu wizards.

Africa, East: The Swahili believe the Owl brings illness to children.

Africa, South: Zulus believe the Owl is the bird of sorcerers.

Africa, West: The Owl is the messenger of wizards and witches, and its cry presages evil.

Algeria: Place the right eye of an Eagle Owl in the hand of a sleeping woman and she will tell all.

Arabia: The Owl is a bird of ill omen, and the embodiment of evil spirits that carries off children at night.

> According to an ancient Arabic treatise, from each female Owl supposedly came two eggs. One held the power to cause hair to fall out and one held the power to restore it.

Arctic Circle: The Owl was created when a little girl was magically turned into a bird with a long beak. But she was so frightened that she flapped about madly and flew into a wall, flattening her face and beak.

> The Inuit believed that the Short-eared Owl was once a young girl who was magically transformed into an Owl with a long beak. But the Owl became frightened and flew into the side of a house, flattening its face and beak.

The Inuit named the Boreal Owl "the blind one," because of its tameness during daylight.

Inuit children make pets of Boreal Owls.

Australia: Aborigines believe bats represent the souls of men and Owls the souls of women. Owls are therefore sacred, because your sister is an Owl--and the Owl is your sister.

Aztecs: One of their evil gods wore a Screech Owl on his head.

Babylon: Owl amulets protected women during childbirth.

Belgium: Legend has it that a priest offered to let the Owl live in his church tower the bird would get rid of the rats and mice that plagued his church.

Artwork by Shane MacDougall.

Bordeaux: Throw salt in a fire to avoid the Owl's curse.

Borneo: The Supreme Being turned his wife into an Owl after she told secrets to mortals.

Brittany: On the way to the harvest, seeing an Owl is the sign of a good yield.

Burma: During a quarrel among birds, the Owl was jumped upon and so his face was flattened.

By eating salted Owl, a person can be cured of gout.

Cameroon: Too evil to name, the Owl is known only as "the bird that makes you afraid."

Carthage: The city was captured by Agathocles of Syracuse (Southern Italy) in 310 B.C. Afterward, Agathocles released Owls and they settled on his troops' shields and helmets, signifying victory in battle.

Celtic: The Owl was a sign of the underworld.

China: The Owl is associated with lightning (because it brightens the night). Placing Owl effigies in each corner of the home protect the home against lightning.

The Owl is associated with the drum (because it breaks the silence).

The Owl is a symbol of too much Yang (positive, masculine, bright, active energy).

England: An early English folk cure for alcoholism was to prescribe raw Owl eggs. A child given this treatment was thought to gain lifetime protection against drunkenness.

Owls' eggs, cooked until they turned into ashes, were also used as a potion to improve eyesight.

Owl Broth was given to children suffering from whooping-cough.

Another traditional English belief was that if you walked around an Owl in a tree, it would keep turning its head to watch you until it wrung its own neck.

An owl is believed to be the only living creature that can abide a ghost.

An owl living in the attic of a house will cause a pregnant woman to miscarry.

Odo of Cheriton, a Kentish preacher of the twelfth century, explained that the Owl is nocturnal because it had stolen the rose, which was a prize awarded for beauty, so the other birds punished it by allowing it to come out only at night.

In parts of northern England it is good luck to see an Owl.

If a person looks into an owl's nest, he will suffer depression for the rest of his life.

The Barn Owl has been used to predict the weather by people in England. A screeching Owl meant cold weather or a storm was coming. If heard during foul weather a change in the weather was at hand.

Ethiopia: A man condemned to death was taken to a table on which an Owl was painted, and expected to take his own life.

Etruria: To the Etruscans of Ancient Italy, the Owl was an attribute of the god of darkness.

France: When a pregnant woman hears an Owl her child will be a girl.

Germany: If an Owl hoots while a child is born, the infant will have an unhappy life.

According to the *Encyclopedia Of Superstitions,* "A charm against the terrible consequences of being bitten by a mad dog was to carry the heart and right foot of an Owl under the left armpit."

Greece: In ancient Greece it was believed that if a child was given an owl's egg, he would never become a drunkard.

The Greeks considered Owls a good omen. An Owl flying over a Greek army at the dawn of battle insured victory.

Greenland: The Inuit see the Owl as a source of guidance and help.

Incas: This culture venerated the Owl for its beautiful eyes and head.

India: Seizures in children could be treated with a broth made from Owl eyes. Rheumatism pain was treated with a gel made from Owl meat. Owl meat could also be eaten as a natural aphrodisiac.

In northern India, if one ate the eyes of an Owl, they would be able to see in the dark.

In southern India, the cries of an Owl were interpreted by number. One hoot was an omen of impending death. Two meant success in anything that would be started soon after. Three represented a woman being married into the family. Four indicated a disturbance. Five denoted upcoming travel. Six meant guests were on the way. Seven was a sign of mental distress. Eight foretold sudden death. And nine symbolized good fortune.

In parts of the Indian sub-continent people believed that the Owl was married to the bat.

Indonesia: Around Manado, on the isle of Sulawesi, People consider Owls very wise. They call them Burung Manguni. Every time someone wants to travel, they listen to the owls. The owls make two different sounds: the first means it is safe to go, and the second means it is better to stay at home. The Minahasa, the people around Manado, take those warnings very seriously. They stay at home when Manguni says so. (Information thanks to Alex van Poppel).

Artwork by Denise Lawrence.

Iran: In Farsi, the Little Owl (*Athene Noctua*) is called "Joghde-kochek." It is said that this bird brings bad luck. In Islam, it is forbidden (*haram*) to eat it.

Ireland: The Irish believe that if an owl flies into a house it must be killed immediately; because if it escapes, it will take the luck of the house with it. The custom of nailing an Owl to a barn door to ward off evil and lightning persisted into the nineteenth century.

Israel: In Hebrew lore the Owl is unclean. It represents blindness and desolation.

Jamaica: To ward off an Owl's bad luck, cry "Salt and pepper for your mammy."

Japan: Among the Ainu people the Eagle Owl is revered as a messenger of the gods or a divine ancestor. They would drink a toast to the Eagle Owl before a hunting expedition.

> The Screech Owl warns against danger.

> They think the Barn Owl and Horned Owl are demonic.

> The Japanese would nail wooden images of owls to their houses in times of famine or pestilence.

Latvia: When Christian soldiers entered any local pagan god's temple, the god would fly away as an Owl.

Lorraine: Spinsters go to the woods and call to the Owl to help them find a husband.

Luxembourg: Owls spy treasures, steal them, and hoard them.

Madagascar: Owls join witches to dance on the graves of the dead.

Malawi: The Owl carries messages for witches.

Malaya: Owls eat new-born babies.

Mayarts: Owls were the messengers of the rulers of Xibalba, the Place of Phantoms.

Mexico: The Owl makes the cold North wind (whereas the gentle South wind is made by the butterfly).

> The Little Owl was called the "messenger of the lord of the land of the dead," and flew between the land of the living and the dead.

Middle East: The Owl represents the souls of people who have died unavenged.

Mongolia, Inner: Owls enter the house by night to gather human fingernails.

Mongolia: The Burial people hang up Owl skins to ward off evil.

Morocco: The cry of Owls can kill infants.

According to Moroccan custom, an Owl's eye worn on a string around the neck was an effective talisman for averting the "evil eye."

Native Americans: To an Apache Indian, dreaming of an Owl signified approaching death.

Cherokee shamans valued Eastern Screech-Owls as consultants because the owls could bring on sickness as punishment.

The Cree people believed Boreal Owl whistles were summonses from the spirits. If a person answered with a similar whistle and did not hear a response, he would soon die.

The Dakota Hidatsa Indians saw the Burrowing Owl as a protective spirit for brave warriors.

The Hopi Indians see the Burrowing Owl as their god of the dead, the guardian of fires and tender of all things underground, including seed germination. Their name for the Burrowing Owl is *Ko'ko*, which means "Watcher of the dark."

The Hopis also believe that the Great Horned Owl helped their peaches grow.

The Kwagulth people of the Northwest coast believed that owls represented both a deceased person and their newly-released soul.

The Kwakiutl Indians were convinced that Owls were the souls of people and should therefore not be harmed, for when an Owl was killed the person to whom the soul belonged would also die.

The Lenape Indians believed that if they dreamt of an Owl it would become their guardian.

The Menominee people believed that a talking contest between a Saw-whet Owl (Totoba) and a rabbit (Wabus) was held to decide whether there would be day or night. The rabbit won and selected daylight, but permitted there to be night time in honor of the vanquished Owl.

The Montagnais people of Quebec believed that the Saw-whet Owl was once the largest Owl in the world and was very proud of its voice. But after the Owl attempted to imitate the roar of a waterfall, the Great Spirit humiliated the Saw-whet Owl by turning it into a tiny Owl with a song that sounds like dripping water.

To the Mojave Indians of Arizona, one would become an Owl after death. This was an interim stage before becoming a water beetle, and ultimately pure air.

The Navajo believed that an owl could tell the future. According to Navajo legend, the creator, Nayenezgani, told the Owl that "in days to come, men will listen to your voice to know what will be their future."

California's Newuks believed that after death, the brave and virtuous became Great Horned Owls. The wicked were doomed to become Barn Owls.

Native peoples of the Sierras believed that the Great Horned Owl captured the souls of the dead and carried them to the underworld.

The Tlingit Indian warriors had great faith in the Owl. They would rush into battle hooting like Owls to give themselves confidence, and to strike fear into their enemies.

A Zuni legend tells of how the Burrowing Owl got its speckled plumage: the Owls spilled white foam on themselves during a ceremonial dance because they were laughing at a coyote that was trying to join the dance.

Zuni mothers place an Owl feather next to a baby to help it sleep.

New Mexico: The hooting of Owls warns of the coming of witches.

New Zealand: To the Maoris, the Owl is an unlucky bird.

Newfoundland: The hoot of the Horned Owl signals the approach of bad weather.

Nigeria: In legend, Elullo, a witch and a chief of the Okuni tribe, could become an Owl.

In certain parts of Nigeria, natives avoid naming the Owl, referring to it as "the bird that makes you afraid."

Persia: Wizards use arrows tipped with a bewitched man's fingernails to kill Owls.

Peru: Boiled Owl is said to be a strong medicine.

Poland: Polish folklore links Owls with death. Girls who die unmarried turn into doves; girls who are married when they die turn into Owls.

An owl cry heard in or near a home usually meant impending death, sickness, or other misfortune.

An old story tells how the Owl does not come out during the day because it is too beautiful, and would be mobbed by other, jealous birds.

Puerto Rico: The Owl is called *mucaro*. Back in the 1800s, the people from the mountain coffee plantations used to blame the little mucaro for the loss of coffee grains. The belief was that coffee was part of the owls' diet, so many owls were killed. There are old Mexican folklore songs on the subject. One goes like this:

Poor Mucaro you're a gentleman
You just want to eat a rat,
Then the rat set up a trap,
He eats the coffee grains
And people blame you.

Rome: The ancient Romans detested Owls because they were thought to be harbingers of death.

Witches in ancient Rome used a screech Owl's feather as part of a potion.

Romania: The souls of repentant sinners flew to heaven in the guises of Snowy Owls.

Russia: Hunters carry Owl claws so that, if they are killed, their souls can use them to climb up to Heaven.

Tartar shamen of Central Russia could assume Owl shapes.

Kalmucks hold the Owl to be sacred because one once saved Genghis Khan's life.

In the Ural Mountains, when other birds migrate, Snowy Owls are made to stay behind as a punishment for deception.

Samoa: The people are descended from an Owl.

Saxony: The Wend people say that the sight of an Owl makes child-birth easier.

Artwork by Denise Lawrence.

Scotland: It is bad luck to see an Owl in daylight.

Shetland Isles: A cow will give bloody milk if it is scared by an Owl.

Siberia: The Owl is a helpful spirit.

Spain: Legend has it that the Owl was once the sweetest of singers, until it saw Jesus crucified. Ever since it has shunned daylight and only repeats the words *"cruz, cruz"* ("cross, cross").

Sri Lanka: The Owl is married to the bat.

Sumeria: Lilith, the goddess of death, was attended by Owls.

Sweden: The Owl is associated with witches.

Tangiers: Barn Owls are the clairvoyants of the Devil.

Transylvania: Farmers used to scare away Owls by walking around their fields naked.

U.S.A.: If you hear an Owl's cry you must return the call, or else take off an item of clothing and put it on again inside-out.

Owls feature in old Hawaiian war chants.

If a pregnant woman hears the shriek of an owl, her child will be a girl.

If an owl hoots during a burial service, the deceased is bound to rise from the grave and haunt the living.

If an owl lands on the roof of your house, it is an omen of death.

If an owl nests in an abandoned house, then the dwelling must be haunted.

Louisianans believe that Owls are old people and should be respected.

Louisianan Cajuns are those individuals who share the French-based culture originally brought to Louisiana by eighteenth century exiles from the French colony of Acadia. Cajuns thought that if you hear an Owl calling late at night you should get up from bed and turn your left shoe upside down to avert disaster.

Illinois: If you kill an Owl, revenge will be visited upon your family.

Various: Constant hooting near your house foretells death, according to countless cultures around the world.

Wales: An Owl heard among houses means an unmarried girl has lost her virginity.

If a woman is pregnant and she alone hears an owl hoot outside her house at night, then her child will be blessed.

VAMPIRES OF ROMANIA

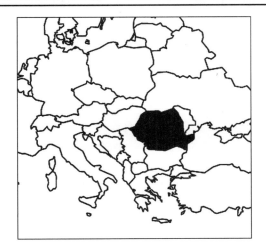

CONCEALMENT-RAU

This phrase, meaning, "the bad one," is a kind of nickname given to the Strigoi, the most common vampires of Romanian legend. *See* entry in this chapter.

MOROI (also Moroii, Muroni)

Moroi is the Romanian name for a "living" vampire, whereas the Strigoi is an undead Revenant. The name is based on the Romanian word for death: *moru*. There are so many different legends about the Moroi that it is likely that this one name has either been used incorrectly to describe a number of different species, or perhaps it is a generic term for vampires. No matter how the name is used, the Moroi is a thing of pure evil.

Male Moroi are usually bald and the females have flushed red faces. These Living Vampires are sorcerers and witches as well as blood drinkers and can shapeshift at will, becoming cats, dogs, black hens, birds of prey, even reptiles. Other accounts claim that while they cannot actually change shape they can astrally project and enter any animal and control its actions.

For centuries the Moroi have spread terror and death throughout Romania, and the creatures are very hard to defend against because they look and act human most of the time. They have families and jobs, they go to church, they have drinks with their friends at the local tavern . . . and all the time they are looking for their next victim. Often a Moroi will walk the darkened streets, byways, and back roads around its town, waiting until it finds someone walking alone, then with dreadful speed and power will attack them and drink them dry.

Some Moroi use spells to lure children out of their beds and homes at night, then take them to a secluded spot to attack them and drain their blood. Or they may wait until the entire household has settled in for the night and then sneak through an upper window, seeking a child sleeping alone.

The Eastern Orthodox Church, which is the dominant religion in Romania, has a different perception of the Moroi: the Moroi are not magicians, they are the undead. In this account, the Moroi are people who die under a curse or who have been excommunicated, and are therefore damned to return from their graves as vampires. This version of the Moroi is close to the Strigoi (*see* entry later in this chapter). The church has, for centuries, upheld the concept that vampires will remain undead until they are granted absolution by the church.

One common folktale suggests that a Moroi is the vengeful spirit of a child murdered by its own parents. In such cases the creature returns to destroy the parents and every other living member of the family until the entire line is wiped out. This kind of Moroi is incredibly savage and is not satisfied with drinking blood, but actually rips open its parents' chests and feasts on their hearts.

THE FEAST OF ST. ANDREW

This celebration is actually one of the most dreaded periods of the year in Romania. St. Andrew was one of the Apostles, sent forth to preach to other nations. He was crucified and killed by the Romans, and each year on the date of his death (November 30) a feast is held in his honor. Along with the feasts of Easter and St. George, St. Andrews Day has been associated with evil for centuries, because it is believed to be a time of great vampiric activity. During the preparation for these feast days the people rub garlic on the doors and windows of their homes in order to protect the inhabitants from vampire attacks.

NOSFERATU

Because of the book *Dracula* by Bram Stoker, the word Nosferatu has been inextricably linked with vampires and most people believe that it is an ancient word that means either "undead" or "not dead." But the term Nosferatu is a fairly modern word derived from an old Slavonic expression, *nosufur-atu*, which in turn was drawn from the Greek term *nosophoros*, or "plague carrier."

This does not mean, however, that Nosferatu and vampires are not linked. Many cultures around the world have found that vampires are often the means by which disease is spread. Disease-carrying vampires include the Adze of Togo, the Bosnian Lampire, the Mara of Canada, Poland, and Scandinavia, the Dalmatian Kozlak, the Nachzehrer of Germany, the Asasabonsam of Ghana, and many others.

Count Orlock, the most famous of the Nosferatu. Archival photo.

In several Third World countries, particularly Malaysia and parts of Africa, vampires and similar evil spirits have been blamed for the spread of AIDS.

It is a particularly unsettling thought that even if one wards off a vampire bite the very presence of the creature in the community can still bring death and suffering. This is one of the many reasons fire was used as a purifying tool by vampire slayers down through the ages.

AIDS

HIV, the Human Immuno-deficiency Virus, is a virus that is transmitted between humans through exchange of bodily fluids, primarily through sexual contact. The AIDS (Acquired Immune Deficiency Syndrome) virus is found throughout the world, and has had devastating impact in many countries, including Romania and many parts of Africa. It is primarily a heterosexual disease, although it is considered a homosexual disease in many first world countries, especially in the United States, largely due to the deaths of homosexual film, TV, and fashion industry celebrities.

AIDS has been a theme in various vampire novels, such as Scott Miller's *In The Blood* (based on his musical of the same name), *Children Of The Night* by Dan Simmons, *Reflections Of A Vampire* by Damion Kirk.

The spread of disease through the blood is nothing new to vampire folklore, since many of the world's undead are directly linked to the spread of disease. It has been speculated that the AIDS epidemic is the direct cause of the increase seen in the number of vampire novels, music, plays, and films over the last couple of decades.

PRYCCOLITCH

This fierce Romanian creature is a combination of vampire and were-wolf, possessing the cunning of the former and the sheer destructive power of the latter. The Pryccolitch is a Living Vampire, rather than a Revenant, but once killed it can rise from its grave if not buried with the proper safeguards (staking, beheading, and use of garlic).

A curse laid on someone's head, heart, or soul—by a witch or a scorned and black-hearted person—can transform a person into a Pryccolitch. Cursing someone, even in jest, can have dire consequences because there are folktales that tell of idle curses resulting in someone being transformed into this bloodthirsty killer.

The transformation into a Pryccolitch begins by the person's soul either going cold or leaving the body entirely. This absence allows evil spirits to enter. These spirits teach the newly transformed monster about its nature, and guide it in its campaign of terror and murder, helping it to choose the right victims and always reminding it to be cautious and sly.

The Pryccolitch can only transform into its monstrous shape while hidden from human eyes. The metamorphosis is very quick but painful, similar to the agonizing transformation shown in the movie *An American Werewolf In London*.

Once transformed into wolf shape, the Pryccolitch hunts freely and kills openly. Pryccolitch accounts from the eighteenth and nineteenth centuries described it as mostly preying on livestock, but earlier accounts were frightening tales of the creature attacking families and wiping out entire villages.

STRIGOI

The Strigoi, the most famous and numerous breed of Romanian vampire, is not a typical Revenant vampire. After burial, the creature can rise and rejoin the community, dwell within it, walk about during daylight hours, wed, raise a family, and even hold a job. But its humanity is a veneer hiding the vampire within.

The name Strigoi is based on a much older Roman term, *strix*, meaning "screech owl," a name that has also come to be identified with vampires and witches. (*See* Vampires Of Rome, p. 437.)

In the early stages of its unlife the creature may need to return to its grave each night, but as it feeds and grows stronger it will pass beyond that limitation. This makes detecting the creature both difficult and dangerous.

The Strigoi. Used with permission, (c) 2003 by Bill Chancellor.

There are many folktales about young people who fell in love with a member of their community (male or female) only to discover on the wedding night, or shortly after the wedding, that their spouse was a Strigoi. The young human lover would suffer from a wasting death that was often blamed on various diseases, while the Strigoi easily played the part of the grieving widow or widower.

Some rural legends say that the Strigoi only drinks human blood for a certain time period, essentially until it has restored its vitality. Once restored to a semblance of humanity, the vampire goes about living as a normal human, and satiates its blood hunger on animals. A few tales hold that after a while the Strigoi becomes entirely human and passes completely beyond the need for blood.

Tangled in the complex rural histories of Romania and the other Slavic countries are a number of references to different types of Strigoi. Some are witches who become vampires after their death and attack children for their blood. Other Strigoi are poltergeist-like creatures that remain invisible but torment their families by hurling things around and generally causing mischief.

Birth defects are cited as leading causes for creating Strigoi. Children born with a caul, teeth, or a tail are believed to be doomed to become Strigoi after their natural deaths. Children born out of wedlock or who die before being properly baptized are likewise fated. Moreover, the seventh son or seventh daughter in a family is suspect, as is the child of a woman who did not eat salt during her pregnancy. Anyone looked at by a vampire carries the taint and may become one after they die, even if that death is by natural causes.

Despite what is suggested in the movies, there are few instances in vampire folklore of a vampire bite causing vampirism in others; but this does occur in the case of the Strigoi. A person bitten by a vampire may return from death as a blood drinker. It is the bite alone that inflicts this curse (no exchange of blood is necessary, thank you anyway, Bram Stoker).

Certain measures can be taken to prevent a person from becoming a vampire. If a child is born with a caul, that membrane needs to be removed and burned before the child can bite it or eat any of it. Once a person has died, the body should be properly prepared so that even a person who was cursed cannot rise as a Strigoi. First, prior to the funeral the coffin should be set where no animal can cross over it or stand upon it. Garlic should be placed around the neck of the deceased, or in its mouth. Wild rose or other wild thorns should be placed or, ideally, planted around the grave as these plants and their thorns have great powers for limiting vampiric movement.

If a vampire is suspected in the area, garlic should be placed on all windows and hung above doors. A paste of garlic can be made and smeared on the lintels, and used to rub down livestock to prevent attack by a Strigoi. Cooking with garlic, or even chewing it, helps keep Strigoi away as they cannot abide the smell of it.

As vampiric activity is at its height on the feast days of Saint George and Saint Andrew, extra precautions should be taken. Garlic can be distributed to parishioners in church and a careful watch made to see who will not (or cannot) eat it.

Once a vampire has been detected—and this usually happens only with very young Strigoi who have not yet managed to blend in with the community—the creature's grave must be located and the monster dealt with in the ritual fashion. The grave should be opened—daylight hours are safest for this activity—and a long stake immediately driven through the chest or stomach to hold the creature in place. Stakes do not kill vampires, even if they are made of hawthorn, but they do keep the vampire from rising.

Next, the vampire's head should be cut off with axe, knife, or sword. Garlic should be crammed into the mouth and the decapitated head turned backward in the coffin.

If the Strigoi is so powerful that it rises even after these actions are taken, the vampire slayers need to step up their campaign. That generally means dismembering the corpse and then burning it to ashes. Once the ashes have cooled, they are mixed with water and fed to the members of the Strigoi's family to cure them of any sickness or evil taint.

In the nineteenth century, some vampire slayers took to shooting the corpse through the heart with a bullet that had been blessed. But the effectiveness of these "sacred bullets" has never been proved.

VARCOLACI

The most powerful Romanian vampire—and indeed a real powerhouse among all forms of vampire—is the Varcolaci. This vampire appears in the folktales of Transylvania as well as Romania. It can shapeshift at will, travel like the wind along an astral thread, and even cause solar and lunar eclipses.

The Varcolaci are humanoid in appearance, with dry, pale skin, and dark hair. Their eyes are deep-set, dark, and fierce, and they possess tremendous physical strength.

The Varcolaci are nocturnal creatures, rising after sunset and leaving their physical forms behind. As spirits, they fly into the sky and, according to legend, drink blood from the moon. In Transylvanian folktales, if a woman alone in a darkened room were to spin threads, she might accidentally create an astral thread along which the Varcolaci could rise into the sky to devour the moon's blood.

The Varcolaci. Artwork by Robert Patrick O'Brien.

As shapeshifters, the Varcolaci can take any form they choose. Sometimes they will appear as a small, black, winged ghost; or as a goat-legged demon; or as a small dragon. A common manifestation is the form of a great wolf with many mouths full of wicked teeth. But in whatever form it adopts, the Varcolaci is immensely powerful and impossible to oppose.

GARLIC

Since the days of the ancient Egyptians, garlic (*allium sativum*) has been to treat wounds, infections, tumors, and a variety of intestinal parasites. It is also a common ingredient in soups and stews, as well as Italian, Greek, and Korean cooking. Garlic also possesses the ability to inhibit the growth of parasites in the intestines, including amoebas that cause dysentery, which is useful in combating the various vampires who spread disease. It is used heavily in the standard vampire exorcism because it is a blood purifier, and many cultures believe that this purification is both physical and spiritual.

The strong aroma of garlic flowers and the pungent odor of raw garlic itself are useful in driving off vampires. Garlic bulbs are often hung above doorways and windows, and lintels are often smeared with a paste made from mashed garlic to act as a barrier against invading evil.

Photo by Jason Lukridge.

VAMPIRES OF ANCIENT ROME

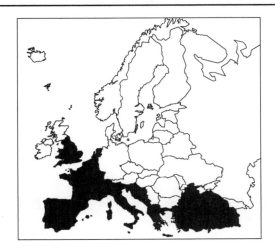

EMPUSA

See Vampires Of Greece.

LAMIA

See Vampires Of Greece.

LEMURE (also known as LARVAE)

According to the mythology of Ancient Rome, when the dead descended to the Underworld the souls were divided into two distinctly different groups: Manes and Lemure. The Manes, by far the largest group, were the honored spirits of dead ancestors. When a spirit received proper honors from his living relatives, and when certain holy rites had been performed, the Manes received permission to ascend from the Underworld and serve as a spiritual guide and guardian to his descendants.

Those persons whose souls were tainted because they lived evil lives were sent back to haunt and torment the living. Known as Lemures (or Larvae), these evil ghosts sowed discord, brought torment to everyone whose lives they touched, and otherwise defiled the world of the living. They actually fed on the pain and misery they caused, so in that respect they were Emotional Vampires.

Though the Lemures were at work all year long, they were particularly powerful during the Festival of Lemuria, held each May.

Charms and spells had little effect on these creatures, but they were sensitive to sound, so the banging of drums was used to drive them off. For this reason drums and other noisemakers became part of regular rites and rituals—purifying the air of all evil spirits.

VAMPIRE SNACKS AT THE COLISEUM

At the gladiatorial games in Ancient Rome, it was fairly common for vendors to strike deals with the guards to purchase the rights to drain the blood of the newly slain. The blood was then sold to spectators as a medicinal draught to prevent epilepsy.

STRIX (also known as STRYX; plural STRIGES)

In ancient Rome, the deadly Strix was a common danger for villagers and city dwellers alike. Striges were Living Vampires, able to live normally among humans during the day and go undetected.

A female vampire-witch, the Strix would transform herself into a crow or owl and fly off looking for prey, invisible against the night sky. When she found a lonely traveler, saw a shepherd watching his flock by moonlight, or spied through an open window a person asleep and vulnerable, the Strix would attack swiftly and glut herself on blood. Though she would attack anyone, she preferred the innocent blood of

The Strix. Artwork by Marie O'Brien.

young children. The classical writer Ovid wrote in his book *Fasti* that Striges attacked children at night in a form resembling that of a screech owl. He wrote that they used their beaks and talons to wound an infant's chest, then drank the blood from these lacerations. Thereafter the Striges would return night after night to trouble their prey until the child wasted away and died.

If the parents discovered (or suspected) that a Strix was preying on their child, their only recourse was to appeal to a demi-Goddess named Carna. This powerful spirit then appeared and went through the home performing sacred rituals which would ban the Strix from returning. Her final act would be to place a branch of white thorn in the window of the infant's room.

It should be noted that white thorn is a species of hawthorn, which is a common proof against vampires throughout Europe, even today.

Photo by Jason Lukridge.

VAMPIRES OF RUSSIA

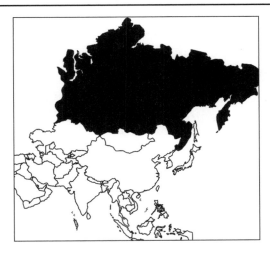

ERESTUN (also known as XLOPTUNY)

Russia has quite a variety of vampire species troubling its long, dark nights. One such creature is the Erestun, a vampire created when a sorcerer takes over a person's body when the victim is on the brink of death. At such times the link between body and soul is tenuous and the sorcerer can, essentially, force the rightful spiritual inhabitant out of the body and occupy it himself. At this point the dying person makes a miraculous recovery. Unfortunately, the Erestun needs to feed on blood in order to maintain the health of its new "vehicle."

The likeliest targets for the Erestun are the relatives of the body's former owner.

ERETIKU (also known as ERETNIK, ERETITSA or ERETNITSA)

These are vampire-sorcerers from Northern Russia whose legends and practices overlap with (and are sometimes identical to) the Erestun.

The root of this vampire's name is *eretic*, or heretic, a deliberate religious blasphemer practicing dark sorcery. It is popularly believed that heretics all become undead creatures after their mortal life has ended. The widespread belief that all heretics return from the dead to harass the living is generally held responsible for the brutality and hysteria surrounding the medieval Russian campaign against heretics.

Often, in tales, the creature is a woman who sold her soul to the devil during her lifetime and returned from the grave to trouble the world of the living. Adopting the form of an old hag by day, the Eretiku would seek out others of her kind and form a coven to meet in the dark shadows of a deep forest ravine.

The East-Central Russian version of the Eretiku is called an Elatomsk. These are often women who had sold their souls to the devil for great magical powers, and after their deaths become "doorknockers," a kind of poltergeist. They sleep in graves and make disgusting and disruptive noises in alehouses, public bathhouses, and other places.

An Eretiku has the power to cause wasting sickness just with the intensity of its baleful stare. In all Slavic cultures it is held that looking into the eyes of the dead is enough to lure one into the grave. That is why it is always stressed that the eyes of a newly dead person should be closed.

LIHO

Few creatures in Russian and Slavic folklore are as fearsome as the one-eyed vampire ghost, the Liho. This bizarre and frightening figure is generally female and personifies trouble, strife, doom, and all other kinds of misery.

The Liho appears in a number of different folkloric story cycles. It assumes various guises and aspects according to variations in regional and even national storytelling. One constant fact, however, is that the creature is powerful and deadly.

Like the Cyclops of the Greek mythology, Liho is a killer and cannibal, savoring the flesh and blood of anyone who falls prey to her wicked appetites. One of the most commonly told Slavic tales about the Liho mirrors the tale of *Ulysses* in many regards. An intrepid metal-smith set out with a plan for defeating the monster that had been preying on his village and most recently devoured his friend, the village tailor. The smith confronted the creature and offered to fashion her a new eye of shiny metal. The Liho agreed, believing that the metal eye would give her sorcerous powers, but the smith said that the procedure was delicate and he had to tie her down in order to keep her from twitching during the procedure. The Liho reluctantly agreed, but sealed her cave first so that the smith could not escape.

The smith bound her with many stout ropes. While she was bound, he used a metal poker to gouge out her eye.

In rage and pain the Liho burst free of the bonds and tried to kill the smith, but he hid from her among her sheep. After a few days of the sheep complaining and needing to be released from the cave so they could graze, the Liho moved the

The Liho. Used with permission, (c) 2003 by Anton Kvasovarov.

rock that blocked the entrance and the smith, dressed now in sheep-skins, slipped out with the livestock.

On the way home, the smith saw a beautiful silver axe sticking out of a tree in the forest. Realizing that the axe was a relic of the Liho's, the smith decided to take it as a trophy. But the haft was enchanted and his hand stuck fast to it. Even the smith's great strength could not break this connection. Behind him he heard the Liho shambling through the forest, crying out that she would quench her thirst with his blood. In panic the smith drew his knife and cut off the hand stuck to the axe. Wounded and nearly dead from blood loss, the smith staggered through the forest and finally managed to find his village. But without his strong right hand he could not work at his trade, and the loss broke his spirit. Within a few years he wasted away and died.

On the day the smith died, however, the Liho grew a new eye and once more began preying on the villagers, feeding on their flesh and blood. To this day rural Slavs say that they can hear her hungry wailing mixed with the howl of the night winds.

UPYR

A Russian Revenant vampire, the Upyr sleeps by day in its grave or in a secluded hiding place, then rises at sunset to hunt for blood. The Upyr is a brutal killer, first attacking the children in a family and then extending its carnage to the adults. Because it is a vicious family destroyer, the Upyr has earned a reputation as one of the most feared and loathed of the Slavic blood drinkers.

Some legends suggest that the Upyr is that rarest of vampire: the kind that can be killed by a stake through the heart. But the folktales generally go on to say that the staking must be followed by decapitation, or with a good burning. So the method of using just a stake has little historical basis for reliability.

Most often it is either a witch or a suicide who becomes a Upyr, both cases being cause for damnation. A Upyr can also be created when a living person, dog, or cat walks over the grave of a newly dead person, a dreadful mistake known in legends as "Corpse Jumping."

The term Upyr is sometimes used as a general term for all kinds of Russian vampires, including the Erestun and Eretiku.

CORPSE JUMPING

There is a common tradition that a person or animal passing over a dead body may cause it to become a vampire. The spirit of the dead can snatch a portion of the life of any living creature and use it to rekindle its own unnatural life. Animals such as dogs or cats are easily capable of corpse jumping, but people, bats, birds, and insects should be restrained as well. The belief, in one form or another, is found in cultures as far apart as Eastern Europe, China, and the Native American Navajo. In China, tigers are believed to possess what is known as a "soul-recalling hair" that hooks part of the spirit when it crosses over a grave.

VOURDALAK (also known as WURDALAK)

The legend of the Vourdalak is an old one, told in various songs and stories, most notably in Leo Tolstoy's 1947 short story, "The Family Of The Vourdalak."

In most tales, the Vourdalak is depicted as a hauntingly beautiful woman who lures travelers to their deaths in secluded spots. Many legends of the Vourdalak seem to blend with that of the Eretitsa by suggesting that the creature is a blasphemer who has made a deal with the dark forces in return for dreadful supernatural powers. She feeds on children, in some cases whole families, and is most feared by her own kindred, for whom she develops a particular appetite.

The Vourdalak. Photo by Jason Lukridge.

IL WURDALAK

The 1963 horror film *Black Sabbath* contains a trilogy of short horror films, one of which is titled "Il Wurdalak," a film adaptation of Leo Tolstoy's 1947 short story, "The Family of the Vourdalak."

This gothic period piece is set in rural Russia and opens with Gorca (Boris Karloff) returning to his family after slaying a vampire. But his homecoming unleashes the curse of the undead and soon only Vladimire, a visiting nobleman, is left to fight the evil scourge. It's a wonderfully creepy and atmospheric yarn with some truly disturbing moments, like the spectral appearance of an undead child. But it is Karloff's haunting presence which gives this episode a special frisson. The film's mythology is also a fairly accurate recounting of the folkloric Vourdalak.

WAMPIR

See the listing for the Upier in the section Vampires Of Poland.

YETI

Though certainly native to the Himalayas of Tibet, Yeti (or some very similar species) are believed to populate the mountain regions of several Russian provinces in what was one Soviet Central Asia.

Mountain climbers have reported seeing them in the Pamiro-Alai mountain range in Tadzhik as recently as 1980. The Russian Yeti are apparently as nonviolent and timid as their Tibetan cousins and may even be of the same species, whereas most of the world's other man-beasts are maneaters.

The various peoples of that region of the former Soviet Union use different names for the Yeti. The Georgians call it the Tkys-katsi; the Azerbaijani call it Mesheadam; in Dagestan it is the Kaptar; the Balkas, Chechens, Kabardins and Ungushes call it the Almasti.

·PART SEVEN·

DEFENSES AGAINST THE UNDEAD

"Thalaba the Destroyer"

"This is not she!" the Old Man exclaim'd;
"A Fiend; a manifest Fiend!"
And to the youth he held his lance;
"Strike and deliver thyself!"
"Strike her!" cried Thalaba,
And, palsied of all power,
Gazed fixedly upon the dreadful form.
"Yea, strike her!" cried a voice, whose tones
Flow'd with such sudden healing through his soul,
As when the desert shower
From death deliver'd him;
But unobedient to that well-known voice,
His eye was seeking it,
When Moath, firm of heart,
Perform'd the bidding: through the vampire corpse
He thrust his lance; it fell,
And howling with the wound,
Its fiendish tenant fled.

Robert Southey
1838

Destroying a vampire is tough and dangerous; warding them off is a bit safer. But it has to be done right because good intentions aren't enough.

There are two approaches to preventing vampire attacks. The first, and most sensible, is to use precautions to protect a corpse so that it is not taken over and transformed demonically into a vampire. The second, used in the event that a vampire has actually risen, is to employ charms of various sorts to either deflect the vampire's attention or repel him.

Proper burial rites have always been important, and for a number of reasons. First and foremost, there is the respect for the dead and the wish that they be buried with dignity and consideration. Even if the body is nothing more than a shell, burial rites honor who the deceased were in life by demonstrating respect for their remains.

Secondly, in the world of the supernatural, a corpse is an empty "shell" or "vessel," an object waiting to be filled. Demons of various kinds wait for the opportunity to inhabit a dead body, using their demonic strength to reanimate it, then satisfying their unnatural hungers by using the stolen body to attack the living. The sacred dead, those who have lived a holy life and were buried with strict adherence to the proper rites and procedures, are safe from this spiritual conquest; but those persons whose lives were lived in sin or who embraced violence and evil become the perfect vessels for demons.

Vampires that are created due to improper burial rites include the Ekimmu of ancient Greece, the Gayal of India, the Kasha of Japan, the Tlahuelpuchi of Mexico, and the Czechoslovakian Nelapsi. Each creature is horrible and powerful, and each one was needlessly brought into the world when proper burial rites would have prevented their creation.

Naturally, proper burial rites and precautions vary from culture to culture, and in some cases there are special rites to be observed if it is suspected that a recently deceased person might be a potential vampire. In the case of the Bohemian Ogoljen, this can be prevented by burying the corpse at a crossroads. The wise men of Aborigine villages in Australia prevent a Mart from rising from the grave by weighing it down with heavy rocks or sometimes breaking the legs of a newly dead corpse to cripple it.

Dirt from the grave works as a charm against the Ogoljen of Bohemia. It is also a potent inhibiting magic which, when placed in the navel of a resting Ogoljen, can prevent the vampire from rising.

Some vampires, like the Czechoslovakian Nelapsi, require extreme and complex methods to prevent them from being created. The villagers first make sure to bump the deceased's coffin on the threshold of his home when they carry it out of the house. Poppy seeds are scattered along the road between the house and the graveyard, then all around the grave and inside the open grave itself. More of the seeds (and perhaps some millet) are used to fill the corpse's nose and mouth. As an added precaution, iron nails are driven deep into the arms and legs to pin the corpse to the coffin. Smaller nails are used to pin the hair and clothes securely to the coffin. A final burial precaution is to pierce the corpse's heart or head with a long hat-pin, a thin iron spike, or a stake made from hawthorn, blackthorn, or oak. Then the villagers go home and thoroughly wash their hands in case they touched the corpse, the coffin, or grave dirt.

In Germany, various preventative strategies are available to reduce the risk of a dead child becoming a Doppelsauger. The key is to make sure the vampire cannot begin to eat itself while in its grave, so it will lack enough strength to break free. Blocks are put in place to prevent the jaws from working, a metal coin is wedged between its teeth, or a semicircular wooden board is placed under the chin to make it impossible for the corpse to bite at itself. The body will often be wrapped up so the vampire cannot use its hands, but cloth from the shroud or burial garments must not come into close contact with the mouth.

Similar methods are used all over the world. In some cases a corpse will be staked, decapitated, and its mouth stuffed with garlic even before it has demonstrated any tendency toward supernatural vigor. Garlic is an excellent multi-purpose defense against vampires. Garlic

Photo by Robert Patrick O'Brien.

bulbs can be hung about houses, garlic paste can be smeared on doors, windows, and livestock, even eating it can prevent vampire attacks. It is also used in prevention rituals, such as stuffing a corpse's mouth with garlic as previously described.

Hawthorn and wild rose are excellent proofs against vampiric activity. They seem to possess the virtue of driving a vampire away or limiting a vampire's movement. In seventeenth century Europe, hawthorn or other wild thorn bushes would be planted on or around a grave site to ward off evil. If they are placed on a grave, vampires such as the Dalmatian Kozlak cannot even rise. A paste made from hawthorn and garlic is used to drive off the Blautsauger of Germany, keeping humans and livestock free from its hunger. The Gypsies used fresh cut hawthorn stakes to impale the legs of a corpse so that if it comes back as the vampiric Mullo it will not be able to rise from its coffin. In ancient Rome, a branch of white thorn (a species of hawthorn) would be hung in a window to ward off the evil Strix. And the Serbian Vlkodlak can actually be killed by piercing its navel with a hawthorn branch and then igniting the branch with death-vigil candles.

In Bulgaria, the vampire slayer known as a Djadadjii will scatter wild roses around the grave of a suspected Krvoijac. Like hawthorn and garlic flowers, wild roses have a powerful restraining effect on some species of vampires; in this case the flowers prevent the Krvoijac from rising.

Should a vampire rise, there is a precaution used all over the world that will confuse the vampire so that it cannot hunt: scattering seeds, grains of rice, beans, or other small dry goods on the ground. For some inexplicable reason, many vampires have an obsession with counting, so a vampire will be compelled to stop and count each and every seed or grain. This bizarre protection is seen across Europe with the Gierach of Prussia, the Mjertovjec of Byelorus, and the Czechoslovakian Nelapsi; in South America with the Azeman of Surinam; in the tropics with the Asema of Trinidad; and in China with the Chiang-Shih.

Various religious charms are proof against some vampires, such as the Bruja of Spain, the Phi Song Nang of Thailand, the Chinese Chiang-Shih, and the Soucoyan of Dominica. But charms are not always religious in nature. The Spanish Bruja is also frightened by sharp objects, so scissors are placed under pillows, on night stands, or even hung above doorways to frighten this vampire-witch away. The Mexican Tlahuelpuchi, an Aztec vampire, is also shy of scissors.

In seventeenth century Europe, it was a fairly common practice to fire a sacred bullet (one blessed by a priest) into the coffin of a recently deceased person.

Unfortunately there is little evidence in folklore that a cross or crucifix has any preventative powers against a vampire. Sorry, Professor Van Helsing.

CHARMS

Magical charms have been used by cultures around the world and throughout history as defenses against evil. A few of the most well-known and effective charms include:

- **THE ALL-SEEING EYE**, a single human eye surrounded by radiating beams of light, is found in many eras and cultures. It symbolizes the protective power of God watching over mankind in general and the wearer of the amulet in particular. It appears on the Great Seal of the United States, and is a symbol of the Freemasons, for whom it represents the Great Architect of the Universe.

All-Seeing Eye. Archival photo.

- **THE FOULED ANCHOR** is the symbol of sailors around the world and is carried to ensure safe travel. In the African-American Voodoo tradition, the Fouled Anchor is used to insure a traveler's safe return home on land as well as sea, and will also bring a straying lover home.

- **ANGELICA ROOT** (also known as Holy Ghost Root, Archangel Root, and Dong Quai) is a healing agent for women and a protection against harm.

- **BLUE STONE** is often used as an ingredient in Mojo Hands (protective pouches of herbs and charms made by African-American Voodoo doctors; *see* entry below). It is used especially for protection from evil and to give good luck to gamblers. Spiritualists also use it to wash floors, in order to purify the home and keep out evil spirits. In addition, hanging a bottle of laundry bluing in a fireplace will keep Satan and his minions out of a house.

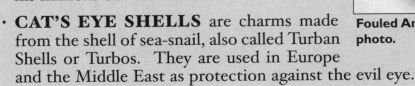

Fouled Anchor. Archival photo.

- **CAT'S EYE SHELLS** are charms made from the shell of sea-snail, also called Turban Shells or Turbos. They are used in Europe and the Middle East as protection against the evil eye.

· **CORNUTO** (or Corno, or Cornicello) is an ancient Italian amulet whose name means "little horn." It is another protection against the evil eye. The long, gently twisted horn-shaped amulet is most often carved from red coral or made of gold or silver. The Cornuto used to be carved like the horn of an animal, not a curled-over sheep or goat horn but rather like the twisted horn of an African eland or something similar. Over the years they have become rather stylized and now look less like an animal's horn. They are primarily found in Italy and in America among descendants of Italian immigrants, and can be bought at any Italian market.

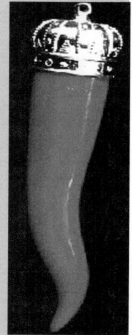

Cornuto. Archival photo.

· **DEVIL'S SHOESTRING** is the common name for several North American plants used as an ingredient in Mojo Hands (a protective pouch of herbs and charms used in Voodoo; *see* entry below). The name refers to a species of viburnum, usually *viburnum alnifolium* (alder-leafed viburnum or hobblebush), but sometimes refers to the related species *viburnum opulus* (cramp-bark) or *viburnum prunifolium* (black haw). All are woodland plants of the honeysuckle family. The "strings" of Devil's Shoestrings are not string-like at all. They are long and flexible, like honeysuckle vine, and they are roots, not canes. Devil's Shoestrings are used for protection, to "trip up the Devil" or "hobble" him so he cannot enter a house.

· The **EYE-IN-HAND** is a talisman used as protection against the evil eye. The charm combines the imagery of Greek and Turkish blue all-seeing eye charms with the downward-facing Arab and Israeli Hamsa Hand (*see* entry below). The Eye-In-Hand is frequently encountered in India and the southern Mediterranean region.

· The **GLASS EYE** is the most common charm found in Greece and Turkey. The blue glass eye "mirrors back" the blue of the evil eye and thus "confounds" it.

- **HAMSA HAND** (Arabic) or **HAMESH HAND** (Hebrew) is an ancient amulet used for protection against the evil eye. The words *hamsa* and *hamesh* both mean "five" and refer to the digits on the hand. An alternative Islamic name for this charm is the Hand of Fatima, a reference to Mohammed's daughter. An alternative Jewish name is the Hand of Miriam, a reference to the sister of Moses and Aaron.

Hamsa Hand. Archival photo.

- **HIGH JOHN THE CONQUEROR ROOT** is one of the staples of African-American folk magic. It is a plant root named after a slave known as John the Conqueror, said to be the son of an African king. It is unknown whether he was real or fictional, but he was an inspiration to slaves who wanted to rebel against their masters but could not do so openly. According to legend, John was taken into captivity but he never became subservient, and his cleverness at tricking his masters supplied a pointed moral to many a story. John the Conqueror may very well be the embodiment of the trickster who is commonly found in African moral folk tales, or possibly an interpretation of the West African deity known variously as Eleggua, Legba, and Eshu. Having John the Conqueror root in a Mojo Hand insures good luck and protection from evil.

- In Ireland, a **HORSESHOE** is placed over the lintel with the points downward to keep witchcraft out and let good luck come in. Some sources suggest that a horseshoe merely prevents bad luck thereby letting the regular benefits of a Christian life occur normally.

- **ICONS** or other images of Gods and Saints have always been kept in the house as protections against evil, or worn as safeguards when traveling. They appear in various religions:

  BUDDHIST and FOLK-BUDDHIST
  - Buddha and Hotei-Buddha

  CATHOLIC and FOLK-CATHOLIC
  - Anima Sola (Lonely Soul)
  - Maximon (Saint Simon)
  - Nino de Atocha
  - Nino Fidencio Saint Anthony
  - Saint Christopher
  - Saint Expedite
  - Saint Jude
  - Saint Martin of Tours (San Martin Caballero)
  - The Seven African Powers (Orishas)

  HINDU
  - Ganesha
  - Hanuman
  - Kali, Durga, Parvati, and other forms of Sakti
  - Laksmi
  - Sarasvati
  - Siva and Bhairava

- **MANO CORNUTO** is an ancient Italian amulet. The name translates as hand (*mano*) and horn (*corno*), and is a charm shaped like the hand gesture in which the index and little fingers are extended while the middle and ring fingers are curled into the palm. This is done to ward off evil, and over the last century or so the charm has been commonly worn by Italians and Italian-Americans.

- The name **MOJO HAND** comes from the West-African word *moju-ba*, meaning a prayer of praise and homage to one of the gods. In American Voodoo, the Mojo Hand is a small flannel prayer bag containing one or more magical items such as sacred objects, lucky stones, pieces of dried root, herbs, or specially made charms.

- **MOMENTO MORI** is a Latin phrase meaning "remember you must die," which refers to the practice of carrying an item that belonged to a recently deceased person, as a keepsake and as a protective charm against their spirit returning to haunt the living. According to the folklore in rural Italy, keeping a souvenir of a dead friend insures that person's ghost or vampire will not trouble you.

- **THE OJO DE VENADO** or **DEER'S EYE CHARM** is a Mexican form of protection against any form of spiritual evil. The charm is made from the seed of Velvet Bean (*mucuna pruriens*), also known as Cowhage.

- A **RABBIT'S FOOT** is considered lucky. Several cultures around the world, including many Western European countries and the American South, believe that carrying a rabbit's foot will bring good luck and prevent evil curses.

- **RATTLESNAKE SKIN** has anti-witch properties. During the early twentieth century, African-Americans from the Deep South commonly sewed a small piece of rattlesnake skin into their clothes to nullify witchcraft.

- **SCISSORS** placed under a pillow, with the points facing the head of the bed, are believed to be a proof against attack by vampires, ghosts, and demons in a number of cultures. The Aztec Tlahuelpuchi vampire is kept away using this method, as are the Brujas of Spain and the Bruxa of Portugal.

- **SALT** has a long history of being used in rituals of purification, magical protection, and blessing. Among spell-casters from the European folk-magic tradition, it is commonplace to lay down a pinch of salt in each corner of a room before performing a spell. This practice has carried over into contemporary African-American Voodoo. Painting a cross on a sack of salt and setting it beside one's front door is also believed to keep evil away.

Salt charm by Faith Maberry.

· **SILVER DIMES** are used in American Voodoo in a number of ways. For example, placing a dime in one's mouth protects against poisoning; boring a hole through a dime and wearing it on a string around one's neck, wrist, or ankle is proof against any Gris-Gris (the negative use of Voodoo); coating a dime with red pepper, wrapping it in brown paper, and keeping it in one's pocket deflects any black magic; and so on. In Ireland, placing a dime under fireplace stones will keep witches out.

·PART EIGHT·

VAMPIRES AROUND THE WORLD

S-Z

"Lamia"

Then Lamia breath'd death breath; the sophist's eye,
Like a sharp spear, went through her utterly,
Keen, cruel, perceant, stinging: she, as well
As her weak hand could any meaning tell,
Motion'd him to be silent; vainly so,
He look'd and look'd again a level--No!
"A Serpent!" echoed he; no sooner said,
Than with a frightful scream she vanished:
And Lycius' arms were empty of delight,
As were his limbs of life, from that same night.

John Keats
1819

VAMPIRES OF SCANDINAVIA

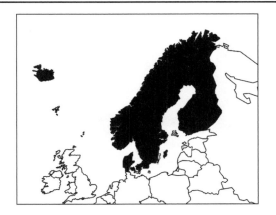

MARA

One of the most fearsome female vampires in the world is the Scandinavian Mara, one of the many breeds of vampire that share qualities with the Succubus. The Mara can adopt different guises, but most frequently appears either as a stunningly beautiful woman or a wrinkled and gnarled old hag. The Mara favors the blood of young men.

The name Mara derives from the old Anglo-Saxon verb *"merran,"* meaning "to crush." The name aptly describes her method of slaughter: she attacks her victims as they sleep, crushing their throats with a terrible strength and then tearing their flesh to get at the blood.

Like the Langsuir of Malaysia and the Cihuateteo of Mexico, the Mara is believed to be the spirit of an unbaptized dead woman.

It requires great courage and skill to defeat a Mara, even while armed. The only defenses against the Mara are edged weapons: knives and swords.

The word "nightmare" is an outgrowth of the words Mara and *nacht* (night), which is wholly appropriate because this monster has disturbed more than a few dreams.

Mara. Artwork by Robert Patrick O'Brien.

VAMPIRES OF SCOTLAND

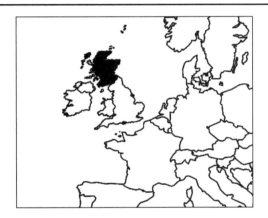

BAOBHAN SITH (also BOBBAN SITH and BEAN SI)

In Scotland the difference between a "vampire" and one of the "faerie folk" is often vague. One case in point is the malicious being called the Baobhan Sith, a Highland succubus that uses her enchanting beauty to lure travelers to a painful death. She has long hair, wears a gray cloak over a flowing green gown (to hide the fact that she is half goat), and sucks blood and life essence from her victims.

Fire and cold iron can kill the Baobhan Sith, but it is nearly impossible to catch or corner her. A vampire slayer needs several assistants with torches to form a ring around her and trap her. The slayer himself must enter the ring and dispatch the Baobhan Sith with a pointed iron shaft or a steel sword. A scythe is also effective, but if the creature is not killed on the first swing she is fast enough to attack the slayer before he can swing again.

BAOBHAN SITH IN FICTION

K. M. Briggs, in her book on the supernatural, *The Anatomy of Puck*, recounts a tale of four hunters seduced and attacked by four beautiful Baobhan Sith. Similar stories abound in fiction and folklore of rural Scotland.

GLAISTIG

The Glaistigs appear most often as beautiful young women. Like the Baobhan Sith, Glaistigs wear flowing green skirts to hide the fact that they have cloven hooves for feet. They dance seductively in order to lure men to secluded places, then enchant the men to dance with them, keeping the revels going on and on until the men collapse from sheer exhaustion. The Glaistigs are blood drinkers, and in the final stages of the dance they tear at their victims' throats and shoulders and feast on the spurting blood.

In some cases the Glaistigs take the form of a crow or raven, and in that guise spy out their next victim.

The Glaistigs fear very little. They have an aversion to horses, so they will generally not bother mounted riders unless, from a distance, they can encourage the riders to dismount and follow them on foot.

When a vampire slayer is choosing a weapon for use against a Glaistig, cold iron is best. Steel is not as effective as a rough iron shaft, sharpened at one end.

LEANAN SIDHE (also LEANHAUN SHEE, LEANHAUN SIDHE)

The Leanan Sidhe is one of the stranger and more enchanting vampires of Celtic folklore. Known as the "Dark Muse," the Leanan Sidhe is a feared blood drinking vampire, yet has been worshiped in various ways by poets throughout Scotland and Ireland. In *Faerie And Folk Tales Of Ireland*, edited by William Butler Yeats, Yeats himself wrote, "This spirit seeks the love of men. If they refuse she is their slave; if they consent, they are hers, and can only escape by finding one to take their place. Her lovers waste away, for she lives on their life. Most of the Gaelic poets, down to quite recent times, have had a Leanhaun Shee, for she

Leanan Sidhe. Photo by Robert Patrick O'Brien with Michael Katz.

gives inspiration to her slaves and is indeed the Gaelic muse—this malignant faerie. Her lovers, the Gaelic poets, died young. She grew restless and carried them away to other worlds, for death does not destroy her power."

Some of the legends of the beautiful and compelling creature speak of the gifts of imagination and insight she bestows on the poets who adore her. Other stories hint that her benefits are not given freely, but come at a price—either blood or life energy, on which she feeds with equal relish.

In Ireland the creature is known as the Leanhaun-Sidhe and is nearly identical to this Highland monster.

SLAUGH (also called SLAUGH SIDHE)

The Slaugh of the Scottish Highlands are a horde of evil vampire-spir-its that fly in great flocks, like murderous birds of prey. The Slaugh are not blood drinkers, but Essential Vampires that feed on pain, misery, and the human soul itself.

According to legends of Ireland and Scotland, the Slaugh are the souls of deceased sinners who haunt the night, trying to capture living souls to enslave. In some folktales, the Slaugh can assume human form in order to deceive their victims. In human form they are pale and ugly, toothless and with small, dark, and very penetrating eyes. Yet for some reason, probably due to enchantment, the Slaugh possess a powerful and compelling attraction.

When they appear they always come from the west. For this reason, when a person is dying the westward-facing windows of the house are always shut and secured. This prevents the Slaugh from stealing the dying person's soul away to damnation, preventing them from reaching heaven.

The Slaugh can be detected most easily by their strong smell, a reek like that of decaying flesh. The odor grows more pungent with age.

Some Slaugh prefer to live in human form yet apart from the human community, favoring old and disused mansions or similar ruins. Some choose to live in sewers (which may account for their odor), while others haunt houses of the living by hiding in crawlspaces and cellars.

Slaugh can only speak in a whisper when in faerie form. In human form they are generally soft-spoken and shy, especially in single numbers. But they are also fiercely territorial and will defend their chosen homes with great violence.

The Slaugh can be killed by ordinary means, but will sometimes return as a ghostly version of their former selves. It is safest to drive them out with prayers, bright lights, and the smell of new cut flowers.

Photo by Jason Lukridge.

REDCAP

Deserted castles, ruins, and graveyards have forever been the hunting grounds of malicious spirits the world over. In Scotland, the blood-thirsty vampire called the Redcap favors these places, taking comfort and strength from ruin and decay. If the Redcap's lonely spot was once the scene of violence or battle, so much the better.

Redcaps are a kind of blood drinking faerie creature that belong to the *Unseelie,* or "unblessed" creatures, as opposed to the *Seelie*, who are "blessed." Their name derives from the fact that they dip their caps in the blood of their victims to dye the caps red.

The Redcaps use a number of methods to snare their victims, some circuitous and some straightforward. For example, if a weary traveler is camped out in a Redcap's territory, the creature will try to open one of the sleeper's veins and then quickly dip its cap in the spill of fresh human blood. Failing that, or being surprised in its attempts, the Redcap will simply slaughter its victim and continue to dye their bloody caps.

Redcaps also like to lay in wait for travelers and then leap out to startle them, frighten their horses, and generally give chase. Sometimes Redcaps are only amused by causing fear and panic, but most of the time they prefer to feed.

There are other Unseelie in Scottish and Irish lore, such as the Kelpies and the Will-o'-the-Wisp, but neither of these is as fell and dangerous as the malicious Redcap.

A Redcap. Artwork by Marie O'Brien.

VAMPIRES OF SERBIA

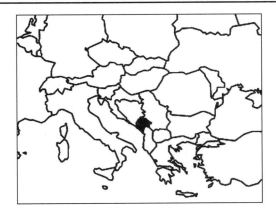

CHILDREN OF JUDAS

The Children of Judas are a cult of red-haired vampires that cause havoc throughout Serbia, Romania, and Bulgaria. They are known for their killing style: they can drain their victims entirely of blood with one bite. Their bite mark is unique in that it resembles the Latin symbol for the number thirty, XXX, which stands for the number of silver pieces Judas received for betraying Jesus.

Judas is seen as a vampiric character because of his actions during Jesus' last few days. Having participated in the Last Supper (a Passover dinner), he drank from Jesus' cup which was symbolically held out to the Apostles as the blood of Christ. That very night Judas went and betrayed Jesus to the authorities, resulting in His arrest and crucifixion. Judas apparently repented of his crime and hung himself in remorse. He is considered by most Christians as the embodiment of evil and is forever damned.

The crucifixion of Jesus as a result of His betrayal by Judas is probably the basis for the belief that crucifixes are anathema to vampires. However, this concept holds far more weight in fiction than it does in folklore.

Though there have not been any reports in recent years of attacks by this vampire society, the Children of Judas concept pops up every now and then in popular fiction. Most recently, in the vampire film *Dracula 2000,* Judas was named as the first vampire, a fact at odds with the more ancient histories of vampirism around the world.

Child of Judas. Used with permission, (c) 2003 by Breanne Levy.

MULLO (also called MULO)

The Serbian Mullo is closely tied to the legends of the Romani vampires. It is the Revenant of a dead Gypsy that returns to feast upon the living. The Mullo has no skeleton and maintains its form through vampiric will. It attacks women and boils them to render flesh from bone, essentially creating another of its own kind.

The Mullo's insatiable sexual hungers are well documented, and the issue of this unholy union is called a Dhampir. Generally it is a Dhampir who alone possesses the skill and power to defeat the Mullo and destroy it. *See* Vampires Among The Gypsies (p. 245) and Part 5: Fighting The Undead (p. 323) for more on Dhampirs.

The Mullo is active day and night, and is unafraid of holy images or sunlight. If a newly buried corpse is suspected of being a Mullo it can be kept from rising by pouring boiling water over its grave. Walking a white horse back and forth over the grave a few times will also work.

The Mullo can be confined to its coffin by piercing its leg with a hawthorn stake or driving a steel needle into the body. Longer wooden stakes driven through the head and chest also keep it from rising. Some legends have it that stealing the Mullo's left sock will somehow make it unable to rise and walk.

VLKODLAK

The Vlkodlak is another fierce Serbian vampire. It has the appearance of a wretched and corrupt drunkard with florid skin the color of blood.

There is something unique and bizarre about the Vlkodlak in that it goes through cycles, like a locust. For seven years it is a blood drinking vampire, then it goes through some inexplicable process of change and becomes human again. While human it ingratiates itself into a new community, then eventually becomes a vampire again and starts a new reign of terror.

The Vlkodlak possesses vast superhuman powers and is said to be able to cause eclipses. Other tales hold that it can merely predict eclipses and times its greatest activity to coincide with them.

The Vlkodlak can be created from someone who has fallen under what is known as the Serbian Curse: a horrific belief among rural Serbs, dating back many centuries, that anyone who chances to see a werewolf and escapes is likely to have fallen under a supernatural taint. After death (whether natural or unnatural), that person will rise as a vampire. Along the same lines, it was held that anyone who eats mutton from a sheep that has been killed by a werewolf will either transform into a werewolf while alive, or will become a vampire after death. These possibilities could also be found in Slovenian lore.

The Vlkodlak can also be created from a person who was conceived through incest, who had committed incest with his own mother, or who died a violent death. To prevent a suspected corpse from rising as a Vlkodlak, the toes and thumbs of the body should be cut off and a nail driven into its neck.

The Vlkodlak can be killed by piercing its navel with a hawthorn branch and then igniting it with death-vigil candles.

Anthropologists and folklorists often disagree as to the nature of the Vlkodlak. Folklorists suggest that it is at very least a vampire and at most a hybrid of vampire and werewolf, while anthropologists believe that the Vlkodlak is more of a euphemism for a male parent who was violently and sexually abusive toward his children, particularly his daughters. According to the anthropologic view, this creature was nothing more than an attempt by eighteenth century peasantry to explain the cruel and sinful behavior of men who should, by all tenets of common decency, be kind and loving fathers.

In either case, whether supernatural or not, the creature they describe is a monster.

Photo by Jason Lukridge.

VAMPIRES OF SIBERIA

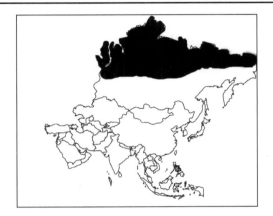

ANIUKHA

Deep in the icy wastes and frozen forests of Siberia there is a legend of a small but deadly vampire called the Aniukha. Perhaps the rarest and least documented of Europe's many vampire species, the Aniukha nonetheless appears in occasional folktales, especially among exiled Jews sent to Siberia during and after the era of Josef Stalin.

This creature has been variously described as being as small as a praying mantis or as large as a squirrel. It runs on all fours like a woodland mammal, but can also stand erect and leap great distances, much like a cat. The Aniukha has a pale body covered in scales with patches of sparse gray or dark brown fur. Its face is like that of an emaciated cat, with huge dark eyes, ears that rise to tufted points, and a short snout filled with very long hollow teeth.

The Aniukha is not physically strong and cannot overpower its prey. Therefore it seeks prey that is otherwise helpless, including infants and the very old and sick.

A dab of garlic paste smeared in a circle on one's breastbone will keep the monster away, though if the garlic is not freshly reapplied every twelve hours the protective virtues fade.

The best method of destroying the monster is to first smear garlic paste on the insides of every door and window, then leave a door or window slightly ajar. The vampire slayer must wait patiently and very quietly until the Aniukha has entered. Once it is inside, the slayer slams the open door or window. With the garlic paste on all exits, the monster cannot escape. With the help of a net that has been smeared with garlic oil, the slayer can then trap the Aniukha and throw it into a fireplace. Nothing but fire will kill it.

Photo by Jason Lukridge.

VAMPIRES OF SLOVENIA

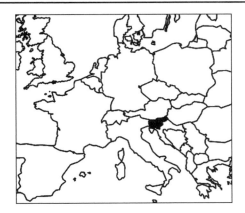

PIJAVICA

The Pijavica is a vampire from the gray lands of Slovenia (formerly part of Yugoslavia). Slovenian folklore has a few different takes on the origin of the Pijavica. The most common is that a person who has committed incest is damned and barred from heaven, and therefore doomed to return to the world of the living as a vampire.

A second belief is that a child born out of incestual relations will be born tainted and will manifest vampiric qualities while alive, and will almost certainly rise from the grave after death.

A third take is that the Pijavica is the result of any sinful practices perpetrated during mortal life (not only incest but other crimes). The sinner will rise as an undead thing after death.

However this beast is brought into the world, the Pijavica is a monstrous blood drinker and killer. More often than not it will return from the dead to prey on its family—the sinful and the innocent alike.

The creature is immensely strong and difficult to kill. If encountered when it is on a hunt, the Pijavica is nearly indestructible. Only fire will kill it when it is awake. If caught asleep (day or night), it can be dispatched with the common rituals of exorcism used throughout Europe: staking to hold it down, decapitation, stuffing the mouth with garlic, and re-interment. In cases where vampire slayers have been unsure of the proper ritual, they simply pour oil into the open coffin and toss in a torch.

Crosses have no effect on the Pijavica, and only strongly barred doors and windows can keep it out. Like nearly all vampires it shuns garlic, so a mash of garlic and wine can be spread around all doors and windows to keep the creature out.

(*See* also Vampires Of Czechoslovakia, p. 163.)

VOLKODLAK

Many cultures have become all too painfully aware of the relationship between vampires and werewolves. Both are shapeshifters and both have unnatural appetites for blood, but in many legends the link between these two creatures extends further than their shared appetites. The Volkodlak of Slovenia is an unsettling example. The Volkodlak is a werewolf, but when it is killed in wolf form it does not die—it returns to unlife as a vampire!

A legendary scholar of the supernatural, the Reverend Montague Summers (*see* following text box) explained the origin of the creature's name: "Volkodlak, Vukodlak [and] Vulkodlak [are] a compound form of which the first half means 'wolf' whilst the second half has been identified, although the actual relation is not quite demonstrable, with *blaka*, which in Old Slavonic, New Slavonic and Serbian signifies the 'hair' of a cow or a horse or a horse's mane." According to Summers, folktales suggest that not only does a werewolf become a vampire in death, but that in some cases those who eat the meat of a sheep killed by wolves will also join the ranks of the undead when they die. This is similar to the Serbian Curse (*see* the Vlkodlak under Vampires Of Serbia for more information).

The Volkodlak. Used with permission, (c) 2003 by Eldred Tjie.

REV. SUMMERS: SUPERNATURAL SCRIBE

The Reverend Alphonsus Joseph-Mary Augustus Montague Summers (1880-1948) was a cleric and historian of the occult from Clifton, near Bristol, in the U. K. Summers' fame as an expert on the occult began in 1926 with the publication of his *History Of Demonology And Witchcraft*. This text was followed by *The Vampire: His Kith And Kin* (1928), *The Vampire In Europe* (1929), and other studies of witches and werewolves. As an editor he also introduced the public to many classic works on the supernatural, including a reprint of *The Discovery Of Witches* by the infamous Matthew Hopkins and the first English translation of *Malleus Maleficarum,* the classic fifteenth century treatise on witchcraft. In later life he also wrote influential studies of another of his lifelong enthusiasms, the Gothic novel; notably *The Gothic Quest: A History Of The Gothic Novel* (Fortune Press 1938) and *A Gothic Bibliography* (Fortune Press 1940).

Though he had once been an Anglican cleric, it is likely Summers was not what he appeared. He had left that church and later claimed (spuriously) to be an ordained Catholic priest. There has been much speculation that Summers was involved in some pretty dark practices of his own.

VAMPIRES OF SOUTH AFRICA

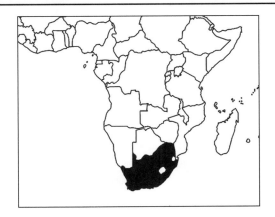

IMPUNDULU

The Impundulu appear to be handsome young men of great virility and sexual appeal, but that is only a disguise. No records exist of what their true forms may be, but it is rumored that their true forms are horrific to look upon. It is widely believed that the form an Impundulu takes is drawn from each victim's darkest fears, so it appears different to each victim and to each it appears to be the epitome of evil.

These vampires are servants of mysterious witches from the eastern Cape region of Southern Africa. They are often used to attack their mistresses' enemies and are given free reign to prey upon their enemies' families and livestock. For the most part they are not sent to kill, but to inflict suffering and hardship. But sometimes the witch will let her rage overrun her sense and the Impundulu will be sent out to kill wantonly.

And kill they do, for the Impundulu have an insatiable appetite for blood which no single killing can assuage. The Impundulu is a killing machine: always hungry for blood, always willing to kill, totally without remorse

Impundulu. Artwork by Marie O'Brien.

or pity. They are eager for the removal of any restraint, and when let loose they kill and keep on killing until they are brought under control again by the witches' spells.

This bloodthirsty beast has been blamed for the wholesale slaughter of whole villages, not to mention entire families. Aside from slaughter, the Impundulu is also a carrier of dread diseases to cattle herds, such as a "wasting disease" very similar to what is often called Mad Cow Disease (*Spongiform Encephalopathy*), and *iphika*, a disease that prevents animals from breeding. Another illness for which they are blamed is characterized by a sudden sharp pain in the chest or head, followed by an immediate and unexpected death. The tribespeople call this being "taken by the bird of heaven."

The Impundulu are as much a curse to their witch mistresses as they are slaves. If a witch does not allow her servant to kill enough humans or animals, the intensity of its bloodlust will grow more powerful than the spell which binds it to the witch's will. In these cases an Impundulu will break free and turn on its mistress. Sometimes the villagers who are under attack will take up torches and pitchforks and storm the witch's home, burning the Impundulu and killing her.

The Impundulu, much like the Incubus of Europe, also has powers of seduction. At times it will turn these powers on its mistress, preying on her sexually, sometimes even feeding on her if the witch is unwary and does not use the proper spells of protection. A well-controlled Impundulu often becomes a lover to its mistress, forming a strange and unholy relationship that might last throughout her lifetime. Legend has it that this is why female witches seldom married.

These creatures are handed down through a family of witches, from mother to daughter. If an Impundulu is not handed down directly from mother to daughter, as where the witch dies suddenly or without issue, then the creature is free to prey at will on whomever it chooses. These ownerless vampires are called Ishologu, and are greatly feared because there are few ways to track them.

An Ishologu can be killed by fire but it has to be trapped and contained long enough for the fire to sap its unnatural strength. This place must be situated so that the attempt does not set fire to the whole region.

MAD COW DISEASE

Bovine spongiform encephalopathy (BSE) is a chronic, degenerative disorder affecting the central nervous system of cattle. This disease was first diagnosed in 1986 in Great Britain, and about ninety-five percent of cases have occurred in the United Kingdom. It has also been seen in other European countries such as Belgium, France, Germany, Spain, and Switzerland. So far it has not reached the United States.

Information provided by the U.S. Food and Drug Administration (www.fda.gov).

ISHOLOGU

See Impundulu.

VAMPIRES OF SPAIN

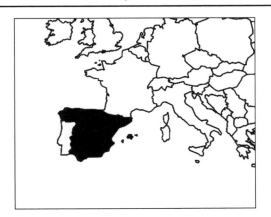

ANIMALITO

Like the Kappa of Japan and the White Ladies of France, Spain's Animalitos are water vampires. *Animalitos* means "small animals" in Spanish, and as the name suggests the creatures are small and bestial, two- or three-feet high. They have dark lizard-like bodies and mouths like dogs. Supple and very fast, the Animalitos attack swimmers and bathers, biting at submerged body parts and feasting quickly and hungrily on blood.

In centuries past, when a common cure for just about any ill would be bleeding the victim, wizard-healers would use Animalitos like leeches. However, the creatures were known for developing an addiction to the blood of specific patients and would seek them out long after they were discharged from the healer's care.

Though supernatural in nature, Animalitos can be killed by sword, gun, fire, or any common method, and will also choke to death on waters polluted with oil. The difficult part is catching one of these elusive monsters, since they possess a cunning ruthlessness, swim with the supple trickery of otters, and are as ferocious as sharks.

BRUJA

The Bruja (feminine) and Brujo (masculine) are nearly identical to the Bruxsa of Portugal. These are immensely powerful vampire witches who can shapeshift into any number of different animal forms and go hunting for human blood. Their favorite meal is the blood of children and infants, especially those children who are particularly beautiful or held to be special in some sacred way. Children born near shrines are particularly favored because taking their blood is considered to be an attack on Heaven itself.

Bruja. Artwork by Michael S. Katz.

Magical amulets and charms are used to protect children. One very potent charm is a small ceramic jar in which is placed virgin's tears and blades of grass plucked at midnight from in front of a traveler's shrine. It is vital to the effectiveness of this charm that the person who plucks the grass not know the name of the virgin whose tears were shed for this mixture, although why this is necessary is one of those mysteries of folk medicine that are lost to time.

One of the Bruja's few fears is sharp objects, so scissors are placed under pillows, on night stands, or even hung above doorways to frighten Bruja off. Small cloves of garlic sewn into the lining of clothes will also protect children and adults alike.

TRAZGOS

A rare and little-known blood drinker from Spain is the Trazgos, a kind of goblin-vampire. The Trazgos stands about four feet tall on average and walks with its body canted forward like a Velociraptor, keeping its weight on the balls of its strong, clawed feet. Unlike a dinosaur, this creature has arms proportioned to its torso, does not have a tail, and has human skin covered with a light reddish fur. Some tales from the Middle Ages insist it has cloven hooves, a pointed tail, and horns; but no tales from before or after that period of time bear this out.

A clever beast, the Trazgos sets traps for travelers much like a wood-land hunter, using devices like deadfalls and foot snares. It lures travelers with various ruses, such as mimicking the cry of a distressed child or a woman's seductive call. Once the traveler has been snared, the Trazgos spits a stinging venom into the helpless victim's eyes. While the person is writhing in blind agony, the creature attacks and feeds on their blood.

To kill the Trazgos, one must use a blade (sword, axe, scythe) that has been soaked for three days in a mixture of sweet oil and mashed garlic. The slayer must kill the creature with a single blow, preferably a decap-itating cut, or it will vanish like a Will-o'-the-Wisp and return the next night unharmed and very angry.

Once a Trazgos has been killed, its body needs to be rubbed down with garlic paste, wrapped tightly in shroud cloth, and tied at three points (neck, waist, and ankles) with seven turns of grapevine. Then it should be staked through the heart with a fire-hardened holy shaft and buried beneath an evergreen. If any of these procedures are missed, the creature will come back to life twice as large and twice as strong, and its first victims will be the vampire slayers who buried it.

VAMPIRO

A general term for vampires in Spain.

Trazgos. Artwork by Marie O'Brien.

VAMPIRES OF SUMATRA

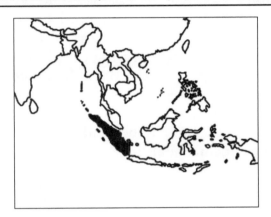

ORANG PENDEK

In Sumatra there is a strange creature that may be the world's only were-ape; or if not a were-ape, then yet another of the world's many species of ape-human hybrids such as the Sasquatch or Kung-Lu (*see* Tibet).

The Orang Pendek stands about five feet tall and is covered in dark hair. European settlers tried to convince the natives that what they were seeing were simply orangutans, but the descriptions really didn't match. Orangutans have shaggy orange hair and are quite docile on the whole. The Orang Pendek's fur is short and brown, and their behavior has often been reported as savage. Both creatures are highly intelligent, but the Orang Pendek apparently have their own language.

Orang Pendek rarely come into populated areas of Sumatra, and even then seldom make contact. But there have been folktales suggesting that in the lonely paths through the forest the Orang Pendek prey on lost travelers and attack them for their blood.

Orang Pendek sightings continue to this day, by persons as varied as Sumatran natives to members of the European press.

PONTIANAK

Centuries ago the vampire species known as the Pontianak flourished on the isle of Sumatra (as well as Malaysia and Java; *see* those entries for further details). Nowadays they are all but extinct thanks to a kind of witch doctor/vampire slayer called a Batak. The Batak has the power to reclaim the soul of a person lost to vampirism, accomplished through herbal medicines. The Batak blends precise amounts of special herbs and garlic into a broth, praying over it as it comes to a full boil. Once it has been prepared, the Batak lets it cool just a little and then forces the concoction down the vampire's throat. This instantly compels the person's soul to return to its body, thereby forcing out the demonic inhabitant. Other medicines and rituals are then used to restore the victim to normal health.

The Batak uses the same ritual and brew if a person has been killed by a vampire. The corpse will not be returned to life, but the victim's immortal soul can return to its body and can thus be properly buried in sacred ground.

The Batak also give advice or prepare medicines to combat other physical or spiritual maladies. For example, a barren woman who desires children is instructed to make wooden images of a child and hold the doll in her lap while praying or meditating so that the magic can make her womb fertile once more.

A popular folktale in Sumatra (which appears in varied form elsewhere in that part of the world) tells of a Batak who spotted a Pontianak clinging to the branches of a large tree while waiting for its next victim. The Batak knew that the Pontianak would transform itself into the form of a gorgeous young woman and use its seductive powers to lure him in before attacking and feasting. As the Pontianak approached to seduce him, he used a garlic-filled charm to weaken her, then spun her around and knocked her to the ground. He kneeled on her and drove a garlic-soaked nail through the back of her head, a trick he knew would lock her in the form of a beautiful woman.

Pontianak. Used with permission, (c) 2003 by Sarah Kirk.

The Batak took the creature home and had intended on experimenting on his captive in order to increase his vampire fighting skills, but some aspect of her power must have remained because he fell in love with her. However, this must have been the only supernatural gift she possessed because not only did she not attack him, she fell in love with him as well! The Batak married her and they lived happily together for decades. They even had a child who was born completely human.

One day their child noticed what seemed to be a tick on his mother's head. When the child tried to remove the tick, he saw that it was a nail. The dutiful child immediately pulled out the nail, thinking he was helping his mother. That was a mistake. Once the nail was removed, the Batak's spell was broken and the mother returned to her true horrific form. Luckily the child was wearing a protective charm his father had given him, and the Pontianak could not attack him. She turned and flew away into the trees, laughing with maniacal joy at her escape.

Thereafter the Batak and his son were unable to capture her and restore her to the form they had known and still loved. The boy grew to hate his father for his deception and later left the village never to return (though there were stories that he became a Batak and wreaked great destruction on the Pontianak of the region). The father, heartbroken, wasted away and died.

One particularly odd postscript to the story: for decades after the death of this particular Batak, the villagers said that the Pontianak would come and perch in the trees above his grave and howl at the night. The howls of the Pontianak did not seem like mocking laughter, but rather a woman's heartbroken sobs.

VAMPIRES OF SURINAME

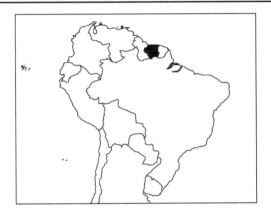

ASEMA

See Vampires Of Trinidad (p. 509).

AZEMAN

The Azeman is a vampire known to haunt many South American countries and islands, with Suriname (formerly Dutch Guyana) in particular. By day she takes the appearance of a wizened old woman, but at night she shapeshifts into a bat or some other creature of the night. The Azeman is only one of a small handful of vampire species who possess this power; despite the prevalence of vampire-into-bat transformations in books and movies, it is very rare in the actual world of vampires.

Like her cousin in Trinidad, the Asema, and indeed many vampires around the world, the Azeman is obsessed with counting and will even forego feeding to count seeds or grains of rice scattered before the door to her victim's house. Seeds spread along a road can even deter it from coming anywhere near a dwelling. Likewise, if a broom is set against the front door, the Azeman will stop to count the bristles one at a time.

When not impeded by brooms or scattered seeds, the Azeman steals in and seeks out a sleeping person whose foot is exposed. With great and subtle care, she uses her needle-sharp fangs to scrape away a piece of flesh from the big toe. When the blood begins to flow, the Azeman drinks hungrily until she is bloated, then crawls out of the house and flies off. Since she is only bat-sized, her feeding is rarely fatal, but the victim is left drained and weakened, and often suffers from the onset of disease.

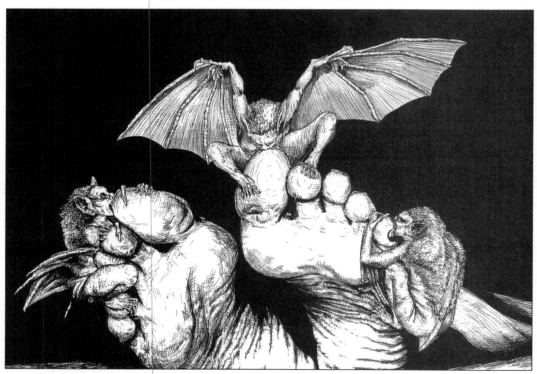

The Azeman. Artwork by Robert Patrick O'Brien.

JARACACAS

See Vampires Of Brazil (p. III).

VAMPIRES OF THAILAND

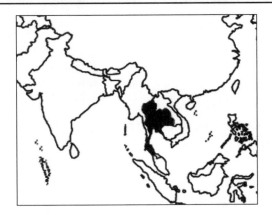

PHI KRASUE

The Phi Krasue is one of the most disgusting of the world's vampire species. Like the Aswang of the Philippines, the Malaysian Penanggalan, and the Vietnamese Ma Cà Rông, the Phi Krasue manifests itself as just a head and otherwise bodiless digestive system. When not out hunting it looks otherwise human, but during the hunt its head rips loose of the body with a spray of blood. This creature does not fly, it crawls: using its unnaturally long tongue like a snail's pseudopod to pull itself along, and dragging its entrails behind.

What makes the monster particularly vile is that its preferred food is excrement, from which it somehow absorbs human life essence. It attacks humans while they sleep and burrows its tongue into their bowels to feed.

The Phi Krasue is nearly impossible to kill, but a seer called a Maw Du can provide specially made charms to ward it off.

PHI SONG NANG

Before Buddhism was established as the primary religion of Thailand, the nation had a vast mythology that included gods and demons of all kinds. Even today some of these legends remain. One such tale is that of the Succubus that is known as the Phi Song Nang.

"Phi" is a general category of supernatural creature that includes witches, ghosts, goblins, elves, and, of course, vampires. Not all Phi are evil, but the Phi Song Nang certainly is. The Phi Song Nang is believed to be the ghost of someone who was buried without proper funeral rites, a woman who has died in childbirth, or even a person who has been killed by animals. It is also feared that victims of sudden, violent deaths might return as blood drinkers.

Much like the Pontianaks of Java and Malaysia, the Phi Song Nang often appears as a lovely and seductive young woman who will lure men to a secret spot, ostensibly for a steamy encounter, then attack them for their blood. Sometimes these men rise from their own unquiet graves as vampires.

If a person is attacked (but not killed) by a Phi Song Nang, a seer called a Maw Du will be called in to examine the victim. By using various spells and incantations the Maw Du is able to determine if a Phi Song Nang is truly at fault. If so, the seer will be able to use other spells to drive out the unholy taint and save the victim's life and soul. Maw Du also prepare and sell a variety of charms useful in preventing attacks by the Phi Song Nang.

Phi Song Nang. Artwork by Marie O'Brien.

VAMPIRES OF TIBET

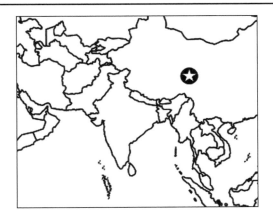

DREGPA

Vampirism is not as common in Tibet as it is in other Asian countries. Supernatural forces that manifest as evil or malicious spirits in Tibet generally do not drink blood, but rather feed off of disharmony. This makes them a rare species of Essential Vampire.

These creatures are part of a class of spiritual beings called Sungma ("Guardians"). There are two distinct types: *'Jig rten pa'i srung ma* ("unenlightened beings") and *'Jig rten las 'das pa'i srung ma* ("enlightened beings").

Dregpa is the common name for the *'Jig rten pa'i srung*, or unenlightened beings. They are lesser deities or spirits. Like humans, they are sentient beings who are still caught up in Samsara (the eternal cycle of birth, suffering, death, and rebirth). Although these beings are often very powerful and wise in secret lore, they are not omnipotent nor omniscient. Their powers, however vast, do have their limits. So they are unenlightened beings who must be subdued and converted to the Dharma (truth) by Buddha or some other great master (Bodhitsava or Lama) with the use of fierce oaths. A Lama will evoke spirits by performing a Rite of the Guardians. The Lama must be extremely careful to use the proper meditative techniques so his spirit will be calm and at peace with the divine. He must also have offerings (actual or visualized in the mind) in order to placate the spirits that are summoned.

According to the Buddhist cosmologic view, a Sungma is a guardian of the Dharma and its practitioners. Each Sungma's retinue includes many violent Dregpa who easily become offended and angered when treated without all due respect and formality. They can do great spiritual harm, and can even cause a wasting sickness by drawing off life energy.

The *'jig rten las 'das pa'i srung ma*, or enlightened beings (also called "transmundane" or "beyond the commonplace world"), also act as Guardians. These Guardians are not lesser gods or spirits like Dregpa, but rather *Sprul Pa*: manifestations of enlightened beings.

A Sprul Pa does not need to be bribed with offerings in order to behave itself and benefit humanity. From the very beginning it is an active manifestation of enlightened compassion. All of the Buddhas and great Bodhisattvas possess the capacity to project these spiritual Guardians. The practitioner makes offerings to these enlightened beings in the same way as with the worldly Guardians, although the Buddha or an enlightened Guardian has no need for our offerings. This is for the practitioner's own benefit in terms of spiritual development: generosity (*sbyin pa*) is the most important among the Ten Perfections (*phar phyin bcu*) that generate good Karma for oneself.

KUNG-LU

Whereas the vast Himalayas are home to the docile Yeti (*see* entry later in this chapter), the lower mountain passes are the hunting grounds of a similar race of giant hulking monsters, the Kung-Lu. Both are gigantic manlike creatures covered in fur, but the similarities end there.

The name Kung-Lu means "great hulking thing." There are ancient tales of wild tribes of Kung-Lu sweeping down on villages and slaughtering everyone before drinking their victims' blood and eating their flesh. Also known as Dsu-The, Ggin-Sung, or Tok, the Kung-Lu sometimes hunt solo, often stealing a human child for their meal.

The Kung-Lu apparently produce no females of their own species and must abduct a human woman to mate with and bear offspring. Male offspring are invariably Kung-Lu, while female offspring become food for these unholy monsters.

Kung-Lu. Artwork by Robert Patrick O'Brien.

THE WRATHFUL DEITIES

In the Tibetan Buddhist religion there are tales of the Wrathful Deities, also known as the Fifty-Eight Blood Drinking Deities. People who are not accustomed to Tibetan Buddhist images are often surprised to hear of creatures as fearsome as the Wrathful Deities, and the common knee-jerk reaction is to label them purely as evil monsters; but that limited view is very wide of the mark. These beings do not attack humans but rather act as harsh guides on the path to enlightenment. Whereas the Peaceful Deities (of which there are forty-two) hope to bring a person's spirit to enlightenment through compassion, the Wrathful Deities will bring a spirit to enlightenment through fear. Although they are not vampires in any traditional sense, they will wear the guise of a monster or create illusions of great destruction in order to literally frighten a person back onto the proper spiritual path.

The Fifty-Eight Wrathful Deities contain five Herukas, "heruka" being a Sanskrit word for semi-wrathful guardian. Herukas are the male Buddha-deities who symbolize the power of enlightenment to over-whelm all evil and negativity in the world. The five Herukas in the Wrathful Deities are all blood drinkers, but blood drinkers are not always evil. Blood is the essential element that symbolizes the hatred and excesses common to humans while alive. Herukas drink blood and use the Fires of Wisdom to transmute blood into the power of compassion. In a sense the Herukas are "anti-vampires."

The most famous Heruka is named Chakrasamvara-Heruka, and when the word Heruka is used alone it usually refers to Chakrasamvara. This twelve-armed and three-headed deity is often depicted wearing a tiger skin, standing upon two corpses in the midst of wisdom flames. In his hands he holds various attributes, symbolizing his magical per-fections. His two primary hands hold *vajra* (scepter) and *gantha* (bell), demonstrating that he has overcome duality.

Chakrasamvara-Heruka. Artwork by Marie O'Brien.

YETI

The legendary Abominable Snowman of the Tibetan Himalayas, or Yeti as it is more properly known, bears many similarities to the Sasquatch of Northwestern Canada, the Bigfoot of California, the Shampe of the Choctaw Indians, the Yowie of Australia, and dozens of others. These creatures are commonly referred to as "hairy men of the forests."

The Yeti is described as being a very large and powerful creature, bestial in appearance, covered in coarse hair, and impossible to catch. Yeti do not seem to be aggressive monsters. There are few reliable reports of them even acting aggressive when surprised, and virtually none of them hunting humans for food.

Reports of the Yeti persist after hundreds of years, and belief in the creature can be found among both the general population and the scientific community. Several legitimate expeditions have been launched to find the creature, many in the mid-twentieth century. The most famous expedition was the 1960 search led by Sir Edmund Hillary, the first man to successfully climb Mount Everest. Sadly, he found nothing.

Yeti. Artwork by Michael Katz.

VAMPIRES OF TOGO

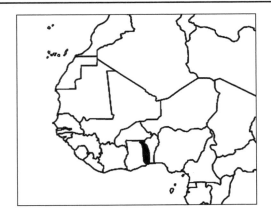

ADZE

Togo is the country that was once called the Slave Coast of Africa (West Africa). The sorcerers and medicine men of the Ewe tribe in southern Togo and southeastern Ghana are believed to be possessed by a kind of vampiric spirit or demon called an Adze.

The Adze is a shapeshifter. It does not appear as a bat or wolf but rather as an insect, such as a firefly, common fly, or large mosquito. These insect-vampires are driven by a powerful thirst for the innocent blood of a village's most beautiful children. In its insect guise, the Adze flits around the village looking for an unattended or sleeping young child or infant, then settles on the child and feeds.

In its vampiric form, the Adze is difficult to kill because it is so difficult to catch. When an Adze is caught or injured it will instantly revert back to human form, revealing its true face. Often it is shown to be a motherless child, or a member of the community who has always demonstrated deviant ways. In its normal human form it can be killed by any ordinary means.

When the Adze cannot find adequate prey—or if their intended prey is protected by a watchful parent—then the Adze can drink coconut water or palm oil. In drought times these insectoid vampires will drink up all of the coconut water, leaving the villagers thirsty. It can also survive on palm oil, which the townspeople use to light their lamps and keep back the dark of night.

The Adze is often thought to intentionally inhabit the bodies of disease-carrying flies, helping to spread plagues. It enjoys seeing beautiful children—or even whole towns—waste away into disease and physical corruption.

WUME

The Togolese have a strong moral sense, and much of their rich oral storytelling tradition is built around tales of right and wrong. The Wume is present in many of these stories as a worst-case scenario for a person's life: live an evil life and you are damned to spend eternity as a hated and feared creature of evil. The Wume was a human being who either died under a curse or who was a criminal in life and was doomed to damnation after death.

The Wume is a persistent vampire; evil, hungry, and very hard to kill. The beast is immensely powerful and very crafty, so no single slayer is likely to overcome it. The preferred method of destruction is to capture it (which takes the combined effort of many men), bind it securely, then find a secret place and bury it deep in an unmarked grave.

VAMPIRES OF TRANSYLVANIA

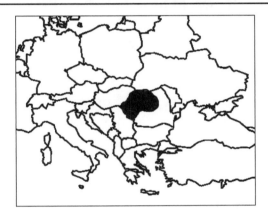

MURONY

Transylvania, Mecca of the pop culture vampire world, does have its own vampire legends; but the famous Count Dracula is not a part of them. Instead, Transylvania is home of the Murony.

The Murony is a shapeshifting creature that can, at will, transform into a cat, toad, hound, or a biting insect. By shifting from shape to shape, the Murony is able to easily ingratiate itself among humans, moving through towns or farms and blending in against the natural background. Its goal is to find a lone person, perhaps someone weak or helpless, then attack them for their blood.

The Murony is a Revenant, so it returns to its grave after feeding. When the locals suspect that a recently deceased person is a vampire, they will dig up the grave and examine the corpse. Long talon-like fingernails are a dead giveaway that the corpse is a Murony. In addition, the corpse will be so engorged with blood that blood will seep out of its eyes, ears, nose, and mouth.

Once the Murony is identified, a long stake is driven through its body to hold it in place, then the ritual decapitation is performed. Garlic is stuffed into its mouth, the head is turned around backward, and the coffin is buried again with many prayers said over it.

STREGOÏCA

Cultures throughout the world have linked sorcery to vampirism—whether it be actual blood drinking, the thirst for life essence, emotional essence, or sheer power. In Transylvania's long history of bloody warfare there were warriors, princes, and kings who were so bloodthirsty and ferocious that they were often referred to as *Stregoïca*, or wizards. Certainly the historical Vlad Tepes (meaning Vlad the Impaler), is as close to a Stregoïca as one can get and not actually be a supernatural monster.

VLAD TEPES (THE IMPALER)

Even though Prince Vladislav was not a vampire, his bloody crimes outstrip anything committed by a supernatural monster. The word *Tepes* stands for "impaler" and he was bestowed with that grisly moniker because of his tendency to punish his enemies by impaling them on stakes, then displaying them publicly for all to see. This was meant to frighten his enemies and scare off anyone (specifically the Turks) who wanted to invade his lands. Vlad Tepes is believed to have killed somewhere between 40,000 to 100,000 people in this fashion, most of them Turkish soldiers in the service of the Ottoman Empire.

Once, Vlad Tepes had 20,000 citizens impaled in a single afternoon. This took place on St. Bartholomew's Day, during an outdoor festival. Vlad sat at a table near the carnage so he could watch. He enjoyed fine food and wine as he watched, and even dipped some of his bread in the blood of the dying so he could savor the taste.

Vlad III was born in Transylvania, and his father became Prince of the neighboring province of Wallachia (in Southern Romania). Like his father before him, Prince Vlad belonged to the Order of the Dragon. The order was created by Emperor Sigismund, the King of Hungary, to uphold Christianity and defend the empire against Turkish invasion. One notable feature of the Order of the Dragon was the wearing of a black and wine-red cape; this was likely an influence on Bram Stoker's Dracula.

Prince Vlad's father, Vlad II, had previously sworn an oath of loyalty to Turkey for having helped him regain his throne. But the great Hungarian warlord and hero John Hunyadi coerced Vlad II back into the service of Hungary's Christian armies. He adopted the name

Vlad the Impaler on St. Bartholomew's Day. Archival woodcut.

Dracul (*Drac* is the Hungarian word for dragon and *ul* means "the") in order to strike fear into the hearts of his enemies. The word Drac could also be defined as "devil," especially among the commoners who were unaware of the meaning of the Order of the Dragon and the symbolism of the dragon on Dracul's shield and coins. After Dracul's death, his son carried on his tradition, but his title was amended with the suffix -*a*, meaning "son of." Hence Dracula was the Son of the Dragon.

Since the Turks of the Ottoman Empire badly outnumbered the Wallachians and Hungarians, the Order of the Dragon needed to use some very serious tactics against them. Their chief weapon was terror. The Turks feared Vlad, and often referred to him as a vampire. Even Prince Vlad's contemporaries hinted that Dracula was either a demon, or had dealings with them. In the writings of the time, words like *Stregoïca* (wizard), *Ordog* (Satan), and *Pokol* (Hell) were used frequently in connection with Prince Vlad.

When the Sultan of Turkey led an invasion force three times the size of Vlad's army, Vlad poisoned wells and burned villages along the way so the Turks would have nothing to eat or drink. By the time the Turks arrived at Vlad's capital city, they were greeted with the sight of 20,000 Turkish captives impaled upon thousands of stakes. This sight, known as "the Forest of the Impaled," had a demoralizing effect on the Turkish army, and they turned around and returned home.

Dracula eventually died on the battlefield, although it was uncertain how he was killed. Different witnesses had him killed in battle by the Turks, murdered by his own officers, or accidentally killed by his own soldiers. His head was taken by the Turks and was displayed on a pike by the Sultan, who wanted to prove to his terrified people that the monster of Wallachia was truly dead. Some claimed that when Dracula's grave was opened in the early 1930s, his body had disappeared. His lifelong thirst for blood could not be quenched by his death, so he walked again as a vampire. But years later a headless skeleton was located nearby, and is believed to be Vlad's remains. The corpse had been wearing expensive clothes, including a wine-red cape.

Stoker had originally planned to name his character Wampyr until he came across the history of Vlad Dracula. It is unknown why Bram Stoker chose Vlad III as his blueprint for Count Dracula. The only connection between the Count and the Impaler is Stoker's book, and Stoker's character was an amalgam of multiple sources from history, folklore, and Stoker's own life.

Vlad Tepes. Archival woodcut.

THE SZÉKELY

The Székely are an ethnic group from Northern Transylvania, now Romania. During the time of Vlad Tepes, Romania's ruling class was composed of Romanian Szekeleys and Hungarian Magyars. Except in a few isolated communities where the ancient customs of the Székely have survived, there is little difference between Székely and Magyars (the dominant ethnic group of Hungary). The Székely (also known as Szeklers or Siculi) came into Transylvania either with or before the Magyars, and they may have been descended from the Turks. Vlad Tepes was not a Szekely, having been born in Southern Transylvania of Wallachian stock, but Bram Stoker's Count Dracula asserted that he was a Székely and proud of his heritage:

> "We Szekelys have a right to be proud, for in our veins flows the blood of many brave races who fought as the lion fights, for lordship. Here, in the whirlpool of European races, the Ugric tribe bore down from Iceland the fighting spirit which Thor and Wodin gave them, which their Berserkers displayed to such fell intent on the seaboards of Europe, aye, and of Asia and Africa too, till the peoples thought that the werewolves themselves had come."

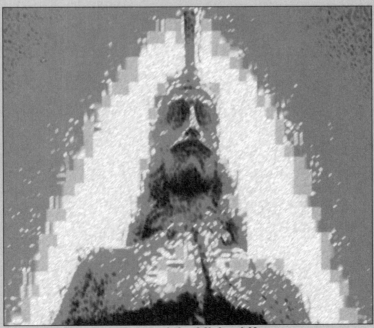

Vlad the Impaler. Artwork by Michael Katz.

THE LAND BEYOND THE FOREST

Bram Stoker obtained much research for his novel *Dracula* on the works of the Scottish writer Emily Gerard, author of the 1885 article, "Transylvanian Superstitions", and the 1888 book, *The Land Beyond The Forest*. Ms. Gerard was born in 1849 at Jedburgh, Scotland and at the age of fifteen went to a convent in Tyrol to learn foreign languages. She was an excellent student and, as a young woman, became a noted novelist and literary critic. In 1879 she began a career as a professional writer and saw her first novel, *Reata*, published in 1880.

Gerard married an Austrian soldier, Chevalier Miecislas de Laszowska. He was eventually stationed in Transylvania, a country she came to love. She researched everything she could about the people, history, culture, and folklore, focusing primarily on death customs and superstitions.

The Land Beyond The Forest (the title of which is a literal translation of the word Transylvania) is a hair-raising novel that tells of a school where the devil himself taught the secrets of the natural and supernatural worlds. Only ten scholars could attend the school at any given time, and the ultimate tuition was that one of the scholars had to stay behind and serve Satan after the classes were over. A steep cost for a twisted education.

Emily Gerard died in 1905.

Photo by Jason Lukridge.

VAMPIRES OF TRINIDAD

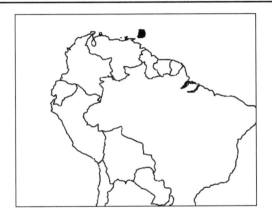

ASEMA

Trinidad's Asema shares many unsavory qualities with other vampires throughout the region, most notably the Haitian Loogaroo and the Azeman of Suriname.

The Asema spends her days in the guise of an old woman (in very rare cases, as an old man). When the sun sets it sheds its skin and its evil supernatural self emerges as a blue ball of light. In this form it will ride the night winds in search of prey, alighting on sleeping humans and drinking their blood.

Sunlight neither harms nor weakens the Asema, but it does make it harder for her to take anyone unawares. The Asema hunts at night strictly because of the advantage offered by darkness.

Popular forms of protection work against Asema. These include eating herbs that will make one's blood bitter, or by eating a lot of garlic. Like many vampires, the Asema can also be foiled by scattering rice or sesame seeds outside one's door, forcing it to linger and count them one at a time.

SUKUYAN

Like the Asema, the Sukuyan shed their skin at nightfall and fly off into the darkness as a ball of blue light. However, they are much faster and can actually travel at speeds approaching the speed of light itself, suggesting that they achieve a kind of energy state of being.

Also like the Asema, the Sukuyan seek out humans, preferably asleep and unaware, and alight on them to drink their blood. The Sukuyan has far more power than the Asema and is a more dangerous and cunning predator. If cornered or trapped, the Sukuyan will shapeshift into an animal form and try to slip away; or it will adopt the form of a predator such as a jungle cat, ape, hunting bird, large dog, or other creature and fight back using a fearsome armament of claws, talons, beaks, or fangs.

In direct combat the Sukuyan can be driven off by steel or flame, but it cannot be killed while it is hunting. Special charms filled with garlic or pollen help keep the monster at bay.

The key to destroying the Sukuyan is to find where it hides its skin and steal it. Denied the chance to return to its skin after feeding, the Sukuyan will eventually fade away and die.

Photo by Jason Lukridge.

VAMPIRES OF TURKEY

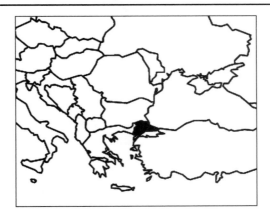

UBER

Actually the Turkish word for "witch," *Uber* is considered by many scholars to be one of the source words for "vampire." The domestic Turkish vampire is very similar to Revenant vampires all through that region of the world. It is a corpse that has risen, usually that of someone who has died during an act of violence, or the corpse of a foreigner who was not a Muslim and died on Turkish soil.

This belief in vampires as pernicious foreigners is part and parcel of the long history of Turkey's conflicts with the Romanian province of Wallachia, the home of Turkey's semi-official "bogey man," Dracula. Not the fictional Dracula, but the actual Wallachian prince named Vlad whose bloody excesses put Bram Stoker's monster to shame.

In the fifteenth century, the Ottoman Empire invaded the three Romanian countries, Wallachia, Transylvania, and Moldavia. The

Turks were bitterly repelled by Prince Vladislav, son of Dracul, more commonly known today as the historical Dracula. Vlad was a powerful ruler, a bloodthirsty warrior, and known as one of the most savage men of his day. He was responsible for the deaths of between 40,000 and 100,000 Turks.

For additional information on the life and death of Prince Vlad, *see* Vampires Of Transylvania.

Whereas vampire movies are popular in Turkey, films about Dracula (especially those setting Dracula in a sympathetic or romantic light) are generally not.

Photo by Jason Lukridge.

DRACULA IN FILMS

There have been scores of films about Dracula the vampire, and even some that touch on the historical Dracula, Vlad Tepes. The following are some of the more significant entries in the genre.

- *The Secrets Of House #5* (1912). This unauthorized Russian version of Dracula was the first true vampire film.

- *Nosferatu, Eine Symphonie Des Grayens (The Undead, A Symphony Of Horror)* (1922). Directed by F.W. Murnau. A silent classic of German expressionist cinema, this was often mistakenly cited as the first vampire film (*Secrets Of House #5* was released ten years earlier). Based loosely on Bram Stoker's novel, though the name *Dracula* could not be used due to a copyright dispute.

- *Nosferatu, Phantom Der Nacht (The Undead, Phantom Of The Night)* (1979). Directed by Werner Herzog. German remake of the original vampire film starring Klaus Kinski.

- *Dracula* (1931). Directed by Tod Browning and starring Bela Lugosi. Based on the play by Deane and Balderston, the film transforms Dracula from a corrupt monster into a suave, continental romantic figure in an opera cloak and tuxedo. Released by Universal Studios.

  Dracula appeared in a number of other Universal films, including:
  > *Dracula's Daughter* (1936).
  > *Son Of Dracula* (1943).
  > *House Of Frankenstein* (1944).
  > *House Of Dracula* (1945).
  > *Abbott & Costello Meet Frankenstein* (1948).

- *Horror Of Dracula* (1958). Directed by Terence Fisher. Starring Christopher Lee as Dracula and Peter Cushing as Van Helsing. Loosely based on Stoker's novel but featuring a very fit and energetic Van Helsing. This was the first and best of the Hammer horror series of Dracula films. Others in the Hammer Dracula series include:
  > *The Brides Of Dracula* (1960).
  > *Dracula Prince Of Darkness* (1966).
  > *Dracula Has Risen From The Grave* (1968).

Taste The Blood Of Dracula (1969).

Scars Of Dracula (1970).

Dracula A.D. (1972).

The Satanic Rites Of Dracula (1973).

- *El Conde Dracula* (1970). Spanish version directed by Jesus Franco and based fairly closely on Stoker's novel. Stars Christopher Lee as Dracula in a story that is a confrontation between youth and age.

- *Dracula* (1973). Made-for-television movie directed by Dan Curtis. Starring Jack Palance (Dracula) and Nigel Davenport (Van Helsing). A more sympathetic portrayal of Dracula as a noble warrior yearning for his lost love is counterbalanced by the first real portrayal of Dracula as superhumanly strong. An underrated classic.

- *Dracula* (1977). BBC/PBS miniseries directed by Philip Saville and starring Louis Jourdan. More faithful to Stoker's work than previous versions, this mini-series captures much of the Gothic mood and growing dream of the novel.

- *Dracula* (1979). Directed by John Badham. Starring Frank Langella (Dracula), Laurence Olivier (Van Helsing), and Kate Nelligan (Lucy). Dracula, played by Langella, is portrayed as a romantic and tragic figure designed to elicit sympathy. Lucy is a twentieth century woman—sexually liberated and very determined to get what she wants.

- *Bram Stoker's Dracula* (1992). Directed by Francis Ford Coppola. Starring Gary Oldman (Dracula), Wynona Ryder (Mina), and Anthony Hopkins (Van Helsing). This adaptation veers between being remarkably faithful to the novel and completely absurd. Again Dracula is cast as a tortured lover and heroic figure despite being a monster. Gary Oldman's interpretation of Dracula is magnificent, but the rest of the cast drops the ball. Even Anthony Hopkins chews up so much of the scenery that his Van Helsing appears to be more of a fruitcake than a scientist.

Additional vampire movies can be found in Appendix IV: Vampires In Film.

VAMPIRES OF VARIOUS CULTURES

INCUBUS (plural INCUBI)

The word *incubus* is a term from Middle English, based in turn on Medieval Latin, and essentially means "nightmare." The Incubus is a kind of psychic vampire that comes to women as they sleep and uses its unholy magical powers to seduce them and have sex with them. This sexual encounter is no mere dream, because a woman who falls victim to an Incubus will often lapse into a coma from which she may never awaken. In cases where the woman does awaken, she is generally weak and moves through life in a dreamy state, pale and wasted, often falling prey to sickness.

If the sexual assault of the Incubus results in a pregnancy, then the child will be a creature of evil, often a sorcerer.

SUCCUBUS (plural SUCCUBI)

The female counterpart to the Incubus is the lewd female vampire-demon called the Succubus. This creature assumes the form of a woman and invades the dreams of men, seducing them and having sex with them. A man will not awaken during this encounter but will continue to dream. Should he wake in the morning, he will consider the experience nothing but an unwholesome sexual dream. In many cultures if a man has a nocturnal emission it is believed to be evidence that he was visited by a Succubus.

Succubus. Used with permission, (c) 2003 by Bill Chancellor.

According to legend, the queen of the Succubi was Nahemah (the Hebrew word for "seduction"). Her disciples were many, though Medieval theologians believed that there were more Incubi than Succubi. Those same theologians believed that female psychic vampires were more vicious than males and their crimes more than made up for the difference in numbers.

Like the Incubus, the Succubus can mate with a human and produce a child. The child of a Succubus, known as a Cambion, is an evil and corrupt sorcerer capable of great harm and mischief.

THE SEDUCTRESS VAMPIRE

This theme recurs throughout folklore and is carried on enthusiastically in popular culture. Seductress Vampires are a kind of Essential Vampire who lure their prey by using supernaturally potent sexual attraction. They feed on their victims by draining life force or other vital essences.

The seductress vampire appears often in poetry such as Samuel Taylor Coleridge's "Christabel" and John Keats' "La Belle Dame Sans Merci" and in fiction, as with Sheridan Le Fanu's immortal *Carmilla*.

Carmilla marked the beginning of a trend of homosexual vampires, and introduced the concept of lesbian seduction to the genre in 1872. *Carmilla* was slated to be produced for the stage in 1932 using a script by Hamilton Deane and John L. Balderston, but production disputes cancelled the tour. (Deane, by the way, is the stage actor who first portrayed Dracula as an elegant man in a tuxedo and opera cloak, an image that is now ingrained in the cultural mind).

Carmilla did make it to the stage in 1957, produced by the Earl of Longford, but was greeted with poor reviews. And in 1931 the first film (partly) inspired by Sheridan Le Fanu's story was released, *Vampyr* (though even a Le Fanu scholar would be hard

Carmilla by Philip Burne-Jones. Archival artwork.

put to actually find the connection). It wasn't until 1960 that French film-maker Roger Vadim made a more straightforward interpretation of Carmilla in his well-received *Blood And Roses*.

Hammer films tried it next with their spicy trilogy based on Carmilla: *The Vampire Lovers* (1970), *Lust For A Vampire* (1971), and *Twins Of Evil* (also 1971).

The story was filmed again in 1989 as *Carmilla*, starring Meg Tilly in the title role and Ione Skye as her vic-tim/lover. The movie was made for cable TV's *Nightmare Classics* series.

The Vampire by Philip Burne-Jones. Archival artwork.

The most recent film version is 1998's *Carmilla*, a very graphic film set in Long Island, New York. The titular vampire preys on vulnerable teenage girls.

Philip Burne-Jones' 1897 painting *The Vampire*, which shows a female vampire reveling in the bloody destruction of a man, was actually painted as a way for the artist to vent about his failed relationship with the actress Stella Campbell. Mrs. Campbell, the most famous actress in London at the time, had broken off her liaison with the young Burne-Jones in favor of the much more famous Shakespearean actor Johnston Forbes-Robertson.

Typical of many thwarted men, Burne-Jones' love turned to a form of hatred and his once-saintly image of Stella Campbell was transformed in his mind to a bloodsucking (or castrating) vampire.

Forms of Seductress Vampires include the ancient Assyrian Akhakharu, the Lamiai of Greece, the Mullo among the Gypsies, the shapeshifting Rakshasas of India, the Irish Leanhaun-Sidhe, the Moldavian Zmeu, the Filipino Mandurugo, the Scottish Glaistig, and the Succubus.

VAMPIRES OF VIETNAM

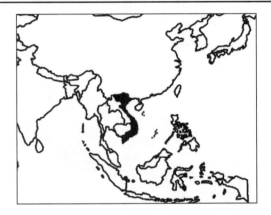

MA CÀ RÔNG

Often seen only as a floating head and entrails (like the Aswang of the Philippines, the Phi Song Nang of Thailand, and the Malaysian Penanggalan), the Ma Cà Rông of Vietnamese legend is a grotesque and deadly creature of darkness. This foul beast does not hunt humans for blood like other vampires but feeds on cow dung (which, even for vampires, is pretty disgusting).

The Ma Cà Rông is brought into being when a person dies at a "sacred hour," called "than trùng." *Than* means "spirit" and *trùng* means "coincidence." So this is not a situation where someone died with a tainted soul; they were just unfortunate to die at an unlucky hour.

Ma Cà Rông. Artwork by Robert Patrick O'Brien.

VAMPIRES OF ZAIRE

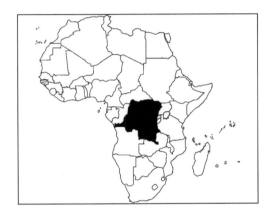

EBOLA: THE VAMPIRE VIRUS

Most people are unaware that the word *nosferatu* means "plague carrier." For centuries the spread of disease has been linked to the supernatural, particularly the belief in vampires. Now the term "vampire" is being used to describe one of the most destructive and frightening viruses in history: Ebola.

Ebola was discovered in the early 1980s when the outbreak of a destructive new virus killed 400 people in Zaire and Sudan. Victims would first develop flu-like symptoms, then double over with severe abdominal cramps and begin burning with a terrible fever. Within hours their capillaries would become clogged with dead blood cells, causing the skin to swell and blister and then actually dissolve away. Meanwhile, blood would bubble out from exposed tissues and flow from the victim's ears, eyes, and nostrils. The victim would begin vomiting a black slime, which happened to be the viscous remains of his internal organs. Death followed shortly thereafter, and blessedly so.

Ebola Zaire was the first formally identified strain of the disease. In 1976 there were 550 cases resulting in 340 deaths, a death rate of eighty percent. The second identified strain was the *Ebola Sudan*, discovered shortly after the first Ebola Zaire outbreak. Ebola Sudan infected 550 people and killed 300 (a fifty-three percent death rate). In 1995 there was another outbreak of the Ebola virus in Kikwit, Zaire, with 293 cases and 233 fatalities, again an eighty percent morality rate.

The Ebola disease can spread like wildfire. It is easily transmitted from person to person and is generally spread through physical contact: an infected person touches an uninfected person, who then touches any opening on his own body. Bodily fluids (blood, vomit, saliva, semen) also carry the infection, so any intimate contact can be a literal kiss of death.

The Ebola virus does not die with its host. Workers who dispose of Ebola victims often contract the disease themselves. Like the vampire, it strikes from the grave.

What makes this virus even more frightening is the mystery that surrounds it. No one actually knows where the virus lives, how it occurs in nature, or why it works with such ferocity in certain areas and at certain times.

Ebola is only one of an increasing number of viruses appearing around the world, naturally occurring microscopic monsters. Some of these pathogens have been around for thousands of years and have long histories of destruction, while others are apparently new. These vampire viruses flare up most often in the world's poorest areas, where health care and sanitation are less common and the people virtually defenseless. Even diseases which had been nearly wiped out in the '60s and '70s, like cholera, bubonic plague, smallpox, and tuberculosis, have begun making a destructive comeback, claiming millions of lives around the world.

Perhaps the next great wave of predatory evil will come not from out of the darkness, but from within humanity's own bloodstreams. Neither garlic nor stake will be of any use against these invisible and unseen viruses, and the vampire hunters of the twenty-first century may well be medical researchers armed with miraculous vaccines.

·PART NINE·

DESTROYING THE UNDEAD

"The Bride of Corinth"

From my grave to wander I am forc'd,
Still to seek The Good's long-sever'd link,
Still to love the bridegroom I have lost,
And the life-blood of his heart to drink;
When his race is run,
I must hasten on,
And the young must 'neath my vengeance sink.

Johann Wolfgang von Goethe
1797

The vampire slayers go about it all wrong in the movies. First off, they generally arm themselves with as few weapons as possible (a cross, a few stakes, some holy water, and a mallet) and go tromping off to a vampire's lair, often just a few hours before sunset. Considering that their prey is usually supernaturally strong, possesses ultra-heightened awareness, and has spent centuries refining its ability to kill, this is beyond foolhardy. The fact that these vampire slayers often survive is a testament to Hollywood's rose-colored view of the world.

Of course, no matter how ancient and crafty a movie vampires is, it will suddenly become struck with some form of stupidity once the end of the movie nears. For example, they may easily grant the slayers entrance to their dwelling, and stand around making dramatic speeches about how many years they've lived and how puny are their opponents' skills and resources; engage in hand-to-hand combat while the sun is about to rise; then trip and fall onto any sharpened piece of wood laying around. Invariably they will fall at just the right angle so that their heart will be pierced by the impromptu stake, and they wither to dust.

All very dramatic . . . and all very wrong! Just assume, for a moment, that a movie vampire is in any way similar to the actual undead; Dracula will serve as a fine example. Here is a creature who was once the ruler of a nation, a fierce and clever warrior known for his cruelty and subtlety who brought crushing defeat to an overwhelming enemy. During five hundred years of unlife he would have amassed a tremendous store of knowledge, and would have learned every trick for thwarting those who would slay him.

It is hard to accept that Professor Van Helsing and his *ad hoc* committee of vampire slayers would actually be able to track him down and destroy him. Someone who had once been Vlad Tepes in life would have controlled any fight, and would have raised the bar on violence and retaliation. He would not have used mere threats against his enemy. If Dracula could not lay hands on Van Helsing because of the professor was using some holy object as protection, Dracula would have simply shot him or burned down the house where they were hiding. When Quincy Morris attacked Dracula with a Bowie knife at the end of the story, the real Dracula would have pulled out a sword and shown him what five hundred years—and quite a number of battles against the Turks—could do for one's speed and dexterity at swordplay.

But books and movies need happy endings, so Quincy stabs Dracula with his big hunting knife, and Van Helsing decapitates him.

Now, what if Van Helsing and his crew had been up against a true vampire from those cold Slavonic forests? What about the Varcolaci, a vampire that can shapeshift, travel like the wind along an astral thread, and even cause solar and lunar eclipses? No cross would stay it, no stake would kill it.

Or the Murony, another shapeshifting creature that could become a cat, toad, hound, or even a biting insect. In beast shape it could have simply outrun any of Van Helsing's vampire hunters and fled into the hills.

Or the Pryccolitch, which has many of the same powers as the werewolf. In bestial form it would have torn Quincy Morris apart.

The kind of vampire Dracula was supposed to be was the Strigoi, a Romanian Revenant that many legends say could actually become human again after feeding on blood for a time. If that were the case, Dracula would have been able to blend in completely with society. The Strigoi, like most vampires, do not fear the cross and can even attend church services. Would Van Helsing have even been able to detect such a monster? Unlikely.

It would be so easy if a cross could hold all vampires at bay and a stake turn them to dust instantaneously. Unfortunately vampires are much harder to kill than that. Because there are so many different species of vampires, each one has different powers and must be destroyed in a different way. A vampire slayer must really know his or her business and should be prepared to go to extreme lengths to get the job done.

First the slayer has to identify the nature of the beast in question. Most countries have only one or two different types of undead, which makes identification a little easier. Some nations, like India, Malaysia, Greece, and Albania (among others) have many different kinds of vampires, and each is distinctly different. But even so, the vampire slayer is rarely faced with more than a handful of choices; and if he knows his business, diagnosing the particular breed of vampire is not too daunting a task.

That's it for the easy part.

Next the slayer has to identify the specific person who is a vampire, then locate their resting place. Though this is not the most dangerous aspect of vampire hunting, it is the longest and most demanding job.

Photo by Robert Patrick O'Brien.

Which brings the vampire slayer to the hardest step: destroying the creature. It is a daunting task, since most vampires are unnaturally strong, bloodthirsty, elusive, secretive, and possess a variety of super-natural powers.

Although different cultures have different methods for destroying vampires, there are some general rules of thumb. For vampires that return to their graves each night (and there are many, many examples

Burning Vampire. Used with permission, (c) 2003 by Eldred Tjie.

of this), a standard exorcism is roughly the same. First the grave needs to be opened, and this is most safely done during daylight hours, and is best to do it with a priest in attendance.

Of course, disinterring a vampire in order to kill it is highly dangerous, even during daylight hours. Few vampires lapse into the trance-like sleep seen in Dracula movies. Dig up a sleeping vampire and it is likely to awaken with rage and bloodlust, and the unwary vampire slayer often becomes a bedtime snack.

Once the coffin has been opened, a long stake should be driven through the monster. The stake may be of wood or metal, and it need not pierce the creature's heart. But it does have to be long enough to pass through the torso and pin the body to the wood of the coffin, or, ideally, pass through the coffin and into the hard earth. This secures the creature and prevents it from rising to feed. Some cultures will go further and use stakes or nails to pin the vampire's arms and legs to the coffin, or to pin the hair and clothes to the coffin as well.

The next step is decapitation. Not much is involved other than a sharp edge and a strong stomach. No sacred blades or holy swords are needed, as shown in some movies. The severed head is sometimes placed between the creature's knees, as seen in the disposal method of the Pijauica of Croatia and with various of the Polish and German vampires. Or the head can be turned around backward in the coffin.

In all cases of decapitation it is recommended that the mouth be stuffed with garlic. Garlic has the power to break the connection between unholy spirit and reanimated flesh.

In some cultures, staking, decapitation, and garlic are enough. But none of these methods by themselves is considered foolproof. Some vampires, once staked and even mutilated, may be strong enough to regenerate and rise, but not if they've been burned.

Fire is the slayer's best weapon. It works on all known species of vampires. Even in cases where other methods are used, fire is either the preferred fallback plan or it is the way to make sure everything else was done right.

Even though stakes, decapitation, and garlic are the most common tools of extermination, there are other disposal methods around the world. The Brazilian Lobishomen is subdued by getting it drunk, at which point it can be overcome by several strong men, crucified to a tree, and then stabbed to death. The corpse is then burned. To kill the Wume of Togo, it must be overpowered by a large number of strong men, bound securely, and buried deep in an unmarked grave. The Albanian Lugat is a nearly indestructible vampire, but some legends hold that it has an Achilles heel: a sword stroke to the back of the leg will effectively hamstring it, so it can be set afire and burned to ash.

Some vampires can be harmed with ordinary weapons. The Australian Garkain can be killed by ordinary means (spears, knives, stones, fire), although getting close enough to deliver the killing blow is difficult because the beast emits a poisonous stench that can kill at several paces. The vampire known as the Chordewa of Bengal, which transforms its evil spirit into the shape of a large black cat, can be harmed while in cat form. If the cat is harmed, the injury will be reflected on the Chordewa when she transforms back to human shape. Bengali vampire slayers know that attacking and killing the cat will slay the vampire.

But there are other vampires scattered throughout the world and described throughout this Field Guide which can only be destroyed by special means. A wise vampire slayer will immerse himself in the culture of each land in order to discover the secret methods of destroying these unholy monsters.

Photo by Jason Lukridge.

THIRTEEN BURIAL METHODS TO PREVENT VAMPIRISM

1. BINDING A CORPSE

A newly awakened vampire seldom possesses great strength; that can only be acquired from its first few feedings. Tightly binding a corpse is often all that is required to keep a vampire from rising. This also prevents the creature from feeding on itself, robbing it of the first meal that could give it the strength necessary to break through its coffin and rise from the grave.

But in some cultures, binding prevents a newly deceased spirit from moving freely enough to enter the Land of the Dead, in effect "binding" it to the earth. This may result in trapping a spirit in a decaying corpses, and creating a vampire that would not otherwise exist.

Example of binding a corpse. Artwork by Robert Patrick O'Brien.

2. BURYING FOOD WITH A CORPSE

As previously mentioned, a newly created vampire needs to feed. Ordinary food will nourish it, but will not provide it with the kind of unnatural strength that feasting on its own flesh will provide. The vampire will remain within the grave for the time being, and it is believed that a well-fed corpse will eventually be content enough to move on into the Land of the Dead and not rise to trouble the living.

3. __BURYING A CORPSE FACE DOWN__

As a rule, newly created vampires are not very bright and easily confused. However, their intelligence grows as they feed. There are many ways of hopelessly confusing a newly awakened vampire, such as the trick of burying it face down in its coffin. As it breaks free of its shroud and bursts through its coffin, it will dig in vain to reach the surface, unaware that it is only burrowing deeper into the earth. Eventually, unable to feed, its strength will fail and its unholy life will fade away, leaving only moldering flesh and bones.

A word of warning: stacking is common in pauper's graves or where space is limited. If a corpse is buried face down over another coffin, the creature will discover the trick and right itself.

4. __BURYING A CORPSE AT A CROSSROADS__

There are countless legends, folktales, and songs about the mystical properties of a crossroads. For many cultures the crossroads symbolizes temptations offered by the Devil. This is the basis for much of the mysticism that is intertwined with the folklore of early blues music.

Crossroads are considered evil, and therefore "unhallowed" ground. A vampire buried at a crossroads cannot rise from its grave because (strangely enough) a person must be buried on hallowed ground in order to rise as a creature of evil. This paradox appears in many cultures, especially in Europe, North America, and South America.

When a vampire buried at a crossroads does manage to rise, the options presented by the many different roads from which to choose is said to confuse the creature, at least those of European descent. As a result the vampire will sit down and ponder its choices until sunrise. The sunlight will not kill the vampire, but will drive it back to its grave for a long day's sleep, and when the vampire rises again the next night it will be faced with the same insolvable quandary. The only escape from this puzzle is for some traveler to happen through the crossroads. A first really good meal will cure the vampire of its confusion and enable it to escape the riddle of the crossroads.

Sometimes they come back. Used with permission, (c) 2003 by Adam Garland.

5. <u>DECAPITATING A CORPSE</u>

In addition to garlic and fire, decapitation is one of the few sure ways of destroying nearly all species of vampire. Ideally, after decapitation the mouth should be stuffed with garlic and the head turned backward in the coffin.

In cases where a vampire is so unnaturally powerful that its energy can even survive decapitation, the head should be buried in a secret grave. A headless Revenant cannot feed, so it must find its head before it can do anything else. If the head is buried in a cask of garlic, on hallowed ground, and in a hidden place, the creature may never find it. Unable to feed, its body will continue to decay and it will perish.

6. <u>FILLING THE COFFIN WITH SEEDS</u>

Some newly risen vampires apparently suffer from obsessive-compulsive disorder. When confronted with a scattering of seeds, dried rice, flower petals, broom thistles, or similar items, they feel compelled to stop and count them. Scatter enough seeds and the vampire will waste the entire night in this endeavor.

Scattering seeds along a road that leads away from a house or town will distract a vampire and lead it on a fruitless chase. If this is done enough nights in a row, the vampire will become so weak from lack of feeding that it may never again have the strength to rise.

Tying a corpse with hundreds of tiny knots is a way of limiting its movements and confusing it with a problem that will appeal to its obsessive nature.

7. <u>GARLIC</u>

Nearly every country that has vampire legends reports that garlic is a powerful agent for limiting vampiric strength, controlling them, barring them from entering a home, and preventing them from rising to feed. Stuff a vampire's mouth with garlic will strip away the vampire's unnatural strength, allowing a vampire slayer the chance to decapitate the creature and successfully complete the ritual of exorcism.

Stuffing the vampire's mouth with garlic also prevents it from feeding on itself.

8. PLACING A HEADSTONE OVER THE GRAVE

A gravestone serves two purposes. The obvious reason is to provide information about the deceased, including name, birth, death, and relations. The second is of a preventative nature, in that the headstone adds ponderous weight to the grave, creating one more obstacle for a newly awakened vampire to overcome when it struggles to rise.

Photo by Jason Lukridge.

9. PLACING HOLY OBJECTS IN THE COFFIN

Few vampires are actually affected by holy objects. Although vampires are spirits of the "other world," they seem unchecked by icons or symbols of faith. Sometimes religious items will work if the vampire was a fairly devout person in life, or if the object in question is of a particularly sacred nature. In some Slavic countries it is believed that placing a crucifix upon a corpse's breast will remind the deceased's spirit of its devotion to the church, so it will therefore abhor its new evil nature. In Romania and Serbia it was once thought that placing a crucifix in a coffin would restore an evil person's faith, so a vampiric spirit would not enter them while in the grave. Other sacred items, such as the Host, only work in very rare cases according to folklore.

Certain shamans, priests, or holy people around the world have had success with creating charms that affect vampires, but for the most part these charms are worn by the living, not buried with the dead.

10. <u>PLACING COINS ON THE EYES OF THE DEAD</u>

Paying a tribute to the spirit world is common in many cultures throughout history, from leaving a coin for Charon (the ferryman across the River Styx) to laying coins on the eyes of the dead. It has essentially been a practice to bribe other spirits not to corrupt or abuse the soul of the departed. In cases where vampirism was suspected—when the deceased was born with a caul, on a Saturday, between Christmas and New Year, or the child of incest or rape—coins were left as a payment so the soul would be accepted into the spirit world, instead of being left to inhabit the corpse and possibly transform into a vampire.

11. <u>STAKING THE CORPSE</u>

Stakes do not kill vampires, despite what has been shown in countless movies and television programs. But when a person is being buried, it is customary in many European countries to drive a stake through the corpse as an added measure (along with proper burial rites) to make sure that the corpse cannot rise if it is reanimated as a vampire. This is a method of binding a corpse, as previously discussed. Unable to rise, the creature will eventually wither and begin to decay.

12. <u>STAKING THE GRAVE</u>

Stakes are also used to pin a vampire down so exorcism rituals can be carried out in relative safety. In cases where the creature is especially powerful and the slayer or priest must remain at a distance, a very long stake (generally of iron) can be driven down through the dirt and the coffin, effectively pinning the vampire in the grave like a butterfly on a collector's board. The exorcism ritual can then be completed in relative safety.

13. <u>WATCHING OVER THE CORPSE UNTIL IT IS BURIED</u>

In any rural area with a history of vampirism, or in cases where some specific aspect of the corpse's birth, life, or death suggest that reanimation is likely, a sentry (or sentries) should be placed by the body until it is safely and correctly interred. A sentry must be sharp, sober, awake, and (depending on the form of local vampire) armed with charms of protection, a sword or other weapon capable of decapitation, a stake of hawthorn, a necklace of garlic, and clear instructions on what to do if the body shows even the slightest sign of reawakening.

Used with permission, (c) 2003 by Alberto Moreno.

STAKING THE VAMPIRE

Staking a vampire has been a feature of folklore and fiction for centuries. In fiction it generally ends the matter. The stake severs the bond between reanimated flesh and demonic spirit, as described in this passage from *Dracula*, where Arthur Holmwood, Van Helsing, and their companions track the newly risen Lucy to her coffin and destroy her:

> "Arthur took the stake and the hammer, and when once his mind was set on action his hands never trembled nor even quivered. Van Helsing opened his missal and began to read, and Quincey and I followed as well as we could.

> "Arthur placed the point over the heart, and as I looked I could see its dint in the white flesh. Then he struck with all his might.

Photo by Robert Patrick O'Brien.

Photo by Robert Patrick O'Brien.

"The thing in the coffin writhed, and a hideous, blood-curdling screech came from the opened red lips. The body shook and quivered and twisted in wild contortions. The sharp white champed together till the lips were cut, and the mouth was smeared with a crimson foam. But Arthur never faltered. He looked like a figure of Thor as his untrembling arm rose and fell, driving deeper and deeper the mercy-bearing stake, whilst the blood from the pierced heart welled and spurted up around it. His face was set, and high duty seemed to shine through it. The sight of it gave us courage so that our voices seemed to ring through the little vault.

"And then the writing and quivering of the body became less, and the teeth seemed to champ, and the face to quiver. Finally it lay still. The terrible task was over.

"The hammer fell from Arthur's hand. He reeled and would have fallen had we not caught him. The great drops of sweat sprang from his forehead, and his breath came in broken gasps. It had indeed been an awful strain on him, and had he not been forced to his task by more than human considerations he could never have gone through with it. For a few minutes we were so taken up with him that we did not look towards the coffin. When we did, however, a murmur of startled surprise ran from one to the other of us. We gazed so eagerly that Arthur rose, for he had been seated on the ground, and came and looked too, and then a glad strange light broke over his face and dispelled altogether the gloom of horror that lay upon it.

"There, in the coffin lay no longer the foul Thing that we has so dreaded and grown to hate that the work of her destruction was yielded as a privilege to the one best entitled to it, but Lucy as we had seen her in life, with her face of unequaled sweetness and purity. True that there were there, as we had seen them in life, the traces of care and pain and waste. But these were all dear to us, for they marked her truth to what we knew. One and all we felt that the holy calm that lay like sunshine over the wasted face and form was only an earthly token and symbol of the calm that was to reign forever."

·APPENDICES·

·APPENDIX ONE·
A VAMPIRE DICTIONARY

A

ALLIUM: The family of plants producing an underground bulb and a flowering spike. The family includes garlic, onion, shallot, leek, chive, and others.

ANEMIA: Derived from the Greek word for "bloodlessness," anemia is a blood disease in which the red cell count is unusually low. Red cells carry oxygen throughout the body, so a person suffering from anemia may exhibit any or all of the following symptoms: pale complexion, fatigue, fainting spells, shortness of breath, and digestive disorders. *See* also Pernicious Anemia.

ASTRAL VAMPIRE: Term coined by Theosophist Franz Hartmann. Refers to the type of vampirism that involves astrally projected spirits of living people who prey on other humans, often draining them of life force or spiritual energy.

B

BEAST SHAPE: Any animal form adopted by a shapeshifter.

BINDING A CORPSE: The practice of restricting a vampire's movements by tying the arms or legs of a corpse to prevent it from rising and wandering. Methods of binding vary from place to place according to local customs. Some cultures believe in tying the legs together, others the arms, and many wrap the entire corpse in bindings so that it cannot move more than a finger. Often a binding is used to keep the jaw shut so that the vampire cannot feast on its own flesh. Garlic is often placed in the mouth of a bound corpse to prevent unnatural life from returning, and coins are placed in the mouth to prevent it from chewing.

BLACK MASS: There was a common belief during the Middle Ages that a person who participated in a Black Mass would return from the dead as a vampire. These masses were blasphemous mockeries of the Roman Catholic mass, generally performed by heretics or Satanists. The Black Mass followed the basic proceedings of a Catholic mass, but each step featured a demonstration of corrupt behavior. A naked woman's body was used as the altar, and a defrocked or renegade priest desecrated an actual consecrated host before conducting a blood sacrifice. It was also believed that a Black Mass could be used to revive a vampire that had been killed, thereby reversing the Ritual of Exorcism.

BLOOD DRINKER: A vampire who feeds (primarily) on blood.

BLOOD PLAY: Also known as Blood Sports, this is a practice where willing participants cut themselves or each other for ritualistic or, more commonly, sado-masochistic thrills.

C

CATALEPSY: A disorder of the nervous system that causes a kind of suspended animation. Symptoms include a loss of voluntary motion, rigidity in the muscles, and a decreased sensitivity to pain and heat. Someone suffering from catalepsy can sometimes see and hear, but cannot move. Breathing, pulse, and other regulatory functions slow down to the extent that, to an untrained eye (such as a villager in the Middle Ages), it would seem as though they were deceased. Many people have been buried alive as a result of this condition, which may account for some reported cases of misdiagnosed vampirism. When the coffin of such a victim was opened, there would be clear evidence that the "corpse" had been awake post-burial. Signs of extreme agitation were often present, and even signs that the buried person had torn at his own skin and clothes and even tried to feed on himself. This condition can last from minutes to days.

CAUL: An amniotic membrane covering the face of some newborns. Many cultures believe this to be an indication of either psychic abilities or the presence of an evil spirit. Many children born with cauls are believed to be fated to become vampires after their deaths.

CORPSE JUMPING: There is a common tradition that a person or animal passing over a dead body may cause it to become a vampire. This stems from the belief that the spirit of the dead can snatch a portion of the life of any living creature and use it to rekindle its own unnatural life. This belief, in one form or another, is found in cultures as far apart as Eastern Europe, China, and the Native American Navajo of the United States. Animals such as dogs or cats are easily capable of corpse jumping, but people, bats, birds, and insects should be restrained as well. In China, tigers are believed to possess what is known as a "soul-recalling hair" that hooks part of the spirit when it crosses over a grave.

D

DERVISH: Muslim mystics who possess powers to fight the undead. Throughout the Balkans, Dervishes were contracted to function as vampire slayers.

DIABOLICAL: A general term referring to any action or force that opposes God's will, usually by an association with demonic or hellish forces, or through a direct pact with the Devil.

Photo by Jason Lukridge.

E

ESSENTIAL VAMPIRE: This type of vampire consumes life energy or "essence" from its victims. It is similar to the Succubus, which consumes sexual essence.

EXCOMMUNICATION: An ecclesiastical censure whereby the person against whom it is pronounced is, for the time, cast out of the communication of the church and excluded from fellowship in all things spiritual. There are two kinds of excommunication, the lesser and the greater. The lesser excommunication is a separation or suspension from partaking of the Eucharist; the greater is an absolute exclusion of the offender from the church and all its rights and advantages, even from social interaction with the faithful.

EXORCISM: The act of driving out evil spirits from persons or places by conjuring; also, the form of conjuring used. In vampire slaying, the Ritual of Exorcism separates the unnatural or demonic life from the reanimated corpse, rendering the earthly remains inert.

F

FEAST OF ST. ANDREW: Held each November 30th and believed to be a time of great vampiric activity in Romania. Along with the feasts of Easter and St. George, St. Andrew's Day has been associated with evil for centuries, and thought of as one of the most dreaded periods of the year in Romania. During preparation for these feast days, people would rub garlic on the doors and windows of their homes in order to protect the inhabitants from vampiric attacks.

FETCH DOG: A supernatural creature who acts like a hunting hound for a Sabbatarian (a person born on a Saturday who spends his life curing illness and fighting the undead).

FOLKLORE: Traditional customs, tales, or sayings preserved orally among a people. From the words "folk" (people) and "lore" (lesson).

G

GARLIC: Garlic (*Allium sativum*) has been used since the days of the Egyptians to treat wounds, infections, tumors, and intestinal parasites.

Also used heavily in the standard Vampire Exorcism because it is a blood purifier, believed by many cultures to be both physical and spiritual. Garlic also possesses the ability to inhibit the growth of parasites in the intestines, including amoebas which cause dysentery, which is useful in combating various vampires that spread disease.

GHOUL: An animated corpse that sustains its own life by eating, more often than not, the flesh of other corpses, but which can also eat humans.

H

HAEMATODIPSIA: A sexual compulsion to drink blood. This is sometimes manifested as sexual satisfaction attained through bathing in blood or smearing blood over one's face and body.

HAWTHORN: Any of the plants of the *Crataegus* plants of the family *Rosaceae* (including Mayflower, May tree, Quickset, Whitethorn, Maybush, Mayblossom, Haw, Halves, Hagthorn, Ladies' Meat, Bread and Cheese tree, etc.) possessing powers both to weaken vampires and ward them off.

HEMATOMANIA: A psychological fixation on blood from which an individual derives satisfaction along the lines of an erotic blood lust. Also known as hematodipsia, this condition is rare but has been seen in several historical and modern examples, including Elizabeth Bathory, the Marquis De Sade, and Gilles De Rais.

HEMAT (OR HEMATO): Greek prefix meaning "blood."

HEMATOPHAGEOUS: Living on a diet of blood. Vampire bats are naturally hematophageous.

HOLY BULLET: Also known as a Sacred Bullet, this is any bullet which has been properly blessed by a priest, monk, or other cleric and is then fired into the coffin of a suspected vampire. This practice was used primarily in the seventeenth century.

HORRIPILATION: The involuntary physical reaction to fear where hair stands on end on one's scalp.

HUMAN VAMPIRES: These are living people who are not supernatural but choose to live as vampires. The term Human Vampire has also frequently been given to a radically different and much smaller sub-group of humanity, specifically that of serial killers who demonstrate cannibalistic behavior. The comparison ends there.

Because some Human Vampires refer to themselves as Living Vampires there has frequently been some confusion. For the purposes of this book Human Vampires and Living Vampires are grouped differently as per the definitions given here and in the text.

Photo by Jason Lukridge.

L

LIVING VAMPIRE: These are supernatural creatures that prey on humans in a vampiric manner but are not undead creatures or ghosts.

M

MAD COW DISEASE: Bovine spongiform encephalopathy (BSE) is a chronic, degenerative disorder affecting the central nervous system of cattle. This disease was first diagnosed in 1986 in Great Britain and about 95 percent of cases have occurred in the United Kingdom. It has also been seen in other European countries such as Belgium, France, Germany, Spain, and Switzerland. So far it has not spread to the United States.

MANDUCATION: The term given to the act of a reawakened vampire eating its own flesh while still trapped in its coffin. In many vampire legends, disinterred corpses show signs of having been partially self-devoured. Some scientists hold that this is proof of premature burial and the resulting starvation and mania; vampire slayers disagree and believe that a reawakening vampire feeds on itself to gain strength so it can rise from its grave.

N

NECROPHAGISM (ALSO NECROPHAGY): A term used in clinical psychology to describe the consumption of pieces of a corpse, typically of someone who has been terribly mutilated. Often done while in a state of high agitation or frenzy, this deviant act is differentiated from true cannibalism in that it is most often directed toward a specific organ or body part, usually of a victim having been murdered only moments before.

NECROPHILIA: An erotic attraction to the dead, sometimes resulting in sexual acts committed on corpses.

NECROCYTOSIS: The death and decay of cells. Rotting.

NECROLYSIS: Separation or exfoliation of necrotic tissue, often leading to a temporarily ruddy appearance to dead flesh. It is presumed that this is the medical basis for the reports of disinterred corpses having a ruddy or healthy appearance.

NEED-FIRE: Also known as a "living fire." This was a special kind of bonfire lit to purify a town, its people, and their livestock. Once lit, the people and animals would either pass between burning mounds, through a veil of smoke, or over the ashes (particular methods varied from culture to culture). Effigies of witches and vampires were often thrown into the fire, symbolic of destroying them. Generally all of the fires in town would have been extinguished first and then rekindled with a brand from the need-fire, again symbolizing new life and health for the village.

NIGHTCOMER: A creature who travels only by night and generally cannot abide the light of day.

P

POLTERGEIST: A spirit, usually mischievous and occasionally malevolent, which manifests its presence by making noises, moving objects, and assaulting people and animals. The term "poltergeist" comes from the German *poltern*, "to knock," and *geist*, "spirit." Some cases remain unexplained despite extensive scientific explanation and may involve actual spirits, while in other cases the phenomena may be produced by subconscious psychokinesis.

Photo by Jason Lukridge.

PORPHYRIA: A rare hereditary blood disease. A victim of porphyria cannot produce heme, a vital component of red blood. Symptoms closely match the modern conception of vampirism, including an extreme sensitivity to sunlight, diminished immune system and inability to heal from wounds, excessive hair growth, and a tightening of the skin around the lips and gums, which would make the teeth--especially the canines--more prominent and visible.

PSYCHIC VAMPIRE: (1) A human who uses charisma, passive aggression, and controlled co-dependency to drain others of emotional, mental, and psychological energy.

(2) The kind of vampire that exists mostly on a spiritual plane and drains life essence from a victim rather than blood. Also known as "Essential Vampire."

R

REINTER: To re-bury a corpse. In vampiric exorcism, the reinterment process was often handled with great care so as prevent any chance of a recurrence of vampiric activity.

REVENANT: A corpse which has been reanimated and has risen as a vampire, ghost, zombie, or angel. For the purposes of this book, Revenant is used to describe human corpses returned from the dead. These vampires are often pale and shambling, their bodies showing signs of decay. Revenants are often immensely strong, mindless, and vicious.

ROSE: Many species of roses possess great virtues for warding off vampires, or rendering them helpless so that rituals of exorcism may be performed. Wild rose, dogrose, blackthorn (sloe), hawthorn, and others are all useful aids to the vampire slayer.

S

SABBATARIAN: A person born on a Saturday who has the power to cure illness as well as detect--and defeat--supernatural creatures such as vampires. The Sabbatarian is often accompanied by a Fetch Dog, a natal spirit that acted like a supernatural hunting hound.

SACRED BULLET: See Holy Bullet

SANGUINARIAN: Derived from the Latin word *sanguineus*, which means bloodthirsty. Sanguinarians are people who have a physical craving for blood. People acting out due to this disorder may be one of the many non-supernatural causes of vampire folktales.

SEXUAL VAMPIRISM: A form of vampirism that feeds primarily on sexual energy, such as in the case of the Incubus and Succubus.

SHAPESHIFTER: Also known as Theriomorph. A creature capable of changing its physical form, usually into other animal shapes. Werewolves are one kind of shapeshifter.

S.I.D.S: Sudden Infant Death Syndrome is the sudden death of an infant under one year of age, and which remains unexplained after a thorough case investigation, including performance of a complete autopsy, examination of the death scene, and review of the clinical history. In many cultures throughout history, vampirism has been blamed for S.I.D.S.

STAKE: A shaft of wood or metal used to impale a vampire and pin it to its coffin so that a vampire exorcism may be performed. Wooden stakes may be made from aspen, ash, buckthorn, holly, juniper, maple, rosewood, and many other woods, depending on the beliefs of individual regions.

SUCCUBUS: A demon or fiend, especially a lascivious one that is supposed to have sexual intercourse with men by night. The Succubus drains life energy from its victim.

SUPERNATURAL: Any creature, being, or event not conforming to the world as understood by science, particularly physics.

T

THERIOMORPH: A human or supernatural being who possesses the ability to shapeshift from human to animal and back again. This is the correct term for the more colloquial "shapeshifter."

V

VAMPIRE: A general term referring to any creature—natural or super-natural--that feeds on the blood, psychic energy, emotion, or life essence of others.

VAMPIRE EXORCISM: The ritualized destruction of a vampire. The most common form of exorcism involves driving a stake (wooden or metal) through the vampire's torso, decapitating the creature, and then stuffing the mouth of the severed head with garlic.

VAMPIRE SLAYER: A person who hunts down and destroys vampires. There are natural vampire slayers, such as the Dhampir, who are born with the ability to hunt and destroy vampires; there are professional vampire slayers who hunt the undead for a living. But most vampire slayers are religious persons, warriors, or villagers who have taken it upon themselves to confront and destroy a vampire in their midst. Also known as Vampire Hunter and Vampire Killer.

VAMPIROLOGY: The unofficial study of vampires, their natures, and their practices. This is not considered a true scientific field of study by the academic world.

Photo by Jason Lukridge.

W

WEREWOLF: A general term used either to describe a person who becomes a wolf (or wolflike beast), or a wolf that assumes human form.

WILL-O'-THE-WISP: The most common name given to mysterious lights that are said to lead travelers from well-trodden paths into treacherous marshes. This legend exists with slight variation throughout the world.

Photo by Jason Lukridge.

·APPENDIX TWO·
A TIMELINE OF VAMPIRES AND WEREWOLVES

Compiled By Jill S. Katz

BCE: BEFORE CHRISTIAN ERA

- **140,000:** Anthropologic evidence shows that early humans and wolves maintained a close connection and possibly lived together in pre-tribal pack communities.

- **135,000:** Recovered DNA traces prove that dogs evolved from wolf ancestors.

- **100,000:** According to research by UCLA biologist Robert K. Wayne, some wolves and early dog species began to be domesticated at this time. Genetic research verifies that dogs evolved only from wolves, not from coyotes or jackals as had been previously believed.

- **75,000:** Examination of prehistoric ruins suggests that humans participated in cults based on wolves, bears, buffalo, and other animals.

- **26,000:** Garkains haunt Neanderthal man in the Aboriginal outback.

- **25,000:** Franco-Cantabrian cave artists depict figures of humans with the heads of animals.

- **13,000:** Eurasian wolves are domesticated.

- **12,000:** The first travelers to North and South America bring domesticated dogs with them. Dog DNA pre-dating Columbus is recently discovered in Latin America and Alaska.

- **6000:** In the excavated ruins of Catal Huyuk in Turkey (formerly Anatolia), cave paintings clearly show hunters wearing the skins and heads of animals, suggesting either a real or psychological link with animal predation methods.

- **4000:** First female blood drinker on record, the Lilitu of ancient Assyria.

- **4000:** According to Hebrew folklore, Adam's first wife, Lilith, flees Eden for the "abode of demons" where she becomes the mother to a race of vampiric demons.

- **4000:** Babylon and Assyria experience the wrath of the Akahuru and other vampire creatures.

- **3000:** Wall paintings in India and Tibet depict vampiric carnage.

- **3000:** The Egyptians build the Sphinx, a creature with the body of a human and the head of a lion.

- **2000:** The *Epic of Gilgamesh* (an actual, historical king of Uruk in Babylonia) makes mention of a lycanthrope (werewolf) in the character of Enkidu, a wild-man created by the sky god Anu. Enkidu and Gilgamesh are initially adversaries, but after the great hero defeats the werewolf they become great friends and share many epic adventures together.

- **1000:** Many of the Greek myths and legends tell of humans and gods transforming into different animals, often to play tricks on humans. Human-animal hybrids, such as the Minotaur, appear in various myths and story cycles.

- **850:** In Homer's *The Odyssey*, the sorceress Circe transforms Ulysses' men into pigs.

- **750:** Romulus and Remus, brothers who are suckled and raised by a she-wolf, found the Eternal City, Rome.

**Eris, the Greek goddess of hate.
Archival artwork.**

- **535:** Babylonian King Nebuchadnezzar becomes afflicted with a mental illness and for nearly four years acts like a wild animal.

- **500:** Herodotus writes that the Scythians, who live in the southern part of the Ukraine immediately north of the Greek towns (and who are thought to be the Iron Age ancestors of the Slavs), believe that the Neuri (the probable ancestors of the Balts) turn themselves into werewolves during a yearly religious festival.

- **400:** The Greek Olympic boxing champion, Darmarchus, is reputed to be a werewolf.

- **37:** The Roman poet Virgil speaks and writes about a were-wolf named Moeris as shown in this excerpt from *The Eclogues*:

Wolf artwork by Shane MacDougall.

> "These herbs of bane to me did Moeris give,
> In Pontus culled, where baneful herbs abound.
> With these full oft have I seen Moeris change
> To a wolf's form, and hide him in the woods,
> Oft summon spirits from the tomb's recess,
> And to new fields transport the standing corn."

CE: CHRISTIAN ERA

(Formerly called AD for Anno Domini)

- **28:** The Christian New Testament gives an account of Jesus exorcizing demonic spirits from two possessed men in the territory of the Gadarenes. These spirits recognize Jesus at once as the Son of God, and ask whether he has come to torture them before their time, requesting that if he is to drive them out, they may be sent into a herd of pigs. This dramatic narrative occurs in Matthew 8:28-34, and also in Mark 5:1-20. Many occult scholars believe that this is an instance of possession similar to that of a person suffering the habitation of an animal spirit, which is the basis of werewolfism.

- **30:** Date approximate, Jesus of Nazareth exorcises demons from Mary Magdalene, who goes on to become one of his most devoted followers and is the first witness to his resurrection from the tomb.

- **35:** Following the death of Jesus of Nazareth, the Apostles (now with Paul, formerly Saul of Tarsus) continue to perform miracles that include the casting out of demons.

- **55:** According to the testimony of St. Justin, Simon of Gitta attempts to usurp the role of Jesus in the early Christian movement by claiming to be the true Messiah. Because of his apparently vast magical powers he is given the name Simon Magus. He is reportedly able to transform himself into different animals, but is discredited by Simon Peter and the other Apostles. However, even after their rebuke, he continues to practice his dark arts and is regarded by the Catholic Church as the first heretic: the "Father of Heresies."

- **111:** Pliny, quoting Euanthes, writes that a man of the family of Antaeus was selected by lot and brought to a lake in Arcadia, where he hung his clothing on an ash and swam across. This resulted in his being transformed into a wolf, and he wandered in this shape for nine years. If he attacked no human being, he would be at liberty to swim back and resume his former shape.

- **150:** *The Golden Ass*, written in Latin by Lucius Apuleius, tells the story of the journey of the hero Lucius through Thessaly, the land of witchcraft. His curiosity leads to his accidental transformation into an ass, and he finds himself trapped in a world of ever-increasing moral depravity.

- **175:** The story of Lycaon supplies the most familiar instance of the werewolf in Greek mythology. According to a story by the scholar and geographer Pausanias, the Lycanians were transformed into wolves as a result of eating human flesh. Witnesses to this unholy act suffered the same fate and became werewolves themselves.

- **432:** St. Patrick arrives in Ireland and discovers that some of his flock are werewolves. He uses his holy powers to heal the people of this unholy affliction and drives lycanthropy out of Ireland.

- **Middle Ages:** White Lady Melusina is believed to kill travelers along French roads.

- **500s and 600s:** Japan's villages are plagued by Tsutsuga shapeshifters.

- **600:** St. Ailbhe (also spelled Albeus) was a bishop and preacher, one of the saints whose life has been woven into the myths and legends of Ireland. He was a known disciple of St. Patrick and in some church records it is claimed that he was left in the woods as an infant and suckled by a wolf.

- **650:** Paulus Aegineta, a celebrated surgeon from the island of Aegina, writes that "melancholic lycantropia" is a black and dismal frame of mind. Those who suffer from this condition leave their homes, wander in cemeteries, and believe themselves to be werewolves.

- **655:** Empress Saimei Tenno sends a sage from her court to magically banish Tsutsugas forever.

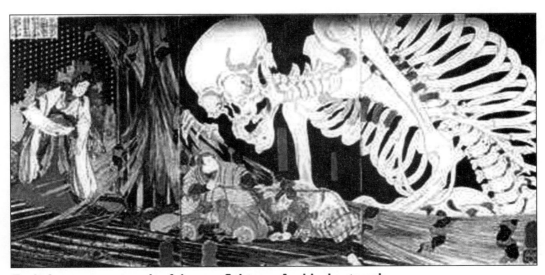

Early Japanese artwork of demon fighters. Archival artwork.

- **725:** Date approximate. *Beowulf* is written, the earliest extant poem in a modern European language. The poem tells the tale of a battle between Vikings and a family of monsters. Scholars and occult theoreticians variously believe the "monsters" to be primitive cannibalistic tribesmen, Neanderthals that had managed to survive extinction, or even a culture of werewolves.

- **731:** The church scholar known as the Venerable Bede (self-described as a "Servant of Christ and Priest of the Monastery of Saints Peter and Paul which is at Wearmouth and Jarrow") relates tales of were-creatures that hunt by moonlight.

- **840:** Agobard, a Carolingian prelate and reformer, writes about demonic forces in his *Liber Contra Insulam Vulgi Opinionem*. He describes malignant beings from the mountains who appear in half-human, half-animal shapes.

- **1000:** Burchard, Bishop of Worms (a town in Germany), decries stories of werewolves by arguing that only God possesses the power to change the shape of men, and that tales of wild folk living in the woods and changing into animals are false. It is his view that the term "werewolf" is merely a euphemism for "outlaw" or "heretic."

- **1047:** The first European use of the word vampire is used in the phrase *Upir Lichy*, which translated various as "wicked vampire" or "extortionate vampire." The term was used to describe the excesses of Vladimir Jaroslav, Prince of Novgorod in Northeast Russia

- **1101:** Prince Vseslav of Palock in the Ukraine dies. While alive he was believed to be a werewolf, and after death he became a lycanthropic bogeyman in rural ghost stories.

- **1131:** Hugues de Camp d'A Vesnes of France destroyed the Abbey of Saint Riguier in order to gain access to two of his enemies, le Compt d'Auxi and le Compt de Beaurain-sur-Canche. Both men had fled to the Abbey to seek asylum and the church's protection against Hugues, who was reputed to be a werewolf. Three thousand people died during the attack and burning of the Abbey.

- **1182:** Giraldus Cambrensis (also known as Gerald de Barry), a distinguished writer, historian, and ecclesiastic of the early Middle Ages, relates the story of a pack of demon-inspired humans who become werewolves during the Christmas season, apparently as a deliberate affront to God.

- **1190:** Walter Map publishes his *De Nugis Curialium (On the Trivialities of Courtiers)*, which includes a few early accounts of vampiric creatures in England.

- **1195:** *The Ancient English Romance of William and the Werewolf* is written by Guillaume De Palerne (with Frederick Madden)

- **1196:** Perhaps following Map's example, William of Newburgh writes his *Historia Rerum Anglicarum*, or *The History of the Affairs of England*. His stories also include reference to vampires.

- **1198:** Marie de France composes "*Bisclavret*," a poem about a noble baron who is also a werewolf.

- **1214:** Gervaise of Tilbury reports cases in Auvergne in which men are seen to take the forms of wolves during a full moon.

- **1216:** King John Lackland (1167-1216; youngest son of Henry II and Eleanor of Aquitane, and signer of the Magna Carta) dies from poisoning and is believed to have returned as a werewolf.

- **1220:** Caesarius of Heisterbach, monk of the Cistercian monastery of Heisterbach near Bonn, and author of *Dialogue of Miracles*, describes numerous accounts of shapeshifting and other magical practices.

- **1250:** Norse writer Kongs Skuggsjo relates how St. Patrick prayed to God to punish some men who howled him down while he attempted to convert them to Christianity. God bestowed a proper punishment, condemning the men to howl like wolves at each full moon. This is almost certainly the origin of the link between werewolfism and the full moon, and has since been corrupted to suggest that people only become werewolves during the full moon, which is not so.

- **1257:** The Church officially sanctions torture as a means of forcing people to confess that they are heretics, werewolves, and witches.

- **1300:** *The Story of the Volsungs* (also known as *The Volsunga Saga*) was written in the Icelandic (Old Norse) language in the thirteenth century A.D., author unknown. It relates a story of an outlaw father and son who become werewolves and establish a dynasty.

The Draugr (a vampire from Iceland). Sculpture by Robert Patrick O'Brien.

- **c. 1178 to 1200:** At the request of the Countess Yolande (daughter of Baldwin IV, Count of Flanders), an alliterative poem is composed called "*Roman de Guillaume de Palerne*" ("The Romance of William of Palerne"). Authorship of the poem is unknown. The poem tells the story of lovers who seek to escape and are successfully aided by a "grateful animal" (here a werewolf, which later resumes human shape as a king's son). Somewhere around 1350, Sir Humphrey de Bohun translates "*Roman de Guillaume de Palerne*" and gives it the new title "The Romance Of William of Palerne, or, William & the Werewolf." The story is again translated in 1949 by Celtic scholar Cecile O'Rahilly.

- **1343:** The Prussian Baron Steino de Retten (Lauenburg) is suspected to be a vampire.

- **1346 to 1353:** An epidemic of the plague arrives in Europe. People believe that it has vampiric qualities: the illness floats in the air like mist and attacks its victims, and that it will disappear with the sound of the church bells. One third of all Europeans die as a result of the Black Death.

- **1407:** At the cruel witch trials in Basel, Switzerland, several people are accused of being werewolves and are then burned for this unholy condition.

- **1414:** Sigismond of Hungary makes the Orthodox Church officially recognize the existence of vampires during the Ecumenical Council.

- **1407:** Accounts of the Scottish witch trials state that werewolves are tortured and burned at the stake.

- **1407:** Serial killer and child murderer Gilles de Rais of France is arrested for murdering young boys and drinking their blood. He is put on trial as a werewolf and convicted.

- **1440s:** "Vlad the Impaler," Vladislav Basarab, the son of Vlad Dracul, is born in Transylvania in 1427 and given the nickname "Dracula" (which means "son of the dragon"). He spends many years gaining and losing control of the Wallachian throne and becomes known as one of the most sadistic rulers in history. He is given the name Vlad Tepes, which means "Vlad the Impaler," for his favorite form of torture. It is thought that he performs or orders the murder of approximately 100,000 people during his reign. Tepes later becomes the primary inspiration for Bram Stoker's *Dracula* in 1897.

- **1502:** Frenchman Pierre Bourgot claims he has broken the neck of a nine-year-old girl and eaten her, and as a result he is executed for being a werewolf.

- **1517:** Swedish historian and geographer Olaus Magnus writes that Livonian werewolves are initiated by draining a specially prepared cup of beer, and repeating a set formula.

- **Early 1500s:** Gervase of Tilbury writes *Otia Imperialia* for his patron, the Holy Roman Emperor Otto IV. This is the first English translation of this major medieval text, and makes mention of werewolves.

- **1521:** Philibert Montot, Pierre Bourgot, and Michel Verdun are tried by Jean Boin, Inquisitor of Besancon, for having made a pact with the devil and for being werewolves. These men become known as the Werewolves of Poligny and are executed.

- **1540:** Cabbalist Giambattista della Porta (ca 1540-1615) writes that in Naples it is customary to place a wolf's head over the door, jaws agape, to ward off witches and vampires.

- **1541:** In Pavia, Italy, a farmer transformed into a werewolf attacks a party of men and slaughters them. He is tracked down and caught. He tells his captors that the only difference between himself and a natural wolf is that in a true wolf the hair grows outward, whilst in him it grows inward. In order to put this assertion to the proof, the magistrates, themselves most certainly cruel and bloodthirsty wolves, cut off his arms and legs; the poor wretch dies from the mutilation.

- **1573:** A hermit named Gilles Garnier is captured and executed for a number of werewolf murders in Dole, France.

- **1578:** Jacques Rollet is put on trial in Paris and found guilty of being a werewolf. While in the shape of the wolf, he had supposedly devoured a little boy. He was burned at the stake at Place de Greve.

Detail from a 16th century illustration of a werewolf attacking a family. Archival artwork.

• **1588:** In a village in the Auvergne region a story spreads of a traveler who cut the hand off an attacking wolf and later found that it had transformed into a woman's hand. The woman with the missing hand is tracked down and burned at Riom as a werewolf.

• **1589:** Peter Stubbe, (a.k.a. Peter Stube, Peeter Stubbe, or Peter Stumpf) is the subject of one of the most famous werewolf trials in history. After being tortured on the rack, Stubbe confesses to having practiced black magic since he was twelve years old. He claims the devil had given him a magical belt which enabled him to metamorphose into "the likenes of a greedy deuouring Woolf, strong and mighty, with eyes great and large, which in the night sparkeled like unto brandes of fire, a mouth great and wide, with most sharpe and cruell teeth, A huge body, and mightye pawes." [Sic.] He also claims to have killed and eaten animals and humans for twenty-five years. The court, appalled by these crimes, sentences him to have his skin torn off by red-hot pincers before being beheaded.

Detail of 16th century illustration of hunters catching a werewolf that turned out to be Peter Stubbe.

The beheading and burning of Peter Stubbe. Archival artwork.

• **1590:** Michel Jaques confesses he became a wolf several times after anointing himself with an unguent given to him by Satan.

· **1598:** One of the most infamous lycanthropes of all time is the dreaded Werewolf of Chalons, also known as the Demon Tailor. He is arraigned in Paris on December 14th on murder charges that are so appalling that the court orders all documents of the hearing to be destroyed. Even his real name has been expunged from history.

· **1598:** In the Jura Mountains, a little boy and girl are attacked by a gigantic wolf. The girl is killed but the boy manages to fend off the creature and escape, though he dies later of wounds sustained in the fight. When the monster is tracked down, the villagers find that it has become Perrenette Gandillon, a mentally challenged woman from St. Claude. Later her entire family is arrested and each of them demonstrates ferocious animalistic qualities. Some modern scholars believe that the Gandillons all suffered from rabies, though the historical records still contend that they were a family of werewolves.

· **Late 1500s:** Gilles Garnier of France is found to have drunk the blood of young women for sustenance.

· **Late 1500s:** Clara Geisslerin is accused of witchcraft and vampiric activities.

· **1600s:** Priests begin blessing bullets to shoot those suspected of being vampires.

· **1600-1610:** Hungarian countess Elizabeth Bathory is convicted of killing over six hundred young girls and bathing in their blood in order to retain her own youth. She and her cohorts are all tried and convicted, but Bathory alone is sentenced to life in prison. Her co-conspirators are all sentenced to death. Of particular note is the fact that she was raised in Transylvania. Bathory became known in popular fiction as "Countess Dracula," although she was not a supernatural vampire nor was she related in any way to Vlad Tepes.

· **1602:** Michée Bauloz, Jeanne de la Pierre, and Suzanne Prevost are tried and condemned as werewolves. They claim to have eaten every part of a captured child except his right hand, "which God hadn't permitted."

· **1603:** In France, Jean Grenier is sentenced to life imprisonment for crimes committed as a werewolf. He dies in 1610.

· **1645:** *De Graecorum Hodie Quirundam Opinationabus* is written by Leo Allatius and is considered the first modern treatment of vampires.

· **1657:** *Relation de ce Qui S'est Passe a Sant-Erini Isle de l'Archipel* is written by Father Francoise Richard to show a link between witchcraft and vampirism.

· **1685:** The townspeople of Anspach, Germany are plagued by a werewolf that reportedly killed many women, children, and animals. The people believe that the werewolf is the reincarnation of the town's detested Burgomaster who had recently died.

Detail from seventeenth century illustration of werewolf attack. Archival artwork.

· **1692:** In Jurgenburg, Livonia, an 80-year-old man named Theiss claimed to be a Benandanti (a werewolf fighting against evil) and that he and a band of other werewolves descended into Hell to fight a coven of witches that were causing crop blights and other famine in the area. The judges were astounded by the story of Theiss and his fellow "hounds of God," and even though church law demanded that any supernatural beings be punished, they sentenced him to a mere ten lashes.

· **Early 1700s:** Vampire hysteria is seen throughout Eastern Europe.

· **1700s:** The Mara is brought to Canada by unknowing Slavs.

· **1720s:** Austrian Peter Plogojowitz is thought to be an actual vampire. Plogojowitz was said to have died at age 62, but after his death is reported to have visited his son asking for food. Both Plogojowitz's son and neighbors are found dead and drained of blood the next day.

· **1727:** Arnold Paole claims to have been bitten by a vampire while serving time as a soldier in the Austrian service. He is purported to have died and returned three weeks later. The four people who claim to have seen him all end up dead shortly thereafter. By 1731, numerous people are claiming that the dead have risen and attacked them. The Emperor of Austria sends Regimental Field Surgeon Johannes Fluckinger to examine the bodies. All suspected dead are disinterred and discovered to be in a state of decomposition not as bad as they should be, and bleed when cut. They are staked and witnesses claim to hear the deceased groan in pain. They are then burned so they will not rise again.

· **1730s-1740s:** Many essays are written on vampirism throughout Europe. The English see the word "vampyre" for the first time thanks to translations of a German treatise.

· **1735:** "Birth" of the Jersey Devil of Leeds Point, New Jersey.

· **1746:** In Austria, Dom Augustin Calmet publishes his treatise on vampires, *"Dissertations sur les Apparitions des Ages des Demons et des Espits, et sur les Revenants, et Vampires de Hundrie, de Boheme, de Moravie, et de Silesie."* The Empress of Hungary's personal physician, Calmet investigated the existence of vampires and found no evidence of any true existence of the creatures. Empress Marie Theresa then passes a law prohibiting Austrians from digging up graves or destroying dead bodies, which had been practiced by Austrians in an attempt to deter vampires rising.

· **1748:** *"Der Vampir,"* the first modern vampire poem, is written by Heinrich August Ossenfelder.

· **1765:** In the rural area of Gevaudan, one hundred deadly attacks occur between 1765 and 1767. The attacks are attributed to a wolf-like creature. Some call the creature a *"Loup-garou,"* or werewolf. The animal is said to resemble a wolf but has six claws and is the size of a horse. Many people are sent to the region by Louis the XV to stop the killings, including Gregoire de Fronsac. Around seventy-five wolves are killed in the hunts but the killings continue. In 1767 a mysterious, deformed mutant animal is killed, and thereafter the savage attacks stopped. This series of events was made into the movie *Le Pacte des Loups* (*The Brotherhood of the Wolf*) in 2002. Drawings of the deformed animal still exist to this day.

· **1773:** The poem "Leonore" is written by Gottfried August Bürger. It tells the tale of a woman who comes back from the dead.

· **1798-1800:** The first English vampire poem, "Christabel," is written by Samuel Taylor Coleridge .

· **1800s:** Operas, poems, and stories about vampires spring up in Germany, England, Italy, and many other countries.

· **1810:** Northern England buzzes with reports that sheep are being murdered and exsanguinated.

· **1819:** The "vampire trap" is created for the stage version of James Planche's *The Vampire*. It has two spring-loaded doors placed in the floor or wall that open and immediately shut, making the actor seem to disappear through the floor or wall.

· **1840s:** England sees the introduction of Penny Blood stories and Penny Gaff theater productions. These are horror stories that the critics pan as "Penny Dreadfuls."

- **1854:** Griswold, Connecticut gives the United States its first vampiric family. The Ray family has members dying in quick succession of and the family thinks the reason is that the dead members are coming back and draining the blood of those still alive. The remaining Rays and some friends dig up the graves of the deceased and burn the bodies.

- **1867:** James Brown, a sailor from Portugal, is caught drinking the blood of one of his dead shipmates, the second he had killed that day.

- **1872:** Vincenzo Verzeni murders two people and drinks their blood in Bottanucco, Italy.

- **1874:** Stories of sheep being exsanguinated appear in Ireland.

- **1894:** H. G. Wells writes the first science fiction vampire story "The Flowering of the Strange Orchid."

- **1887:** Dr. William Robert Woodman, William Wynn Westcott, and L. MacGregor Mathers found the Order of the Golden Dawn, a hermetic society whose members are taught the principles of occult science (including tarot, alchemy, and geomancy) and the magic of Hermes. Other members include Nobel Prize-winning poet William Butler Yeats and occultist Aleister Crowley. Among the many beliefs taught by the Order, rumors abound that the Order also fosters beliefs in werewolves and vampires. Many members of the Order emphatically deny this.

- **1897:** *Dracula, Or The Un-Dead* by Bram Stoker is published.

- **Early 1900s:** The Vampire of Muy, Victor Ardisson, is found guilty of illegal exhumation and necrophilia.

- **1910s:** The Vampire of Dusseldorf, Peter Kurten: Kurten was molested as a young boy by his father and was also taught to torture dogs at age nine by a local dogcatcher. He becomes a thief, commits acts of bestiality on sheep, and then starts to murder the animals he abuses. His sadism eventually progresses to humans, mostly young women, whom he strangles or murders with an axe and sometimes drinks their blood. After spending a few years away from

Early twentieth century Dracula playbook. Archival artwork.

Dusseldorf and living a respectable life, he returns and resumes his crime spree. This time, he stabs his victims repeatedly. Kurten is finally captured after admitting all to his wife and asking her to turn him in to the police. Although he admits to dozens of crimes, Kurten is only convicted of nine murders and seven attempted murders. His excuse for the murders is that he wanted to get back at a society that had done wrong by him.

- **1910:** A Portugese man named Salvarrey admits to being a vampire after being the sole suspect in the murder of an exsanguinated girl.

- **1912:** *The Secrets of House No. 5* is produced in England; it is believed to be the first vampire movie.

- **1913:** *The Werewolf* is the first werewolf film.

- **1920s:** The Vampire of Hanover, German Fritz Haarmann: Haarmann murders young men and drinks their blood. He is convicted of twenty-four murders, but it is believed that he actually killed closer to fifty. He also worked as a butcher and claimed to have sold some of the meat from his victims to unwitting customers.

- **1920s:** Numerous European countries produce movie versions of *Dracula*. One of these films, *Nosferatu*, is considered too close to the original and the director is sued by the Stoker estate.

- **1928:** *The Vampire: His Kith and Kin* by Montague Summers is released, becoming the twentieth century's first major non-fiction work on the subject. However, as Summers bases much of his "research" on Bram Stoker's novel, *Dracula*, much of the information is tainted by elements of pop culture. Though still an enjoyable read, the book is not as definitive a work as it was first believed to be.

- **1929:** *The Vampire in Europe* is released, also by Montague Summers, continuing along the same lines of research.

- **1933:** *The Werewolf* by Montague Summers is released. The book attempts to link werewolfism to serial killing throughout the ages. It stands for years as the definitive non-fiction werewolf book.

- **1940s:** The Acid Bath Vampire, John George Haigh: as a boy, Haigh is told by his father that his mother was an angel and his father was marked by the devil. Although he rarely acted up, on the occasions that he did, his mother would hit the back of his hand with her hairbrush, drawing blood. This is supposed to have started his interest in the taste of blood. As an adult, his taste for blood grows to the point that he murders a man and drinks his blood. He then disposes of the body in a vat of acid. He is later arrested for theft, but tries to avoid imprisonment by pleading insanity. His proof that he was insane? He admits to the murders and disposals he had performed. Although he had admitted to more, he is convicted of nine murders in total.

- **1942:** "Asylum" by A. E. Van Vogt is the first story about a vampire alien.

- **1954:** Richard Matheson writes *I Am Legend*, a novel that portrays vampirism as a disease (*bacilli vampiri*).

- **1954:** The Comics Code bans the walking undead, vampires, and werewolves from comic books.

- **1967:** *Dark Shadows* introduces vampire Barnabas Collins to daytime TV.

- **1970s:** Vampire research societies, foundations, and fan clubs spring up all over the United States and England. Movies, TV shows, and books branch out to include more and more vampire stories.

- **1978:** The Dracula Killer: Richard Chase of Sacramento, California is convicted of murdering people and drinking their blood. He claims it keeps him from disintegrating.

- **1980s:** Russia's Citizen X: Andrei Chikatilo is sentenced to death after murdering some fifty-three people. Chikatilo admits to cannibalism and desecrating the bodies of his victims. His murders are not reported to the general public at the time for fear of public hysteria.

- **1982:** *The Were-Wolf and Vampire in Romania* by Harry Senn is published by Columbia University Press and emerges as one of the twentieth century's most authoritative works on its subjects.

- **1989:** Transylvania becomes open to tourists after Nikolai Ceaucescu is removed from power in Romania.

- **1997:** *Buffy the Vampire Slayer* airs on television, inspiring a surge of copycat shows and movies.

- **1998:** *The Vampire Book: An Encyclopedia of the Undead* is published by J. Gordon Melton, becoming a landmark book of historical and fictional accounts of vampirism.

- **1999:** *The Werewolf Book: An Encyclopedia of Shape-Shifting Beings* by author Brad Steiger is published. It is the most authoritative work on the subject since *The Werewolf* by Montague Summers.

·APPENDIX THREE·
A VAMPIRE BIBLIOGRAPHY

Many of the books in this list have been published in a number of different editions, so much so that it would be more confusing than useful to try to include all of the publishers, editions, versions and volumes. Therefore only titles and authors are provided.

FICTION - ANTHOLOGIES

· *After Midnight* stories by Carol Finch, Colleen Faulkner and Karen Ranney

· *Blood and Roses: Vampires in 19th Century Literature* edited by Adele O. Gladwell
· *Blood Kiss: Vampire Erotica* edited by Cecilia Tan
· *Blood Lines: Vampire Stories from New England* edited by Martin H. Greenberg
· *Blood Thirst : 100 Years of Vampire Fiction* edited by Leonard Wolf
· *Brothers of the Night: Gay Vampire Stories* edited by Michael Rowe & Thomas S. Roche

· *Celebrity Vampires* edited by Martin H. Greenberg
· *Cherished Blood: Vampire Erotica* edited by Cecilia Tan
· *Classic Vampire Stories* edited by Leslie Shepard
· *Classic Vampire Stories: Timeless Tales to Sink Your Teeth Into* edited by Molly Cooper

· *Dark Angels: Lesbian Vampire Stories* edited by Pam Keesey
· *The Darkest Thirst: A Vampire Anthology* edited by Thomas J. Strauch
· *Daughters of Darkness: Lesbian Vampire Stories* edited by Pam Keesey
· *Dead Brides: Vampire Tales* by Edgar Allan Poe

- *The Dracula Book of Great Vampire Stories* edited Leslie Shepard
- *Dracula in London* edited by P.N. Elrod

- *Erotica Vampirica: Sensual Vampire Stories* edited by Cecilia Tan

- *Fields of Blood: Vampire Stories from the American Midwest* edited by Martin H. Greenberg

- *Isaac Asimov's Vampires* edited by Gardner Dozois & Sheila Williams

- *The Kiss of Death: An Anthology of Vampire Stories* edited by Thomas J. Strauch

- *Love in Vein* edited by Poppy Z. Brite
- *Love in Vein II* edited by Poppy Z. Brite & Martin H. Greenberg

- *Mammoth Book of Dracula: Vampire Tales for the New Millennium* edited by Stephen Jones
- *Mammoth Book of Vampire Stories by Women* edited by Stephen Jones
- *Mammoth Book of Vampires* edited by Stephen Jones
- *Midnight Mass* edited by Martin H. Greenberg

- *Night Bites: Vampire Stories by Women* edited by Victoria A. Brownworth

- *Penguin Book of Vampire Stories* edited by Alan Ryan

- *Sisters of the Night* edited by Barbara Hambly and Martin H. Greenberg
- *Sons of Darkness* edited by Michael Rowe & Thomas S. Roche
- *Southern Blood: Vampire Stories from the American South* edited by Martin H. Greenberg
- *Strangers in the Night* stories by Anne Stuart, Chelsea Quinn Yarbro & Maggie Shayne
- *Streets of Blood: Vampire Stories from New York City* edited by Martin H. Greenberg

- *The Time of the Vampires* edited by P.N. Elrod and Martin H. Greenberg

- *The Ultimate Dracula* edited by Byron Preiss

- *Vampire Detectives* edited by Martin H. Greenberg
- *The Vampire Omnibus* edited by Peter Haining
- *Vampire Slayers* edited by Martin H. Greenberg & Elizabeth Ann Scarborough
- *Vampire Stories* edited by Richard Dalby
- *The Vampire Stories of Nancy Kilpatrick* by Nancy Kilpatrick
- *Vampire Stories of R. Chetwynd-Hayes* edited by Stephen Jones
- *Vampires: Encounters with the Undead* edited by David J. Skall
- *Vampires: The Greatest Stories* edited by Martin H. Greenberg

- *A Whisper of Blood* edited by Ellen Datlow

FICTION - SERIES

THE ADVERSARY CYCLE by F. Paul Wilson
1. *The Keep*
2. *The Tomb*
3. *The Touch*
4. *Reborn*
5. *Reprisal*
6. *Nightworld*

AMERICAN VAMPIRE edited by Martin H. Greenberg

ANGEL Spin-off from *Buffy the Vampire Slayer*
   This is a partial list of a fast-growing series:
1. *City of* by Nancy Holder
2. *Haunted* by Jeff Mariotte
3. *Hollywood Noir* by Jeff Mariotte
4. The *Hollower* by Christopher Golden, Hector Gomez, Sandu Florea
5. *Autumnal* by Christopher Golden, Tom Sniegoski, Christian Zanier, Eric Powell
6. *Earthly Possessions* by Christopher Golden, Tom Sniegoski, Andy Owens
7. *Long Night's Journey* by Brett Matthews, Chris Dreier, Joss Whedon
8. *Not Forgotten* by Nancy Holder, Joss Whedon, David Greenwalt
9. *Shakedown* by Don Debrandt
10. *Close to Ground* by Jeff Mariotte
11. *Image* by Mel Odom
12. *Redemption* by Mel Odom
13. *Avatar* by John Pasarella
14. *The Summoned* by Cameron Dokey
15. *Bruja* by Mel Odom
16. *Soul Trade* by Thomas Sniegoski
17. *Avatar* by John Passarella

ANITA BLAKE VAMPIRE HUNTER by Laurell K. Hamilton
1. *Guilty Pleasures*
2. *The Laughing Corpse*
3. *Circus of the Damned*
4. *The Lunatic Café*
5. *Bloody Bones*
6. *The Killing Dance*
7. *Burnt Offerings*
8. *Blue Moon*
9. *Obsidian Butterfly*
10. *Narcissus in Chains*
11. *Cerulean Sins*

ANNO DRACULA by Kim Newman
1. *Anno Dracula*
2. *The Bloody Red Baron*

THE AUSTRA FAMILY SERIES by Elaine Bergstrom
1. *Shattered Glass*
2. *Blood Alone*
3. *Blood Rites*
4. *Daughter of the Night*

BUFFY THE VAMPIRE SLAYER – Various Authors
This is a partial list of a fast-growing series:
1. *Bad Blood* by Bennett Watson
2. *Blooded* by Christopher Golden, Nancy Holder
3. *Buffy the Vampire Slayer* by Richie Tankersley Cusick
4. *Uninvited Guests* by Brereton Watson
5. *Child of the Hunt* by Christopher Golden, Nancy Holder
6. *Coyote Moon* by John Vornholt
7. *Deep Water* by Laura Anne Gilman, Josepha Sherman
8. *Out of the Madhouse: The Gatekeeper Trilogy, No 1* by Christopher Golden, Nancy Holder
9. *Ghost Roads: The Gatekeeper Triology , No 2* by Christopher Golden, Nancy Holder
10. *Sons of Entropy: The Gatekeeper Trilogy, No 3* by Christopher Golden, Nancy Holder
11. Ghoul Trouble by John Passarella
12. Halloween Rain by Christopher Golden, Nancy Holder
13. Immortal by Christopher Golden, Nancy Holder
14. *Night of the Living Rerun* by Arthur Byron Cover
15. *Obsidian Fate* by Diana Gallagher
16. *Return to Chaos* by Craig Shaw Gardner
17. *Sins of the Father* by Christopher Golden
18. *Prime Evil* by Diana G. Gallagher
19. *Resurrecting Ravana* by Ray Garton
20. *Sons of Entropy* by Christopher Golden, Nancy Holder
21. *The Angel Chronicles* by Richie Tankersley
22. *The Dust Waltz* by Daniel Brereton
23. *The Evil That Men Do* by Nancy Holder
24. *The Harvest* by Richie Tankersley Cusick
25. *The Origin* by Christopher Golden
26. *The Remaining Sunlight* by Andi Watson
27. *The Xander Years* by Jeff Mariotte
28. *Unnatural Selection* by Mel Odom
29. *Visitors* by Laura Anne Gilman, Josepha Sherman

THE CARPATHIANS by Christine Feehan

1. *Dark Prince*
2. *Dark Desire*
3. *Dark Gold*
4. *Dark Magic*
5. *Dark Challenge*
6. *Dark Fire*
7. *Dark Legend*
8. *Dark Guardian*

THE DARKANGEL TRILOGY by Meredith Ann Pierce

1. *The Darkangel*
2. *A Gathering of Gargoyles*
3. *The Pearl of the Soul of the World*

THE DIARIES OF THE FAMILY DRACUL by Jeanne Kalogridis

1. *Covenant with the Vampire*
2. *Children of the Vampire*
3. *Lord of the Vampires*

THE EROTIC VAMPIRE SERIES edited by Cecilia Tan

1. *Blood Kiss: Vampire Erotica*
2. *Cherished Blood: Vampire Erotica*
3. *Erotica Vampirica: Sensual Vampire Stories*
4. *A Taste of Midnight: Vampire Erotica*

JONATHAN BARRETT by P.N. Elrod

1. *Red Death*
2. *Death and the Maiden*
3. *Death Masque*
4. *Dance of Death*

LAWS OF THE BLOOD by Susan Sizemore

1. *The Hunt*
2. *Partners*
3. *Companions*

MIDNIGHT ROMANCE SERIES by Nancy Gideon

1. *Midnight Kiss*
2. *Midnight Temptation*
3. *Midnight Surrender*
4. *Midnight Enchantment*
5. *Midnight Gamble*
6. *Midnight Redeemer*
7. *Midnight Shadows*
8. *Midnight Masquerade*

THE NECROSCOPE SAGA by Brian Lumley
Necroscope series
1. *Necroscope*
2. *Necroscope II : Vamphyri!*
3. *Necroscope III : The Source*
4. *Necroscope IV: Deadspeak*
5. *Necroscope V: Deadspawn*
The Vampire World series
1. *Vampire World I: Blood Brothers*
2. *Vampire World II: The Last Aerie*
3. *Vampire World III: Bloodwars*
The Lost Years series
1. *Necroscope: The Lost Years*
2. *Necroscope: Resurgence The Lost Years : Volume II*
E-Branch trilogy
1. *Necroscope: Invaders*
2. *Necroscope: Defilers*
3. *Necroscope: Avengers*

THE VAMPIRE CHRONICLES by Anne Rice
1. *Interview with the Vampire*
2. *The Vampire Lestat*
3. *The Vampire Lestat: A Graphic Novel*
4. *The Queen of the Damned*
5. *The Tale of the Body Thief*
6. *Memnoch the Devil*
7. *The Vampire Armand*
8. *Merrick*
9. *Blood and Gold*

NIGHT WORLD SERIES by L.J. Smith
1. *Secret Vampire*
2. *Daughters of Darkness*
3. *Spellbinder*
4. *Dark Angel*
5. *The Chosen*
6. *Soulmate*
7. *Huntress*
8. *Black Dawn*
9. *Witchlight*
10. *Strange Fate*

NOSFERATU CHRONICLES by Mick Farren
1. *The Time of Feasting*
2. *Darklost*
3. *More Than Mortal*

THE OLIVIA SERIES by Chelsea Quinn Yarbro
1. *Flame in Byzantium*
2. *Crusader's Torch*
3. *A Candle for D'Artagnan*

POWER OF THE BLOOD SERIES by Nancy Kilpatrick
1. *Child of the Night*
2. *Near Death*
3. *Reborn*

RAVENLOFT BOOKS – Various Authors
1. *Vampire of the Mists* by Christie Golden
2. *Knight of the Black Rose* by James Lowder
3. *I, Strahd: The Memoirs of a Vampire* by P.N. Elrod
4. *Tales of Ravenloft* edited by Brian Thomsen
5. *Baroness of Blood* by Elaine Bergstrom
6. *I, Strahd: The War Against Azalin* by P.N. Elrod

SABERHAGEN'S DRACULA by Fred Saberhagen
1. *The Dracula Tape*
2. *The Holmes-Dracula File*
3. *An Old Friend in the Family*
4. *Thorn*
5. *Dominion*
6. *A Matter of Taste*
7. *A Question of Time*
8. *Seance for a Vampire*
9. *A Sharpness on the Neck*

THE SAGA OF DARREN SHAN by Darren Shan
1. *Cirque du Freak: A Living Nightmare*
2. *The Vampire's Assistant*
3. *Tunnels of Blood*
4. *Vampire Mountain*
5. *Trials of Death*

THE SAINT-GERMAIN CHRONICLES by Chelsea Quinn Yarbro
1. *Hotel Transylvania*
2. *The Palace*
3. *Blood Games*
4. *Path of the Eclipse*
5. *Tempting Fate*
6. *The Saint-Germain Chronicles*
7. *Darker Jewels*
8. *Better in the Dark*
9. *Mansions of Darkness*
10. *Writ in Blood*
11. *Blood Roses*
12. *Communion Blood*
13. *Come Twilight*
14. *A Feast in Exile*
15. *Night Blooming*

THE SHADOW SAGA by Christopher Golden
1. *Of Saints and Shadows*
2. *Angel Souls and Devil Hearts*
3. *Of Masques and Martyrs*

SISTERS OF THE NIGHT by Chelsea Quinn Yarbro
1. *The Angry Angel*
2. *Soul of an Angel*

THE TREMAYNE VAMPIRE SERIES by Linda Lael Miller
1. *Forever and the Night*
2. *For All Eternity*
3. *Time Without End*
4. *Tonight and Always*

THE VAMPIRE by Michael Romkey
1. *I, Vampire*
2. *The Vampire Papers*
3. *The Vampire Princess*
4. *The Vampire Virus*
5. *The Vampire Hunter*

VAMPIRE: THE MASQUERADE from White Wolf Publishing
1. *As One Dead*
2. *The Book of Nod*
3. *A Dozen Black Roses*
4. *The Masquerade of the Red Death* trilogy
   a. *Blood War*
   b. *Unholy Allies*
   c. *The Unbeholden*
5. *Pomegranates Full and Fine*
6. *Prince of the City*
Vampire Clan novels
1. *Toreador*
2. *Tzimisce*
3. *Gangrel*
4. *Settite*
5. *Ventrue*
6. *Lasombra*
7. *Ravnos*
8. *Assamite*
9. *Malkavian*
10. *Brujah*
11. *Giovanni*
12. *Tremere*
13. *Nosferatu*

THE VAMPIRE DIARIES by L.J. Smith

1. *The Awakening*
2. *The Struggle*
3. *The Fury*
4. *Dark Reunion*

THE VAMPIRE FILES by P.N. Elrod

1. *Bloodlist*
2. *Lifeblood*
3. *Bloodcircle*
4. *Art in the Blood*
5. *Fire in the Blood*
6. *Blood on the Water*
7. *A Chill in the Blood*
8. *The Dark Sleep*
9. *Lady Crymsyn*

VAMPIRE LEGACY by Karen E. Taylor

1. *Blood Secrets*
2. *Bitter Blood*
3. *Blood Ties*
4. *Blood of My Blood*
5. *The Vampire Vivienne*

VICTORIA NELSON SERIES by Tanya Huff

1. *Blood Price*
2. *Blood Trail*
3. *Blood Lines*
4. *Blood Pact*
5. *Blood Debt*

WINGS IN THE NIGHT by Maggie Shayne

1. *Twilight Phantasies*
2. *Twilight Memories*
3. *Twilight Illusions*
4. *Beyond Twilight*
5. *Born in Twilight*
6. *Twilight Vows*
7. *Twilight Hunger*

FICTION - STAND-ALONE NOVELS

- *Absence of Faith* by E. Carter Jones
- *After Twilight* by Amanda Ashley, Christine Feehan and Ronda Thompson

- *Batman and Dracula* by Doug Moench
- *Bedbugs* by Rick Hautala
- *Beneath a Blood Red Moon* by Shannon Drake
- *The Black Castle* by Les Daniels
- *Blood and Chrysanthemums* by Nancy Baker
- *Blood Covenant* by Mary Lamb
- *Blood Feud* by Sam Siciliano
- *Blood Dreaming: A Collection of Gothic Ku* by Lewis Sanders
- *Blood Hunt* by Lee Killough
- *The Blood of the Covenant* by Brent Monahan
- *The Blood of the Goddess* by William Schindler
- *Blood Memories* by Barb Hendee
- *Blood to Blood* by Elaine Bergstrom
- *Blood Thirst* by L. A. Freed
- *Blood Walk* by Lee Killough
- *Bloodsong* by Karen Marie Christa Minns
- *Bloodsucking Fiends* by Christopher Moore
- *BloodWind* by Charlotte Boyett-Compo
- *Blythe: NightVision* by David Quinn, Hannibal King
- *The Book of Common Dread* by Brent Monahan
- *The Book of the Dark* by William Meikle
- *Bound in Blood* by David Thomas Lord
- *Breed* by Owl Goingback
- *Breeder* by Douglas Clegg
- *Bring on the Night* by Don & Jay Davis

- *Candle Bay* by Tamara Thorne
- *Canyons* by P.D. Cacek
- *Carmilla* by Joseph Sheridan Le Fanu
- *Carmilla: The Return* by Kyle Marffin
- *Carrion Comfort* by Dan Simmons
- *Children of the Night* by Dan Simmons
- *Children of the Night* by Mercedes Lackey
- *The Children's Hour* by Douglas Clegg
- *Come the Night* by Angelique Armae
- *Companions of the Night* by Vivian Vande Velde
- *The Cowboy and the Vampire* by Clark Hays and Kathleen McFaul
- *Crimson Kiss* by Trisha Baker

- *Crimson Night* by Trisha Baker
- *Dancing with the Devil* by Keri Arthur
- *The Dark Blood of Poppies* by Freda Warrington
- *Dark Changeling* by Margaret L. Carter
- *Dark Hunger* by Mayra Calvani
- *Dark Rapture* by Michele Hauf
- *Dark Salvation* by Jennifer Dunne
- *A Darker Dream* by Amanda Ashley
- *The Darkness Therein* by Kate Hill
- *Darkspawn* by Lois Tilton
- *Daughter of Darkness* by Steven Spruill
- *Dawn of the Vampire* by William Hill
- *Dead Until Dark* by Charlaine Harris
- *Deadly Obsession* by Patricia A. Rasey
- *Deep Midnight* by Shannon Drake
- *Deeper than the Night* by Amanda Ashley
- *The Delicate Dependency* by Michael Talbot
- *Demon in My View* by Amelia Atwater-Rhodes
- *Desmond* by Ulysses G. Dietz
- *Doctors Wear Scarlet* by Simon Raven
- *Dracul: An Eternal Love Story* by Nancy Kilpatrick
- *Dracula* by Bram Stoker
- *Dracula Cha Cha Cha* by Kim Newman
- *Dracula the Undead* by Freda Warrington
- *Dracula: A Symphony in Moonlight & Nightmares* by Jon J. Muth
- *Dracula's Tomb* by Colin McNaughton

- *Embrace the Night* by Amanda Ashley
- *Enemy Mine* by Jewell Dart
- *Eye Killers* by A.A. Carr

- *Fevre Dream* by George R. R. Martin
- *Fitcher's Brides* by Gregory Frost
- *The Flesh, the Blood and the Fire* by S. A. Swiniarski

- *Galen* by Allan Gilbreath
- *A Gift of Blood* by JennaKay Francis
- *The Gilda Stories: A Novel* by Jewelle Gomez
- *The Golden* by Lucius Shepard
- *Gothique* by Kyle Marffin
- *The Guardian* by Beecher Smith

- *The Heat Seekers* by Katherine Ramsland
- *His Father's Son* by Nigel Bennett and P.N. Elrod
- *The Hour Before Dawn* by Patricia A. Rasey
- *The Hunger* by Whitley Strieber

- *Hunting Zoe* by Steve Gerlach
- *I Am Dracula* by C. Dean Andersson
- *I Am Legend* by Richard Matheson
- *The Immaculate* by Kate Hill
- *In the Forests of the Night* by Amelia Atwater-Rhodes

- *The Judas Glass* by Michael Cadnum

- *Keeper of the King* by Nigel Bennett and P.N. Elrod
- *Kiss of the Vampire* (a.k.a *The Night Inside*) by Nancy Baker

- *Lady Crymsyn* by P.N. Elrod
- *The Last Vampire* by Whitley Strieber
- *The Last Vampire* by T.M. Wright
- *The Letters of Mina Harker* by Dodie Bellamy
- *Lilith's Dream: A Tale of the Vampire Life* by Whitley Streiber
- *Live Girls* by Ray Garton
- *The London Vampire Panic* by Michael Romkey
- *Living Dead in Dallas* by Charlaine Harris
- *Lord of the Dead* by Tom Holland
- *Lost Souls* by Poppy Z. Brite
- *Love Bite* by Sherry Gottleib
- *Love in the Dark* by Christien Churchill
- *Love Lies Dying* by Steve Gerlach

- *Madonna of the Dark* by Elaine Moore
- *Midnight Embrace* by Amanda Ashley
- *Midnight Predator* by Amelia Atwater-Rhodes
- *Mina: The Dracula Story Continues* by Marie Kiraly
- *Monastery* by Patrick Whalen
- *The Mountain King* by Rick Hautala

- *... never dream* by Scott Charles Adams
- *The Night Inside* (a.k.a. *Kiss of the Vampire*) by Nancy Baker
- *Night Players* by P.D. Cacek
- *Night Prayers: A Vampire Story* by P.D. Cacek
- *Night Thirst* by Patrick Whalen
- *Nightchild: A Clans Novel* by J.A. Cummings
- *The Nocturne* by Steve Gerlach

- *One Foot in the Grave* by Wm. Mark Simmons
- *One With the Hunger* by J. C. Wilder

- *The Pines* by Robert Dunbar
- *The Priest of Blood* by Douglas Clegg
- *Prince of the Night* by Jasmine Cresswell
- *Prince of Dreams* by Susan Krinard

- *Progeny of the Adder* by Leslie H. Whitten
- *Quenched* by Mary Ann Mitchell
- *Quincy Morris, Vampire* by P.N. Elrod

- *Raga Six* by Frank Lauria
- *Rage* by Steve Gerlach
- *Raven* by S.A. Swiniarski
- *Red Moon Rising* by Billie Sue Mosiman
- *Renfield: A Tale of Madness* by Kyle Garrett and Galen Showman
- *The Ruby Tear* by Rebecca Brand
- *Rulers of Darkness* by Steven Spruill

- *'Salem's Lot* by Stephen King
- *Scarabus* by Karen Koehler
- *Sealed in Blood* by Margaret L. Carter
- *Search for a Soul* by Rosemarie E. Bishop
- *The Secret Life of Laszlo, Count Dracula* by Roderick Anscombe
- *Shades of Gray* by Amanda Ashley
- *Shadow's Embrace* by Astrid Cooper
- *Shadows After Dark* by Ouida Crozier
- *Shadows Bite* by Stephen Dedman
- *Shaman Moon* by Owl Goingback
- *Shattered Glass* by Elaine Bergstrom
- *Shattered Mirror* by Amelia Atwater-Rhodes
- *The Silver Kiss* by Annette Curtis Klause
- *Sips of Blood* by Mary Ann Mitchell
- *Slave of My Thirst* by Tom Holland
- *Some of Your Blood* by Theodore Sturgeon
- *Space Vampires (a.k.a. Lifeforce)* by Colin Kapp
- *Soul of the Vampire* by Minda Samiels
- *Stainless* by Todd Grimson
- *Street Hungry* by Bill Kent
- *The Stress of Her Regard* by Tim Powers
- *The Sun Will Find You* by Chris Muffoletto
- *Sunglasses After Dark* by Nancy Collins
- *Sunlight Moonlight* by Amanda Ashley

- *A Taste of Blood Wine* by Freda Warrington
- *A Terrible Beauty* by Nancy Baker
- *They Thirst* by Robert McCammon
- *Thirst* by Michael Cecilione
- *Thirst* by Pyotyr Kurtinski
- *Those of My Blood* by Jacqueline Lichtenberg
- *Those Who Hunt the Night* by Barbara Hambly
- *Traveling With the Dead* by Barbara Hambly
- *Turnbull Bay* by Liberty

- *Unexpected Unexplained: Vampires* by Kristie Lynn Higgins

- *The Vampire Apocalypse: Books One: Revelations* by Katriena Knights
- *The Vampire Journals* by Traci Briery
- *Vampire Junction* by S.P. Somtow
- *The Vampire Memoirs* by Traci Briery
- *Vampire Nation* by Thomas M. Sipos
- *The Vampire Tapestry* by Suzy McKee Charnas
- *The Vampire Viscount* by Karen Harbaugh
- *Vampire Vow* by Michael Schiefelbein
- *The Vampire's Beautiful Daughter* by S.P. Somtow
- *Vampire's Waltz* by Thomas Staab
- *Vampire$* by John Steakley
- *The Vampyre* by John Polidori
- *Vampyrrhic* by Simon Clark
- *Vanitas: Escape from Vampire Junction* by S.P. Somtow
- *Varney the Vampyre; or, The Feast of Blood* by James Malcolm Rymer
- *Vlad Dracula: The Dragon Prince* by Michael Augustyn

- *Walk in Moonlight* by Rosemary Laurey
- *Watchers of the Wall* by William Meikle
- *When Darkness Falls* by Shannon Drake
- *Wicked Angels* by Michele Hauf
- *Worse than Death* by Sherry Gottleib

Photo by Jason Lukridge.

NON-FICTION

- *The Alchemy of Immortality* by P.V.N. Frater
- *American Vampires: Fans, Victims, Practitioners* by Norine Dresser

- *Beginners Guide -- Vampires* by Teresa Moorey
- *Beyond the Highgate Vampire* by David Farrant
- *Blood and Roses: Vampires in 19th Century Literature* edited by Adele O. Gladwell
- *Blood Bound: Guidance for the Responsible Vampire* By Deborah Addington and Vincent Dior
- *The Blood is the Life: Vampires in Literature* by G. Heldreth Leonard and Mary Pharr
- *Blood Lines: The Little Book of Vampires* by Barbara Steward
- *Blood Read* edited by Joan Gordon, Veronica Hollinger & Brian W. Aldiss
- *Bloodlust: Converstaions with Real Vampires* by Carole Page
- *Bloodsucking Witchcraft: An Epistemological Study of Anthropomorphic Supernaturalism in Rural Tlaxcala* by Hugo G. Nutini, John M. Roberts
- *Bloody Countess* by Valentine Penrose
- *The Book of Vampires* by Dudley Wright

- *Channeling the Vampire* by Gary Lynn Morton
- *Children of the Night* by Tony Thorne
- *A Clutch of Vampires* by Robert T. McNally
- *Compleat Vampyre: The Vampyre Shaman, Werewolves, Witchery & the Dark Mythology of the Undead* by Nigel Jackson
- *The Complete Book of Vampires* by Leonard Ashley, R.N.
- *The Complete Idiot's Guide to Vampires* by Jay Stevenson, Ph.D.
- *The Complete Vampire Companion* by Rosemary Ellen Guiley and J. B. MacAbre
- *Countess Dracula* by Tony Thorne

- *The Darkling: A Treatise on Slavic Vampirism* by Jan Louis Perkowski
- *Daughters of Lilith: An Analysis of the Vampire Motif in 19th Century Literature* by Carol A. Senf
- *Dhampir: Child of the Blood* by VW Johnson
- *A Dictionary of Vampires* by Peter Haining
- *Different Blood: The Vampire as Alien* by Margaret L. Carter
- *Digging for Dracula* by John Sean Hillen
- *Do Vampires Exist? A Special Report from Dracula Fan Club* by Jeanne Keyes Youngston
- *The Dracula Book* by Donald F. Glut
- *The Dracula Cookbook of Blood* by Ardin C. Price
- *The Dracula Killer* by Lt. Ray Biondi, Walt Hecox
- *Dracula: The Shade and the Shadow* by Elizabeth Miller

- *Dracula: Sense & Nonsense* by Elizabeth Miller
- *Dracula: The Vampire and the Critics* by Margaret L. Carter
- *Dracula Was a Woman* by Raymond T. McNally
- *The Embrace: A True Vampire Story* by Aphrodite Jones
- *Evolution of the Vampire* by Grant Hetherington

- *Fallen Angels: Demons, Fiends & Spirits of the Dark* by Robert Masello
- *The Fantastic Vampire: Studies in the Children of the Night; Selected Essays from the Eighteenth International Conference on the Fantastic in the Arts* by Greenwood Publishing Group
- *Food for the Dead: On the Trail of New England's Vampires* by Michael E. Bell
- *Forests of the Vampires: Slavic Myth* Charles Phillips & Michael Kerrigan

- *Ghost: Investigating the Other Side* by Katherine Ramsland

- *Hex Files: The Goth Bible* by Mick Mercer
- *The Highgate Vampire* by Sean Manchester
- *The History of Ghosts, Vampires and Werewolves* by Douglas Hill

- *In Pursuit of Premature Gods & Contemporary Vampires* by Stephen Kaplan
- *In Search of Dracula* by Raymond T. McNally & Radu Florescu
- *In Search of Vampires: The History of Dracula and Vampires* by Raymond T. McNally
- *In the Shadow of the Vampire* by Jana Marcus

- *The Life and Deeds of Vlad the Impaler* by Constantin Giurescu
- *Liquid Dreams of Vampires* by Martin V. Riccardo
- *The Living and the Undead* by Gregory Waller
- *Living Dead: A Study of the Vampire in Romantic Literature* by James B. Twitchell
- *The Lure of the Vampire* by Martin V. Riccardo
- *Lust for Blood: The Consuming Story of Vampires* by Olga Gruhzit Hoyt

- *The Monster of Dusseldorf: The Life and Trial of Peter Kurten* by Margaret Seaton Wagner
- *Monsters, Maidens and Mayhem* by Brad Steiger
- *The Mystery of Vampires and Werewolves* by Chris Oxlade

- *The Natural History of the Vampire* by Anthony Masters
- *A Night in Transylvania: The Dracula Scrapbook* by Kurt Brokaw
- *Northern Shadows: An Illustrated Guide to Canadian Vampires* by John Arkelian

- *The Origin of the Vampire: How it All Started* by John Edward Walker
- *Ou Sont Passes Les Vampires?* By Ioanna Andreesco

- *Piercing the Darkness: Undercover with Vampires in America Today* by Katherine Ramsland
- *Politics of Atrocity and Lust: The Vampire Tale as a Nightmare History of England in the 19th Century* by Alok Bhalla
- *Popular Legends* by Mrs. Ellet
- *Porphyria: The Woman Who Has the Vampire Disease* by Tammy Evans
- *Prism of the Night: A Biography of Anne Rice* by Katherine Ramsland
- *Private Files of a Vampirologist: Case Histories & Letters* edited by Jeanne K. Youngson

- *The Quotable Vampire* edited by David Proctor

- *Reading the Vampire* by Ken Gelder
- *Real Vampires* by Daniel Cohen
- *The Really Fearsome Blood-Loving Vampire Bat* by Theresa Greenaway
- *Rebirth of the Undead* by E. Beatty.; D.L. Crabtree
- *Reflections on Dracula* by Elizabeth Miller
- *Return From the Dead* by Douglas Hill

Photo by Jason Lukridge.

- *The Science of Vampires* by Katherine Ramsland.
- *Shadow of a Shade: A Survey of Vampirism in Literature* by Margaret L. Carter
- *Sheridan Le Fanu* by Nelson Browne
- *Something in the Blood* by Jeff Guinn and Andy Grieser
- *Speaking with Vampires: Rumor and History in East and Central Africa* by Luise White
- *Stage Blood: Vampires of the Nineteenth Century Stage* by Dudley Wright
- *The Story of Vampires* by Thomas Aylesworth

- *Terror By Night* by Douglas Hill
- *Transformations* edited by Time-Life Books and Jim Hicks
- *Treatise on Vampires and Revenants* by Dom Augustine Calmet
- *The Trial of John George Haigh* by Lord Dunboyne
- *True Vampires of History* by Donald F. Glut

- *The Undead* by Dickie James
- *Unexplained Unexpected: Vampires* by Kristie Lynn Higgins
- *The Unknown Darkness: Profiling the Monsters Among Us* by Katherine Ramsland and Gregg McClary

- *V Is for Vampire : An A to Z Guide to Everything Undead* by David J. Skal
- *The Vampire: An Anthology* by Ornella Volta
- *The Vampire: A Casebook* by Alan Dundes
- *The Vampire Book: The Complete Encyclopedia of the Undead* by J. Gordon Melton
- *The Vampire Companion: The Official Guide to Anne Rice's "The Vampire Chronicles"* by Katherine Ramsland
- *The Vampire, Dracula and Incest: The Vampire Myth, Stoker's Dracula, and Psychotherapy of Vampiric Sexual Abuse* by Daniel Lapin
- *The Vampire Encyclopedia* by Matthew E. Bunson
- *The Vampire Gallery* by J. Gordon Melton
- *The Vampire Hunter's Handbook* by Sean Manchester
- *The Vampire in Europe: True Tales of the Undead* by Montague Summers
- *Vampire Informania* by Martin Jenkins
- *The Vampire in Human Form: A Study in Depravity* by R.M. Eberling
- *The Vampire: In Legend & Fact* by Basil Copper
- *The Vampire in Literature: A Critical Bibliography* by Margaret L. Carter and Robert Scholes
- *The Vampire Interview Book: Conversation with the Undead* by Edward Gross; Marc Shapiro
- *The Vampire Killers* by Clifford L. Linedecker
- *The Vampire Lectures* by Laurence A. Rickels
- *Vampire Legends in Contemporary American Literature: What Becomes a Legend Most* by William Patrick Day
- *The Vampire of Tradition: A Casebook* edited by Alan Dundes
- *The Vampire Omnibus* edited by Peter Haining
- *Vampire: The Complete Guide to the World of the Undead* by Manuela Dunn-Mascetti
- *Vampires* by Elwood D. Baumann
- *Vampires* by Randy Burgess
- *Vampires* by Nancy Garden
- *Vampires* by Douglas Hill
- *Vampires* by Vincent Hillyer
- *Vampires* by Bernhardt T. Hurwood
- *Vampires Almanac* by Robert Welch
- *Vampires and Vampirism* by Dudley Wright
- *Vampires & Werewolves? Mysterious Monster of the Past* by Paul Hugli
- *Vampires: Blood Suckers from Beyond the Grave (Strange But True Stories)* by Rowan Wilson
- *Vampires, Burial & Death: Folklore & Reality* by Paul Barber

- *Vampires: Emotional Predators Who Want to Suck the Life Out of You* by Daniel and Kathleen Rhodes
- *Vampires in the Carpathians* by Petr Bogatyrev, Stephen Reynolds, Patricia Ann Krafcik, Bogdan Horbal
- *Vampires, Mummies and Liberal: Bram Stoker and the Politics of Popular Fiction* by David Glover
- *Vampires, Myths & Mysteries* by Vincent Hillyer
- *Vampires or Gods?* by William Meyers
- *Vampires: Restless Creatures of the Night* by Jean Marigny
- *Vampires, Werewolves and Ghouls* by Douglas Hill
- *Vampires, Werewolves & Demons* by Lynn Myring
- *Vampires, Werewolves & Demons: Twentieth Century Reports in the Pshychiatric Literature* by Richard Noll
- *Vampires and Other Creatures of the Night* by Rita Golden Gelman
- *Vampire Hunter's Guide to New England* by Christopher Rondina
- *Vampire in Verse: An Anthology* by Steven Moore
- *Vampire Legends of Rhode Island* by Christopher Rondina
- *Vampire Readings: An Annotated Bibliography* by Patricia Altner
- *Vampires Among Us* by Rosemary Ellen Guiley
- *Vampires and Other Ghosts* by Thomas Aylesworth
- *Vampires and Vampirism: Legends from Around the World* by Dudley Wright
- *The Vampire's Bedside Companion* by Peter Underwood
- *Vampires, Burial & Death: Folklore & Reality* by Paul Barber
- *Vampires: Encounters with the Undead* by David J. Skal
- *Vampires of the Slavs* by Jan L. Perkowski
- *Vampires: Restless Creatures of the Night* by Jean Marigny, translated by Lory Frankel
- *Vampires: The Occult Truth* by Konstantinos
- *Vampires Unearthed* by Martin V. Riccardo
- *Vampires Unstaked: National Images, Stereotypes and Myths in East Central Europe* by A. Gerrits
- *Vampires, Zombies and Monster Men* by Daniel Farson
- *Vampirism and Sadism* by Phillip Terry
- *Vampirism: A Sexual Study* by Phillip Carden
- *Vampirism: Literary Tropes of Decadence and Entropy* by Michael James Dennison
- *Vampiro: The Vampire Bat in Fact and Fantasy* by David E. Brown
- *The Vampyre: A Bedside Companion* by Christopher Frayling
- *The Vampyre's Almanac* by Father Sebastian
- *Vampyres: Lord Byron to Count Dracula* by Christopher Frayling
- *Visions of the Fantastic* by Allienne Becker

- *Werewolf and Vampire in Romania* by Harry Senn
- *The Witches' Companion: THe Official Guide to Anne Rice's "Lives of the Mayfair Witches"* by Katherine Ramsland

EARLY EUROPEAN VAMPIRE NON-FICTION
A CHRONOLOGICAL LISTING
Compiled and Provided by Melinda K. Hayes.
Information from Melinda Hayes' *Vampire Resource Page* and
Vampiri Europeana Page. Used by permission of Melinda Hayes,
(c) Copyright Melinda Hayes 2003.
(http://isd.usc.edu/~melindah/vampire.htm)

Revised by Jill S. Katz

1. Neubirge, Wilhelm. Rerum anglie, 12--?

2. Die Geschicht Dracole Waide. Nuremberg, Germany: Wagner, 1488. Anonymous German printed pamphlet.

3. Ein wünderliche und erschröliche Hystorie. Bamberg, Germany: Hans Spörer, 1491.

4. Bonfini, Antonius. Rerum Hungaricarum decades tres. Basel, Switzerland, 1543.

5. Bonfini, Antonius. Rerum Hungaricarum decades tres. Basel, Switzerland, 1545.

6. Kosmograffia zeska: to jest gyisanij o polozenii krajin neb ziemij y obyciejijch naroduow wseh swieta. Prague, Czech Republich, 1554.

7. Bonfini, Antonius. Rerum Hungaricarum decades tres. Cluj, Romania, 1561.

8. Böhm, Martin. Chronik von Lauban a. a., 1567.

9. Bonfini, Antonius. Rerum Hungaricarum decades tres. Basel, Switzerland, 1568.

10. Cureo, Joachimo. Gentis Sileziae annales contexti ex antiquitate sacra et scriptis recentioribus a Joachimo Cureo, Wetten-Friestadiensi. Wittenberg, Germany, 1571.

11. Bonfini, Antonius. Rerum Hungaricarum decades tres. Basel, Switzerland, 1575.

12. Wier, Joannis. De lamiis liber: item de commentitiis ieiuniis. Cum Rerum ac verborumcopioso indice. Basil, Switzerland: ex Officina Oporiniana, 1577.

13. Bonfini, Antonius. Rerum Hungaricarum decades tres. Frankfurt am Main, Germany, 1581.

14. Lonicer, Philippus, Editor. Theatrum historicum des Andreas Hondrof. Frankfurt am Main, Germany, 1590.

15. Hajek, Václav. Böhmische Chronica des Wenceslai Hagecii. Prague: A. Weidlich, 1596.

16. Böhm, Martin. "Vom Schmätzen im Grabe," in Die drei grossen Landtplagen: 23 Predigten erkleret durch Martinum Bohemum Laubanensum, predigern daselbst, by: Böhm, Martin. Wittenberg, Germany: 1601.

17. Pietro Luccari, Giacomo de. Copioso ristretto degli annali de Ragusa. Venice, Italy, 1605.

18. Lojerus, Petrus. Discours et histoire des spectres. Paris, France, 1608.

19. Kornmann, Heinrich. Henrici Kormanni ex Kirchajina de miraculis mortuorum. Typis Joannis Wolfii, sumptibus Joannis Jacobi Porsii, 1610.

20. Pico della Mirandola, Johannes Francisci. Strix seu de ludificatione daemonum dialogi tres. Strasbourg, France, 1612.

21. Praetorius, Johannes. Anropodemus Plutonicus, das ist, eine neue Weltbeschreibung, von allerley wunderbaren Menschen. Magdeburg, 1668.

22. Rohr, Philippus. Dissertatio historico-philosphico de masticatione mortuorum, quam dei superiorum induitu, in illustri Academ. Lips. sistent praeses M. Philippus Rohr & respondens Benjamin Frizschius, [24] p., 4°. Leipzig, Germany: Typis Michaelis Vogtii, 1679.

23. Mencke, Johann Buchard. Acta eruditorum Latina. Leipzig, Germany: 1682, 1712, 1722.

24. Roch, Heinrich. Neue Laussitz-Böhm- und Schlesische Chronica. Leipzig, Germany: bey Johann Herborde Klossen, 1687.

25. Valvasor, Johann Weidchard Freyherr von. Topographia Carolinae: mit Zusätzen und Anmerkungen v. Ersamus Francisci, die Here des Herzogtums Crain. Laibach, 1689.

26. Bonfini, Antonius. Historia pannonica. Cologne, Germany: sumptibus haeredum Joannis Widenfeldt & Godefridi de Berges, 1690.

27. Mercure historique et politique (Le Haye). 1693.

28. Mercure galant (Paris). Vol. 5. 1694.

29. "Die Gespenster von Freundthal," in Curiöser Geschichtskalender des Herzogtums Schlesien. Leipzig, Germany: 1698.

30. Henel ab Hennenfeld, Nicolaus. Silesiographia renovata. Editor: Fibiger, M. J. Breslau, 1704.

31. Schertz, Karl Ferdinand Frh. von. Magia posthuma. Olmütz, 1706.

32. Grossgebauer, Philipp. Schediasmate de esu mortuorum, von dem Schmatzen der Toten. Weimar, Germany, 1708.

33. Garmann, Christoph. L. Christ. Frid. Garmanni ... de miraculis mortuorum libri tres. Dresden; Leipzig, Germany, 1709.

34. Dlugosz, Jan. Historia polonica. Frankfurt, Germany, 1711.

35. Academiae Caesareo-Leopoldinae naturae curiosorum ephemerides. Vol. centuriae 1-10. Frankfurt am Main; Leipzig, Germany: 1712.

36. Dlugosz, Jan. Historia polonica, vol. 2. Leipzig, Germany, 1712.

37. Tournefort, Joseph Pitton de. Voyage du Levant (A voyage into the Levant), 1717.

38. Tournefort, Joseph Pitton de. Relation d'un Voyage du Levant, fait par ordre du roi, contenant. Amsterdam, Netherlands: aux dépens de La Compagnie, 1718.

39. "Gespräche von neuen und alten Staats-Angelegenheiten," in Der europäische Niemand, welcher Niemanden zu beleidigen, Jedermann aber nützlich zu sein beflissen ist, etc., no. 2 (1719).

40. Sammlung von Natur- und Medicin: Geschichten, an Licht gestellt von einigen Breslauischen Medicis. Breslau, 1719.

41. Rzaczynski, Gabriel. "Tractat XIV: Extraordinaria mortuorum adducens," Sandomir: Typis Collegii Soc. Jesu, 1721.

42. Rzaczynski, S. J. "Der polnische Upier," in Naturgeschichte des Königreichs Polen, by: Rzaczynski, S. J. Sandomir: 1721.

43. Leipziger Zeitung. 1725.

44. Ranfft, Michael. De masticatione mortuorum in tumulis. Leipzig, Germany, 1725.

45. Rzazynsky, Gabriel. Historia naturalis curiosa regni Poloniae. Sendomir, 1721.

46. Wienerisches Diarium. Vol. 58, 13. Vienna, Austria: July 21, 1725, February 13, 1732.

47. "Lipsia literata, vel relationes dissertationum in academia lipsiensi evulgatarum," in Fortgesetzte Sammlung von alten und neuen theologischen Sachen (1726).

48. Sammlung von Natur- und Medicin- wie auch hierzu gehörigen Kunst- und Literatur- Geschichten, so sich an. 1725. Leipzig; Breslau: Verlegts David Richter, 1727.

49. Ranfft, Michael. De masticatione mortuorum in tumulis Leipzig, Germany, 1728.

50. Turóczi, Laszlo. Ungaria suis cum Regibus compendio data, 1729.

51. Stein, Otto zum Graf. "Dialog über das Schmatzen der Todten," in Reiche der Geister, by: Stein, Otto zum Graf. Leipzig, Germany: 1730.

52. Stein, Otto zum Graf. "Die Geschichte von Asvitus und Asmundus," in Reiche der Geister, by: Stein, Otto zum Graf, 1730.

53. Stein, Otto zum Graf. Otto Graffens zum Stein Unterredungen von dem Reiche der Geister (Diologi menstrui in spiritum regnum habitorum). Leipzig, Germany, 1730.

54. Acten-Mässige. Umständliche Realition von denen Vampiren oder Menschen-Saugern. Leipzig, Germany, 1732.

55. "Ad relationem Fliningerianam." Est. 1732.

56. "Anonymi Cogitationes de mortuis viventium tyrannis vulgo dictis, sive de Vampyrismo plurmarum in Europa orientalie sitarum regionum morbo endemio," in Commercium Litterarium, Editors: Götz, Johann Christoph, Schultz, Johann Heinrich, and Treu, Christoph Jacob, vol. Hebd. 22. Nuremberg, Germany: 1732.

57. Auserlesene theologische Bibliotec, oder gründliche Nachrichten von denen neuesten und besten theologischen Büchern und Schrifften, pt. 62. Leipzig, Germany, 1732.

58. Blochbergern, Michael. Eines Weimarischen Medici mutmäßliche Gedanken von denen Vampyren oder sogenannten Blut-Saugern, welchen zuletzt das Gutachten der Königlichen Preußischen Societät derer Wissenschaft von gedachten Vampyren mit beigefügtet ist. Leipzig, Germany, 1732.

59. Colerus, Johann Christoph. Auserlesen Theologische Bibliotheck, oder gründliche Nachrichten von denen neusten und besten Theologischen Büchern und Schrifften. Vol. 62, 69. Leipzig: 1732.

60. Crell, Johann Christian, Editor. Remarquable curieuse Briefe, oder deutliche Beschreibung Alter und Neuer merckwürdiger Begebenheiten, die sich hin und wider guten Theils im Churfürstentum Sachsen und incorporirten Landen zugetragen, 137 couvert. Leipzig, Germany, 1732.

61. Demelius, Christoph Friedrich. Philosophischer Versuch, ob nicht die merkwürdige Begebenheit derer Blutsauger in Niederungarn, anno 1732 geschehen, aus denen principiis naturae, ins besondere aus der sympathia rerum naturalium und denen tribus facultatibus hominis könne erleutert werden. Weimar, 1732.

62. Dieterich, Albert. Dissertatio physica de cadaueribus sanguisugis, sub praesidio Jon. Christ. Stockii. Jena, 1732.

63. Eudoxo. Auserlesene Theologische Bibliothek oder gründliche Nachrichten von neusten und besten Theologischen Büchern und Schriften, pt. 62 and 69. Leipzig, Germany, 1732.

64. Franckfurter Zeitungen dieses Jahrs. Vol. 38. 1732.

65. Freundt de Weyenberg, Johann Jacob. Laurea Medica, id est: inauguratio septem medicinae doctorum Vienae habita in divi Stephani proto-martyris Metropolitana coram Senatu populóque Academico, Excellentissimo, Reverendissimo, Illustrissimo ac Amplissimo auditorio. Promotore Joanne Jacobo Freundt de Weyenberg... Decano. Die XII. Novembris Anno MDCCXXXII. Vienna, Austria: typis Andreae Heyinger, Universitatis Typogr., 1732.

66. Fritsch, Johann Christian. Eines Weimarische Medici muthmassliche Gedancken von denen Vampyren, oder sogenannten Blut-Saugern. Leipzig, Germany, 1732.

67. Geelhausen, Johann Jacob. "An Johann Christoph Götz, Wien 9. 4. 1732," in Commercium litterarium, (Nuremberg), editors: Götz, Johann Christoph, Schultz, Johann Heinrich, and Treu, Christoph Jacob, no. 18. Nuremberg, Germany: 1732.

68. Geistliche Fama mitgringend einige neuere nachrichten von göttlichen Gericht, Wegen Führungen und Erweckungen. Sarden, 1732.

69. Glaser, Johann Friedrich. "An Johann Christoph Götz, Wien 13. 2. 1732," in Commercium litterarium, (Nuremberg), editors: Götz, Johann Christoph, Schultz, Johann Heinrich, and Treu, Christoph Jacob, no. 11. Nuremberg, Germany: 1732.

70. Götz, Johann Christoph, Schultz, Johann Heinrich, and Treu, Christoph Jacob, Editors. Commercium litterarium ad rei medicae et scientiae naturalis incrementum institutum quo quicquid novissime observatum agitatum scriptum vel peractum est succinte dilucideque exponitur. Accedunt praefatio et indies necesarii. Nuremberg, Germany: Sumptibus Societatis Litteris Io. Ernest. Adelbulneri, 1732.

71. Joerdens, Christian Friedrich. "Meditationes extemporales super relatione de vampyrs serviae," in Commercium litterarium, editors: Götz, Johann Christoph, Schultz, Johann Heinrich, and Treu, Christoph Jacob, no. 28. Nuremberg, Germany: 1732.

72. Kramer, Johann Georg Heinrich. "Cogitationes de vampyris serviensibus," in Commercium litterarium, editors: Götz, Johann Christoph, Schultz, Johann Heinrich, and Treu, Christoph Jacob, no. 37. Nuremberg, Germany: 1732.

73. Liberius, Arnold. Neueröffnete Welt- und Staats- Theatrum, welches die in allen Theilen der Welt, sonderlich aber in Europa vorfallenden Staats- und Kriegs- und Freidensaffären ... hinlänglich erläutert. Erfurt: 1732.

74. Loescher, Valentin Ernst. Fortgesetzte Sammlung von alten und neuen theologischen Sachen. Leipzig, Germany: 1732, 1736, 1739, 1746.

75. Martini, Augusto. Actenmäßige und umständliche Relation von denen Vampyren oder Menschen-Saugern, welche sich in diesem und vorigen Jahren im Königreich Servien hervorgethan; nebst einem Raisonnement darüber, und einem Sendschreiben eines Officiers, des Printz-Alexanderischen Regiments aus Medvedia in Servien, an einen berühmten Doctorem der Universität Leipzig. Leipzig, Germany, 1732.

76. Nieder-Sächsische Gelehrten-Zeitungen. 1732.

77. Pohl, Johannes Christophorus and Hertel, Johann Gottlob. Dissertatio de hominibus post mortem sanguisugis, vulgo sic dictis vampyren, auctoritate inclyti philosophorum ordinis publico eruditorum examini die xxx aug. an. MDCCXXXII. submittent M. Io. Christophorus Pohlius, Lignicens. Silesius et Io. Gottlob Hertelius, philos. et med. stud., Langenheimii. Leipzig, Germany, 1732.

78. Putoneus [Johann Christoph Meinig]. Besondere Nachrichten, von denen Vampyren oder sogenannten Blutsaugern, wobei zugleich die Frage: Ob es möglich, daß verstorbene Menschen wiederkommen, den Lebendigen durch Aussaugung des Bluts den Tod zuwege bringen, und dadurch ganze Dörffer und Menschen und Vieh ruiniren können? gründlich untersucht worden von Putoneo. Leipzig, Germany, 1732.

79. Relationis historicae semestralis autumnalis continuatio, Jacobi Franci Historische Beschreibungen. Frankfurt am Main, Germany: 1732.

80. Rohlius, Joh. Chph. and Hertelius, Jo. Glo. Diss. de hominibus post mortem sanguisugis, vulgo dictis Vampyren. Leipzig, Germany, 1732.

81. "Schreiben eines guten Freundes an einen andern guten Freund (Epistola ab amico ad amico etc.), die Vampyren betreffend, (...) sammt einer Beylage fernern Gutachtens sub signo (Ring mit Punkt), 26. 3. 1732," in Commercium litterarium (Nuremberg), editors: Götz, Johann Christoph, Schultz, Johann Heinrich, and Treu, Christoph Jacob, no. XXII. Nuremberg, Germany: 1732.

82. Stein, Otto zum Graf. Graffens zum Stein unverlohrnes Licht, und Recht derer Todten unter den Lebendigen, oder gründlicher Beweiß der Erscheinung der Todten unter den Lebendigen, und was jene vor ein Recht in der obern Welt über dieses noch haben könne, untersucht in Ereigung der vorfallenden Vampyren, oder sogenannten Blut-saugern im Königreich Servien und anderen Orten in diesen und vorigen Zeiten. Berlin; Leipzig, Germany, 1732.

83. "Der Todten Essen und Trincken," in Geistliche Fama, mitbringend verschiedene Nachrichten und Begebenheiten von göttlichen Erweckungen, Wegen, Führungen und Erweckungen, editor: Dippel, Johann Conrad, vol. Sammelband 1733. Sarden: 1732.

84. Visum et repertum über die so genannten Vampirs, oder Blut-Aussauger, so zu Medwgia in Servien, an der Türckischen Granitz, den 7. Januarii 1732 geschehen. Nuremberg, Germany, 1732.

85. Vogt, Gottlob Heinrich. Kurtzes Bedencken von den acten-mäßigen Relationen wegen deren Vampiren, oder Mensch- und Vieh-Aussaugern ingleichen über das davon in Leipzig herausgekommene Raisonnement vom Welt-Geiste, an gute Fruende gesandt von Gottlob Heinrich Vogt. Leipzig, Germany: August Martini, 1732.

86. "Von dem Königreich Servien in Ober-Hungarn," Verlegts Carl Friedrich Jungnicol, Buchhändler und Buchdrucker, 1732.

87. "Von denen im Königreich Servien von neuen wieder verspührten Vampiren, oder so genannten Menschen-Saugern," Erfurt, Germany: Verlegts Carl Friedrich Jungnicol, Buchdrucker und Buchhändler, 1732.

88. W. S. G. E. Curieuse und sehr wunderbare Relation, von denen sich neuer Dingen in Servien erzeigenden Blut-Saugern oder Vampyrs, aus authentischen Nachrichten mitgetheilet, und mit historischen und philosphischen Reflexionen beglietet von W.S.G.E. S.l.: s.n., 1732.

89. Lettres historiques et politiques (le Haye), vol. 92 (February 1732).

90. "Gutachten," in Vampyren oder Blut-Aussaugern, editor: Königlichen Preussischen Societät derer Wissenschafften. Berlin, Germany: March 11, 1732.

91. Mercure de France. Paris, France: May 1732.

92. Stock, Johannes Christianus. Dissertatio physica de cadaveribus sanguisugis, i.e. von denen sogenannten Vampyren oder Menschen-Säugern. Jena, Germany, May 13, 1732.

93. Gazette d'Amsterdam. Vol. 44. Amsterdam: May 30, 1732.

94. Burchard, Johann and Mencke, Freidrich Otto. Neuer Zeitungen von gelehrten Sachen des Jahres. Leipzig, Germany: July 16, 1732, Feb. 26, 1733, June 29, 1733, Oct. 14, 1734, March 19, 1736.

95. Carl, Johann Samuel. "An Johann Christopf Götz, Berlenburg 24. 9. 1732," in Commercium litterarium, Recensio Synoptica (Nuremberg), editors: Götz, Johann Christoph, Schultz, Johann Heinrich, and Treu, Christoph Jacob. Nuremberg, Germany: 1733.

96. Erhard, Balthasar. "An Jacob Christoph Treu," in Commercium litterarium, Recensio Synoptica (Nuremberg), editors: Götz, Johann Christoph, Schultz, Johann Heinrich, and Treu, Christoph Jacob. Nuremberg, Germany: 1733.

97. Fritzsch, Johann Christoph. "An Johann Christoph Götz, Weimar 4. 7. 1732," in Commercium litterarium, (Nuremberg), editors: Götz, Johann Christoph, Schultz, Johann Heinrich, and Treu, Christoph Jacob, no. 32. Nuremberg, Germany: 1733.

98. Gmelin, Johann Conrad. "An Christoph Jacob Treu, Petropolis 1. 11. 1732," in Commercium litterarium, Recensio Synoptica (Nuremberg), editors: Götz, Johann Christoph, Schultz, Johann Heinrich, and Treu, Christoph Jacob. Nuremberg, Germany: 1733.

99. Götz, Johann Christoph, Schultz, Johann Heinrich, and Treu, Christoph Jacob, Editors. Commercium litterarium ad rei Medicae & scientiae naturalis incrementum institutum, quo, quicquid novissime observatum, agitatum, scriptum vel peractum est, exponitur 1731 und 1732. Nuremberg, Germany, 1733.

100. Harenberg, Johann Christoph. Vernünftige und christliche Gedancken über die Vampirs oder bluhtsaugende Todten, so unter den Türcken und auf den Grenzen des Servien-Landes den lebenden Menschen und Viehe das Blut aussaugen sollen, begleitet mti allerley theologischen, philosophischen und historischen aus dem Reiche der Geister hergeholten Anmerckungen und entworffen von Johann Christoph Harenberg, Rector der Stiffts-Schule zu Gandersheim. Wolffenbütel, Germany, 1733.

101. Sarganeck, Georg. "An Christoph Jacob Treu, 9. 6. 1732," in Commercium litterarium, Recensio Synoptica (Nuremberg), editors: Götz, Johann Christoph, Schultz, Johann Heinrich, and Treu, Christoph Jacob. Nuremberg, Germany: 1733.

102. Segner, Johann Andreas. "Brief an Johann Christoph Götz," in Commercium litterarium, Recensio Synoptica (Nuremberg), editors: Götz, Johann Christoph, Schultz, Johann Heinrich, and Treu, Christoph Jacob. Nuremberg, Germany: 1733.

103. Zopf, Johann Heinrich. Dissertatio de vampyris serviensibus quam supremi numinis auspicio praeside M. Joanne Henr. Zopfio gymnasii assindiensis directore, publice defendet, responens Christianus Fridericus van Dalen, Emmericensis. Duisburg ad Rhenum: Johannis Sas, 1733.

104. Albrecht, D. Johann Wilhelm. Tractat. de effectibus musices in corpus animatum, 1734.

105. Camuzat, Denis François. Histoire critique des journaux. Amsterdam, Netherlands: J. F. Bernard, 1734.

106. Kottwitz, Alexander Frhr. von. "An Michael Ernst Ettmüller, Belgrad 26. 1. 1732," in Tractat von dem Kauen und Schmatzen der Todten in Gräbern, worin die wahre Beschaffenheit derer Hungarischen Vampyrs und Blut-Sauger gezeigt, auch alle von dieser Materie bißher zum Vorschein gekommene Schrifften recensiert werden, by: Ranfft, Michael. Leipzig, Germany: Teubners Buchladen, 1734.

107. Ranfft, Michael. Tractat von dem Kauen und Schmatzen der Todten in Gräbern, worin die wahre Beschaffenheit derer hungarischen Vampyrs und Blut-Sauger gezeigt, auch alle von dieser Materie bißher zum Vorschein gekommene Schrifften recensiert werden, [10], 291, [11] p. 8°. Leipzig, Germany: Teubners Buchladen, 1734.

108. Bel, Matthias. Adparatus ad Historiam Hungariae, sive collectio miscella, Monumentorum ineditorum partim, partim editorum, sed fugientum. Conquisiuit, in Decades partitus est, & Praefationibus, atque Notis illustrauit. Sumtu Philohistorum Patriae. Posonii: Typis Joannis Paulii Royer, 1735.

109. Geyer, Johann Daniel. Müßiger Reise-Stunden gute Gedancken von denen Todten Menschen-Saugern an die hochpreißlichen Praesidem und Collegas S.R.I. Academiae Naturae Curiosorum. Dresden, Germany: bei Gottlob Christian Hilschern, 1735.

110. Závodsky, Georg. "Diarium rerum per Hungariam, ad anno MDLXXXVI, usque ad annum MDCXXIV," in Apparatus ad Historiam Hungariae, editor: Bel, Matthias, pp. 350-380. Posonii: Typis Joannis Paulli Royer, 1735.

111. Argens, Jean-Baptiste de Marquis d'. Lettre juives ou correspondance philosphique, historique, et critique, entre un juif voyageur à Paris & ses correspondans en divers endroits, chez Pierre Paupie. la Haye, France, 1736.

112. Mercure historique et politique (Le Haye). Vol. 101. 1736.

113. Tharsander. "Die Vampyren und schmatzende Todten," Berlin; Leipzig, Germany: Ambrosius Haude, 1736.

114. Ad nova acta euridoturm quae Lipsieae publicantur supplementa. Leipzig, Germany, 1737.

115. Hellmund, Günther. "Judicium necrophagiae, das Gericht derer Todten-Fresser und Blut -Sauger (Vampyrs)," in Unbekannte Gerichte Gottes. Frankfurt am Main, Germany: 1737.

116. Schlesische historisches Labyrinth Breslau; Leipzig, Germany: Bey Michael Hubert, 1737.

117. Stebler, Franz Anton Ferdinand. "Sub vampyri, aut sanguisugae larva a verae philosophiae et rationalis medicinae placitis detectum ac dejectum depravatae imaginationis spectrum," in Acta Academia Naturae curiosae. Nuremberg, Germany: 1737.

118. Argens, Jean-Baptiste de Marquis d'. Aaron Monceca, an Isaak Onis, einen Caraiten, und ehemaligen Rabbi von Constantinopel. London, England, 1738.

119. Argens, Jean-Baptiste de Marquis d' and Paupie, Pierre. Lettres juives ou correspondance philosophique, histoirque, et critique, entre un juif voyageur à Paris & ses correspondans en divers endroits. new, augmented ed. la Haye, France, 1738.

120. Harenberg, Johann Christoph. "Vernünftige und christliche Gedancken über die Vampirs oder bluhtsaugende Todten, so unter den Türcken und auf den Grenzen des Servien-Landes den lebenden Menschen und Viehe das Blut aussaugen sollen, begleitet mti allerley theologischen, philosophischen und historischen aus dem Reiche der Geister hergeholten Anmerckungen und entworffen von Johann Christoph Harenberg, Rector der Stiffts-Schule zu Gandersheim," in Supplem ad vixu Erudit lips an 1738 (Leipzig), vol. 2 (1738).

121. "Auszug zweier Schriften von den Vampyren oder Blut-Saugern in Servien (Putoneus, besondere Nachrichten von denen Vampyren, und Actenmässige &ampc. Relation von denen Vampyren)" Bibliotheca, acta et scripta magica. Gründliche Nachrichten und Urtheile von solchen Büchern und Handlungen welche die Macht des Teufels in leiblichen Dingen betreffen. Zur ehre Gottes, und dem Dienst der Menschen, Editor: Hauber, Eberhard David, vol. 1, no. pt. 10, pp. 702-708. Lemgo: Gedruckten bei Joh. Heinrich Meyer, 1739.

122. "D. Luthers Urtheil von den Vampyren (Tischreden Cap. XXIV fol. 211)," in Bibliotheca, acta et scripta magica. Gründliche Nachrichten und Urtheile von solchen Büchern und Handlungen welche die Macht des Teufels in leiblichen Dingen betreffen. Zur ehre Gottes, und dem Dienst der Menschen, editor: Hauber, Eberhard David, vol. 3, no. 36, p. 794. Lemgo: Gedruckten bei Joh. Heinrich Meyer, 1739.

123. Harenberg, Johann Christoph. Von Vampiren. Wolffenbütel, Germany, 1739.

124. "Nachricht von einem seltsamen Gespenst in Ober-Ungarn," in Bibliotheca, acta et scripta magica. Gründliche Nachrichten und Urtheile von solchen Büchern und Handlungen welche die Macht des Teufels in leiblichen Dingen betreffen. Zur ehre Gottes, und dem Dienst der Menschen, editor: Hauber, Eberhard David, vol. 1, no. pt. 11, pp. 709-719. Lemgo, Germany: Gedruckten bei Joh. Heinrich Meyer, 1739.

125. Charisius, Ludwig Christian. Medicinisches Bedencken von denen Vampyren, oder sogenannten Blutsaugern, ob selbte vorhanden, und die Krafft haben, denen Menschen das Leben zu rauben? Königsberg, February 28, 1739.

126. Argens, Jean-Baptiste de Marquis d' and Paupie, Pierre. Lettres juives, ou correspondance philosophique, histoirque, et critique, entre un juif voïageur en différens Etats de l'Europe, & jes correspondans en divers endroits. nouvelle edition augmenté de XX nouvelles lettres, de quantité de remarques, & de plusieurs figures. la Haye, France: Chez Pierre Paupie, 1742.

Artwork by Robert Patrick O'Brien.

VAMPIRE POETRY

A

· Adams, Mary Beth. ETERNAL LOVE
· Adams, Mary Beth. THE LOVE OF A VAMPIRE
· Aiken, Conrad. THE VAMPIRE
· Alecsandri, Valilie. THE VAMPYRE (STRIGOIGUL)
· Amorosi, Ray. VAMPIRE.
· Ash. KING OF THE APOCALYPSE
· Ashley, Leonard. ENVOY
· Ashley, Professor L.R.N. MY SHADOWS
· Atlas, Kelly Gunter. DARK PRINCE
· Atlas, Kelly Gunter. MY PHANTOM LOVE
· Atlas, Kelly Gunter. NIGHT VISITOR

B

· Baglini, Lisa. ALL WE HAVE, MY DARK KIN, IS EACH OTHER
· Baglini, Lisa. DARK CHILD
· Baglini, Lisa. DREAMSOUL
· Baines, Joanne Q. FOR ETERNITY
· Banks, J.A. EMBRACE
· Barach, Jeffrey A. DENIAL IS SO EASY
· Barnidge, Mary Shen. APPARITION
· Barnidge, Mary Shen. VAMPIRE
· Barreca, Regina. DRACULA'S WIVES
· Baudelaire, Charles Pierre, LE VAMPIRE (The vampire), in Les fleurs du Mer (The Flowers of Evil)
· Baudelaire, Charles. METAMORPHOSIS OF THE VAMPIRE.
· Beheim, Michael, GEDICH OVER THE WAYVODEN II DRAKUL
· Behrens, Richard David. THE GATE
· Bellero, Antonia T. BLOOD SONG
· Beret, Renee. THE HEART JARS LOOSE
· Bettridge, Michael G. THE BRIDES OF NOSFERATU
· Blood, Drucilla. BLOOD DREAM
· Blood, Drucilla. IN THE VELVETEEN SHADOWS
· Bluth, Bertha. CHILDREN OF ELVES
· Bobrowski, Johannes, IN THE EMPTY MIRROR
· Bond, Alex. BETTER LUCK NEXT TIME
· Bornstein, Linda. NIGHTIE CLAD VIRGIN
· Bosler, Renee. LIKE THAT STORY I READ ONE TIME
· Bosler, Renee. NIGHT II
· Brautigam, Richard. VAMPIRE

- Breiding, G. Sutton. JOURNAL VAMPIRE
- Brekke, Kristine. CARMILLA
- Brekke, Kristine. CRYING BLOOD
- Brekke, Kristine. EXISTENT DREAM
- Brekke, Kristine. THE CANDY SHOP
- Brennan, Carl. BRIDGETTE'S LOVER
- Brennan, Carl. BRIGETTE
- Brown, Joey. THE NIGHT WIND
- Brown, Natalie. NIGHT OF DARKNESS
- Brown, Natalie. THE DREAM OF THE VAMPIRE
- Buburuz , Cathy. BLOODMATE
- Buburuz , Cathy. LADIES
- Buburuz , Cathy. MIDNIGHT REMINISCENCE
- Buburuz , Cathy. NIGHT CHILD
- Buckaway, C.M. VAMPIRE SEQUENCE
- Burger, Gottfried August. LENORA
- Byars, Anne S. BECKONED FROM THE MIST
- Byars, Anne S. I AM THE DARKNESS
- Byron, George Lord, NEVERTHELESS YOU
- Byron, Lord George Gordon. THE GIAOUR

C
- Carey, Fran. NEVER FORGIVIN
- Carisle, Johann. LOVEPAIN OF ETERNAL NIGHT
- Carter, John. BLACK WIDOW
- Carter, John. LADY DEATH
- Carter, Lin. WALPURGISNACHT
- Carter, M.L. THE AMNESIA VICTIM
- Carter, M.L. THE IMMORTAL COUNT
- Carter, Margaret L. LOVER'S PARTING
- Carter, Margaret L. MEMO TO PROFESSOR WEYLAND
- Carter, Margaret L. THE AMNESIA VICTIM REMEMBERS
- Carter, Margaret L. THE VAMPIRE COUNTESS' LOVE SONG
- Carthers III, Thurmond J. I WANT TO
- Cassandra. BREATHLESS
- Catalyst, Clint. IN THE CEMETERY
- Chiez-Gothe, Vanese. THE VAMPYRE PRINCE
- CHILDREN OF THE NIGHT
- Clark, Terry Don. EVIL IN THE CITY
- Clark, Terry Don. BLUES
- Clark, Terry Don. THE BEATNIK
- Clark, Terry Don. THE DEVIL'S CHILD

· Delacroix, Vanyell. DAMNING EVIDENCE
· Delacroix, Vanyell. REFLECTIONS
· Delacroix, Vanyell. IMMORTAL INCARCERATION
· Delacroix, Vanyell. MY NIGHTLY FARE
· Delacroix, Vanyell. LET ME
· Delacroix, Vanyell. NOSFERATU NIGHT
· Delacroix, Vanyell. THE BLOOD
· Delacroix, Vanyell. ETERNAL ESCAPADE
· Delacroix, Vanyell. LUNACY
· Delacroix, Vanyell. BLOOD ROSE
· Delacroix, Vanyell. ETERNAL LOVE
· Derene, Jeff. DESMOD
· Derenne, Jeff. ACCORDIAN WINGS
· Devor, Danielle. NOSFERATU
· DeWitt, Charles. THE VAMPIRE
· Ditts, Joseph. BLOOD BROTHERS
· Dominie, Fay. AWAKENING
· Dominie, Fay. CHILD OF THE NIGHT
· Dominie, Fay. CRY OF THE VAMPIRE
· Dominie, Fay. EMBRACES
· Dominie, Fay. KISS OF ETERNAL LIFE
· Dominie, Fay. LIPS THAT HIDE
· Donne, Christine. THE COLOR OF DEATH
· Dorf, Carol. DUSK, BENEATH THE BRIDGE
· Dumars, Denise. CARNATIONS
· Dunn, R.S. CONFESSIONS OF DRACULA'S DENTIST
· Dunn, R.S. GRIPE OF THE VAMPIRES
· Dunn, Robert S. AUNTIE SPAM
· Durrell, Lawrence. A WINTER OF VAMPIRES

E
· Eilizabeth, Kim. DARK FATHER.
· Elizabeth, Amy. THE BLOOD OF LIFE
· Elizabeth, Kim. A HEART BEATS BENEATH THE CHASM
· Elizabeth, Kim. AS ONE
· Elizabeth, Kim. BEYOND THE CROSSING OF EREBUS
· Elizabeth, Kim. BORN FROM BLACK LIGHT
· Elizabeth, Kim. EVIL MOON.
· Elizabeth, Kim. FORGIVE ME FATHER
· Elizabeth, Kim. FROM A DEAD GIRL
· Elizabeth, Kim. FROM BENEATH THE TOMB
· Elizabeth, Kim. IMMORTALIZED GODDESS

- Gilbert, Ken. IT'S GOTTA BE THE FULL MOON
- Gilbert, Ken. KNOCK! KNOCK! (WHO'S THERE?)
- Gilbert, Ken. MONSTERS OF HALLOWEEN #.
- Goethe, Johann Wolfgang von, LA FIANCÉE DE CORINTH (The Bride of Corinth)
- Goff, Chris. THE VAMPIRE
- Goldberg, Claudia. NIGHT THIRST
- Goldberg, Claudia. NO LIFE
- Gonzales, Sue. BLOOD DRAINS
- Gorman, Brice P. NIGHT
- Graffeo, Warren. THE IMMORTAL
- Grayton, Alex. CRYPTIC DREAMS
- Grayton, Alex. THE LESSER CHOICE
- Grey, John. AS HE CHANGES
- Grey, John. BEHIND THE IRON CURTAIN
- Grey, John. CHANGES IN LIFESTYLE
- Grey, John. DARK ONE
- Grey, John. ENTERTAINING A NOTION
- Grey, John. GARLIC
- Grey, John. HOLDING YOU
- Grey, John. IN OUR TOWN
- Grey, John. LATEST DATE
- Grey, John. LETTING THE PAST OUT
- Grey, John. LOVE WITH WIRANDA IN LAKE WITHER
- Grey, John. LOVING THE TWO
- Gwydion. NOTE FROM HIS MISTRESS

H
- Hafer, Patrick. CEMETERY CLERGY
- Hagele, Linda. I LONG TO SEE THE SETTING SUN
- Hainesworth, William S. AS LIGHT FADES, AS DARKNESS FALLS
- Hakes, Jana. BLOOD LUST
- Hakes, Jann. AFTERTASTE
- Haldeman, Joe. TIME LAPSE
- Hale, Nathan. LAST LIGHT
- Hale, William. THE KISS
- Hanna, Amy Renee. ISOLATION
- Hanna, Amy Renee. THE SACRIFICE OF LOVE
- Hanna, Amy Renee. GONE
- Hanna, Amy Renee. REALLY OLD, UNTITLED, VAMPIRE POEM
- Harris, Cherie. THE NIGHT HAS BEGUN
- Hartner, Johnny. KISS OF THE VAMPIRE

- Hartwick, Sue-Anne. ETERNAL
- Hartwick, Sue-Anne. ISOLATION
- Hartwick, Sue-Anne. NIGHT SHAPE
- Harwick, Sue-Ann. NIGHT
- Hay, C. David. CEMETERY
- Hay, O. David. NIGHT WATCH
- Hayes-Reese, Cathern. HE HAD TO BE DIFFERENT
- Heffley, Carl. CAT-WINDS
- Heffley, Carl. DWELLERS IN THE DARKNESS
- Heffley, Carl. FRAGMENT
- Heine, Heinrich, DIE BESCHWÖRUNG
- Heliman, Gary. THE DESERTED CASTLE
- Helou, Brenda. THE CHILD
- Henslet, Chad. GRAVEN IMAGE
- Hensley, Chad. BED OF ROSES
- Hensley, Chad. HUNGERING FOR APPARITIONS
- Hewitt, Christopher. THE YOUNG BAT
- Hilbert Jr., Ernie. HIS
- Hilbert, Ernie. MORTAL
- Hinz, Kim. BECOMING
- Hinz, Kim. I SIT HERE SILENT EVERY NIGHT
- Ho Sang, Stephanie and Carolyn. ODE TO IMMORTALITY
- Hobbs, W. C. WHEN THE SUN HIDES ITS FACE
- Hogan, Cathy. FOG
- Hogan, Cathy. HALLOWEEN IS COMING
- Hogan, Cathy. HALLOWEEN
- Hogan, Cathy. NIGHT
- Hogan, Cathy. THE HOUR HAS GONE
- Holzapel, Rudi. SHE'S EXPECTING
- Hood, Robin. BLOOD RAIN
- Hood, Robin. HEARTBURN
- Huffman, Marlys Bradley. FUNERAL WREATH
- Humphries, Dwight E. BLOOD
- Humphries, Dwight E. COME NIGHT
- Humphries, Dwight E. IN DARKNESS

J
- J. THE BALLAD OF THE VAMPIRE STALKING
- Jacob, Charlee. MY LOVE COMES DRESSED ONLY IN ETERNITY
- Jacob, Charlee. THE DARKNESS IS MEDIEVAL IN ALL CENTURIES
- Jansen, Leonard. LIFE/DEATH CYCLE
- Jarrell, Patty. FANTASY

· Jarrell, Randall. HOHENSALZBURG: FANTASTIC VARIATIONS ON A THEME OF ROMANTIC CHARACTER
· Joyce, James. ULYSSES: STEPHEN'S VAMPIRE POEM

K

· Kaplan, Stephen. AMERICAN VAMPIRES
· Keats, John, LA BELLE DAME SANS MERCI
· Keats, John. LAMIA
· Kerr, Walter H. VAMPIRE
· Keyes, Lisa. THE HAPPY VAMPIRES
· Keyes, Margaret C. & Jeanne Youngson. THE VAMPIRE'S LOVE SONG
· Keyes, Margaret G. HICKORY, DICKORY
· Keyes, Margaret G. MAYBE I'M IN THE WRONG BUSINESS
· King, Teresa. BURIED TREASURE
· Kipling, Rudyard. THE VAMPIRE
· Klein, Victor. NECROMANCER'S ENDEAVOR
· Klein, Victor. NETHERSHORE
· Knapp, Ramona. THE VAMPIRE
· Knapp, Ramona. NOT WORTH A TEAR
· Knapp, Ramona. BURNING CITIES
· Knox, Hugh. HE SINGS TO THE LIVING
· Kofmel, Kim. DARK DREAMS
· Kofmel, Kim. NIGHT FLYER
· Kolmar, Gertrud, TROGLODYTIN
· Kowit, Steve. DRACULA
· Kucera, Karl, Elisabeth NÁDASDY

L

· La Borde, Barbara. COUSINS LEAVE COFFINS
· Lace. HE LOOKS INTO MY EYES STARING
· Lady Mej. GIFTS
· Ladfy Mej. EMPTY SHE CRAWLS IN
· Laico, Kim Elizabeth. BLACK X'S.
· Laico, Kim Elizabeth. THE BECKONING.
· Laico, Kim. ALL HALLOWMAS DAY
· Lake, Rhonda. HORROR
· Lake, Rhonda. MOURNING
· Lament. HIDDEN LAYERS
· La Morte, Xela. THE JOY OF MIDNIGHT
· Lander, Tracey. DARKLOVE
· Lane, Misty. DARK MOVEMENTS
· LaPointe, James. FOR THE LOVE OF A VAMPIRE

- Lathrop, Jan. IN MEMORY OF LOUIS V
- Laurencot, Lisa S. COTILLION
- Laurencot, Lisa S. MOONLIGHT SONATA
- Layton, Peter. DEEP THIN
- Leverel, Michelle. LUST IN BLOOD
- Levian, Lotus. FALLEN
- Levian, Lotus. ERA PAST
- Levian, Lotus. FURY
- Liddell, Henry. VAMPIRE BRIDE
- Lifshin, Lyn. MADONNA VAMPIRE
- Louisianax. LOUIS, MY ETERNITY
- Louisianax. EMPATHY
- Louisianax. ELEGAIC
- Louisianax. CRIMSON GLORY
- Louisianax. DARK LIGHT
- Louisianax. RESTLESS BLOOD
- Louisianax. INFERNAL ANGEL
- Louisianax. FINAL SEDUCTION
- Louisianax. DARK ANGEL
- Louisianax. THE INCUBUS
- Louisianax. DARKNESS ETERNAL, UNEARTHLY FIRE
- Louisianax. ETERNIA, SOUL OF NIGHT
- Lovell, Amy. A DRACULA OF THE HILLS
- Lowidski, Witt. A DEAD TEA PARTY.
- Lowidski, Witt. A VISION
- Lowidski, Witt. DRAK BIDS ON HOME OWNERSHIP
- Lowidski, Witt. DRAK FLIES
- Lowidski, Witt. REST ASSURED
- Lowidski, Witt. TRANSITIONAL BIOGRAPHY
- Lunde, David. CARPATHIAN INN
- Lynge, Dan. KINDRED

M
- Malak, Itz. CHILDREN OF THE NIGHT
- Mandelbaum Esq., W. Adam. DISTURBED REST
- Manfredi, Noreen. DEMON
- Markay, Quinten. ANGELIQUE
- Markay, Quinten. GRAVEYARD IN THE RAIN
- Markay, Quinten. MASKS
- Markiewicz, Sheila. FIRST TIME V.
- Marlow, John Robert. MORE THAN HUMAN
- Marra, Sue. VAMPIRE'S CHILD

- Marrick, Louis. MACABRE SONNET
- Martin, Cheryl. THE DEAD DO NOT SLUMBER
- Martin, Lisa Marlene. NIGHTBREED
- Marunycz, Jacki. CRIMSON LAMENT
- Marunycz, Jacki. A CEMETERY AWAKENING
- Maxwell, James Clerk. THE VAMPYRE
- McCarthy, Joanne. THE DREAM
- McCasland, Dallance. EBON & SCARLET
- McCasland, Dallance. LAMIA
- McCellan, Michael W. THE CASTLE
- McClasland, Dallance. INSOMNIA
- McClellan, Michael W. EROGENOUS ZONE
- McCoy, Ranee. DON'T BE AFRAID
- McEntire, Lisa R. LUST FOR BLOOD
- Mérimée, Prosper GUSSLE, ODER AUSGEWÄHLTE ILLYRISCHE DICHTUNGEN
- Merrill, James. A NARROW ESCAPE
- Merwin, W.S. THE INDIGESTION OF THE VAMPIRE
- Mickiewicz, Adam. MY SONG LIES DARKLY IN IT'S TOMB
- Miller, Fern Stephanie. THE CASTLE
- Monargadon, Allician. VAMPIRE METAMORPHISM
- Morgan, Ken. I NEED YOU
- Morgan, Ken. THE NIGHT
- Morse, Jody A. CONFESSION
- Morse, Jody A. PRISONERS OF VAMPIRES
- Ms. Vampire. AWAKENING VAMPIRE
- Ms. Vampire. VAMPIRE
- Ms. Vampire. CALLING
- Ms. Vampire. NIGHTFLYER
- Ms. Vampire. MEMORIES OF A VAMPIRE
- Ms. Vampire. THE VAMPIRES
- Murphy, Shannon K. THE ETERNAL OUTSIDER
- Murphy, Shannon. LOUIS
- Mythical. AS A VAMPIRE AMONG THEM

N
- Neidigh, Kim L. THE CONSUMING
- Neidigh, Kim. THE COLOR RED
- Niedermeier, Rainer Anton, POSTMODERNES
- Norris, Gregory L. BLOODREAMS
- Nottestad, Roy Martin. BLOODLESS
- Nottestad, Roy Martin. MOONCHILD
- Novalis, HINÜBER WALL ICH

O

- Orr, Geregory. THE VAMPIRE
- Ossenfelder, August. THE VAMPIRE
- Ossenfelder, Heinrich August, DER VAMPIR
- Overby, Mark. ANGEL AND THE ROSE
- Owens, W. THE DARK LOVER
- Owens, W. DARKNESS
- Oz, Jane & Amy Bear. THE PRICE, PLEASE
- Oz, Jane. DO VAMPIRES EXIST?
- Oz, Jane. ECSTASY
- Oz, Jane. FOR ADULTS ONLY
- Oz, Jane. IMMORTALITY
- Oz, Jane. LUCY'S FATE
- Oz, Jane. NO ONE WANTS TO DIE
- Oz, Jane. SO SMALL, SO DEAR, SO INNOCENT
- Oz, Jane. THE CURSE OF THE LIVING CLASS

Artwork by Robert Patrick O'Brien.

P

· Paddock, Shelley. NIGHTFIRE
· Palmer, Herbert E. THE VAMPIRE
· Pandora. DOMINI
· Pandora. DROPLETS OF RED
· Pandora. LUST FOR BLOOD
· Pandora. THE LAKE
· Pearson, Sharon. DARKNESS
· Pedrick, Jean. VAMPIRE
· Pepkin, Dusan, KRVAVÉ LÁZNE
· Peters, Robert. THE BLOOD COUNTESS
· Phillips, Kitty. IN OLD NEW ORLEANS
· Pierce, Lisamarie. BLACK AND WHITE SHADOW
· Poe, Edgar Allen. THE SLEEPER
· Pond, Tammy. LONLINESS
· Pond, Tammy. MUSINGS
· Ponzol, Marilyn. DRACULA'S DARK MAJESTY
· Powell, Shirley. LEGIONS OF BATS
· Prelutsky, Jack. THE VAMPIRE
· Puschkin, Alexander, LIEDER DER WESTSLAWEN

R

· Raab, Lawrence. VAMPIRES
· Raab, Lawrence. VOICES ANSWERING BACK: THE VAMPIRES
· Rasnic Tem, Steve. NOCTURNE
· Rathbone, Wendy. A CAREFUL BURNING
· Rathbone, Wendy. FOREPLAY
· Rathbone, Wendy. LOVING IN THE NIGHT
· Rathbone, Wendy. MIRROR FLIGHT
· Rathbone, Wendy. MOON GODDESS
· Rathbone, Wendy. THE NEW DEATH
· Ray, R.R. M.M. AT HOME
· Ray, R.R. ODE TO LUCY
· Rebelledo, Efron. THE VAMPIRE
· Reedman, Janet P. DREAMS
· Resch, Kathleen. A VAMPYRE LEGEND
· Resch, Kathleen. REVENANT
· Reyes-Blanco, Maria. ALONE
· Reyes-Blanco, Maria. GUESS WHO
· Riccardo, Denise. SOFT DESCENT
· Riccardo, Martin V. CRIMSON SAP
· Riccardo, Martin V. DEADPAN
· Riccardo, Martin V. LILITH'S DAUGHTER
· Riccardo, Martin V. MODERN FANGSTER HAIKU

- Scheluchin, Andre. NIGHT SWEATS RED
- Schreiber, John. MY GIRL
- Schreiber, John. MY GIRL
- Schultz, Don. CONSTANCE GREY
- Schultz, Don. THE LUST SUPPER
- Schwader, Ann K. AFTER SECOND WAKING
- Schwader, Ann K. BLACK BUTTERFLIES
- Schwader, Ann K. DARK LADY SUNRISE
- Schwader, Ann K. NINETY-EIGHT POINT SIX
- Schwader, Ann K. NOCTURNE/ABADE
- Schwob, Marcel, KINDERKREUZZUG
- Scognamillo, Giovanni. AND LET US COME TO THE BLOODLAND
- Sessler, Jolene. THE CROSSROADS
- Sessler, Jolene. THE NIGHT
- Sheppard, Monica. HEAVEN'S BLEEDING
- Sheppard, Monica. NEVER ENDING BLOODSONG
- Shifman, Mary. CROSSROADS
- Shifman, Mary. DAYDREAMS
- Shifman, Mary. FLIRTING WITH DEATH
- Shifman, Mary. MATERNAL INSTINCT
- Showalter, David. DESTROY
- Showalter, David. HAND
- Simon, M.B. HITCHWHORER
- Simon, N.M. MIS-STAKES DO HAPPEN
- Smith, Karen J. FATAL CHARM
- Smochina, N, P, ELEMENTE ROMANESTI IN NARATIUNILE SLAVE ASUPRA LUI VLAD TEPES
- Snell, Bertrande Harry. VAMPIRE
- Snodgrass, W.D. VAMPIRE'S AUBADE
- Southey, Robert. THALABA THE DESTROYER
- Spriggs, Nancy. NIGHT TALK
- Stagg Esq., John. VAMPYRE
- Stathis, Nancy. MIDNIGHT HUNGER
- Stefanescu, Elena, AM IESIT OARE (Did I Really Come Out?)
- Stefanescu, Elena, ASA CREZI TU? (Is that What You Think?)
- Stefanescu, Elena, ASTRI AI HAOSULUI (The Heavenly Bodies of Chaos)
- Stefanescu, Elena, CAND ZARESTI APUSUL (When You See the Sunset)
- Stefanescu, Elena, CASTELUL DRACULA (Dracula's Castle)
- Stefanescu, Elena, CAT PUTEM FI DE MICI! (How Small Can We Be?)
- Stefanescu, Elena, CATA DURRERE! (What a pain!)
- Stefanescu, Elena, CE CREZI, DRACULA? (What Do You Think, Dracula?)

- Storm, Sue. NIGHT VISIT
- Storm, Sue. THE LAST VAMPIRE
- Strauch, Michaele. THE HUNT
- Stravropoulos, Stephanie. THE DAY BEFORE WALPURGIS
- Stúr, Karla, Wzteklice DIE BESESSENE
- Sturm, Robbie. BROKEN PROMISES
- Sturm, Robbie. DRACULA'S VENGEANCE
- Sutherland, Donald. AWAKENED BY A VAMPIRE
- Sweeney, Toni V. MIDNIGHT GOTHIC
- Swinburne, Algernon Charles, SATIA TE
- Symons, Arthur. THE VAMPIRE
- Syndal, James. IN TRANSYLVANIA

T
- Tammerie. DARK'S DEEP EMBRACE
- Tammerie. HER DARK, DARK EYES
- Tammerie. THE BOYAR
- Tattunigma. NO RETRIBUTION
- Tattunigma. SILENCING THE LAMBS
- Taylor, Nancy Ellis. THE HIGH ART OF HUNGER
- Teer, T.J. ALONE
- Teer, T.J. KISS ME LOVE
- Teer, T.J. NIGHTSHADE
- Thacher, Ellen. EYE OF NIGHT
- Thornburg, Thomas R. VAMPYRE
- Turner, Peter. LOVE PREVAILS DEATH
- Turner, Peter. SILENT SAVAGERY
- Turner, Peter. STARE INTO MY DARKNESS
- Turner, Peter. A LOST LOVE IN THIS ETERNAL NIGHT
- Turner, Peter. SHAMELESS EXPRESSION
- Turner, Peter. LOVE OF A VAMPIRE
- Turner, Peter. BLOOD
- Turner, Peter. THE VAMPIRE
- Turner, Peter. THE HIGHWAYMAN
- Turner, Peter. THE REMORSELESS KILLER

V
- Vachott, Sándor, BÁTHORY ERZSÉBET: TÖRTÉNETI BESZÉLY, KÉT ÉNEKBEN
- VAMPIRE LIMERICK
- Vasterling, L.K. ABILITIES.
- Vasterling, L.K. DINNER TIME

- Vasterling, L.K. DOOMED PASSIONS
- Vasterling, L.K. GARLIC
- Vasterling, L.K. HUNGER PAINS.
- Vasterling, L.K. LOVE'S TRANSFORMATION
- Vasterling, L.K. MONSTERS
- Vasterling, L.K. THE LONG ROAD
- Vlad. BLOOD AND MUSIC
- Vogl, Johann Nepomuk, DIE BURGRAU ZU CSEITHA
- Volcane. AS THE DARKNESS FALLS
- Volcane. BLOOD LUST
- Volcane. COME FORTH
- Volcane. LOVE
- Volkman, Joann. BLACKNESS EMBRACES ME
- Volkman, Joann. BLOOD TOAST
- Volkman, Joann. DARK GIFT
- Volkman, Joann. IN MY DARKEST HOUR

W

- Walsh, Francis W. DROWNING IN A SEA OF CRIMSON
- Walsh, Mr. Francis W. LOCK YOUR DOOR!
- Watson, Amanda. HYMN FOR THE MOON
- Weisbrodt, Michael. VAMPYR
- Weisbrodt, Michael. WALK ON
- Weiss, Sanford. DRACULA AND ME. Kayak
- Welcher, Rosalind. COBWEBS
- Welcher, Rosalind. MOONLIGHT
- Welcher, Rosalind. SHADOWS
- Wellman Manly Wade. THE ONLOOKER
- Wellman, Manly Wade. THE VAMPIRE'S TRYST
- White, Chris. BITEY, THE VEGGIE VAMPIRE
- White, Michael. DRACULA WAS A SINNER BUT GOD FORGAVE HIM.
- Wilber, Richard. THE UNDEAD
- Wilbur, Rick. THE IMPALER IN LOVE
- Wilson, Shawn M. CREATURE OF THE NIGHT
- Wolfgang Von Goethe, Johann. THE BRIDE OF CORINTH

Y

- Yeats, Will Butler. OIL AND BLOOD
- Young, Ree. MEMORIES
- Young, Ree. THE LONG VOYAGE
- Youngon, Jeanne. NO REST FOR THE WICKED
- Youngson, Jeanne. A LITTLE KNOWLEDGE

· Youngson, Jeanne. AN OFFER YOU SHOULDN'T REFUSE
· Youngson, Jeanne. AN OLD REFRAIN
· Youngson, Jeanne. BEWARE
· Youngson, Jeanne. BOO HOO
· Youngson, Jeanne. DISTURBING THOUGHT
· Youngson, Jeanne. DRACULA'S BRIDE
· Youngson, Jeanne. FUNNY YOU SHOULD ASK
· Youngson, Jeanne. HOSPITALITY WILL GET YOU NOWHERE
· Youngson, Jeanne. LISTEN TO THE GLISTENING SILENCE
· Youngson, Jeanne. LOOKING FORWARD
· Youngson, Jeanne. LUNA
· Youngson, Jeanne. MARY ELIZABETH ELEANORE FRYE
· Youngson, Jeanne. NO LONGER FREE
· Youngson, Jeanne. OLD COUNT DRACULA
· Youngson, Jeanne. SOMETHING....GORY
· Youngson, Jeanne. THE COUNT
· Youngson, Jeanne. THE LAST WORD
· Youngson, Jeanne. THE PASSIONATE FANTASOPHILE
· Youngson, Jeanne. THE TV LATE, LATE SHOW
· Youngson, Jeanne. THINGS ARE TOUGH ALL OVER
· Youngson, Jeanne. TIT TAT TOE
· Youngson, Jeanne. TO COUNT DRACULA
· Youngson, Jeanne. TO MY VALENTINE COUNT DRACULA
· Youngson, Jeanne. TONIGHT'S THE NIGHT
· Youngson, Jeanne. UNK
· Youngson, Jeanne. WHITBY
· Youngson, Jeanne. YOU ARE BEE-UTIFUL
· Youngson, Jeanne. ZOLTAN, HOUND OF DRACULA

Z

· Zimmerman, Thomas. GEMS OF DARKNESS

·APPENDIX FOUR·
VAMPIRES IN FILM

A

Abbott and Costello Meet
  Frankenstein 1948

Abrakadabra 1986

Addicted to Murder 1995

Ahkea Kkots 1961

Allen and Rossi Meet Dracula and
  Frankenstein 1974

Aloha Little Vampire Story 1987

Anak Pontianak 1958

Andy Warhol's Dracula 1974

Angelis Y Querubines 1972

As Sete Vampiras 1984

Atom Age Vampire 1960

B

Barry McKenzie Holds His Own
  1974

Bat People 1940

Batman 1964

Batman Fights Dracula 1967

Batula 1952

Beast of Morocco 1966

Beautiful Dead Body (a.k.a. Sexy
  Kama Sutra) 1987

Beiss Mich, Leibling 1970

Beloved Vampire 1917

The Best of Dark Shadows 1965-71

Beverly Hills Vamp 1989

Billy the Kid vs. Dracula 1966

Bite 1997

Black Day for Bluebeard 1974

Black Sabbath 1963

Black Sunday 1961

The Black Vampire 1974

Black Vampire 1988

Blacula 1972

Blade 1998

Blade II 2002

Bloedverwanten 1977

The Blonde Vampire 1922

Blood 1974

Blood and Black Lace 1964

Blood and Donuts 1995

Blood and Roses 1961

Blood Bath 1966

Blood Ceremony 1973

The Blood Demon 1967

The Blood Drinkers 1966

Blood Fiend 1966

Blood For Dracula 1974

Blood Lust 1970
Bloodlust 1961
Bloodlust 1992
Bloodlust: Subspecies 3 1994
Bloody Mallory 2002
Blood Moon 1970
The Blood of Dracula 1957
The Blood of Dracula's Castle 1969
The Blood of Pontianak 1958
Blood of the Vampire 1958
Blood-Spattered Bride 1969
Bloodstone: Subspecies 2 1993
Bloodstorm: Subspecies 4 1998
Blood Suckers from Outer Space 1984
The Bloodless Vampire 1965
Bloodsuckers 1971
Bloodsuckers From Outer Space 1984
Blood Thirst 1965
Bloodthirsty 1998
The Bloody Countess 1973
The Blue Sextet 1971
The Body Beneath 1970
Bongo Wolf's Revenge 1970
Bram Stoker's Dracula 1992
Bram Stoker's Original Dracula 1978
Brides of Dracula 1960
Buffy the Vampire Slayer 1992
Bunnicula The Vampire Rabbit 1979
Bury Him Darkly 1974

C

Captain Kronos: Vampire Hunter 1972
Capulina Contra Los Vampiros 1971
Carmilla 1990
Carmilla 1968
Carry On Screaming 1966
Casa de los Espantos 1963
The Case of the Full Moon Murders 1974

Castle of Blood 1963
Castle of Dracula 1968
The Castle of the Living Dead 1964,
Cast A Deadly Spell 1991
Casual Relations 1973
Cave of the Living Dead 1964
Cemetery Girls 1972
Ceneri E Vampe 1916
Ceremonia Sangrientia 1972
Chabelo Y Pepito Contra Los Monstruos 1973
Chamber of Fear 1968
Chanoc Contra El Tigre Y El Vampiro 1970
Chappaqua 1966
Chi O Suu Bara 1974
Chi O Suu Ningyo 1970
Children of the Night 1991
Chiosu Me 1970
Chosen Survivors 1974
Cinque Tombe Per un Medium 1965
City of the Walking Dead 1980
Close Encolunters Of The Vampire 1986
Condemned To Live 1935
Contes Immoraux 1969
The Corpse Vanishes 1941
Count Downe - Son of Dracula 1973
Count Dracula 1970
Count Dracula 1978
Count Dracula and His Vampire Bride 1973
Count Dracula, The True Story 1979
Count Erotica, Vampire 1971
Count Yorga, Vampire 1970
Countess Dracula 1970
Crazy Safari 1992
The Crime Doctor's Courage 1945
The Curse of Dracula 1957
The Curse of Dracula 1979
Curse of the Undead 1959

Curse of the Vampires 1970
Crypt of the Living Dead 1973

D
Dakki, the Vampire 1936
Dance of the Damned 1989
Dance of the Vampires 1968
Danse Vampiresque 1912
Dark Lady Of Kung Fu (a.k.a. Dark Lady Of The Butterfly) 1986
Dark Shadows 1968
Darkness 1992
Daughter of Darkness 1990
Daughter of Dr. Jekyll 1957
Daughters of Darkness 1971
Dead of Night 1976
Dead Men Walk 1942
Deafula 1975
Death on a Barge 1973
The Death of P'Town 1963
The Deathmaster 1971
Deathship 1980
De Dodes o 1913
Def By Temptation 1990
Dendam Pontianak 1957
Der Fluch der Grunen Augen 1965
The Devil And The Ghostbuster 1988
The Devil Bat 1940
The Devil Bat's Daughter 1946
The Devil is Not Mocked 1972
The Devil's Commandment 1956
The Devil's Mistress 1966
Devils of Darkness 1965
Devil's Vindata 1992
The Devil's Wedding Night 1973
Dick and the Demons 1974
Die Zartlichkeit der Wolfe 1973
Die Zwolfte Stunde 1922
Dir Schlangengrube und Das Pendel 1967

Disciple of Death 1972
Disciples of Dracula 1975
Diversions 1976
Does Dracula Really Suck 1961
Dr. Terror's Gallery of Horrors 1967
Dr. Terror's House of Horrors 1964
Dracula 1920
Dracula 1931
Dracula 1931
Dracula 1957
Dracula 1958
Dracula 1969
Dracula 1973
Dracula 1976
Dracula 1972
Dracula 1979
Dracula 2000 2000
Dracula: A Cinematic Scrapbook 1991
Dracula and Son 1979
The Dracula Business 1974
Dracula Contra El Dr. Frankenstein 1971
Dracula Exotica 1981
Dracula, Father and Son 1976
Dracula Goes to R.P. 1974
Dracula Has Risen From the Grave 1968
Dracula in Italy 1975
Dracula in the House of Horrors 1974
Dracula Meets the Outer Space Chicks 1968
Dracula, Pere et Fils 1976
Dracula, Prince of Darkness 1965
Dracula Rises From the Coffin 1982
Dracula Rising 1992
Dracula Rocks 1979
Dracula Saga 1972
Dracula Sucks 1969
Dracula Sucks 1979

Dracula Today 1971

Dracula (The Dirty Old Man) 1969

Dracula Vs. Dr. Frankenstein 1974

Dracula Vs. Frankenstein 1971

Dracula Walks the Night 1972

Dracula's Baby 1970

Dracula's Blood 1974

Dracula's Daughter 1936

Dracula's Dog 1975

Dracula's Feast of Blood 1974

Dracula's Great Love 1972

Dracula's Last Rites 1980

Dracula's Lusterne Vampire 1970

Dracula's Wedding Day 1967

Dracula's Widow 1988

Dragstrip Dracula 1962

Dragula 1973

Drakula 1921

Drakula Istanbulda 1952

Drakulita 1969

Dungeon Master 1968

Used with permission, (c) 2003 by Bill Chancellor.

E

El Ataud del Vampiro 1959

El Baul Macabro 1936

El Castillo de los Monstruos 1957

El Charro de las Calaveras 1966

El Conde Dracula 1970

El Extrano Amor de los Vampiros 1977

El Fantasma de la Operetta 1955

El Gran Amor Del Conde Dracula 1972

El Imperio de Dracula 1967

El Mundo de los Vampiros 1960

El Retorno De Los Vampiros 1972

El Vampiro 1957

El Vampiro Aechecha 1962

El Vampiro de la Autopista 1970

El Vampiro Negro 1953

El Vampiro Sagriento 1961

El Vampiro y el Sexo 1968

Enchen me al Vampiro 1964

Encounters of The Spooky Kind 1981

Encounters of The Spooky Kind 2 1990

Ercole al Centro della Terra 1961

Erotikill 1981

Escala en HI-FI 1963

Every Home Should Have One 1970

The Evil Touch 1974

Evils of the Night 1985

The Exorcist Master 1993

The Eye of Count Flickenstein 1966

F

Face of Marble 1946

Fantasmagorie 1963

Fantasy Mission Force 1983

The Fearless Vampire Killers or: Pardon Me, But Your Teeth Are in My Neck 1967

First Man Into Space 1958

First Vampire In China 1986

Five Lucky Ghosts Part 2 (a.k.a. Spooky Family 2, a.k.a. Ghost Legend) 1991

Five Venoms Vs. Wu Tang (a.k.a. 5 Venoms Vs. The Ghost, a.k.a. The Venoms Vs. The Vampires) 1987

Fools 1970

The Forest Vampires 1914

The Forsaken 2002

Frankenstein, El Vampiro y Cia 1961

Frankenstein Meets Dracula 1957

Fright Night 1986

Fright Night II 1988

From Dusk Till Dawn 1996

From Dusk Till Dawn 2: Texas Blood Money 1999

From Dusk Till Dawn 3: The Hangman's Daughter 2000

The Funeral 1972

G

Ganja And Hess 1973

Gandy Goose in the Ghost Town 1944

Garu, The Mad Monk 1970

Gebissen Wird Nur Nachts - Happening Der Vampire 1971

Ghost Bride

Ghostly Love 1990

Ghost's Hospital 1988

Ghoul Sex Squad

Go For a Take 1972

Goliath and the Vampires 1964

Graf Dracula Beisst Jetzt in Oberbayern 1979

Grandpa's Monster Movies 1988

Grave of the Vampire 1972

Graveyard Shift 1986

The Green Monster 1974

The Groovy Goolies 1970

Guess What Happened To Count Dracula 1969

H

Habit 1997

Hannah, Queen of the Vampires 1972

Hanno Cambiato Faccia 1971

The Hardy Boys and Nancy Drew Meet Dracula 1977

Haunted Cop Shop 2 1986

Hello! Dracular 1987

Heubhyeolgwi yeonyeo 1981

High Priest of Vampires 1971

The Hilarious House of Frightenstein 1974

Horror of the Blood Monster 1970

Horror of Dracula 1958

Horror of Dracula 1966

The Horror of It All 1964

Horroritual 1972

Hotel Macabre 1976

House of Dark Shadows 1970

House of Dracula 1945

House of Dracula's Daughter 1973

House of Frankenstein 1944

House on Bare Mountain 1962

The House That Dripped Blood 1971

How They Became Vampires 1973

Howling VI: The Freaks 1990

The Hunger 1983

I

I Am Legend 1974

I Bought a Vampire Motorcycle 1990

I, Desire 1982

I Like Bats 1986

I Married a Vampire 1983

I Was A Teenage Vampire 1959

I, The Vampire 1972

Il Mostro dell'Opera 1964

Il Plenilunio swllw Vergine 1973

Il Risviglio di Dracula 1968

Il Vampiro Dell'Opera 1962

Immoral Tales 1969

In Search of Dracula 1975

The Innerview 1973

Innocent Blood 1992

An Innocent Vampire 1916

Insomnia 1965

Inspector Ghostbuster

Interview With the Vampire 1994

In the Grip of the Vampire 1913

Is There a Vampire in the House? 1972

Isabell, A Dream 1958

Isle of the Dead 1945

It Lives Again 1978

It Lives By Night 1973

It's Alive! 1974

It's Alive III: Island of the Alive 1986

It! The Terror From Beyond Space 1958

I Vampiri 1956

J

The Jail Break 1946

Jerry and the Vampire 1917

The Jitters (a.k.a. Year of The Kynosee) 1988

Johnathan, Vampire Sterben Nicht 1970

John Carpenter's Vampires 1998

Jumping Corpses

Jupiter 1971

K

Kali: Devil Bride of Dracula 1975

Killer Klowns From Outer Space 1988

Kiss Me Quick 1963

Kiss of the Vampire 1915

Kiss of the Vampire 1963

Kronos 1972

Kung Fu From Beyond The Grave 1982

Kuroneko 1968

Kyuketsu Ga 1956

Kyuketsu Gokemidoro 1968

L

La Bestia Desnuda 1968

La Danza Macabra 1963

Lady Dracula 1973

La Fee Sanguinaire 1968

La Fille De Dracula 1972

La Huella Macabra 1962

La Invasion de los Muertos 1972

La Invasion de los Vampiros 1962

La Llamada del Vampiro 1971

La Maldicion de los Karnsteins 1963

La Maldicion de Nostradamus 1960

L'Amante del Vampiro 1962

L'Amanti D'Oltretomba 1965

La Marca del Hombre Lobo 1968

La Maschera del Demonio 1960

La Messe Nere Della Contessa Dracula 1972

La Nipote Del Vampiro 1969

La Noche de Todos de Horrores 1973

La Noche de Walpurgis 1970

La Notte Dei Diavolli 1971

La Saga De Los Draculas 1972

La Senal del Vampiro 1943

Las Luchadoras Contra La Momia 1965

La Sorciere Vampire 1967

La Sombra del Murcielago 1966

La Sorella Di Satana 1965

The Last Man on Earth 1964

La Stragi del Vampiri 1962

Last Rites 1980

Last Vampire

Las Vampiras 1968

The Latest in Vampires 1916

La Torre de Vampiri 1914

La Vampira Indiana 1913

La Vampire Nue 1969

The League of Extraordinary Gentlemen (2003)

Le Circuit De Sang 1973

The Leech Woman 1960

Le Frisson des Vampires 1970

Legacy of Satan 1973

Legend of a Ghost 1908

Legend Of The Living Corpse (a.k.a. Shaolin Brothers, a.k.a. The Legend of The Living Gorps) 1980

Legend of the Seven Golden Vampires 1975

Le Manior du Diable 1897

Le Nosferat ou les eaux Glacees du Calcul Egoiste 1974

Leonor 1975

Le Pacte des Loups 2001

Le Puits Fantastique 1903

Le Rouge aux Levres 1970

Le Sadique Aux Dents Rouge 1971

Le Sangre de Nostradamus 1960

Les Vampires 1915

Le Vampire 1923

Le Vampire de Dusseldorf 1964

Les Chemins de la Violence 1972

Les Femmes Vampires 1967

Let's Scare Jessica To Death 1971

Levres de Sang 1976

Lifeforce 1985

Lilith and Ly 1919

The Little Shop of Horrors 1960

The Little Vampire 1969

The Living Dead at the Manchester Morgue 1974

London After Midnight 1927

The Lost Boys 1987

Love After Death 1969

Love at First Bite 1979

LONDON AFTER MIDNIGHT. Archival photo.

Love Bites 2000
Love Life of a Vampire 1973
Love...Vampire Style 1971
L'Ultima Preda del Vampiro 1960
L'Ultimo Uomo Della Terra 1964
L'Urlo del Vampiro 1962
Lust for a Vampire 1970
Lust for a Vampire 1971
Lust Never Dies
The Lust of Dracula 1971
Lust of the Vampire 1967

M

Maciste Contro Il Vampiro 1961
Madhouse 1974
Mad, Mad Ghost 1992
Mad, Mad, Mad Monsters 1972
The Mad Love Life of a Hot
    Vampire 1971
Mad Monster Party 1967
Mad Vampire
The Magic Christian 1969

Magic Story (a.k.a. Young Master
    Vampire) 1986
Magic Touch
Malikmata 1967
Mama Dracula 1988
The Man Upstairs 1958
Mark of the Vampire 1935
Martin 1977
Mary, Mary, Bloody Mary 1975
Men of Action Meet Women of
    Dracula 1969
Memorias de una Vampiresa 1945
Messiah of Evil 1974
Mickey's Gala Premier 1933
The Midnight Hour 1986
Mighty Mouse Meets Bad Bill
    Bunion 1945
Mind F*** 1990
Mini-Munsters 1973
Miss Magic
Mister Vampire 1916
Modern Vampires 1999
Mondo Balordo 1968
The Monster Club 1981
Monster in the Closet 1987
Monster Rumble 1961
The Monster Squad 1987
Moonrise 1992
Morning Star 1962
Munster, Go Home! 1966
Musical Vampire 1992
Mutant 1983
Mutanto, the Horrible 1961
Mr. Vampire 1986
Mutt and Jeff Visit the Vampire
    1918
My Best Friend is a Vampire 1988
The Mysteries of Myra 1916
The Mystery in Dracula's Castle
    1973

N

Nacht des Grauens 1916

National Lampoon's Class Reunion 1982

Near Dark 1987

Nella Stretta Morsa Del Ragno 1971

New Mr. Vampire (a.k.a. Kung Fu Vampire Buster) 1986

New Mr. Vampire II

Ng Manugang ni Drakila 1964

Nick Knight 1989

Night Angel 1990

Night Journey 1996

Nightland 1995

NightLife 1989

Nightmare in Blood 1976

The Nightmare Sisters 1988

Nightwing 1978

Night of Dark Shadows 1971

Night of the Devils 1987

Night of the Living Dead 1968

Night of the Walking Dead 1975

Night of the Sorcerers 1971

The Night Stalker 1972

The Night Strangler 1972

Nocturna 1978

Nostradamus y el Genio de la Tinieblas 1960

Nosferatu 1922

Nosferatu the Vampire 1979

Not of This Earth 1988

Not of This Earth 1995

O

Old Dracula 1974

Old Mother Riley Meets the Vampire 1952

The Omega Man 1971

Once Bitten 1985

Onna Kyu Ketsuki 1959

Orgy of the Dead 1966

Orlak, El Infierno de Frankenstein 1961

P

Pa Jakt Efter Dracula 1971

Pale Blood: An Erotic Vampire Thriller 1990

Parque de Juegos 1963

Pastel de Sangre 1971

Paul Bowles In Morocco 1971

Pawns of Satan 1961

Pity For The Vamps 1956)

Plan Nine From Outer Space 1956

Planet of the Vampires 1965

A Polish Vampire in Burbank 1985

Pontianak 1957

Pontianak Gua Musang 1964

Pontianak Kembali 1963

Preview Murder Mystery 1936

Prince Dracula 1978

The Public Eye 1973

NOSFERATU. Archival photo.

Q
Queen of the Damned 2002

R
Rabid 1977
Razor Blade Smile 1998
Red Blooded American Girl 1990
Red Lips 1994
Red Sleep 1992
The Reflecting Skin 1990
The Reluctant Vampire 1992
Rendevous 1973
A Return to Salem's Lot 1987
The Return of Count Yorga 1971
The Return of Dracula 1957
The Return of the Vampire 1943
The Return Of Dr. X 1939
The Revenge of Dracula 1958
Robo Vampire 1988
Rockula 1974
Rockula 1990

S
Sabrina, The Teenaged Witch 1971
Saint George and the Seven Curses 1961
Salem's Lot: The Movie 1979
Sangre de Virgines 1967
Sangre Eterna 2002
Santo Contra El Baron Brakula 1965
Santo en la Venganza de las Mujeres Vampiro 1968
Santo Y Blue Demon Contra los Munstruos 1968
The Satanic Rites of Dracula 1974
Saturday the Fourteenth 1981
Saved From the Vampire 1914
Scars of Dracula 1970
School For Vampires 1990

Science Fiction Films 1970
Scream and Scream Again 1970
Scream, Blacula, Scream 1973
The Secret Sex Life of Dracula 1972
The Secrets of House No. 5 1912
Seddock, L'Erede di Satana 1960
Seven Dead in the Cat's Eyes 1972
Seven Brothers Meet Dracula 1974
Sexy Probitissimo 1964
Sexyrella 1968
Shadow of Dracula 1973
Shadow of the Vampire 2001
Shaolin Drunkard (a.k.a. Wu Tang Master)
She Was Some Vampire 1916
Shikari 1964
The Shiver of the Vampire 1972
Shock Treatment 1974
Slave of the Vampire 1959
Sleepwalkers 1992
Son of Dracula 1943
Song of the Vampyres 1977
Sons of Satan 1973
Space Ship Sappy 1957
Spermula 1976
The Spider Woman Strikes Back 1946
Spiritual
Spirit Vs. Zombi 1989
Spooks Run Wild 1941
Slaughter of the Vampires 1971
Strange And Mischievious Young Boy (a.k.a. Little Vampire 2: Kids From Another World)
Subspecies 1991
Sumpah Pontianak 1958
Sundown, Vampires in Retreat 1989
Super-Giant 2 1956
Sweet Hunters 1969
The Sweetness of Sin 1968

T

Tale of a Vampire 1992
Tales of Blood and Terror 1969
A Taste of Blood 1967
Taste the Blood of Dracula 1970
Teen Vamp 1988
Tempi Duri per i Vampiri 1959
Tendre Dracula, Ou Les Confessions D'un Buveur de Sang 1973
Terror of Pontianak 1958
The Thing from Another World 1951
Thirst 1979
The Thirsty Dead 1975
Those Cruel and Bloody Vampires 1973
3D Army
Three Wishes
Till Death 1972
To Die For 1989
To Die For II:Son of Darkness 1991
To Oblige a Vampire 1917
To Sleep With A Vampire 1992
Tore Ng Diyablo 1969
Tracked by a Vampire 1914
Transylvania 6-5000 1963
Transylvania 6-5000 1985
Transylvania Twist 1990
Tremplin 1969
A Trip With Dracula 1970
Trouble Every Day 2001
Tunnel Under the World 1970
Twins of Evil 1972

U

Ugetsu Monogatari 1953
The Ugly Vampire 1968
The Understudy: The Graveyard Shift II 1988
Universal Ike, Jr. and the Vampire 1914

U (cont.)

Upior 1968
Un Sonho de Vampiros 1970
Un Vampiro para Dos 1966

V

Vaarwhel 1973
Vadim's Dracula 1978
Valerie A Tyden Divn 1970
Valley of the Zombies 1946
Vamp 1986
Vampe di Gelosia 1912
Vampir 1971
Vampira 1974
Vampira 1961
Vampire 1950
Vampire 1967
Vampire 1969
Vampire 1970
Vampire 1979
The Vampire 1911
The Vampire 1912
The Vampire 1913
The Vampire 1914
The Vampire 1915
The Vampire 1920
The Vampire 1928
The Vampire 1957
The Vampire 1957
The Vampire 1973
The Vampire 1974
Vampire 2000 1972
Vampire a du Mode 1928
Vampire At Midnight 1988
Vampire Bat 1933
The Vampire-Beast Craves Blood 1967
Vampire Child (a.k.a. Vampire Strikes Back) 1987
Vampire Circus 1972
Vampire Cop 1991
Vampire Expert (teleseries) 1995

Vampire Expert II (teleseries) 1996
Vampire Happening 1971
Vampire Hookers 1979
Vampire Hunter D. 2000
The Vampire Hunters (a.k.a. Era Of Vampires) 2002
Vampire Journals 1997
Vampire Kids 1991
Vampirella 1974
Vampire Love 1957
Vampire Lovers 1970
Vampire Lust For Blood 1971
Vampire Men of the Lost Planet 1970
The Vampire of the Coast 1909
The Vampire of the Desert 1913
The Vampire of Dusseldorf 1965
A Vampire Out of Work 1916
The Vampire People 1966
The Vampire Princess Miyu 1988
Vampire Returns (teleseries)
Vampire's Bite 1972
The Vampire's Clutch 1915
The Vampire's Curse 1969
A Vampire's Dream 1970
Vampire's Ghost 1945
Vampires In China
Vampire's Kiss 1989
Vampire's Love 1969
A Vampire's Nostalgia 1968
Vampires D'Alfama 1963
Vampiresas 1930
Vampire Shows His Teeth
Vampires Live Again 1987
Vampires: Los Muertos 2002
Vampires of the Night 1914
Vampirisme 1967
The Vampire's Trail 1910
Vampire Vs. Sorceror 1992
Vampire Vs. Vampires (a.k.a. One-Eyebrow Priest) 1989
Vampyr 1932

Vampyrdanserinden 1911
Vampyres: The Lost Girls 1975
Vampyros Lesbos - Die Erbin Des Dracula 1970
Vampyrn 1912
Varney, The Vampire 1975
Vasco, the Vampire 1914
Vault of Horror 1973
The Velvet Vampire 1971
Vengeance of the Wurdalak 1973
Vierges Et Vampires 1972
A Village Vampire 1916
VII 1967
Virgin Vampire 1970
Virgins and Vampires 1971
Vlad the Impaler 1973
Voodoo Heartbeat 1972
Vrijeme Vampira 1970

W

Wanda Does Transylvania 1990
Wampiry Warszawy 1925
Was She A Vampire? 1915
Waxwork 1988
Waxwork II: Lost in Time 1991
Wendigo 2002
Who Cares
The Wife and the Vampire 1931
Winter With Dracula 1971
World of the Vampires 1960

Z

Zoltan, Hound of Dracula 1978

·APPENDIX FIVE·
VAMPIRE WEBSITES

The Abandoned Playground
http://pub95.ezboard.com/btheabandonedplayground

After Dark, Mysteries of Blood
http://perso.wanadoo.es/vampiros/

Another Realm
http://www.anotherealm.com/

AppleDoll.com
http://www.appledoll.com/

At Night
http://countdarkness.tripod.com/thenight/index.html

Alt.Gothic.Fashion Board
http://pub80.ezboard.com/bagf61626

Alt.Vampyres.Net
http://www.altvampyres.net/

Anita Blake Compendium
http://halo-productions.com/anita/

Anne Rice Website
http://www.annerice.com/

Aquilus Dot Net
http://aquilus.net/

Beautiful Deadly Children
http://www.beautifuldeadlychildren.fsnet.co.uk/default.html

Bite Me Magazine
http://www.bitememagazine.com/

BloodLust-UK.com
http://www.bloodlust-uk.com/

Bloodykisses
http://www.bloodykisses.com/

Bloody Minded
http://disc.server.com/Indices/26844.html

Bourbon Street - La strada dei vampiri
http://www.bourbon-street.net/

British Horror Films
http://pub55.ezboard.com/bbritishhorrorfilms

By Light Unseen
http://users.net1plus.com/vyrdolak/index.htm

Castle of Vampires
http://www.angelfire.com/darkside/castleofvampires/

Children of Night
http://www.geocities.com/TimesSquare/Lair/7212/

City of Blood
http://www.angelfire.com/ca4/CityofBlood/index.html

Clan of the Kings --Ventrue
http://www.ventrue.net/

Classic Horror Webzine
http://classic-horror.com

Couleur De Sang
http://sang.turmalino.de/

Coven of the Articulate
http://www.angelfire.com/ab2/covenofthearticulate/

Crimson Connection
http://pub34.ezboard.com/bvcclassifieds

Dagonbytes
http://www.dagonbytes.com

The Dark Aesthetic
http://www.geocities.com/Area51/Labyrinth/2497/

Darkclaw´s Darkworld
http://www.beepworld.de/members3/darkclaw/willkommen.htm

Dark Forum
http://www.darkforum.com/

The Dark Heaven
http://www.thedarkheaven.com/

Darkness Embraced
http://www.darkness-embraced.com/

Dark Poetry Deep Inside
http://pub83.ezboard.com/bdarkpoetrydeepinside

DarkRealms
http://pub145.ezboard.com/bdarkrealms43343

Deader is Better: Living Dead Dolls
http://pub47.ezboard.com/fdeaderisbetterfrm1

Dear BloodyKiss
http://www.angelfire.com/ca4/dearbloodykiss/

Demythri's Domain
http://www.geocities.com/Area51/Chamber/7290/

Drac in a Box Gothic Clothing
http://www.dracinabox.com/

Dracula Homepage
http://www.dracula.freeuk.com/

Dracula's Children
http://www.geocities.com/Area51/Comet/4237/index.html

Dracula's Homepage
http://www.ucs.mun.ca/~emiller/

Dracula Tour: Vampire Vacation to Transylvania
http://www.geocities.com/Area51/Dreamworld/5747/

Drink Deeply And Dream
http://memory_and_dream.tripod.com/

Drink Deeply and Dream: The Reality of the Modern-Day Vampire
www.drinkdeeplyanddream.com

DSDV - Damn Society Dwelling Vampyres
http://www.dsdv.com/

Edward745's Dark Fantasies
http://www.edward745.com/

English Vampire Folklore
http://members.lycos.co.uk/Hirudo/engvamps.html

FarSector
www.farsector.com

Feed the Fetish
http://www.geocities.com/feedthefetish/

Female Vampires
www.femalevampires.com

Fetish-Vampires
http://www.fetish-vampires.de/

Funeral in Carpathia
http://au.geocities.com/crystal_jade_au/

Gothic Funeral
www.gothicfuneral.net

Garden State Horror Writers
http://www.gshw.net

Gothic-Iowegian
http://www.gothic-iowegian.com/

Graham Masterton Website
http://homepage.virgin.net/the.sleepless/masthome.htm

Hellnotes
http://www.hellnotes.com/

Horror Critique Group
HorrorCritiqueGroup@groups.msn.com

Horror Writers Association
https://www.horror.org

Hush Hush Little Baby
http://www.geocities.com/hushhush_littlebaby/

Immortal Desires
http://www.angelfire.com/darkside/s_leigh/

International Horror Guild
http://www.ihgonline.org

Kim's Lair
http://hometown.aol.com/VAMPIRFEM/VampireKim.html

Kingdom of Darkness
http://www.geocities.com/Area51/Labyrinth/5504/

Kitten's Korner: VamPress
http://www.geocities.com/Heartland/Valley/1745/vampire.html

La Page de L'Ange Noire
http://foolishblue.ix9.org/

The Last Breath
http://www.angelfire.com/goth/thelastbreath/main.html

Laurell K. Hamilton Official Website
http://www.laurellkhamilton.org/MainPage.htm

Lestat´s Top 20
http://www.topsitelists.com/area51/darkfallenangel/

Lilian Broca -Artist
www.lilianbroca.com

The Lilith Gallery
http://www.lilithgallery.com/

The Literary Vampire
http://www.geocities.com/SoHo/Village/2258/

Lizabet's Vault
http://www.horrorseek.com/vampires/lizabetvault/welcome.html

Lusty's Lair
http://www.lustyslair.com/

Menschenblut.de
http://www.menschenblut.de/

National Vampire Association
http://www.angelfire.com/id/nightless/begin.html

Nelapsi's Queen of the Damned Page
http://www.vampirequeenakasha.freehomepage.com/

Night Angel
http://www.angelfire.com/de2/NightAngelAmortise/

Nocturnal Visions
http://www.nocturnalvisions.freeservers.com/index.html

Poppy Brite Official Website
http://www.poppyzbrite.com

RavenBlack
http://quiz.ravenblack.net/blood.pl?biter

A Ravinn's Nest
http://www.geocities.com/Area51/Labyrinth/9013/iindex.html

Reapers of Blood
http://reapersofblood.org/

Official F. Paul Wilson Page
http://www.repairmanjack.com/home.html

Sangue Demonio
http://www.rancidgolem.veryrude.co.uk/

Sanguinarius: The Vampire Support Page
http://members.tripod.com/~Sanguinarius/gateway.htm

Sanguinox
http://sanguinox.com/

Siania's Vampyre Information Pages
http://www.fortunecity.com/marina/greenwich/424/

Slept So Long
http://queenofthedamnedfansite.cjb.net/

St. Louis After Dark
http://www.slad.net/

Thee Gothic Image
http://www.darksites.com/souls/vampires/jadesin/index.html

Vamp!
vampress.net

Vampgirl.com
http://www.vampgirl.com/index.html

Vamp. Elite
http://personal.msy.bellsouth.net/msy/l/u/lugosi/

Vampire Athenaeum
http://www.vampireathenaeum.org

Vampire Collector's Domain
http://vampirecollector.com/

Vamperotica.com
http://www.vamperotica.com/

Vampettes
http://www.vampettes.com/

VampFangs
http://www.vampfangs.com/

Vampier.pagina.nl
http://vampier.pagina.nl/

Vampir-Club
http://www.vampir-club.de/

The Vampire/Donor Alliance
http://www.darksites.com/souls/vampires/vampdonor/

Vampire Folklore Resources
http://www.sanguinarius.org/~akrieytaz/folklore.html

The Vampire Forum
http://www.vampireforum.co.uk/

Vampire Freaks
http://www.vampirefreaks.com/

Vampire Galleria
http://vampires.freehosting.net/

Vampire Hall
http://www.darksites.com/souls/vampires/slash/

The Vampire ii
http://devoted.to/thevampireii

Vampire Junction
http://www.afn.org/%7Evampires/

Vampirelord's Rest
http://www.vampirelord.com/

Vampire Movies
http://www.netaxs.com/~elmo/vamp-mov.html

The Vampire Pages Soaked In Blood
http://www.oddworldz.com/countdraven/index.html

Vampire Realm of Darkness
http://www.vampires.nu/

Vampire Red
http://www.vampirered.homestead.com/entry.html

Vampires. Children of the Night.
http://www.geocities.com/blade_vampkiller_uk/index.html

The Vampire's Graveyard
http://members.tripod.com/~brujahTRENCH/

The Vampires of Bloody Island
http://www.allinkempthorne.co.uk/Vampires.htm

Vampires of New Dimension
http://vampires-castle.hypermart.net/

Vampires of the World
http://www.btinternet.com/~vampires/index.htm

Vampire's People
http://www.vampirespeople.too.it/

Vampires Soul
http://www.afflictiun.com/

The Vampire Tales!
http://www.thevampiretales.com/

Vampire Wear - Clothing For Immortals
http://www.vampirewear.com/

Vampires.xxx
http://www.sukkubus.pwp.blueyonder.co.uk/vampiresxxx/index.html

Vampirism
http://www.angelfire.com/mi/psyvampyr/vampire.html

Vampiros.cl Arte y Sangre
http://www.vampiros.cl/

Vampnet
http://www.vampnet.com/

Vampress Home of Vampire
http://www.vampress.de/

Vampyre Queen of the Week
http://members.tripod.com/~VAMPQ/

Vampyres Crypt
http://www.vampyreonline.com/

Vampyres Only
http://www.vampyres.com/

Vampyres2000
http://www.geocities.com/vampyres2000/

Vampyress' Grimoire
http://www.geocities.com/Vampyress1138/

The Victim Of Fate
http://www.victimoffate.batcave.net/

View from the Darkside: Gothic Photos
http://www.macabre.net/darkside/

Visions of Vampires
http://www.vampirevisions.de/

The Voluptuous Horror of Countess Bathoria
http://www.bathoria.com/

The Watcher's Zone
http://watcherszone.deadtime.net/

Waxdolly Design Co.
http://waxdolly.freeyellow.com/

The World of BloodRose
http://members.tripod.com/~BloodRose_2/

World Vampire Net
http://www.geocities.com/thekindredtimes/upload/english.html

Artwork by Robert Patrick O'Brien.

·APPENDIX SIX·
VAMPIRE NEWSGROUPS

Newsgroups are informal online organizations, generally run by enthusiastic and talented amateurs with a love for their subject matter. The list of vampire newsgroups changes constantly, but following are some of the groups that provided very useful information and support during the researching of this book.

alt.vampyres

alt.books.anne-rice

alt.books.poppy-z-brite

alt.culture.vampires

alt.horror

alt.tv.buffy-v-Slayer

alt.tv.forever-knight

alt.games.vampire

alt.games.vampire.the

alt.games.vampire.the.masquerade

alt.games.vampire.tremere

alt.vampire

alt.vampire.tremere

alt.games.whitewolf

alt.fan.dean-stark.vampyres

alt.fan.whitevampire

alt.flame.dr-tom.4d.vamps

alt.flame.dr-tom.4d.vamps.acid

alt.vampyres.its-spelled-vampires-you-fools.hwest

alt.vampyres.flap.flap.flap

Photo by Jason Lukridge.

·APPENDIX SEVEN·
THE PROTECTIVE POWERS OF STONES AND MINERALS

Text and photos by Faith Maberry.
Charms courtesy of The Celtress Collection.

Fighting evil forces such as vampires, werewolves, ghosts, demons, and the rest often requires personal protection as well as weapons like torches and stakes. For thousands of years people from cultures all over the world have believed that natural items from the earth-- stones, minerals, plants, soil, and even water--possess a variety of powers for protection, healing, and spiritual advancement.

Mixed gemstones.

Following is a collection of some of the most potent stones used in magical charms to defend against evil and restore to health someone who has fallen under an evil curse. Quite a few of these stones are also used in white magic, to promote contin- ued good health, cultivate love, and help focus one's mind and spirit for meditation.

AGATE

Agate is a stone with powerful energies, often used for love spells and to remove or avoid envious or spiteful thoughts. Agate is also worn as a truth amulet to ensure that one's words are pure. It is associated with strength, courage, longevity, healing, protection, good luck, and love. Agate can also promote abundance when gardening.

AGATE, BLUE LACE

Blue Lace Agate is one of the most powerful soothing stones. This cool blue semi-precious stone relieves stress, calms troubled emotions, eases tensions, and promotes healing energies. This stone is worn for peace and happiness, as it eliminates anger and assists in achieving a higher lever of consciousness and a connection with higher powers. Blue Lace Agate promotes mental clarity, improved reasoning, and faster mental processing.

AGATE, BOTSWANA

Botswana Agate has strong energies associated with increased physical strength, protection, long life, endurance, and general good health. It increases stamina and enhances sexual energy. It stimulates the crown chakra (energy center), balances yin and yang, and energizes the aura.

AGATE, DENDRITIC TREE

Dendritic Tree Agate is a soothing stone with strong healing properties. It enhances gentleness and encourages one to walk lightly through the gardens of light. It both opens and activates the chakras. It is a stone of plentitude providing abundance and fullness in life. This stone is often used in rituals for healing the earth. It is often used as a good luck stone to promote wealth and good fortune.

AGATE, MOSS

Moss Agate is a potent stone that gives energy and strength during stress. It is a soothing stone with strong healing properties. It enhances gentleness and encourages one to walk lightly through the gardens of light. It both opens and activates the chakras. It is a stone of plentitude providing abundance and fullness in life. This stone is often used in rituals for healing the earth. It is also used as a good luck stone to promote wealth and good fortune.

AMAZONITE

Amazonite is a good luck stone, associated with money, good fortune, and gambling success. It is an excellent talisman for games of chance. It is also a soothing stone with healing properties that calm troubled nerves, relieve stress, and ease tension. It lifts the spirits and promotes joy. Amazonite also balances the energies of the body, bringing harmony and a higher connection with universal love.

AMBER

The use of Amber as adornment goes back many thousands of years. It has associations with time, cycles, and longevity. It is thought to contain life energies and is a most valuable magical tool, used for strength, healing, protection, power, love, and luck. Amber's properties make it one of the most widely used and prized magical substances of all times and places on Earth. It is highly protective, and is a potent amulet against negative magic. It is frequently used by witches, wise women, and shamans to strengthen their spells, attract love, improve health, and draw money, power, and success.

AMETHYST

Amethyst is steeped in ancient magic, and often associated with royalty or divinity. Its powers include: psychism (ESP, etc.), protection, peace, healing, courage, love, and happiness. Amethyst is a spiritual stone with no negative vibrations, and is associated with the fifth element, Akasha. A truly soothing stone, it calms fears, raises hopes, relieves stress, and eases tension. It lends courage when worn and is an excellent guardian for travelers. It is often used to increase psychic awareness and sharpen the "sixth" sense. Amethyst is often worn to attract or strengthen love.

Amethyst.

AQUAMARINE

Aquamarine has been used in Magic rituals since ancient times and is a potent stone often used to enhance psychic powers. This semi-precious gemstone allows increased access between the conscious and subconscious minds. It is associated with peace, courage, and purification. Aquamarine is also used for soothing and calming emotional problems. As a charm this stone can be worn to ensure good health, halt fear, and strengthen courage. It also promotes mental alertness. Aquamarine is also a cleansing and purification stone, placed near the bathtub during ritual baths. It is a soothing and calming stone, and much like Amethyst, it promotes peace, joy, and happiness, especially in relationships.

ARAGONITE

Aragonite is a creamy gold gemstone with warm energies. It clears and opens the third chakra, and is used in preparation for meditation. This lovely stone aids communication skills, allowing confidence, clear thinking, and poise, while facilitating communication on a higher plane. Aragonite is used for healing of general aches and pains, and conditions related to the skin, kidneys, and liver. Aragonite also eases tension, eliminates anger, and helps bring the emotions into balance.

AVENTURINE

Aventurine is one of the best all-around good luck stones. It is associated with money, luck, gambling success, healing, and increased mental powers. It enhances and balances the energies of the physical, spiritual, mental, emotional, and auric bodies, bringing all into alignment and increasing power. Aventurine opens and activates the heart chakra. It stimulates creativity and enhances intelligence.

BLOODSTONE

Bloodstone has been used in magic for at least 3,000 years. In ancient Babylon it was used to overcome enemies both mortal and supernatural. In ancient Egypt it was used to break bonds, open doors, and even cause stone walls to fall. Bloodstone has been carried into battle by countless warriors as a charm to ensure victory, protect against injury, and to halt bleeding. Bloodstone lends courage, calms fears, and eliminates anger. It is a popular stone with athletes who wear it to increase physical strength and win competitions. Bloodstone is often used to secure victory in legal matters, increase business, draw wealth and money, and improve agriculture.

Bloodstone.

CARNELIAN

Carnelian is a stone of power. It was used in ancient Egypt to still anger, envy, and hatred, and is still used today as a potent protector against negativity and the evil eye. This stone is associated with healing, courage, self-confidence, good luck, and peace. It strengthens astral vision, and protects against enchantments, negativity, and lightning storms. When placed by the bed it is said to prevent nightmares. This stone is also worn to stimulate sexual energy.

CAT'S EYE

This stone comes in light-reflecting shades of gray, green and brown. It is widely used as a spiritual shield against the "evil eye." Cat's Eye is often used in Mojo bags along with various protection herbs, such as Nettle, to provide protection against magic and attacks from supernatural predators that hunt at night.

CITRINE

Citrine is a protective stone that guards against negativity and nightmares, and ensures restful sleep. Citrine represents the element of air and is associated with positive energy, warmth, joy. It promotes optimism, and repels negative energy. Citrine is also a stone of communication. Often worn or carried in the pocket by speech givers, it lends courage and strengthens communication skills. It helps one to think clearly with organized thoughts, and bolsters confidence.

EMERALD

Emeralds have long been highly valued for their beauty and their use in magic. These stones are blessed with potent energies associated with love, wealth, good luck, and protection. They are believed to protect against demonic possession, storms at sea, and miscarriage. They are also considered a traveler's guardian. Emeralds are excellent in any wealth or money-attracting spell, and are used to improve memory.

FLUORITE

Fluorite stimulates mental powers, improving intellect, quelling strong emotions, and bringing all into balance. It assists in gaining an accurate perspective which then allows the making of changes necessary to improve relationships, health, intellect, and emotional well-being. Fluorite can provide for purification and cleansing.

GARNETS

Garnets are often used in magic to tap into extra energy for ritual purposes. They are associated with healing, protection, strength, and love. Wear garnets to enhance bodily strength, endurance, and vigor. Many years ago it was thought to drive off demons and night phantoms. Today it is used to strengthen the aura and create a shield of positive vibration that repels negativity on contact. Garnets are often used in healing rituals, and are exchanged between parting friends to ensure that they will meet again. Known as the passion stone, the garnet is a balancer of the yin and yang energies, and increases psychic sensitivity.

GOLDSTONE

Goldstone is a brownish stone with zillions of tiny gold flecks that capture the light and sparkle like the stars at night. The stone promotes beauty, offers protection, and brings good luck. It helps align healing energies and brings them into balance to promote wellness.

GOLDSTONE, BLUE

Blue Goldstone is deep blue with a myriad of tiny gold flecks that capture the light and sparkle like the stars at night. Like Goldstone, Blue Goldstone promotes beauty, offers protection, brings good luck, and aids healing.

HEMATITE

Hematite is a metallic stone in silver-black, with energies of healing, protection, and love. Hematite is said to be powerful in drawing illness from the body, and a necklace of small stones is excellent for this purpose. Hematite is also a stone often used for divination and grounding.

Hematite.

HOWLITE

Howlite is a white stone with gray markings. It is used to promote kindness and peace and can be used to eliminate anger, pain, stress, and rage. It promotes good intentions, and combines the power of reason with observation and patience, providing for discernment, retentive memory, and a desire for knowledge. Howlite is useful in assisting one to attain enlightenment, higher thinking, and purity of heart.

IOLITE

Iolite is a soothing stone often used for stress relief and to calm troubled emotions. It increases mental endurance and strengthens the mind. It is one of the major stones used in the third eye/crown area during healing, guided meditations, and astral travel. Iolite produces an electrical charge when in contact with one's aura field that strengthens and aligns this field. Iolite is also used to draw and strengthen love.

JADE

Jade is most commonly known for its rich apple green shade, but can also be white, pink, yellow, black, gray, or brown. There are two different kinds of this stone: jadeite and nephrite. Jade is believed to strengthen the organs (heart, kidneys, and immune system), increase fertility, smooth out the emotions, dispel negativity, and grant both courage and wisdom. When carved into religious symbols it acts as a charm against evil. Green jade is used as a charm to induce prophetic dreams.

JADE, MOUNTAIN (DOLOMITE)

Mountain Jade, or Dolomite, is associated with strengthening and balancing the energies of the chakras. It helps to bring all aspects of the physical, mental, emotional, spiritual, and ethereal body into alignment. Dolomite is also used to strengthen the muscular structure and improve lung and urogenital function.

JADE, YELLOW

Yellow Jade is a stone of love, healing, longevity, wisdom, and protection. It has been used since ancient times to attract love, and is given as a sign of love. It is considered to be a fortunate stone bringing good luck and prosperity.

JASPER

Jasper is a warm gemstone with powerful energies, and has been used in magic for thousands of years. Jasper is associated with healing, protection, beauty, and health. Its healing energies work continuously in a slow steady manner, beginning gradually and continually intensifying. It can be used for any healing purpose, but its fame is associated with pregnancy and childbirth, and illnesses in the blood. Jasper is a strong protective stone and works against physical and non-physical hazards. It is used in defensive magic, and against negative energy it sends negativity back to its source, the evil eye. Jasper is often worn to attract good luck, to enhance beauty and grace, to ward off illness, and to protect during travel. Jasper is also excellent for grounding, especially after heavy magic rituals, psychic, or spiritual work.

JASPER, DALMATIAN

Dalmatian Jasper has black spots on a whitish background. This protective stone facilitates awareness and balance. It is used for protection during astral travel, and helps to unite the physical energies with the ethereal to balance the form and direct one toward one's goals. It has also been used to stimulate contact with the faerie realm, is useful in meditation, and to balance yin and yang energies.

JASPER, LIZARD

Lizard Jasper, also called Zebra Jasper, is a stone in shades of green with silvery-white striations. It can be used to promote healing on all levels, to assist in the release of the causes of illness, and to impart hope. Lizard Jasper has been used to support changes in life, to initiate modifications in behavior patterns, and stimulate action. It is also used for spiritual advancement, to facilitate personal growth, and assist in achieving higher goals.

JASPER, YELLOW

Jasper has been used in magic since ancient times. Yellow Jasper is a gorgeous gemstone valued for its potent energies of protection, especially during travel. It also is worn to stabilize the emotions, increase awareness, promote mental processes, and to enhance natural and inner beauty. It is said to relieve pain and protect from physical and nonphysical hazards. Yellow Jasper is particularly useful as a traveler's talisman.

LAPIS

Lapis is steeped in ancient magic and traditions. It has timeless associations with kings, queens, and deities. In ancient Sumer it was believed to contain the soul of a deity, and anyone who wore the stone would possess the deity's magic powers. Lapis is a soothing stone with healing energies. It is also an uplifting and spiritual stone that dispels depression, promotes spirituality, relieves stress, and calms the body with its peaceful vibrations. Lapis is also used for protection, to draw love, to strengthen the bond between lovers, and to increase psychic awareness. It fills the heart with joy, lends courage, and aids meditation.

LABRADORITE

Labradorite has iridescent color flashes much like Moonstone. It is a spiritual stone that represents the powers of the universe. It is a stone of energy, healing, power, and increased intuition. It detoxifies the body and brings the physical, mental, emotional, and spiritual into balance. It is often used to lend extra power in magic, and send energy towards one's magical goals.

MOONSTONE

Moonstone is intimately connected with the moon, and has long been dedicated to Moon Goddesses. It is a stone of love that not only draws love in, it also aids lovers with working out difficulties. Moonstone is also associated with divination, psychism, protection, and fertility. Wear it when gardening and see the garden burst with life and fertility. Place it near the bed to ensure restful sleep. Use it during dieting to strengthen willpower and self-control.

MALACHITE

Malachite is a magical stone that has long been used to lend extra energy during magical rituals and spells, and to send power to magical goals. It is associated with power, protection, love, peace, wealth, and business success. Malachite guards against negativity and physical danger. Considered a traveler's talisman, it is particularly powerful in preventing falls. It expands the heart's ability to love, and draws love to you. Malachite also dispels depression, promotes tranquility, and ensures restful sleep.

MOTHER OF PEARL

Mother of Pearl has long been valued as a powerful amulet for fertility, protection, long life, and wealth. It is related to the fifth element, Akasha, and has been used in ritual jewelry throughout the ages. Mother of Pearl is particularly useful as a talisman of protection, especially around water. Mystically it relates to the ocean, to depth and movement. It is also used for protection from physical harm, injury, and illness. It is a symbol of wealth and is widely used to bring good luck, good fortune, prosperity, and wealth.

MOUKAITE

Moukaite (pronounced moo-kite) comes from Australia. It typically has mixed shades of brown, tans, gold, pinks, and white. This stone offers protection, good luck, and grounding. It can also be used to increase communication skills, boost confidence, and bring all aspects (physical, emotional, spiritual, etc.) into balance to facilitate personal growth.

OBSIDIAN

Obsidian (also called Black Obsidian) has long been valued as a stone with strongly protective energies. It repels negativity, and protects from all types of harm including negative magic, hexes, jinxes and evil intent. Obsidian is also used for aligning with higher powers, banishing grief, enhancing self-control, grounding, and divination. Obsidian balances the yin and yang energies, and helps one become the master of his/her own future.

[OBSIDIAN], APACHE TEAR

Apache Tear is a translucent form of Obsidian, and is valued for its strong protective energies. It is also associated with good luck, comfort in times of grief, divination, and grounding.

OBSIDIAN, IRIDESCENT

Iridescent Obsidian is pure black with occasional color flashes much like Moonstone. It is used for protection, as well as defense against negativity. It breaks and prevents hexes and psychic attacks, and is also used for divination, psychism, and grounding.

OBSIDIAN, SNOWFLAKE

Snowflake Obsidian is deep black with gray markings that sometimes looks like snowflakes. It is used for protection, grounding, centering, divination, and peace. Snowflake Obsidian also facilitates inner change for personal growth. It is a stone of purity, bringing purity and balance to the body, mind, and spirit. This stone also has beneficial energies that bring success in business matters and other challenges.

OPAL

Opals are versatile, potent, and full of energies. They are associated with astral projection, psychic powers, beauty, money, luck, love, and power. The Opal contains the colors and powers of every other stone, so it can be "programmed" or charged with virtually every type of energy and used in spells involving all magical needs. Opals are worn to bring out inner beauty, draw prosperity, bring wealth, increase personal power, and recall past incarnations.

ONYX

Onyx has long been valued as a stone with strongly protective energies. It repels negativity, and protects from all types of harm, negative magic, and evil intent. Onyx is also used for aligning the total person with the higher powers, for banishing grief, enhancing self-control, grounding, and centering. Onyx also balances the yin and yang energies.

PYRITE

Pyrite is a powerful protective stone that guards against negative energies, evil intent, hexes, and jinxes. It was used in ancient Mexico for divination, and by Native American Shamans to lend energy and power to their medicine bags. In addition to protection, it is also carried to bring good luck.

PERIDOT

Peridot is a green semi-precious gemstone associated with healing, good luck, and protection. It is said to increase willpower and bolster courage. It is often worn to protect from enchantments and the evil eye. It is also used to attract love and calm anger.

QUARTZ CRYSTAL

Quartz Crystal is a stone of power. It is often used for healing, protection, love, divination, and psychism. Quartz Crystal increases the energies of any stone, and can be programmed with any intent. A spiritual stone that facilitates higher thinking, it can clear the consciousness, open the chakras, or lend extra energy to one's magical goals.

Quartz.

QUARTZ, ROSE

Rose Quartz is a stone of Love. It is used to open the heart chakra, attract love, and promote peace and fidelity in established relationships. It is a soothing stone with healing energies that calm troubled emotions and bring them into balance.

QUARTZ, SMOKY

Smoky Quartz Crystal is a stone of power. It is often used for healing, protection, love, divination, and psychism. Quartz Crystal increases the energies of any stone, and can be programmed with any intent. It is a spiritual stone that facilitates higher thinking. Use it to clear the consciousness, open the chakras, or lend extra energy to one's magical goals. Smoky Quartz elevates mood, relieves depression, overcomes negative emotions, and is excellent for grounding.

RHODOCROSITE

Rhodocrosite is pink with white striations, and is used for energy, peace and love. It is worn to lend extra energy in times of extreme physical activity and has peaceful vibrations that are soothing to the emotions and the body. It de-stresses, calms, and eases tension, as well as balances the emotions. This is also a stone of love, used in rituals to both draw and strengthen love. It increases self-esteem and bolsters confidence.

RHODONITE

Rhodonite is a pink stone. Like rhodocrosite, it has peaceful vibrations that are soothing to the emotions and the body. It de-stresses, calms and eases tension, as well as balances the emotions. This is also a stone of love, used in rituals to both draw or strengthen love. It increases self-esteem and strengthens the confidence.

RIVERSTONE

Riverstone is a symphony of creams, tans, beige, and grays. This is a stone of beauty, strength, and endurance, and is said to bring long life, protection, and good luck to one who carries or wears it.

SERPENTINE

Serpentine is used to open, clear, and activate the chakras, the energy centers of the body. This stone is often used to improve communications, and facilitate the exchange of ideas and information. Serpentine is used as a good luck stone to bring confidence and positive energy or Chi.

SODALITE

Sodalite is a blue gemstone flecked with white. Often mistaken for Lapis, Sodalite does not have the golden pyrite often contained in Lapis. Sodalite is a healing stone, especially for emotionally-related diseases or those caused by stress, nervousness, or fear. It is also used to increase wisdom, improve mental abilities, to bring about inner peace, and is excellent for meditation.

SUNSTONE

Sunstone is a stone of power and energy. It is often used to balance, clear, and activate the chakras, or energy centers of the body. This stone is also used to strengthen courage, eliminate fear, increase vitality, and alleviate stress. Sunstone offers protection from negative forces from other realms, and facilitates and strengthens one's connection with one's Spirit Guide.

TOPAZ

Topaz is associated with protection, healing, money, and love. It is said to relieve depression, arthritis, anger, fear, and all disturbing emotions. It is used to protect against envy, disease, injury, sorcery, lunacy, and negative magic. Topaz is also worn to draw true love. It stimulates creativity, joy, and brings success, including wealth.

TOPAZ, BLUE

Blue Topaz has the same properties as Topaz.

TOURMALINE

Tourmaline is associated with love, friendship, money, business, health, peace, energy, courage, and astral projection. It is used for grounding, protection, removing negative energy, and is associated with the element of earth.

Blue Topaz.

TURQUOISE

Turquoise has potent magical properties, long considered sacred to Native Americans and others worldwide. It is a stone with strong healing vibrations and was a valuable tool in the Shaman's medicine bag. It is worn to restore and maintain good health. Turquoise is also a protective stone that guards against injury and the evil eye. This beautiful stone is also a strong tool for good luck, good fortune, and money, and has additional associations with love, courage, and friendship.

TIGER EYE

Tiger Eye is a warm stone that promotes energy flow through the body and inner peace. It is excellent for attracting money and wealth, as well as good luck. It lends courage and confidence, and strengthens convictions. Tiger Eye is a protective stone that guards against all forms of harm. It is also associated with improving divination powers, and is often used to delve into past lives.

UNAKITE

Unakite is a stone of balance, protection, and good luck. It can be used to balance the emotions, and bring them into alignment with the spiritual body. Unakite can also be used to promote health, especially with respect to a woman's body, and facilitates the health of the unborn; an excellent amulet for anyone who is pregnant or plans to have children. This stone has been used to protect from illness, disease, and physical dangers.

ZOISITE

Zoisite is green with black markings, with spots of genuine ruby scattered about. This is a stone of exceptional good luck, used for prosperity, money, wealth, good fortune, healing, protection, and power. It is also used to prevent nightmares.

·APPENDIX EIGHT·
THE VAMPIRE SLAYERS' QUICK REFERENCE GUIDE

Here is a breakdown of the various categories of vampires. Individual entries can be located using the main index.

ASTRAL VAMPIRE
Bebarlangs
Erestun
Tarunga

ESSENTIAL VAMPIRE
Akakharu
Baobhan-Sith
Bas
Bebarlangs
Chordewa
Dearg-Due
Dregpa
Eng Banka
Eretica
Glaistig
Impundulu
Incubus
Kephn
Keres
Leanan Sidhe
Leanhaun Sidhe
O Toyo
Shtriga
Skinwalkers
Slaugh

Sriz
Succubus
Zmeu

HUMAN VAMPIRE
Atakapa
Ramanga
Skinwalkers
Stregoica

LIVING VAMPIRE
Adze
Akakharu
Algul
Alp
Aluka
Animalitos
Asasabonsam
Asema
Aswang
Atakapa
Azeman
Baital
Bajang
Baobhan-Sith
Bas
Bebarlangs

Bruja
Brukolaco
Bruxsa
Callicantzaro
Canchus
Chordewa
Chupacabra
Dakhanavar
Dames Blanche
Danag
Draugr
Dregpa
Empusa
Eng Banka
Erestun
Eretiku
Estrie
Garkain
Ghul
Gierach
Glaistig
Green Ogresses
Impundulu
Incubus
Jaracacas
Jersey Devil
Jigakkwar
Kali
Kappa
Kasha
Kephn
Keres
Kudlak
Lamiai
Leanhan Sidhe
Leanhaun Sidhe
Lil
Lilith
Little Old Woman
Lobishomen
Lofa
Loogaroo
Loup-garou
Mandurugo
Maneden
Mashan
Mormo

Moroi
Nobusuma
Nodeppo
Nora
Obayifo
Old Woman Bat
Pelesit
Pijauica
Polong
Pryccolitch
Redcap
Shampe
Shita
Shtriga
Skinwalkers
Slaugh
Soucouyan
Sriz
Striga
Strigoi
Strix
Succubus
Sundal
Bolong
Talamaur
Tarunga
Tlacique
Tlahuelpuchi
Toad Woman
Trazgos
U'tlun'ta
Varcolaci
Vjestitiza
Vourdalak
Wendigo
Wrathful Deities
Xipe-Totec
Yama
Yara-Ma-Yha-Who
Yatu-Dhana
Ye'iitsoh
Zmeu

PSYCHIC VAMPIRE
Talamaur

REVENANT
Alp
Bajang
Bhuta
Blautsager
Blautsauger
Chiang-Shih
Churel
Cihuateteo
Craqueuhhe
Doppelsauger
Drakul
Ekimmu
Farkaskoldus
Gayal
Ghul
Gjakpires
Hannya
Kathakano
Kozlak
Krvoijac
Kudlak
Lampire
Langsuir
Lemures
Lugat
Maca Rong
Mara
Masan
Mjertovjec
Moroi
Mrart
Mullo
Murony
Nachzehrer
Nelapsi
Neuntoter
O Toyo
Obur
Ogoljen
Ohyn
Otigiruru
Oupire
Owengas
Penanggalan

Phi Song Nang
Pijauica
Pijavica
Pisachas
Pontianak
Prêt
Sampiro
Sriz
Stregoni Benefici
Strigoi
Tenatz
Tlahuelpuchi
Upier
Upor
Upyr
Ustrel
Utukku
Vilkacis
Vlkodlak
Volkodlak
Vrykolaka
Wume

SEXUAL VAMPIRE
Akakharu
Baobhan-Sith
Dearg-Due
Green Ogresses
Impundulu
Incubus
Leanhaun Sidhe
Liderc Nadaly
Lilith
Mullo
Nakshasa
Succubus
Sundal
Bolong
Toad Woman
Zmeu

BLOOD DRINKER

Adze
Akakharu
Algul
Alp
Aluka
Animalitos
Asasabonsam
Asema
Aswang
Azeman
Baobhan-Sith
Blautsager
Blautsauger
Bramaparush
Bruja
Brukolaco
Bruxsa
Callicantzaro
Canchus
Chedipe
Chiang-Shih
Children of Judas
Chupacabra
Cihuateteo
Craqueuhhe
Dakhanavar
Dame
Blanches
Danag
Dearg-Dul
Doppelsauger
Drakul
Draugr
Empusa
Erestun
Estrie
Farkaskoldus
Galistig
Gjakpires
Green Ogresses
Hannya
Impundulu
Jaracacas
Jersey Devil

Kali
Kappa
Kathakano
Kozlak
Krvoijac
Lamiai
Langsuir
Leanhan Sidhe
Liderc Nadaly
Lilith
Lobishomen
Lofa
Lugat
Mandurugo
Maneden
Mara Masan
Mashan
Mjertovjec
Mormo
Moroi
Murony
Nelapsi
Neuntoter
Nora
Obayifo
Obur
Ogoljen
Ohyn
Otigiruru
Oupire
Owengas
Pelesit
Penanggalan
Phi Song Nang
Pijauica
Pijavica
Polong
Pontianak
Prêt
Rakshasa
Redcap
Shampe
Soucouyan
Striga
Strigoi

Strix
Sukuyan
Sundal Bolong
Tenatz
Tlacique
Tlahuelpuchi
Trazgos
Tsutsuga
U'tlun'ta
Upier
Upor
Upyr
Ustrel
Varcolaci
Vlkodlak
Vrykolakas
Wrathful Deities
Xipe-Totec
Yama
Yara-Ma-Yha-Who
Zmeu

FLESH-EATER
Atakapa
Bhuta
Bramaparush
Brukalaco
Craqueuhhe
Dames Blanche
Doppelsauger
Draugr
Garkain
Ghul
Green Ogresses
Jigarkhwar
Kasha
Lamiai
Loup-garou
Mashan
Nachzehrer
Ohyn
Penanggalan
Pisachas
Pontianak
Rakshasa

Shita
Sundal Bolong
Wendigo
Yatu-Dhana

NIGHTCOMER
Algul
Chiang-Shih
Cihuateteo
Dakhanavar
Gjakpires
Kephn
Lil
Mara
Mrart
Penanggalan
Rakshasa
Shampe
Tlahuelpuchi
Upyr

SHAPESHIFTER
Adze
Alp
Asema
Aswang
Azeman
Bajang
Bhuta
Blautsager
Bruja
Chordewa
Drakul
Ekimmu
Empusa
Gjakpires
Glaistig
Kudlak
Lamiai
Liderc Nadaly
Loogaroo
Loup-garou
Lugat
Mandurugo
Moroi

Mullo
Murony
Pontianak
Pryccolitch
Rakshasa
Sampiro
Shtriga
Skinwalkers
Soucouyan
Striga
Strix
Sukuyan
Sundal Bolong
Tenatz
Tlacique
Tsutsuga
U'tlun'ta
Upor
Varcolaci
Vjestitiza
Ye'iitsoh
Zmeu

·INDEX·

N

THE VAMPIRE SLAYERS' GUIDE TO THE ARTISTS

ROBERT PATRICK O'BRIEN

Bob O'Brien was raised in the suburbs of Philadelphia. As a professional artist he has worked in every aspect of the business, from body art to fine art, and works in many media, from silk-screening to special makeup FX. Bob is a core member of Strider Nolan Publishing. Contact Bob at stridernolan4@yahoo.com.

MARIE ELENA O'BRIEN

Marie Elena O'Brien has had a lot of experience with vampires, for example, having played Mina Murray in Tom Savini's stage production of Dracula. Marie Elena can usually be found moonlighting in NYC as a stage and film actor, writer, occasional crooner or all-around freelance artist. She over-indulges in Coen brother movies and graphic novels, has had more hair colors than Gaiman's Delirium, and has an inexplicable fear of danishes.
Marie is a frequent contributor to Strider Nolan projects. She can be reached at vixensmojopin1@msn.com

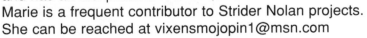

JASON LUKRIDGE

Though trained as a sculptor, Jason Lukridge has worked as a photographer since 1998. An avowed experimental photographer, Jason works in both film and digital formats.
Jason is a frequent contributor to Strider Nolan projects.
Contact Jason at jasonlukridge@yahoo.com

LILIAN BROCA

Lilian Broca is a graduate of Pratt Institute (MFA) living and working in Vancouver, Canada. Her works hang in numerous prestigious public and private collections throughout North America. Her website is www.lilianbroca.com

MATEJ JAN

Matej Jan is a technical artist at 3D-Level (game development team). While mostly doing concept art, texture painting and low polygon modeling, his works also include different fantasy and science fiction themed artworks, done in both 2D and 3D. He lives in Slovenia, home of the Pijavica and Volkodlak vampire species. His artwork can be viewed at www.3dlevel.com/flamer.
Contact Matej at matejjan@hotmail.com

SARAH KIRK

Sarah Kirk was born in Cornwall, England and graduated from Sheffield Hallam University in 2002 with a BA (Hons) Fine art. She currently lives in London while working on her Masters in Digital arts, and plans to become a professional games artist.

STEFANI RENNEE DE OLIVEIRA SILVA

Stefani Rennee de Oliveira Silva is an artist living in Sao Paulo, Brazil. He is a graphic designer and illustrator. He is currently a member of Arcana Studio (www.arcanastudio.com).
To contact the artist: rennee@ig.com.br

KRISTA MCLEAN

Krista McLean currently resides in Vancouver, Canada. She holds a B.F.A from the University of Victoria, Canada. Her artwork includes both traditional and digital media. Her website iswww.ghoulgirl.com.
She can be contacted at flossie11@hotmail.com.

BILL CHANCELLOR

Bill Chancellor is professional illustrator living in Texas. His art has appeared on the covers of various magazines including *Cult Movies*, *Scarlet Street*, and *Screem Magazine* as well as the covers of numerous DVD's for Allday Entertainment. Contact Bill at bchancellor@earthlink.net

BREANNE LEVY

Breanne Levy is a professional photographer and poet from Willow Grove, Pennsylvania. She can be contacted at Bre@temple.edu.

ALBERTO MORENO

Alberto Moreno is a professional artist working for a videogame company, making 2D and 3D. He lives in Spain. His website is www.grihan.com. Contact Alberto at amoreno@grihan.com.

PHILIP STRAUB

Philip Straub, a native of Syracuse, New York has been a professional illustrator for over 8 years. He has illustrated over 30 children's books and created background and concept art for over 10 CD Rom games. His work has appeared in some of the finest illustration annuals including; The Society of Illustrators, Spectrum, and Exposé. Philip can be contacted at www.philipstraub.com

ELDRED TJIE

Specialising in ink art, Eldred is also a freelance animator and aspiring comic book artist. Eldred can be contacted at asylum13@yahoo.com

ANTON KVASOVAROV

Anton Kvasovarov is a digital artist living in Vologda City in Russia and works as a conceptual artist for book and CD covers. His themes mostly concern pagan art such as characters from old Russian and Slavic mythology. Contact Anton at: ancient@bk.ru; anton@digital-artist.org
Portfolio: http://anton.digitalart.org/

ADAM GARLAND

Adam Garland teaches Computer Animation and FX Capilano College in British Columbia, and does freelance art for computer games. He's also a freelancer, creatng art for greeting cards, coloring books, and movies.
Adam can be reached at cowsmanaut@hotmail.com

PEDRO LARA SALAZAR

Pedro Lara Salazar hails from Costa Rica. He is both a comic book creator and computer graphics designer. His work can be found at www.hybridos.net, a collective forum for artists and web designers, as well as www.gfxartist.com. He can be contacted at pedro@hybridos.net.

JACK SCHRADER

Jack Schrader is a graduate in painting from the University of Oregon. He has illustrated books and done cartooning and other graphic designwork for many years. He lives in Vancouver, USA with his wife, Esther, and is currently perfecting his skills as a watercolorist, ukulele and slack-key guitar player. Contact Jack at traderkeaka@comcast.net

MICHAEL KATZ

Michael Katz is an illustrator and writer from Glenside, Pennsylvania.

SHANE MacDOUGALL

As well as writing, the author is a professional illustrator.